Their Gazes Caught— and Held

His hands lingered, and she could feel the pressure of his gloves, generating a heat that seeped through her clothes and into her skin.

"Your riding is extraordinary," he told her. "As is your candor, your determination—and you."

"I'm also a mess." Anastasia couldn't believe those words had just popped out of her mouth. When had she ever been preoccupied with her appearance?

Only now.

Tearing her gaze from Damen's, Anastasia regarded herself: the ruined gown flowing around dirt-stained stockings—not to mention her hair, which now tumbled free, cascading over her shoulders and back. "It seems to me I'm in a perpetually rumpled state," she said.

Damen shook his head slowly. "Not rumpled. Genuine. Uninhibited. Free-spirited. There's a big difference." He tugged off one of his gloves, capturing a strand of her hair and rubbing it between his fingers. "You embrace life, live it to its fullest. Never make light of that. It's a great blessing."

Anastasia's heart began hammering against her ribs. "You're speaking from experience."

"Um-hum." His knuckles caressed her cheek. "I'm much the same way. I seize life with both hands, savor every opportunity it hands me." His gaze fell to her lips. "Every one."

He lowered his head, capturing her mouth beneath his.

THE MUSIC BOX

"*The Music Box* is a trip into Wonderland, full of adventure and mystery with a magical romance to warm readers' hearts!"

—*The Literary Times*

"Breathtakingly brilliant! Andrea Kane . . . has taken intrigue and passion to new heights."

—*Rendezvous*

"Ms. Kane's mystery/romance will . . . bring a sparkle of love and laughter to your life."

—Bell, Book and Candle

"Ms. Kane has worked her special magic with this delightful story. . . . *The Music Box* is simply enchanting. Don't miss it!"

—CompuServe Romance Reviews

THE BLACK DIAMOND

"Andrea Kane is the reigning queen of prize-winning historical romance. *The Black Diamond* is a beautiful tale of love, an exciting tale of adventure, and an adrenaline-pumping rush of nonstop action."

—Painted Rock.com

"Andrea Kane is a 'diamond of the first water' in the galaxy of historical romance stars."

—*Romantic Times*

LEGACY OF THE DIAMOND

"Andrea Kane starts her Black Diamond series with a bang! It has everything: action, adventure, sensuality, and the gripping storytelling style that has become her trademark."

—*Affaire de Coeur*

Books by Andrea Kane

My Heart's Desire
Dream Castle
Masque of Betrayal
Echoes in the Mist
Samantha
The Last Duke
Emerald Garden
Wishes in the Wind
Legacy of the Diamond
The Black Diamond
The Music Box
"Yuletide Treasure"—Gift of Love Anthology
The Theft
The Gold Coin

Published by POCKET BOOKS

ANDREA KANE

THE GOLD COIN

SONNET BOOKS

New York London Toronto Sydney Tokyo Singapore

This book is a work of fiction. Names, characters, places and incidents are products of the author's imagination or are used fictitiously. Any resemblance to actual events or locales or persons, living or dead, is entirely coincidental.

An *Original* Publication of POCKET BOOKS

A Sonnet Book published by
POCKET BOOKS, a division of Simon & Schuster Inc.
1230 Avenue of the Americas, New York, NY 10020

Copyright © 1999 by Andrea Kane

ISBN: 0-671-01888-4

First Sonnet Books printing August 1999

10 9 8 7 6 5 4 3

SONNET BOOKS and colophon are trademarks of Simon & Schuster Inc.

Front cover illustration by Lisa Litwack
Tip-in illustration by Gregg Gulbronson

Printed in the U.S.A.

To family—those special people
whose hearts and lives
are tied to yours.

Acknowledgments

To Gryphon Books, for their commitment, patience, and professionalism in digging up reference books for me on the 19th-century English banking system. Many thanks—you've spared me more sleepless nights than I can count.

To my family, the true-to-life embodiment of what Anastasia and Breanna's grandfather believed family ought to be. I love you.

THE
GOLD COIN

Prologue

Kent, England
August 1803

*T*hey made the pact when they were six.

They hadn't planned on making it. But drastic circumstances required drastic actions. And drastic circumstances were precisely what they found themselves in on that fateful night.

Fearfully, the two little girls hesitated at the doorway.

Crackling tension permeated the dining room. They peeked inside, freezing in their tracks as angry voices assailed them. They scooted backward, pressing themselves flat against the wall so as not to be spied.

"What the hell is wrong with discussing profits?" Lord George Colby barked, his sharp words hurled at his brother. "The fact that our business is making a fortune should please you as much as it does me."

"Tonight is not about profits, George," Lord Henry reminded him in a voice that was taut with repressed ire. "It's about family."

"Family? As in brotherly devotion?" A mocking laugh. "Don't insult me, Henry. The business is the only meaningful thing you and I share."

"You're right. More and more right every day. And I'm getting damned tired of trying to change that."

"Well, so much for sentiment," George noted scornfully. "And so much for this whole sham of a reunion."

"It wasn't meant to be a reunion." Clearly, Henry was striving for control. "It's Father's sixtieth birthday celebration. Or had you forgotten?"

"I've forgotten nothing. *Nothing.* Have you?"

The pointed barb sank in, blanketing the room in silence.

"They're fighting loud," Anastasia hissed, inching farther away from the doorway, and shoving one unruly auburn tress off her face. "Especially Uncle George. We're in trouble. *Big* trouble."

"I know." Her cousin Breanna gazed down at herself, her delicate features screwed up in distress as she surveyed her soiled party frock—which was identical to Anastasia's, only much filthier. "Father sounds really mad. And if he sees I got all dirty . . . and ruined the dress Grandfather gave me . . ." She began rubbing furiously at the mud and grass stains, pausing only to wipe streaks of dirt from her forearms.

Anastasia watched, chewing her lip, knowing this whole disaster was her fault. She'd been the one who insisted they sneak out of Medford Manor to play while the grown-ups talked. Now she wished she'd never suggested it. In fact, she wished it had been she, rather than Breanna, who had fallen into the puddle outside. Her father would have forgiven her. He was gentle and kind—well, at least when it came to her. When it came to almost everyone, in fact. Except for one person: his brother. He and Uncle George, though twins, were practically enemies.

Maybe that was because they were so different—except for their looks, which were identical, right down to their vivid coloring: jade green eyes and thick cinnamon hair, both of which she and Breanna had inherited. But in every other way their fathers were like day and night. Her own father had a quick mind and an easy nature. He embraced life, creative business ventures, and his family, while Uncle George was stiff in manner, rigid in expectations, and downright intimidating when crossed.

Especially when the one who crossed him was his daughter.

"Stacie!" Breanna's frantic hiss yanked Anastasia out of her reverie. "What should I do?"

Anastasia was used to being the one whose ideas got them both in and out of trouble. But this time the trouble they'd be facing was bad. And the person who'd be paying the price would be Breanna. Well, that was something Anastasia couldn't—*wouldn't*—allow.

Her mind began racing, seeking ways to keep Uncle George from seeing Breanna—or at least from seeing her frock.

Absently, Anastasia studied her own party dress, noting that other than a fine layer of dirt along the hem, it was respectably clean.

Now *that* spawned an idea.

"I know! We can change dresses." Even as she spoke, she spied Wells, the Medford butler, striding down the endless corridor, heading in their direction. Any second he would spot them—if he hadn't done so already. It was too late for scrambling in and out of their dresses.

"No," she amended dejectedly. "We don't have time. It would've worked, too, 'cause our dresses look exactly the same—" Abruptly she broke off, her eyes lighting up as she contemplated another, far better and more intriguing possibility. "So do we."

Breanna's brows drew together. "So do we . . . what?"

"Look exactly the same. Everyone says so. Our fathers are twins. Our mothers are sisters—or at least they were until yours went to heaven. No one can ever tell us apart. Even Mama and Papa get confused sometimes. So why don't you be me and I'll be you?"

"You mean switch places?" Breanna's fear was supplanted by interest. "Can we do that?"

"Why not?" Swiftly, Anastasia combed her fingers through her tangled masses of coppery hair, trying—with customary six-year-old awkwardness—to arrange them in some semblance of order. "We'll fool everyone and save you from Uncle George."

"But then *you'll* get in trouble."

"Not like you would. Papa might be annoyed, but Uncle George would be . . ."

"I know." Breanna's gaze darted toward Wells, who was now almost upon them. "Are you sure?"

"I'm sure." Anastasia grinned, becoming more and more intrigued by the notion. "It'll be fun. Let's try it, just this once."

An impish smile curved Breanna's lips. "A whole hour or two to speak out like you do. I can hardly wait."

"Don't wait," Anastasia hissed. "Start now." So saying, she lowered her chin a notch, clasping the folds of her gown between nervous fingers in a gesture that was typically Breanna. "Hello, Wells," she greeted the butler.

"Where have you two been? I've looked everywhere for you." Wells's eyes, behind heavy spectacles, flickered from Anastasia to Breanna—who had thrown back her shoulders and assumed Anastasia's more brazen stance.

"All of us, most particularly your grandfather, have been worried sick. . . . Oh, no." Seeing the condition of Breanna's gown, Wells's long, angular features tensed.

"It's not as bad as it looks, Wells," Breanna assured him with one of Anastasia's confident smiles. "It was only a little trip and a littler fall."

A rueful nod. "You're right, Miss Stacie," he agreed. "It could have been worse. It could be Miss Breanna who'd taken the spill. I shudder to think what the outcome of *that* would have been. Now then . . ." He waved them toward the dining room, frowning as he became aware of the heavy silence emanating from within. "Hurry. Tell them you're all right. It will certainly brighten your grandfather's birthday."

With an uneasy glance in that direction, he scooted off, retracing his steps to the entranceway.

The girls' eyes met, and they grinned.

"We fooled him," Breanna murmured in wonder. "*No one* fools Wells."

"No one but us," Anastasia said with great satisfaction. She nudged her cousin forward. "Let's go." An impish twinkle. "After you, Stacie."

Breanna giggled. Then, head held high, she preceded Anastasia into the dining room—despite the soiled gown—just as her cousin would have.

Once inside, they waited, assessing the scene before them.

The elegant mahogany table was formally set, its crystal and silver gleaming beneath the glow of the room's ornate chandelier. At the head of the table sat their beloved grandfather, his elderly face strained as he looked from one son to the other. At the sideboard, George bristled, splashing some brandy into a glass and glaring across the room at his brother, who was shaking his head resignedly. Henry nodded as he listened to the soothing words his wife, Anne, was murmuring in his ear.

Grandfather was the first to become aware of his granddaughters' presence, and he beckoned them forward, his pursed lips curving into a smile of welcome. "At last. My two beautiful . . ." His words drifted off as he noted Breanna's stained and wrinkled gown. "What on earth happened?"

"We took a walk, Grandfather," Breanna replied, playing the part of Anastasia to perfection. "We were bored. So we went exploring. We climbed trees. We tried to catch fireflies. It was my idea—and my own fault that I fell. I forgot all about the time, and I was rushing too fast on my way back. I didn't see the mud puddle."

The Viscount Medford's lips twitched. "I see," he replied evenly.

Anastasia walked sedately to her grandfather's side. "We apologize, Grandfather," she said, intentionally using Breanna's sweet tone and respectful gaze. "Stacie and I were having fun. But it is your birthday. And we should never have left the manor."

"Nonsense, my dear." He leaned over and caressed his granddaughter's cheek. His insightful green gaze swept over her, his eyes surrounded by the tiny lines that heralded sixty years of life. Then he shifted to assess her cousin's more rumpled state. "You're welcome to explore to your hearts' content. The only reason for our concern was that it's becoming quite dark and neither of you knows your way around Medford's vast grounds. But now that you're here, no apology is necessary." He cleared his throat. "Anastasia, are you hurt?" he asked Breanna.

"No, Grandfather." Breanna shot him one of Anastasia's bold, infectious grins. "*I'm* not hurt. But my gown is."

"So I noticed." The viscount looked more and more as if he were biting back laughter. "How did you fall?"

"I slipped and landed in a puddle. As I said, I was in too much of a hurry."

"Aren't you always?" George muttered, abandoning the sideboard and marching over to the table. Purposefully, he ignored the girl he assumed to be his niece, instead gesturing for his daughter—or at the least the girl he thought to be his daughter—to take the chair beside him. "Sit, Breanna. You've already delayed our meal long enough." A biting pause. "Perhaps your cousin should change her clothes before she dines?" he inquired, inclining his head to give his brother a pointed look.

"Papa? Mama?" Breanna glanced at her uncle Henry and aunt Anne. "Would you prefer I change?"

Anastasia's father shook his head. "I don't think that will be necessary."

"Darling," Anne inserted, her brows drawn in concern, "are you sure you aren't hurt?"

"Positive," Breanna assured her with that offhanded shrug Anastasia always gave. "Just clumsy. I really am sorry."

"Never mind," the viscount interrupted, gesturing for the girls to be seated. "Dirty or not, you're a welcome addition to the table." He tossed a disapproving scowl in George's direction. "A breath of fresh air, given the disagreeable nature of the conversation."

"It wasn't a conversation," George replied tersely. "It was an argument."

"When isn't it?" his father countered, shoving a shock of hair—once auburn, now white—off his forehead. "Let's change the subject while we enjoy the fine meal Mrs. Rhodes has prepared."

Despite his urging, the meal, however delicious, passed in stony silence, the only sound that of the clinking glassware and china.

After an hour, which seemed more like an eternity, the viscount placed his napkin on the table and folded his hands before him. "I invited you all here tonight to celebrate. Not only my birthday, but what it represents: our family and its legacy."

"Colby and Sons," George clarified, his green eyes lighting up.

"I wasn't referring to the business," his father replied, sadness making his shoulders droop, his already lined face growing even older, more weary. "At least not in the economic sense. I was referring to us and the unity of our family—not only now, but in years to come."

"All of which is integrally tied to our company and its profits." George sat up straight, his jaw clenched in annoyance. "The problem is, I'm the only one honest enough to admit that's what business—*and* this family— are all about: money and status."

Viscount Medford sighed. "I'm not denying the pride I feel for Colby and Sons. We've all worked hard to make it thrive. But that doesn't mean I've forgotten what's important. I only wish you hadn't either. I'd hoped . . ." His glance flickered across the table, first to Anastasia, then to Breanna. "Never mind." Abruptly, he pushed back his chair. "Let's take our brandy in the library."

Anne rose gracefully. "I'll get the girls ready for bed."

"We won't be staying," George said, cutting her off, his jaw clenching even tighter as he faced his brother's wife. "So you needn't bother."

She winced at the harshness of his tone and the bitterness that glittered in his eyes. But she answered him quietly, and without averting her gaze. "It's late, George. Surely your trip can wait until morning."

"It could. I choose for it not to."

Anastasia and Breanna exchanged glances. They both hated this part most of all—the icy antagonism Breanna's father displayed when forced to address his brother's wife.

The antagonism *and* its guaranteed outcome.

They'd be split up again soon. And Lord knew when they'd see each other next.

Quickly, Breanna rose. "Breanna and I will wait in the blue salon, Uncle George," she said, still playing the part of her cousin. "We'll stay there until you're ready to leave."

George was too caught up in his thoughts to spare her more than a cursory nod.

It was all the girls needed.

Without giving him an instant to change his mind, they scampered out of the room. Pausing only to heave sighs of relief, they bolted down the hall and dashed into the blue salon.

"We were wonderful!" Anastasia squealed, plopping onto the sofa. "Even *I* wasn't sure who was who after a while."

Breanna laughed softly. "Nor I," she agreed, squirming onto the cushion alongside her cousin.

"Let's make a pact," Anastasia piped up suddenly.

"Whenever we're together and one of us gets in trouble—the kind of trouble that would go away if people believed I was you or you were me—let's switch places like we did tonight. Okay?"

After a brief instant of consideration, Breanna arched a brow. "Good for me, but what about you? When could you ever be in enough trouble to need to be me?"

"You never know."

"I suppose not." Breanna sounded decidedly unconvinced.

"So? Is it a pact?" Anastasia pressed, bouncing up and down on the sofa.

Apparently her enthusiasm was contagious, because abruptly Breanna grinned. "It's a pact."

With proper formality they shook hands.

A knock interrupted their private moment together.

"Girls?" Their grandfather entered the salon, closing the door behind him. "May I speak with you both for a moment?"

"Of course, Grandfather." Anastasia eased over and patted the space between her and Breanna, a curious glint in her eye. "Come sit with Brea—with Stacie and me," she hastily rectified.

"Thank you—Anastasia." With a whisper of a smile, the viscount lowered himself between the girls, chuckling as he saw surprise, then disappointment, flash across Anastasia's face.

"You knew?" she demanded.

"Of course, my headstrong Stacie. *I* knew," he clarified, leaning over and patting each of their hands. "But no one else did. Especially not your father," he assured Breanna. "A brilliant tactic on both your parts. I do, however, suggest you swap frocks right after our chat, in case your visit is cut short. I'll do my best to keep peace in the library, but I'm not sure how long your fathers will stay in the same room together."

"Good idea," Anastasia agreed at once.

"Not good," Breanna amended with utter resignation. "Just wise."

Both girls fell silent.

A shadow crossed the viscount's face, and he gazed sadly from Anastasia to Breanna and back. "You're both extraordinarily special. I only wish your fathers could share the bond you do. But I'm afraid that's impossible."

"Why do they fight, Grandfather?" Breanna asked. "And why does Papa dislike Aunt Anne so much?"

The viscount sighed, feeling far older than his sixty years. What could he say? How could he tell them the truth when they were far too young to understand?

He couldn't.

But what he could do was to ensure their futures. Their futures and that of the Colby family.

"Tell me, girls," he asked, "which would you value more, gold or silver?"

Anastasia shrugged. "That depends on which of us you ask. I love gold—it's the color of the sun when it rises and the stars when they glow in the sky. Breanna loves silver—it's the color of the trim on her favorite porcelain horse, and the color of the necklace and earrings her mama left her."

"It's also the color of the pond here at nighttime," Breanna pointed out. "When the moon hits it, it looks all silvery and magical."

Their grandfather's smile was gentle. "I'm glad you feel so much at home at Medford Manor," he said, moved by the irony that neither of his granddaughters had equated value with actual monetary worth. "You do know that gold is worth more than silver, like a sovereign is worth more than a crown?"

Breanna frowned. "Of course. Father says things like that all the time. But that's not what you asked."

"No," the viscount agreed in an odd tone. "It's not, is it?" With that, he dug into his pocket, extracted two shiny objects, one silver, one gold. "Do you see what I have here?"

Both girls leaned closer, studying the objects. "They're coins," Anastasia announced.

"Indeed they are. Identical coins, other than the fact that one is silver, the other gold." He held them closer. "They're also very special. Can you see what's engraved on them?"

"That's Medford Manor!" Anastasia exclaimed, pointing. "On both coins."

"Um-hum. And on the back of each coin is the Colby family crest." The viscount caressed each veneer lovingly, then slipped the gold coin into Anastasia's hand, the silver one into Breanna's. "They remind me of you two: very much alike and yet so very different, each unique and rare, both worth far more than any bank's holdings." He squeezed their little fingers, closing them around their respective coins. "I want you both to promise me something."

"Of course." Breanna's eyes were wide.

"Each of you hold on to your coin. They're special gifts, from me to you. Keep them safe, somewhere you'll always be able to find them. Don't tell anyone else about the coins, or about your hiding places. We'll make the whole thing our secret. All right?"

Solemnly, the girls nodded.

The viscount gazed intently from one girl to the other. "The day may come when you're asked to give up your coins, for what might seem to be a very good reason, even one that's offered by someone you trust. Don't do it. Don't *ever*, under any circumstances, give the coins to anyone else, not even to your fathers." His mouth thinned into a grim line. "They wouldn't understand the coins' significance, anyway. But you will—perhaps not now, not entirely, for you're too young. Someday, however, you will. These coins represent each of you, and your commitment to our family. Wherever your lives take you, let them remind you of this moment and bring you back together again, to renew our family name and sustain it, knowing that you yourselves are the riches that bequeath it its value. Do that for me—and for each other."

Somehow both girls understood the importance, if not the full meaning, of what they were being asked. Together, they murmured, "We will, Grandfather."

"Good." With that, he rose, kissing the tops of each of their heads. "I'll leave you now, so you can exchange clothes. Remember what I said: you're extraordinarily special. I don't doubt you'll accomplish all your fathers didn't and more." He straightened, regarding them for a long, thoughtful moment. "I only wish I could make your paths home easier," he murmured half to himself.

Crossing the room, he stepped into the hall, shutting the door behind him to ensure the girls' privacy and protect them from discovery. Then he veered toward the entranceway, determined to complete one crucial task before returning to the library to assume his role as peacemaker.

"Wells," he summoned, beckoning to his butler.

"Yes, sir?"

The viscount withdrew a sealed envelope from his coat pocket. "Have this delivered to my solicitor at once. It's imperative that he receive it—and that I receive written confirmation of that fact."

"I'll see to it immediately, my lord," Wells replied.

Nodding, the viscount handed over the envelope, fully aware of how drastic an action he was taking, how explosive the results might be.

He only prayed the rewards would outweigh the consequences.

1

Kent, England
July 1817

She was home.

Glancing out the carriage window, Anastasia drank in the sprawling countryside and the lovingly familiar roads of Kent, the winding path of oak trees and lush, colorful gardens that led to Medford Manor.

More than ten years had passed since she'd last been here. And yet she remembered that final day as if it were yesterday—a foggy, drizzly March morning when she and her parents had left England.

It had been the worst day of her life.

No, actually it had been a culmination of worst days, beginning a fortnight earlier when her beloved grandfather had died. Then had come the funeral—where she'd wept and wept—and the reading of the will, a formality that did nothing to ease her hollow sense of loss. She and Breanna had huddled together in the back of Mr. Fenshaw's office, alternately crying and comforting each other as the solicitor summarized the provisions their grandfather had made—something about dividing his assets in half and passing ownership of Colby and Sons to their fathers, to be shared equally.

Those are only things, Anastasia had wanted to scream. *None of them can bring Grandfather back.*

But she'd bitten her lip, swallowed her grief, and said nothing.

The next day, the unthinkable had happened.

Her father had taken her aside, explained that he, Mama, and she were about to embark on the adventure of a lifetime. They were sailing for the States, opening an American branch of Colby and Sons in the thriving city of Philadelphia, starting a whole new life in a whole new country.

Anastasia had understood—far more than he'd realized.

With Grandfather's passing, the Colby family had ceased to exist. The final vestiges of it had died along with him, been dispensed along with his possessions. Uncle George and her father no longer had a reason to strive for the mutual tolerance they'd exerted during their father's lifetime. In fact, they wanted nothing more than to put an ocean between them.

Well, to her father that might have meant new beginnings and the thrill of expansion.

To Anastasia, it had meant something entirely different: that she'd never see Breanna again.

Which was why, on that foggy spring morning, she'd felt as if she were living a nightmare. She was bidding a final farewell to everything she held dear: Grandfather, England, Medford Manor—and Breanna.

She and her cousin had exchanged a tearful good-bye on the steps of Medford Manor—a brief one, given that Uncle George refused to take Breanna to see them off.

Not only didn't he share her anguish, he was also far too busy moving into his new home. He was, after all, the new Viscount Medford, a title he'd craved for years and which passed to him by right since he was older than his twin by twelve minutes.

Thus, Breanna and Anastasia had parted, hugging each other fiercely, exchanging their good-bye's amid promises to write every week.

They'd kept their word.

Throughout the years, weekly letters had sailed back and forth from England to the States, as the girls kept each other apprised of their lives. How different those lives had become—Breanna being groomed for the role of a proper English lady and Anastasia enjoying the slightly less sophisticated but more independent role afforded by life in Philadelphia. She'd never quite felt she belonged; she wasn't an American, for England was still, would always be, her home. Yet she wasn't a traditional English noblewoman either. And while she never stopped yearning for her country, she had to admit she felt a tremendous admiration for the American ideals and those who held them.

She'd also seen a thousand opportunities for expansion in the States; a great untapped world of natural resources to cultivate and trade. She'd asked her father dozens of questions, learned as much as she could about Colby and Sons: what an import and export company did, the kinds of goods her father traded, the contacts he made, even the lengths he went to to ensure neutral trade continued during the years America and Britain were at war.

Abruptly, eighteen months after the war ended, Anastasia's foundation was snatched away. Her mother died of a fever, leaving her father grief-stricken and in shock. He never recovered. Eight months later, he passed away in his sleep, leaving Anastasia utterly, excruciatingly, alone.

Henry Colby's American solicitor, Mr. Carter, had sent for Anastasia, explaining that her father's will was held in England, given that Henry had assumed his daughter would choose to return there upon his death. However, if such was not the case, Mr. Fenshaw could forward the will to Philadelphia, where Mr. Carter would read it.

Anastasia had smiled softly, realizing how well her father had understood where her heart was. She'd thanked Mr. Carter, arranged to have him continue to oversee her father's local assets and to act as the American agent to Colby and Sons—a role he'd been groomed for—then packed her bags and booked passage on the next packet ship to Liverpool.

Breanna's letter had arrived in Philadelphia that very day, begging Anastasia to come home, to come straight to Medford Manor and move in with them. *Even Father agrees this is the best thing for you*, she'd added with a touch of ironic amusement.

Gratefully, Anastasia had decided to do just that. The last thing she wanted was to be totally alone. And being with Breanna again would bring great joy at a dismal time.

The ship had docked three days ago, at which time Uncle George's carriage had been ready and waiting. She'd spied the family crest instantly, and had nearly wept with happiness at the familiar sight.

She hadn't minded the length of the drive from Liverpool to Kent. She'd used the time to savor the winding country roads, the quaint villages and towns the carriage rolled through. She'd reacquainted herself with her country, reveled in the sheer joy of being back after more than a decade away.

And now, at long last, Medford Manor loomed ahead, a beacon of light at the end of a very dark tunnel.

Anastasia leaned out the carriage window, watching the manor draw closer, the gardens flowing around her like a cluster of dear friends, welcoming her home.

The front door burst open as the carriage rounded the drive, and a young woman rushed down the steps.

Anastasia didn't need to ask who it was.

It was like peering into a looking-glass, seeing a mirror image of herself gazing back at her. Even now, at almost twenty-one years old, they still looked like twins.

"Stacie!" Breanna waved frantically, and Anastasia nearly knocked over the footman in her haste to alight.

"Breanna!" She flung her arms around her cousin, alternately laughing and crying, more overwhelmed by this moment than even she'd realized.

The two girls, now women, drew back, stared at each other in joy and wonder.

"After all this time, I can't believe I'm seeing you." Anastasia grinned. "Seeing *me*," she corrected, taking in Breanna's delicate features and vibrant coloring.

"It is amazing," Breanna agreed, returning her cousin's scrutiny with rapt fascination. "I always wondered if we'd still look alike after all this time. Well, now I know." Her eyes sparkled. "I have a twin." She gripped Anastasia's hands. "I can't believe you're finally here."

"Nor can I. I feel as if an eternity's passed since I left. And yet, in some ways, it's like I never left at all. Never and forever all rolled into one." As she spoke, Anastasia gazed up at the manor, a knot of emotion tightening her throat. Here, after all these years, was the estate on which she and Breanna had frolicked as children. Only now their childhood was over, and she was entering Medford Manor with the maturity and self-sufficiency of an adult.

It was a sobering thought.

"Forever and never . . . yes, I feel the same way," Breanna agreed. "But more the former than the latter. Without your letters, I don't know what I would have done. I can't tell you how I missed you." She paused, watched the play of emotions on her cousin's face. "Stacie," she added softly. "I'm so sorry about your parents."

"I know you are." Anastasia blinked away her tears. "Now let's go inside. We have a decade to catch up on."

As if on cue, Wells stepped outside—an older, grayer Wells, perhaps, but Wells nonetheless, his sharp features softening as he gazed at Anastasia.

"Miss Stacie . . . forgive me, Lady Anastasia—welcome."

Anastasia abandoned the formalities and hurried up the steps to hug the elderly butler. "Thank you, Wells," she whispered, a tremor catching in her voice. "And I'm still Stacie. Everything else might have changed, but that's the same."

He chuckled, looking a bit misty-eyed. "I'm glad to hear that." He shook his head in wonder. "There's one other thing that hasn't changed. You and Miss Breanna still look too much alike to distinguish one of you from the other. It's startling. I remember your father saying he couldn't tell . . ." Wells's mouth snapped shut.

"It's all right," Anastasia told him gently. "Mentioning Papa doesn't make it hurt any more than it already does. Besides—" Her chin came up a notch as she sought the internal strength she'd come to count upon. "He's with Mama now. Which is precisely what he wanted."

"And you're with us." Breanna ascended the stairs, squeezed Anastasia's shoulders, and led her inside the house. "Let's get you settled. You must be exhausted. Mrs. Charles has made sure your room is all ready. We gave you the one right next to mine—so we can talk all night, just like we used to."

Anastasia stepped into the house, feeling a surge of warmth encompass her. It was like greeting a long-lost friend, or being enfolded in safe, loving arms. Medford Manor was precisely as she remembered it, its tasteful Oriental carpet running the full length of what had seemed to a child's eyes to be an endless hallway filled with paintings and flanked on either side by two elegant, winding staircases.

All that was missing was Grandfather.

Again, grief coiled in her stomach.

"It's just the same as it was then," Breanna told Anastasia, touching her arm gently. "Just as Grandfather would have wanted it."

"Yes. It is." Anastasia drank in every tiny beloved detail, a twinge of surprise accompanying the realization of just how true Breanna's statement was. "Actually, I thought Uncle George would have made a few changes, given that this is his home now and that he and Grandfather didn't exactly have similar taste. Or similar views, for that matter."

"The same honest Stacie," Breanna noted with fond

amusement and perhaps a touch of awe. "You're right. They didn't. I suspect Father scarcely notices what the house looks like. Decorating doesn't interest him—business does."

"Breanna, you didn't tell me your cousin had arrived." George Colby interrupted their conversation, emerging from the sitting room and making his way slowly toward them. "Anastasia—welcome to Medford Manor."

Anastasia tensed a bit at the well-remembered patronizing tone, and her gaze darted over to study the man who was her father's twin.

She'd been almost afraid to see him again; afraid he'd remind her so much of her father that her loss would become impossible to bear. But that wasn't the case. Uncle George hadn't aged well. He was far grayer than her father had been, his face more lined, his shoulders stooped. And his eyes, though the same striking jade green hue as that of all the Colbys, were lackluster, devoid of the intelligent spark that had lit her father's eyes or the laughter and insight that had glistened in her grandfather's.

The years had not been kind to her uncle. Then again, kindness was not a trait he valued—nor one he deserved.

"Thank you, Uncle George," she greeted him cautiously. "It's good to see you. And I'm very grateful to you for inviting me to stay here."

He nodded, surveying her with a cool, assessing look. "I wouldn't have it any other way. After all, you shouldn't be alone—not at a time like this, and certainly not in a strange country. Not when you have family right here in England to help ease your loss." He cleared his throat. "I trust your journey was uneventful?"

"It was tiring, but fine." She realized he was making an attempt at polite conversation. Still, she couldn't help feeling as if he were delivering a rehearsed speech, and she were responding in kind.

"Stacie's exhausted, Father." Breanna spoke in that same measured, respectful tone she'd used as a child. "I'd like to show her to her room, perhaps let her rest awhile."

"Yes, of course." The viscount gestured toward the second level. "Go ahead. Wells will see that your bags are brought up. Luncheon will be served promptly at two."

"Thank you," Anastasia murmured, already heading toward the stairs. She was tired, yes, but she was also eager to see her new room, to spend time with Breanna.

To find a place for herself again.

Waiting for Breanna to catch up, Anastasia ascended the steps, rounding the second-floor landing and following her cousin down the corridor to the fourth room on the right.

"I hope you like it," Breanna said, waving her into her new chambers. "Gold and green used to be your favorite colors. I hope they still are."

"They are," Anastasia assured her, smiling at the sight of the drapes and bedcovers, both a deep green brocade, and the floral needlepoint hanging over the canopied bed—a path of goldenrods amid a tree-lined grove. "Oh, Breanna, it's lovely."

"I wanted to do more. I also wanted to meet you at the ship. But there's only so much Father will allow . . ." Breanna's voice trailed off, and she shut the door behind them. "Anyway, feel free to decorate any way you choose," she continued. "From this moment on, it's your room."

Anastasia dropped onto the edge of the bed, tucking a strand of hair behind her ear as she assessed the chambers. "My room. At Medford Manor. It's hard to believe." She studied her cousin with compassionate awareness. "Don't give another thought to not having met me at the ship. I know Uncle George too well to have contemplated the notion. Oh, he's being very solicitous. Still—" Her voice dropped to a mock baritone. "—'Breanna, you didn't tell me your cousin had arrived' and 'luncheon will be served promptly at two.'" She rolled her eyes. "Something tells me he hasn't changed a bit."

"No, he hasn't." Breanna's lips curved slightly. "Then again, neither have you. You're still as forthright as ever. Only your accent has changed."

"My accent?"

"Um-hum. You no longer speak proper English. Now you sound like . . . like . . ."

"Like I've lived ten years in America?" Anastasia teased.

"Well . . . yes." Breanna's eyes sparkled with curiosity. "Tell me about Philadelphia. Your letters made it sound so different from here."

"Not entirely different. But less restrictive." Anastasia leaned back on her elbows. "Protocol isn't valued as highly as it is in England. Chaperons aren't mandatory, there isn't as wide a chasm between servants and those who employ them. America is less set in its ways than England is. Which makes sense, given that it's a new country."

Breanna lowered herself to a chair. "It sounds a lot like you—unorthodox, set on forging its own path. Will you miss living there?"

"Some aspects of it, yes. Others, no. It's true I fit in, but I never really belonged. We were always glaringly English. It was especially obvious during the war. If Papa hadn't had such a good rapport with the American farmers and manufacturers, we probably would have had to leave, to go to Canada or come home. But they trusted him. He had integrity—and connections in nearly every neutral country. I guess that when it comes right down to it, profits are profits. And Colby and Sons ensured a healthy revenue for all, war or no war. Father was his usual inventive self, devising creative routes to deliver goods without violating either England or America's war policies." She broke off, shot her cousin a questioning look. "Why are you staring at me like that?"

"How do you know so much about your father's business?" Breanna demanded.

"It's not just Father's business. It's our entire family's business, yours and mine included." Seeing Breanna's incredulous expression, Anastasia felt her lips twitch. "Now that I consider it, I suppose my interest in Colby and Sons must seem rather extreme to you. A proper Englishwoman involved in matters of business and money-making? Shocking."

"Not shocking, just . . . unusual." Breanna sighed. "We *do* have a lot of catching up to do."

"Let's start with you." Anastasia leaned forward, propping her chin on her hand. "Your letters left far more to the imagination than mine did. For example, I know Uncle George brought you out two Seasons ago. Yet you never went into any detail about the balls you attended, the gentlemen you met. And when I pressed you for details, you avoided the subject altogether. Why is that?"

Breanna lowered her lashes, contemplated the folds of her gown. "The truth? Or what everyone believes to be the truth?"

"I think you know the answer to that."

A nod. "I've never told this to a soul. Then again, I'm not in the habit of discussing my private life with anyone—other than you." Breanna inhaled sharply. "Father is very specific about his plans for my future. Yes, he brought me out, but it was all a formality. My first Season was scarcely under way when a business emergency—an alleged business emergency," she amended, "necessitated our returning here, where we stayed for the duration of the Season. Last year we didn't go to London at all—supposedly because I was recovering from a severe bout of influenza. A bout of influenza, which, to be blunt, I never had."

Anastasia sat straight up, her gaze fixed on her cousin's veiled expression. "I don't understand. You're saying Uncle George is intentionally keeping you from meeting eligible noblemen? That makes no sense. Knowing him, I should think he'd be eager to marry you to the Prince Regent himself."

Breanna's lashes lifted, but she didn't smile. "If that were feasible, I'm sure Father would try to arrange it."

"Breanna, what aren't you telling me?" Anastasia felt the old surge of protectiveness swell inside her. "You know you can trust me," she added, when her cousin remained silent.

"Of course I do. It isn't that. Frankly, it's just that this whole situation is horribly embarrassing." Breanna laced her fingers together, stared down at them. "I feel like a prize horse."

"A prize horse." Anastasia's mind was racing, fitting

pieces together. "Then you're being groomed for something." A pause. "Or some*one*."

"A very specific some*one*," Breanna acknowledged. "Father's plans are to wed me to the wealthiest and most successful nobleman he's acquainted with, and then share in his wealth and position."

"And who would that be?"

"The Marquess of Sheldrake."

"Oh." Anastasia's mouth snapped shut.

She needn't ask who the Marquess of Sheldrake was. He was the one and only Damen Lockewood.

She'd heard his name all her life; first, from her grandfather, who had begun his company at the same time that Damen's father had opened his first bank, and later from her father, who had developed his most powerful contacts in America thanks to Damen and the long-standing relationship between the Colbys and the Lockewoods.

According to Anastasia's father, it was Damen who'd always been the true genius of the family, even though in official terms he'd become head of the House of Lockewood only nine years ago, upon his father's death. Since that time, however, he'd made the House of Lockewood the most influential merchant bankers in England, if not perhaps the world. His advice and counsel were sought by nearly all the nations of Europe, and his business acumen and powerful connections with statesmen and financiers alike garnered his family its reputation.

So, yes, Anastasia knew who the Marquess of Sheldrake was.

She also knew her Uncle George. And, given that Lord Sheldrake was rich, titled, and acclaimed throughout Europe—not to mention serving on the Board of Directors at Colby and Sons—it stood to reason he'd be Uncle George's choice for a husband for Breanna.

Money. Wealth. Status. *And* enhancing his business. Those were the only things that mattered to Uncle George.

Obviously, he truly was the same man her father had disliked, had turned away from all those years ago.

"Stacie? Aren't you going to say anything?"

"I presume you've met the marquess," Anastasia replied. "Because I haven't. He was still at Oxford when we sailed for Philadelphia."

"Yes, I've met him. Many times, right here at Medford Manor. He advises Father on all his important business matters."

"And?"

"And . . . what?"

"What do you think of him?"

Breanna sighed. "He's very handsome, very charming, and—as you would expect—very intelligent."

"But . . . ?"

"But nothing. He kisses my hand when he arrives and again when he leaves. The rest of the time he spends talking with Father, except on those embarrassing occasions when Father coerces him into having dinner with us. On those nights, he sits across the table from me—doubtless feeling as uncomfortable as I—makes polite conversation, and says good night." A tiny shrug. "He's very gracious, considering how obvious Father's intentions are. Still, gracious and enamored are a far cry from each other. And the ability to exchange pleasantries is hardly a basis for a marriage. Although Father insists otherwise."

"Uncle George would insist the sky was green if that

would convince you and Lord Sheldrake to marry," Anastasia stated bluntly. "What I want to know is what *you* think. You've spoken of the marquess's reaction to you. What about your reaction to him? Could you have feelings for this man?"

"Feelings." Breanna repeated the word as if it tasted foreign on her tongue. "I'm not sure how to answer that. Lord Sheldrake is a fine man. I like and admire him. Are those feelings?"

"No."

Breanna started at her cousin's adamant reply, the resolute lift of her chin, and burst out laughing. "Oh, Stacie, I've missed your audacity more than you can know. I'm so glad you're home." She dismissed the subject of Damen Lockewood with a wave of her hand. "Enough about me. Let's discuss you. You must have met dozens of gentlemen in Philadelphia."

Anastasia frowned, but took her cousin's cue, letting the subject drop—for now. "I did. And they were all pleasant enough. But I suppose I never thought of them as anything other than acquaintances passing through my life. Part of me always knew I'd be returning to England. Papa knew that, too, which is why he never pressed me toward a commitment. Except once in a while when he'd remember that I was no longer eighteen. Then he'd push me, ever so gently, toward a particular gentleman." A pointed look. "Only I'd push back. I won't even consider marriage unless I fall in love. Neither should you."

A tentative knock on the bedchamber door interrupted their conversation.

"Yes?" Breanna called.

A young, uniformed girl poked her head in and glanced uneasily about as if she were afraid of intruding. "Pardon

me . . ." Spying Breanna—and then Anastasia—her eyes
widened in amazement. "My goodness."

Swiftly, Breanna rose and beckoned her in. "You're not
losing your mind, Lizzy. Come in and meet my cousin.
Anastasia—this is Lizzy. She assists Mrs. Charles at just
about everything."

"Hello, Lizzy," Anastasia greeted her.

The young girl continued to stare. "I can't believe it.
You're the same. I mean, you look the same. I mean . . ."
Blushing, she dropped a curtsy. "I'm sorry. Pleasure to
meet you, my lady."

"As it is to meet you."

"Did you need something, Lizzy?" Breanna pressed
gently, as the maid continued to shake her head in
wonder.

"Oh, yes." Lizzy stuck her hand in her apron pocket,
fumbling until she'd extracted an envelope. "This just
arrived for Lady Anastasia. Mrs. Charles asked me to
bring it right up."

"Thank you." Anastasia stepped forward and took the
letter with a smile. "And thank Mrs. Charles. I can't wait
to see her again."

Nodding, Lizzy backed away until she butted up
against the door. Reluctantly, she turned and slipped out.

"I think we're going to be getting a lot of that sort of
reaction," Anastasia commented in amusement. She tore
open the envelope.

"I suspect you're right." Breanna watched Anastasia
read her message. "What is it?"

"A letter from Mr. Fenshaw. He's arranged the reading
of Father's will for tomorrow. Uncle George and I are
expected at his office at one o'clock." Anastasia paused,
her brows knitting together in puzzlement. "He asks that

you be there as well. Not for the will reading, but for another matter. A matter of great importance to both you and me. He's instructing us to bring the confidential gifts Grandfather gave us when we were six."

Her chin shot up, and her gaze met Breanna's. "The coins."

2

Mr. Fenshaw's office was in an unassuming brick building on Chancery Lane in London. George Colby's carriage arrived there just before one—not a surprise, given that the viscount was never late—at which time he hurried Anastasia and Breanna out of the carriage and up the steps.

The slight bang that accompanied the closing of the door alerted the solicitor to their arrival, for he walked out of his inner office, slipping his spectacles onto his nose as he came forward to greet them.

"Good day, George, Breanna." He blinked as his pale gaze shifted to Anastasia. "Or is this Breanna?"

Anastasia shook her head. "No, Mr. Fenshaw. You were right the first time."

He blinked again. "Anastasia, goodness. The resemblance is astonishing." He bowed ever so slightly, giving her a gentle smile. "I don't suppose you remember me. But I remember you—an active little girl with a mind of her own. I'm terribly sorry about your parents. They were fine people, both of them."

"Yes, they were." A flash of memory flitted through Anastasia's mind; a gray-haired gentleman with red cheeks, thick spectacles, and a kind smile offering her a peppermint stick. "Actually, I do remember you. You had the most delicious peppermint sticks in London."

Fenshaw chuckled. "You did so enjoy that candy." He inclined his head, his expression compassionate. "How are you, my dear? Under the circumstances, that is."

"Not as devastated as I was a few months ago. I'm very fortunate to have Uncle George and Breanna. Returning to them and to Medford Manor has made my loss a little more bearable."

"I'm glad."

"I realize we're early, Fenshaw," George interrupted. "But if it's all right with you, we'll proceed. I have another business matter to see to this afternoon and I want to leave for Kent before dusk."

"As you wish." Fenshaw gestured them into his inner office. "Please, come in. Now that everyone is here, we can begin at once."

"Everyone?" George shot him a perplexed look as he crossed the threshold behind his daughter and niece. "Who else . . . ?" He broke off, staring in surprise at the tall, broad-shouldered man who rose to his feet as they entered. "Sheldrake. I don't understand."

Sheldrake? Now *that* brought Anastasia's head around quickly.

"Nor do I," the marquess was replying, shrugging his dark head. He extended his hand to shake George's. "All I know is that Fenshaw asked me to attend. So here I am." He glanced past George, then bowed politely at Breanna—whom he clearly had no difficulty recognizing, despite the presence of Anastasia by her side. "Breanna, how are you?"

"I'm well, my lord."

"I'm glad to hear that." Damen Lockewood's gaze flickered to Anastasia, and a slight smile curved his lips. "Ah, it seems I don't need an introduction."

"Nor do I," she returned. "Although in your case, it's your name I recognize, rather than your appearance." Eager to remedy that fact, Anastasia stepped forward, curtsying quickly so she could rise and inspect this man she'd heard so much about.

He was tall—over six feet—and powerfully built, with steel-gray eyes, a square jaw, and hard, patrician features. His raven-black hair was cut short at the nape, yet a few strands of it swept over his broad forehead—perhaps the only aspect of him that was even remotely disheveled. His blue tailcoat, silk waistcoat, and white shirt and trousers were of the latest style, worn with the casual elegance of a man who was accustomed to such attire. He carried himself with an air of self-assurance—not arrogance, exactly, but more an awareness that he knew his own capabilities and was not afraid to acknowledge them.

There was something infinitely intriguing about the Marquess of Sheldrake.

"I'm pleased to meet you, my lord," Anastasia continued, watching a corner of Damen Lockewood's mouth lift at her flagrant scrutiny. "My father spoke very highly of you. So did my grandfather. Which leads me to believe that your reputation as a shrewd banker and clever investment adviser is more than just a rumor."

A chuckle escaped his lips. "I'm relieved to hear that. My clients will be as well." He brought Anastasia's fingers to his lips. "Welcome home, my lady." His amusement vanished. "With regard to your father and grandfather, I had the utmost respect for them both. They were fine men and, as I remember, your mother was a lovely, gracious lady. Please accept my condolences on your loss."

"Thank you," she replied softly.

"It's always a pleasure to see you, Sheldrake," George spoke up. "But I still don't understand why you're here." He arched a questioning brow at Fenshaw.

"All of you, have a seat," Fenshaw responded, retreating behind his desk and extracting a folded document from his drawer. "I believe the next few minutes should answer all your questions."

Everyone complied, and Anastasia's interest in Damen Lockewood was forgotten as the finality of what was about to occur sank in. She steeled herself for yet another facet of this painful good-bye with her father, seating herself between Breanna and Lord Sheldrake, and clutching Breanna's hand as Mr. Fenshaw commenced the will reading.

" 'I, Henry Colby, being of sound mind, do hereby give, devise, and bequeath . . .' "

The words droned on, stating her father's last wishes, the provisions he'd made for his sizable assets. Initially, there were no surprises. Henry had left everything he possessed—including his funds in both England and America, together with his share in Colby and Sons—to his beloved Anne. And, in the event that his wife predeceased him, to his daughter Anastasia, and to her children thereafter.

With regard to Anastasia's proper guardianship:

Should she choose to remain in Philadelphia upon his and Anne's death, and should she, at that time, be unmarried and under the age of twenty-one, appropriate instructions had been left with Frederick Carter, his American solicitor, and would be read and carried out by the same. Should she, however, choose to return to England as he believed she would, his brother George would assume the role of her guardian, to properly reintroduce her to English society and to do his best to ensure her future happiness and well-being. To that end, and for that sole purpose alone, the sum of ten thousand pounds had been deposited at the House of Lockewood, from which George could withdraw whatever amounts were necessary to provide for Anastasia's coming-out.

At that point, Mr. Fenshaw paused and looked up, something about the intensity of his expression, the gravity of his stare as he glanced from one of them to the other, making them all aware that something unexpected was about to occur.

"Continue, Fenshaw," George instructed, waving his hand impatiently so as to hear the remainder of his brother's provisions.

Fenshaw cleared his throat. " 'With regard to the above guardianship, I have several stipulations to make. First, Anastasia shall not be forced to abide any circumstances she finds intolerable; specifically, unduly harsh or unfeeling treatment, or excessive discipline that might result in squelching her spirit. Second, she shall never be forced to marry against her will, for while she needs a guardian's hand to guide her through the portals of society, she must be allowed to wed as her heart dictates.

" 'If either of these stipulations is violated, if Anastasia should find herself unhappy or ill-treated in any manner, she will advise Mr. Fenshaw of such, at which point alternate provisions will be made for her guardianship. Should that occur, the funds set aside for Anastasia's coming-out will be transferred to her newly appointed guardian and will no longer be available to my brother, George.

" 'Second, and more painful, is the matter of managing my daughter's newly acquired inheritance. It is no secret that my brother, George, and I do not agree about the importance of money, nor about the fervor through which it is earned or hoarded. Therefore, and excepting the sum set aside for Anastasia's coming-out, I specify that George's guidance and control over my daughter's life be limited only to non-financial matters. Specifically, in the event Anne and I should both die either before Anastasia is well and truly wed, or before her twenty-first birthday, I hereby appoint an administrator to oversee my daughter's inheritance, including her interest in Colby and Sons, and to advise her in her capacity as beneficiary. The man I have chosen to serve as that administrator is Damen Lockewood.

" 'His lordship is a man of great honor and integrity, as well as one whose knowledge of my assets is surpassed only by his wisdom at investing them. He shall, therefore, be the sole overseer of Anastasia's financial resources, until or unless she weds, at which point the responsibility shall be transferred to her husband, or in the event of her death without husband or issue prior to the age of twenty-one, at which point my funds shall be equally divided between my brother George and his daughter Breanna.' "

Halting, Mr. Fenshaw took an uncomfortable sip of water from the glass perched on his desk. "That, in essence, is that."

Scarcely had the words been uttered when George rose to his feet. His movements were controlled, deliberate, but Anastasia could feel the anger emanating from him.

"Those stipulations are absurd, Fenshaw," he stated, pressing his palms flat on the desk and leaning toward the solicitor. "Henry must not have been himself when he devised them."

"I assure you, he was quite himself, my lord," Fenshaw replied with the kind of quiet certainty that indicated he'd readied himself for just such a reaction. "The will was drawn eleven years ago, just before Henry took his family to America. We've been in constant touch ever since, and he remained adamant that the will stay as is. Mr. Carter, Henry's American solicitor, was advised to adhere to the terms and conditions as well, the only difference being he was given different guardianship provisions to comply with in the event Anastasia chose to remain in Philadelphia. However, in either case, the marquess was designated to administer Henry's estate for the next three months."

"Three months?" Damen spoke up for the first time, his tone probing rather than stunned. His expression was intent as he studied Mr. Fenshaw, his entire demeanor suggesting that he liked to be in possession of all the facts before he reacted.

"Yes," Anastasia heard herself reply, her voice sounding thin to her own ears. She was grappling with an onslaught of emotions besieging her all at once—emotions that required all her energy to sort out and master. There was bittersweet comfort that her father had taken the time to so carefully consider her future, weak-kneed relief that her uncle George would have minimal control over her life.

And bone-deep resentment that this total stranger sitting beside her would have ultimate say over her financial decisions. Especially given the plans she'd made in her father's memory.

Just pondering this unexpected constraint made her chin come up a mutinous notch. "Yes," she repeated, staring directly at Damen Lockewood. "Three months. I'll be twenty-one in October."

One dark brow lifted ever so slightly. "I see." His sharp gaze flickered past Anastasia and Breanna, focusing on George and assessing his obvious displeasure. "Does this provision of Henry's will present a problem for you, George?"

The marquess was certainly direct, Anastasia thought, automatically tensing as she awaited her uncle's response. No one spoke so boldly to George Colby—not without expecting to be cut off at the knees. Then again, few if any had Damen Lockewood's power.

She sneaked a peek to her left. Sure enough, her uncle was shaking his head, even as a muscle worked furiously in his jaw.

"No, Sheldrake," he managed to say. "A shock, perhaps, but not a problem."

"Are you certain?" Damen pressed. "Because if so, we'd best discuss it—now."

Curiously, Anastasia angled her gaze at the marquess, noting his unwavering stare and unruffled composure.

Doubtless her uncle George noted them, too.

"Consider it from my standpoint," he offered. "By appointing you to administer his funds, my brother has

all but labeled me a financial buffoon. It's bad enough he
intimated—in a less-than-subtle manner—that I might
somehow mistreat Anastasia. But this . . ." He shook his
head. "I always knew how deeply he disliked me, and
how deeply he disapproved of my preoccupation with our
business. But I never thought he'd doubt my judgment to
the point where he'd refuse to grant me control, not only
of his funds but of his interest in Colby and Sons. It's
disgraceful."

Damen frowned. "I don't think Henry is doing any
such thing. I think he wants an unbiased eye kept on the
family business—which I do anyway, given my involvement in your company—and a knowledgeable banker
who will advise Lady Anastasia in a manner that reflects
the way her father would advise her were he alive. Dislike
is not the issue here, George. Objectivity is."

Even as he spoke, Damen nodded his conviction.
"Actually, I think Henry's decision is a prudent one, one
that will ensure his daughter's happiness and continued
prosperity, as well as that of his company. Remember, I
have far more contacts in America than you. I can easily
oversee the Philadelphian branch of Colby and Sons." A
pointed cough, and Anastasia could swear the marquess
was speaking more to her than to her uncle. "Besides, it's
only for three months. After that, your niece will be
mistress of her own fate." His lips twitched the tiniest bit.
"Unless, of course, some gentleman sweeps her off her
feet before that time and she decides to wed."

"I seriously doubt that will happen, my lord," Anastasia informed him, torn between annoyance at his absurd
comment and admiration at the shrewd, concise way he
had of explaining things so as best to soothe her volatile

uncle's pride. "My feet are planted firmly on the ground and not likely to be swept anywhere."

This time Damen made no attempt to hide his grin. "Very well, then, three months it is." He made to rise. "Shall we set up an appointment to review your newly acquired assets?"

"Wait." Fenshaw forestalled Anastasia's reply, holding up a deterring palm. "There's another matter to be addressed before you leave."

Anastasia frowned. "I thought you said you'd concluded Papa's will reading."

"I have." The solicitor folded up the will and tucked it away, extracting a second document from inside his desk. "But now that you've returned to England, I have another legal matter to conclude." He paused, amending his own choice of words. "Actually, your return to England made this far easier for me. Had you opted to remain in Philadelphia, I would have had to summon you anyway. The terms must be carried out by you and Breanna prior to your respective twenty-first birthdays—which will occur in October and December of this year."

"Is this matter you're referring to the reason I was summoned to this meeting as well, Mr. Fenshaw?" Breanna asked.

"Yes, Breanna. It is."

"Henry left a document other than his will?" George demanded.

"No, my lord. Your father did."

George blinked, although neither Breanna nor Anastasia were stunned by Mr. Fenshaw's announcement. Given the wording of his written message, they'd expected something of this sort.

Fenshaw smoothed out the page, looking from one cousin to the other. "The late viscount's provisions are simple. Prior to his death, he set aside a sizable trust fund for each of you, to be inherited upon your respective twenty-first birthdays."

"How large a trust fund?" George asked.

"Fifty thousand pounds apiece."

"Good Lord." George sucked in his breath. "I was never told about this fund."

"Nor was your brother," Mr. Fenshaw advised him. "No one knew of the trust funds' existence but your father and myself. And, of course, Lord Sheldrake, whose bank holds the funds." His gaze flickered in Damen's direction, then leveled on Anastasia and Breanna. "There is a condition to your receiving this money. Many years ago, your grandfather gifted each of you with a coin. Do you recall that fact?"

"Yes, Mr. Fenshaw," Anastasia replied, answering for them both. "We do."

"And did you bring those coins with you today, as instructed?"

"No, Mr. Fenshaw, we did not."

The solicitor looked intrigued. "And why not?"

"Because when Grandfather gave us the coins, he told us to put them in a safe place—permanently. Which is what we've done."

"I see." Mr. Fenshaw turned a quill over in his hands. "That presents a problem."

"What coins?" George bit out. "What problem? What is this all about?"

"In a minute, my lord," Mr. Fenshaw assured him. He continued addressing the girls. "You say you don't have the coins with you. Let me explain why you need to produce them. At the time your grandfather gifted them to you, did he not tell you the coins had great significance, if not great value?"

"He did."

"You're about to discover what he meant. In order to collect your inheritances, you must both turn your coins over to me. At that time, I will sign the money over to you, due and payable on your twenty-first birthdays."

Neither girl moved.

"Breanna, what coin is Mr. Fenshaw referring to?" George demanded, turning to face his daughter. "You've never spoken a word to me of a coin."

Breanna paled but didn't falter. "Grandfather asked that we keep it between us. No one was to know about the coins but him, Stacie, and me."

Her father drew a harsh breath, looking as if he wanted to lash out at her for deceiving him, yet unwilling to do so given the advantageous outcome of her silence. "An odd arrangement," he said at last, his syllables clipped. "However, there's no point in berating you for something you did as a child. We'll simply go home, get the coin, and you can give it to Mr. Fenshaw, thus satisfying your grandfather's peculiar terms."

"I can't do that, Father."

George started. "What did you say?"

"We can't turn over the coins, Uncle George," Anastasia confirmed. "Not even for an inheritance, no matter how vast. Grandfather's instructions were for us to keep the coins safe, and to never, under any circumstances, give them to anyone else." An uncomfortable pause. "Not even to our fathers."

Her Uncle George swore softly under his breath.

Trying to ignore his anger, Anastasia focused her gaze on Mr. Fenshaw. "When I was six, I didn't fully understand Grandfather's reasons. But I think I do now. He wanted Breanna and me to hold fast to something he feared was doomed to die along with him: our family. The coins display our family crest on one side, and Medford Manor on the other. They're a symbol—one that Grandfather felt was up to us to sustain. He said nothing about trading them in; in fact, he emphasized the contrary, insisting we keep them with us always. Well, if those were his wishes, then keep them we will. Unless you can read something from that document that gives us reason to believe Grandfather changed his mind. But in all due respect, an inheritance isn't that reason."

"Your logic is ridiculous . . ." George began anew.

Again, Mr. Fenshaw held up his palm, never looking away from Anastasia. "You refuse to give me your coin?"

"Yes, Mr. Fenshaw, I do. Please understand. I mean you no disrespect. You're a dear family friend. But even if my own father were to have asked, I wouldn't have given him that coin. Not when Grandfather specifically told me not to."

"I see." Fenshaw averted his head, studied Breanna. "And you?"

Breanna straightened her shoulders and folded her hands rigidly in her lap—as defiant a gesture as Anastasia had ever seen her make. "I feel the same way Stacie does," she declared without hesitation. "My coin remains where it is."

"You're both mad," George exclaimed, coming to his feet. Briskly, he rubbed the back of his neck. "Fenshaw, let me talk to them. We still have several months before their birthdays. I'm certain they'll change their minds by then."

"There's no need," Fenshaw responded.

"Pardon me?"

"I said, there's no need. I've heard all I must." He set down his quill, interlacing his fingers on the desk. "Clearly, your grandfather was right about you. You have all the qualities he most prayed you would have, loyalty not being the least of them. You've more than passed his test."

"Test?" both girls asked simultaneously.

"Yes. The viscount did indeed want you to keep those coins, not only then but forever—for all the reasons Anastasia just enumerated. He wanted to be certain you couldn't be tempted to part with them, not even for a large inheritance." Fenshaw's round cheeks glowed. "A fabricated inheritance, I might add."

George seemed to wilt on his feet. "You mean, there is no inheritance?"

"Oh, there's an inheritance, just not the one I spoke of."

"You said fifty thousand pounds apiece."

"Yes. The actual inheritance is one the late viscount began amassing the day Anastasia was born, compiled from profits he made over the ensuing years. It totals over four hundred thousand pounds—two hundred thousand pounds apiece."

"Four hundred thousand . . ." George murmured faintly.

"Actually, it's closer to six hundred thousand pounds," Damen supplied. "Including all the interest that's accrued over the years."

George swallowed, his eyes a bit glazed as they shifted

from Damen to Fenshaw. "You're saying my father kept that amount of money separate and apart from what he left Henry and me?"

"That's exactly what I'm saying," Fenshaw confirmed. "For reasons of his own, your father wanted that sum to go directly to his granddaughters, rather than by way of his sons. So he made provisions to do just that—and modified those provisions the day he gave your daughter and niece their coins. Had Breanna and Anastasia willingly turned over their coins for fifty thousand pounds apiece, the entire four—pardon me—six hundred thousand pounds would have been donated to charity. Further, if both the girls were to die childless, the remainder of the fortune would go to charity after their deaths."

Mr. Fenshaw pointed to the bottom of the document. "It's clearly stipulated here that the money is to pass only to Breanna and Anastasia, then on to their children; or, should either of them die childless, the full amount is to pass to the other cousin. Under no circumstances were either you or Lord Henry to have access to this fortune."

"He would donate it to charity," George repeated woodenly. "My own father would have given away his money rather than leave it to me."

"To you *or* Lord Henry," Fenshaw reminded him. "Sir, I don't think the late viscount's decision was meant as an indignity, either to you or your brother. It was simply his way of ensuring the continuity of the Colby family."

Anastasia was scarcely listening at this point, so dazed was she by the steps her grandfather had taken. The six hundred thousand pounds was staggering enough. But what it represented—his faith in her and Breanna, in their ability to preserve what their fathers could not—*that* was even more overwhelming.

"Stacie?" Breanna touched her sleeve, speaking in an undertone so as to keep their conversation separate and apart from her father's discussion with Mr. Fenshaw. "Are you as astounded as I am?"

"I'm reeling," Anastasia replied. She inclined her head toward her cousin. "Breanna, do you realize how sure Grandfather was that you and I could do what our fathers could not?"

Solemnly, Breanna nodded.

"We won't let him down," Anastasia said fiercely. "Not under any circumstances." She tensed as her uncle snapped out a few final words to Mr. Fenshaw, reminding herself that—on the subject of not-under-any-circumstances—her uncle's resentment was at the top of the list. Combating it was going to be a formidable challenge, indeed.

"Pardon me, my lady." Damen Lockewood's voice broke into her thoughts.

Anastasia pivoted in her chair, watching as the marquess rose, regarding her from beneath hooded lids.

"I have two meetings I'm already late for," he informed her in a crisp, businesslike tone. "Before I leave, I'd like to set up that appointment regarding your inheritance. Would tomorrow at eleven be convenient?"

Feeling dwarfed by his height and less than pleased by that decided disadvantage, Anastasia stood as well, tilting back her head to meet his gaze. "Tomorrow?" A rush of irrational resentment surged anew. What was the man's hurry? Did he hope to quickly rid her of all financial responsibilities, take over full authority of her financial investments?

If so, he was going to be in for the surprise of a lifetime.

"I admire your initiative, my lord," she replied coolly.

"You're certainly eager to assume your role as my business adviser. By the way, how is it possible to be late for two meetings at the same time?"

He looked more amused than put off. "The House of Lockewood has its main offices right here in London. The building runs almost the full length of Bishopsgate Street. Inside are many offices in which I confer with clients. Sometimes I meet with one while another reviews documents I've prepared." His lips curved. "I assure you, I give my full attention to each and every person I advise. You won't be neglected."

Anastasia had a strong urge to strike him. "Trust me, my lord, being neglected was the least of my worries. As for our meeting, it will have to wait. I can't possibly impose upon Uncle George to return to London again tomorrow."

"Understandable." The marquess acknowledged the obstacle she'd erected, never breaking stride as he scaled it. "Fine. I'll ride to Kent, then. Expect me tomorrow morning at eleven."

The more insistent he became, the deeper Anastasia dug in her heels. "That's very considerate of you. But I have no need of your assistance. Rest assured, I won't squander my funds away by morning. And I don't want to inconvenience my uncle."

"Ah, of course not. Let's address that issue, shall we?" Without awaiting her reply, the marquess glanced over her head, assessing George's fervent conversation with Mr. Fenshaw and interrupting it with the slightest lift of his brows. "Pardon me, George. I need to meet with your niece about her inheritance. Would it be possible for me to drop by Medford Manor at eleven o'clock tomorrow?"

"H-m-m? Why, yes, I suppose so." George's forehead

was still deeply furrowed, his lips thinned in a tight line of annoyance as he contemplated the morning's revelations.

Abruptly, Damen's request sank in, and George whipped out his timepiece, blinking in surprise when he saw it was nearing three o'clock.

"Actually your visiting tomorrow morning would work out nicely," he announced with a frown. "As I mentioned earlier, I have another meeting this afternoon—one I'm already an hour late for, and which I suspect will go on for some time. Your riding out in the morning would ease my time constraints. If it's agreeable with you, I'll have my driver take Breanna and Anastasia back to Kent directly from here, while I stay on to conduct my business. After that, I can spend the night in Town and ride home with you tomorrow."

Lord Sheldrake nodded. "That's perfectly acceptable."

"Good." For the first time since entering Mr. Fenshaw's office, Uncle George looked pleased by an outcome. "We'll arrive at Medford Manor by eleven o'clock. You'll stay for lunch, of course."

"How can I resist one of Mrs. Rhodes's fine meals?" the marquess responded, gathering up his portfolio and putting a purposeful end to the discussion. "So, on that pleasant note, I'll be on my way. Fenshaw, I'll be in touch. George, Breanna—I'll see you both tomorrow. And Lady Anastasia—" He bowed, a corner of his mouth lifting as his gaze found hers. "It was a pleasure meeting you. Oh, and by the way," he added in an offhanded tone—although Anastasia could swear she saw a baiting look flash in those steel-gray eyes—"I wasn't concerned about your squandering your funds, at least not for the next three months. You can't. You'd need my signature to do so."

3

*T*he Thames was bustling as the business day came to a close.

Iron cranes loaded and unloaded cargo from the various ships tied up in the harbor, and a stream of workers shuttled freight into the slew of waiting warehouses.

This surge of activity was clearly visible from the offices of Lyman Shipping Company. Overlooking the river, the company's spacious front room window provided a lovely view of Westminster Bridge and of the dignified cluster of buildings surrounding Westminster Hall.

The charm of the view was lost on George Colby.

Scowling, he peered into the gathering dusk, feeling choked by fate and its unexpected limitations.

"I expected to be paid today, Medford," Edgar Lyman reminded him for the second time, his voice fraught with tension. Abandoning his chair, the stocky man with the square jaw and watery blue eyes paced about his office, palms sweating as he rubbed them together. "I need that money."

"I know. I thought I'd have it." George ran a hand

through his hair, then rubbed the nape of his neck in frustration. "Unfortunately, the cash I expected to come into will be delayed—temporarily."

"Then the shipment will have to be delayed—temporarily."

"The hell it will." George's head whipped around, his eyes darkening with anger. "Don't threaten me, Lyman. You won't like the results."

"I wasn't threatening you." Lyman recoiled from George's menacing tone, taking a precautionary step backward. "I'm just stating a fact. Expenses are mounting. So are risks. Meade's pressuring me. He wants higher wages. Says there's more at stake now."

"Then deal with him," George snapped. "Meade's your problem, not mine. But that merchandise is expected. Arrangements have been made to receive it. It will go out—*on* schedule. I don't care if you have to use your personal funds to get it there. I've certainly spent enough of mine. You'll make your profit. You always do. So does Meade—more than that browbeating son of a bitch is worth. Now get that shipment out by week's end."

A resigned nod. "Fine. I'll take care of it. But with regard to payment . . ."

"I said, I'm working on it. An unexpected obstacle's been thrown in my path."

"An insurmountable obstacle?"

George's lips thinned into a grim line. "No obstacle is insurmountable. I'll either bypass it or remove it. Just as Meade is your problem, this is mine. And I'll resolve it. Soon." He walked to the door. "Contact me when the shipment reaches port."

Alone in his London Town home, George abandoned the facade of self-assurance. Cursing under his breath, he poured himself a brandy, tossing it off in three swallows.

Damn life and its ugly, unforeseen twists. Damn Anne for giving birth to that little chit. Damn Henry for his exasperating stipulations. And now, the most stunning twist of all—damn their father for leaving a bloody fortune to two stupid girls who hadn't a notion what to do with it.

Six hundred thousand pounds. *Six hundred thousand pounds.* Every pence of which should have been his. Instead, he hadn't even known of its existence. And, now that he did know, he'd been advised—in the very same breath—that he couldn't touch a single pound of it. Not now. Not ever.

Furiously, he refilled his goblet, his thoughts jumping from his father to his brother.

Henry's estate wasn't worth a third of their father's unexpected trust fund, but it was a sizable estate nonetheless. More important, it was money George had counted on having access to. Why else would he have invited his niece to come live at Medford Manor? Oh, he'd expected Henry to have found a way to limit his power, probably by directing Fenshaw to keep an eye on things, possibly even assigning the solicitor some say in the management of Anastasia's inheritance. Neither of those restrictions would have amounted to a major stumbling block. The situation would simply have required a touch of creativity—something George was more than capable of providing. But for Henry to snatch his inheritance away entirely? To leave full control of it to a non-family member, no matter how trusted? That was a blatant slap in the face—and a major impediment to his plan.

Which brought him to the man Henry had entrusted his funds to: Damen Lockewood.

Having the marquess in charge was indeed a double-edged sword. On the one hand, George felt confident that his own relationship with Sheldrake was good—good enough that he might be able to use it to make inroads to Henry's money. On the other hand, Sheldrake was smart as a whip *and* ethical—especially when it came to financial matters. So how the hell could George avail himself of Henry's estate without alerting the marquess to his intentions?

Then there was the additional matter of Colby and Sons, which George had fully anticipated having to himself after today's will reading. Not directly, of course. He'd second-guessed Henry's decision to bequeath his shares of the company to Anastasia. Nevertheless, that wouldn't have posed a major problem. After all, George's grieving niece was living under his roof now. And things being what they were, he was confident he could have convinced her, with relative ease, to let him represent her interests in the family business. But now, with Sheldrake managing her shares? George would have to tread very carefully. As it was, the marquess was integrally involved in their company. This new duty would make his role that much more pivotal—and the profits that much more difficult for George to skim.

He *had* to get his hands on those profits—fast.

That realization brought him full circle, back to the ultimate shock: his father's six hundred thousand pounds. The old man had always been too bloody sentimental. But to leave a fortune of that size to a pair of women? Mere girls at that, he reminded himself. The pathetic old fool must have snapped altogether.

George's fist struck the sideboard. None of this was doing him any good. The bottom line was that his hands were tied. He had no access to his father's trust fund and—thanks to Henry—he'd also be hard-pressed to get at the remaining Colby resources. Dammit, he needed that cash. And he needed it now.

But how to get it, without answering any questions or arousing any suspicions . . . now *that* was his dilemma. He'd have to go about things slowly. And the logical approach was to begin with what was legally available to him.

Anastasia's coming-out funds.

True, it was only ten thousand pounds. But it *was* a start. And a start was all he needed—for now.

Late morning sunlight trickled into Anastasia's bedchamber, a sticky summer breeze heralding yet another July day.

Breanna sat, perched at the edge of the carved armchair, watching as Anastasia brushed her hair at the dressing table. "Stacie, what is it?" she asked. "You've been frowning since we left Mr. Fenshaw's office yesterday. What's troubling you so much?"

"H-m-m?" Anastasia looked up, realizing Breanna had spoken to her. "I'm sorry. What did you say?"

"The same thing I said to you last night before we went to bed. You're obviously upset. Is it grief? Are you missing your parents? Did yesterday's will reading worsen the pain? If so, tell me. I'd like to help."

Anastasia lowered her eyes, staring at the handle of her brush with a wistful expression. "If anyone could help, it would be you. And, yes, I miss Mama and Papa. I always will. That's what's weighing on my heart. But my mind—now that's another story."

"And what story is that? Is it the money Grandfather left us? Are you worried over how he'd want us to spend it?"

"Oddly enough, no. I have a feeling we'll know just what to do with that money when the time comes. I think Grandfather believed that, too."

"I agree." Breanna fell silent, waiting expectantly.

Anastasia chewed her lip, met her cousin's gaze in the looking glass, and sighed. "Actually, it's the money Father left me that's on my mind. Or, more specifically, the man who'll be overseeing how I spend it." She lay down her brush, turning to face Breanna. "It's nearly eleven o'clock," she blurted. "Before I force myself to go downstairs and attend this meeting, tell me more about Damen Lockewood."

"Ah." Breanna propped her chin on her hand, regarding her cousin with amused interest. "Damen Lockewood. That was my third guess. He really rankled you, didn't he?"

"Why do you say that?"

"Oh, I don't know—probably because you sprang up and confronted him like a hissing cat about to strike."

A rueful grin. "Was I *that* obvious?"

"Let's say you weren't subtle."

"Wonderful." Anastasia rolled her eyes. "Now I'll not only have an arrogant, opinionated overseer, I'll have an arrogant, opinionated overseer who dislikes me."

"I didn't say he dislikes you," Breanna refuted, tucking a stray ringlet back into her smooth knot of upswept hair. "In fact, if I had to wager a guess, I'd say he was more fascinated by you than annoyed. You are unique, Stacie. What's more, I doubt many women challenge Lord Sheldrake's authority, much less his skill."

"I didn't challenge his skill." In one impatient motion, Anastasia gave up trying to arrange her own auburn waves, letting them tumble unimpeded down her back. "I'm sure he's every bit the financial genius Papa claimed him to be. But that doesn't mean I want him as a guardian—monetary or otherwise."

"So I gathered." Breanna gave a quizzical shrug. "Why not? Surely you can benefit from his knowledge."

"I'm sure I can. But I'm *not* sure I want to." Rising, Anastasia shook out the folds of her lime green day dress. "What do you know of him—besides the fact that he's brilliant, wealthy, and, if Uncle George has his way, your future husband?"

A flush stained Breanna's cheeks. "I wouldn't place much faith in the last. As for the rest, yes, he's both brilliant and wealthy. He's also charming, handsome, and polite. I'm not sure how much more I can tell you. From what little I saw during my sole London Season, I suspect he's never at a loss for female companionship. On the other hand, I truly believe business is his primary passion—and his primary pastime. While he did attend a few balls that Season, he didn't seem particularly enthused and he didn't stay long. I only danced with him twice. As for other women . . ."

"What type of investor is he?"

Breanna blinked. "Pardon me?"

"When he invests your father's money, is he narrow-minded in his choices, rigid in his approach? Or is he willing to try new things, hear new ideas?"

"How on earth would I know?"

Anastasia's hand balled into a frustrated fist, her arm helplessly slicing the air before falling to her side. "I suppose you wouldn't. But I need to. I have specific ideas for how that money should be invested—how Papa would *want* it to be invested. And I must know if . . ."

A knock on the door interrupted them.

"Come in," Anastasia called.

"Pardon me." Kate, the rotund, smiling, middle-aged woman who'd been assigned—in whatever limited capacity her new mistress would allow—the role of Anastasia's lady's maid, entered the room. "The viscount and Lord Sheldrake have arrived," she informed Anastasia. "They're awaiting you in the yellow salon." A concerned, motherly look. "Shall I fix your hair, m'lady? I can put it up like Lady Breanna's, or weave some pearls through the crown and . . ."

"Thank you, no, Kate." Anastasia waved away the suggestion. "I'll just tie it back. That should suffice. After all, I'm going to a meeting, not a ball." So saying, she snatched up a satin ribbon, tugging it into place as she walked. "Very well. Let's get this over with." She glanced at Breanna. "Are you coming?"

Her cousin stood, a spark lighting her eyes. "I wouldn't miss it for the world."

Both George and Lord Sheldrake rose to their feet when Anastasia and Breanna entered the salon. Anastasia's gaze bypassed her uncle altogether, going straight to the man who, for the next three months, held her financial future in his hands.

The marquess was as impeccably groomed and mannered today as he had been yesterday, his commanding presence—those bold good looks and that profound self-assurance—seeming to fill the room. Alongside his chair was propped the same portfolio he'd carried to Mr. Fenshaw's office yesterday, only this morning it was twice as thick as it had been then.

"Excellent," George pronounced, nodding his approval at the girls' promptness. "You're both here." His glance flickered from Anastasia to Breanna and back again—and Anastasia had the distinct impression he hadn't a notion which of them was his daughter.

"Ah, Breanna." Clearly, Lord Sheldrake didn't suffer from the same affliction. He stepped forward and walked straight to Breanna, bowing and kissing her hand. "Good morning. You look lovely, as always." He turned to Anastasia, his expression altering from cordial to assessing. "Good morning, my lady. I trust you slept well and are ready for our meeting?"

Staring into those probing silver-gray eyes, Anastasia wondered if he was taunting her or merely making light conversation. "I slept soundly, my lord," she assured him. "I'm quite rested and ready to discuss my inheritance."

"Good. Then let's get started." The marquess turned to George. "Where can your niece and I meet in private?"

The viscount's jaw dropped. "In private? I don't think . . ."

"You know very well how I do business, George," Lord Sheldrake broke in quietly. "My discussions with my clients are confidential. As of yesterday, Lady Anastasia is my client. Now, where can she and I meet?"

George inhaled sharply, then gave a terse nod. "Why don't you stay right here? Breanna and I will busy ourselves elsewhere and meet you in the dining room in, say, an hour."

"Fine." The marquess moved back to his chair, gathered up his portfolio and removed some papers, placing them on the end table alongside the sofa. That done, he drew himself up, hands clasped behind him, and shot George an expectant look.

Reluctantly, the viscount signaled Breanna, then strode out of the salon. Breanna followed suit, but hovered in the doorway for an instant, tossing Anastasia an I-can't-wait-to-hear-the-details look. Then she followed her father into the hallway, shutting the door in her wake.

Lord Sheldrake waited until the quiet click heralded the privacy he'd sought.

"Have a seat," he instructed Anastasia, gesturing off-handedly at the mahogany settee opposite the sofa. Brow furrowed, he resumed perusing his stack of papers. "This shouldn't take long. I'll explain all your father's assets to you as simply as I can, then give you my recommendations with regard to investments. Or, if you'd prefer, I can just take care of things myself, and not trouble you at all. Whatever your preference, I will, of course, keep records of all the transactions I conduct on your behalf in the event you want to see where your inheritance has been invested and how its value grows."

"Stop." Anastasia held up her palm, certain she'd scream if he continued for one more moment. "First, you needn't exert yourself searching for simple words of explanation. I am very familiar with financial terms. I'm also well acquainted with the options available to me— especially those I'd be interested in pursuing. In addition, given that the money in question is mine and not yours, I insist not only on being apprised but on approving each and every investment decision involving my inheritance. And last, *I* have some recommendations to offer *you*."

Damen Lockewood's head came up, and he stared at her, utter astonishment written all over his face. "Do you now?" he murmured at length. Abruptly, his lips twitched. "I suppose that shouldn't surprise me."

"But it does."

"Yes, it does—this time. Which is quite a coup for you, given that I'm rarely caught off-guard. However, what I *never* am is stupid—stupid enough to make the same mistake twice. So, from here on in, I won't be surprised."

He tossed down his papers and folded his arms across his chest—scrutinizing her in a way that indicated he was abandoning his customary tactics. Then he advanced toward her, a challenging gleam in his eye. "Very well, my lady. I suggest we try a different approach. You tell me what you already know of your assets, what additional information you need, and how and where you suggest investing them. First, I'll listen. Then I'll give you my input, after which decisions will be made. How would that be?"

Anastasia's brows rose. "You'd really agree to that kind of exchange? You'd actually hear me out?"

"I would." A slow smile spread across the marquess's face. "It appears that now *I've* surprised *you*."

"I have to admit you have. Somehow, I didn't expect you to be so . . . so . . ."

"Open-minded?" he supplied.

Anastasia nodded. "Yes. Open-minded."

"Well, I am—sometimes. Other times, I'm every bit as rigid as you anticipated I'd be. Which quality I demonstrate depends upon the wisdom of what I hear. Fair enough?"

"I suppose it will have to be."

One dark brow shot up. "Meaning?"

"Meaning you were careful to say that decisions would be made. I notice you didn't qualify who would make those decisions."

A corner of Lord Sheldrake's mouth lifted. "No, I didn't, did I?" He chuckled, gesturing toward the sofa. "Nonetheless, I did agree to listen to your ideas, if not to defer to them. So, can we sit down, or must we continue to do battle standing up?"

Reluctantly, Anastasia gathered up her skirts and crossed over, perching at the edge of the settee and waiting, stiff-backed, until the marquess had followed suit. Only after he'd lowered himself to the adjoining sofa did she relax. Bad enough that the man towered over her when they were both on their feet. But with him standing and her seated, she felt dwarfed by his size and power—a perception that made her feel at a distinct disadvantage, something she was unwilling to allow.

"I'm neither armed nor dangerous," he interrupted, as if reading her mind.

"I realize that." Anastasia started, taken aback by the magnitude of his insight. She eyed him intently. Armed? Dangerous? That was a matter of opinion. This man needed no weapon to be a formidable adversary. He was intelligent, powerful, and self-assured. He also had an impressive array of contacts and an unrivaled level of success—both of which she intended to profit from, and which had factored heavily into the amended strategy she'd devised last night.

"Is it true you privately convene with kings all over the Continent to offer them financial counsel?" she blurted out, inspired by the possibilities her own thoughts had conjured up. "Is your courier system really faster than that of any sovereign? Is that one of the reasons for your success? Do you get advance information that gives you an edge in determining your own investments, as well as those of your clients'?"

At first, amusement flickered in his eyes, but as the questions continued to be fired, it faded, eclipsed by a hint of wariness. "What inspired this deluge of questions?" he asked when she'd paused for air. "Is it idle curiosity? Or is it more? Because if you're prying, I don't discuss my clients or the nature of their business ventures with anyone. And if you're verifying my credentials, I assure you, I'm as qualified as your father deemed me to be."

Anastasia couldn't help but feel a grudging admiration for the marquess's integrity. "Part harmless curiosity, my lord," she assured him candidly. "And part personal interest. I wasn't doubting you, nor was I prying. I'm simply fascinated by how extensive your dealings are, and how notable your contacts. As I told you yesterday, your reputation precedes you."

The wariness vanished as quickly as it had come. "In that case, I'll merely say thank you." A twinkle. "I'm glad I've piqued your interest—and equally glad I've impressed you."

"I didn't say I was impressed," Anastasia amended, her own eyes dancing. "Not yet, anyway. You'll have to work harder to accomplish that feat."

To her surprise, Lord Sheldrake laughed aloud. "You, Lady Anastasia, are quite a handful. Physical resemblance aside, it's hard to believe you and Breanna are related."

"Breanna has had more restrictions than I," Anastasia said, defending her cousin swiftly. "I was fortunate. I lived in America, and my parents encouraged my curiosity and, to a great extent, my independence. Breanna's situation is quite different."

"Yes, I know. Quite different." The marquess pursed his lips, diverting the subject before Anastasia had a chance to figure out his underlying meaning. "Tell me, what makes you think I meant that as a compliment?"

"Pardon me?"

"You rushed to Breanna's defense, and I commend you on your loyalty. Still, what makes you think I find being a handful an admirable trait?"

"*You* might not, my lord, but *I* do."

Again, laughter rumbled from Lord Sheldrake's chest. "I rather expected as much."

"Good. I'm glad I didn't surprise you," she returned with a perky grin. "That would have violated your one-surprise-per-person rule."

"True." Schooling his features, Lord Sheldrake leaned back and crossed one long leg over the other in a deceptively casual stance. "Tell me what you had in mind for your father's inheritance."

Anastasia realized instantly that the abrupt change in subject was meant to catch her off-guard. Well, it wouldn't. She was too well-prepared with this particular response. She'd rehearsed it half the night, modifications and all.

Gripping the folds of her gown, she raised her chin, met the marquess's gaze head-on. "What I have in mind is twofold: to invest directly in America's expanding industry, and to open a bank that will meet a growing nation's demands—one that will make an enormous profit in the process."

Lord Sheldrake's expression never changed. "Were these your father's ideas?"

"I believe they were his wishes. But the ideas are mine."

"I see." He cleared his throat. "There are already banks in America."

"Not like the one I have in mind. Mine would be as vital to America as the House of Lockewood is to Europe. Which is why I want your cooperation—not only as my adviser, but as my partner."

Dead silence.

Then: "You want me to co-invest in this endeavor?"

"Yes. Although, to be blunt, I never considered the idea until yesterday. I intended to do this on my own. Then, when I found out that Papa had appointed you to oversee my funds, my mind began to race. Your insights, your contacts, my firsthand knowledge of the States; abruptly, it struck me that my bank—*our* bank—would be twice as successful, twice as quickly, if we combined our resources. Surely you can see what a splendid opportunity it is?"

Lord Sheldrake rubbed his palms together, contemplating his answer. "Lady Anastasia," he said at last, "part of being a sound investor is avoiding putting all your eggs in one basket. Another is determining which ventures have a higher percentage of success, and which have greater risks and somewhat uncertain rewards. England and the Continent offer both stability and proven opportunities. The colonies are still a vast unknown."

Anastasia's jaw set. "They're not colonies anymore, my

lord. They're states. And just because you've always done things one way doesn't mean there isn't a better way to do them. It only means you have yet to find that other way. Reluctance breeds complacency, which often leads to failure."

An astute glance. "You've rehearsed this argument well."

"I had all night to do so. I anticipated your reluctance since yesterday afternoon when Mr. Fenshaw proclaimed you my financial adviser. I just didn't know whether that reluctance would extend only to investing your own money or whether you'd be dubious of the entire notion. I suppose now I have my answer."

Lord Sheldrake raised his head, met her stare. "I suppose you do. But I want you to understand why I'm reluctant. It's not because I refuse to explore new avenues, nor because I resent your suggestions. It's because I'm not convinced this is the right time to do what you're suggesting. In a few years, maybe. But not now. Not with a country that's still as wobbly on its legs as a new colt—a country, I might add, with whom we've just been at war."

"A few years? That makes the issue rather moot, since I won't need to consult with you then. Nor will I need to do so in a few months, for that matter." Anastasia's hand balled into a fist, pressed into the brocaded cushion of the settee. "But I don't want to wait a few months. I intend to get started right away—for my father. He was a man of great foresight; he welcomed new, creative business challenges. Several times we talked about expanding the role of Colby and Sons in the States, finding a way to lend capital to the growing number of merchants we did business with. He would have been the first to applaud my endeavors."

"I agree that Henry was very enterprising. But he was also smart. He wouldn't have suggested throwing away money. Nor would he have poured all his assets into one risky investment."

Anastasia bit back her disappointment, reminding herself that this was only a setback, not a defeat. "We could argue this point all day. You see things one way; I, another." She rose. "You've given me your answer. You won't be taking part in my venture. Very well. I'll manage it alone. Father's estate is worth over a hundred fifty thousand pounds, and that's not including his home in England and his home in Philadelphia, nor his shares in Colby and Sons. Tell me exactly how much of the estate is in cash assets which are, therefore, immediately available to me."

"None of it."

Anastasia's head jerked around, and she stared at the marquess. "Pardon me?"

"Your father's cash assets total close to two hundred thousand pounds—*none* of which is available to you." Calmly, Lord Sheldrake unfolded himself from the sofa and came to his feet. "My job is to advise you—and to manage your funds. I can't, in good conscience, allow you to squander away your inheritance."

Twin spots of color stained Anastasia's cheeks. "Are you saying you're refusing me access to my own money?"

"No, I'm merely saying I'm refusing to let you invest that money in an American bank." He regarded her intently, clearly aware that she was angry and, therefore, trying to soften the blow. "I'm not doing this to be cruel or tyrannical. I hope you believe that. But if you don't . . ." A shrug. ". . . that's something we'll both have to live with. I won't compromise my integrity just to convince you that my intentions are honorable. Think of it this way: I can't stop you forever. Starting in October, you'll be overseeing your own funds, and you can invest as you choose. I only hope that three months gives me enough time to influence your thinking; that, with a little financial guidance from me, you'll have regained your senses by then."

"Or perhaps I'll have used those three months to influence other businessmen, those who aren't afraid to try something new by financing my venture," Anastasia shot back, feeling angry and frustrated and resentful— more so because she wasn't wholly sure where those emotions stemmed from. Oh, she was furious at being thwarted, at having someone else in control of her life. But she was also bothered by Lord Sheldrake's rejection, more bothered than she'd anticipated. And she couldn't help but feel a grudging surge of admiration at his utterly principled way of doing business—even if she did loathe the outcome.

So who was she angry at, him or herself?

An intrigued spark had lit the marquess's eyes. "You intend to seek out other investors?"

"Given your negative response, yes."

His lips twitched. "I wish you luck."

Damn, the man was arrogant.

"This meeting is over, my lord." Anastasia gathered up her skirts and started to walk by him. "I appreciate your time, and your integrity. I *don't* share your opinions."

Unexpectedly, he caught her arm as she passed. "And I respect your passion for this venture. Can we agree to disagree, or is that too unconventional a notion, even for you?"

Anastasia froze, uncomfortably aware of the strong hand gripping her forearm, more aware of her own powerful, if confusing, reaction to it. Half of her wanted to yank herself away, the other half to stay precisely as she was, to explore the odd sensations elicited by Lord Sheldrake's touch. Both reactions were too extreme, too irrational, given the inconsequence of the contact, the casual nature of their acquaintance. Perhaps it was just the fervor of their discussion, the intensity of their differing opinions. And yet . . .

Slowly, her gaze lifted to meet his. "No, my lord," she replied, trying to read his thoughts, and to understand her own. "It's not too unconventional for me. As of now, we agree to disagree."

"Excellent."

Was it her imagination, or did his grip tighten? She wasn't certain. What she was certain of was that his gaze narrowed, probed hers, and that despite the finality of his tone, he made no move to release her.

A heartbeat later, he spoke. "I, in return, promise that I won't interfere with your efforts to win over England's businessmen. If you find someone eager to invest—wonderful. I not only won't stand in his way, I'll applaud your abilities of persuasion."

Anastasia felt an unwilling smile tug at her lips. "Is that a challenge, my lord?"

His teeth gleamed. "And if it is?"

"Then I accept." Her gaze shifted back to her arm, where she could actually feel the warmth of his fingers seeping through her gown, singeing her skin with an unknown and strangely disconcerting heat. "We'd best go to lunch," she suggested, her tone oddly strained.

Slowly, he nodded. "Yes. We'd best."

4

*L*unch was an hour and a half of delicious food, fine wine, and tension so thick you could cut it with a knife.

It wasn't for lack of conversation. George saw to that. Seated at the head of the table, he scarcely let a moment pass before directing yet another financial question at Damen Lockewood. The marquess, seated on George's left, answered every question, his gaze politely encompassing not only George but Breanna—who sat directly across the table from him—and occasionally Anastasia, seated to her cousin's right. For his part, George never spared a glance at either girl, keeping his body angled toward the marquess, and his eyes, which seemed overly bright, glued to him as well. George's voice and expression were strained, and Anastasia suspected he was still peeved that he hadn't been privy to her financial advisory session.

She stifled a smile. How relieved her uncle would be if he knew he'd missed nothing of consequence. No grand business ventures had been planned, no innovative ways to invest her inheritance had been explored. To the contrary, other than learning the value of her father's estate and having Lord Sheldrake shoot down her investment plans, the entire meeting had been immaterial.

She looked up at that moment, met the marquess's scrutinizing gaze, and instantly averted her eyes.

Perhaps not *entirely* immaterial.

"Before we finish dessert, I have a bit of news I'd like to share." George leaned forward, for the first time addressing everyone at the table. "I've given Anastasia's situation a great deal of thought. It was Henry's wish that I bring her out, introduce her to all the right people. I've decided to do just that."

With a tight smile of self-approval, he continued. "I'm going to host a house party—a *substantial* house party—in Anastasia's honor. Several hundred people will be invited. It will include two or three days of diversions, including a grand ball to introduce Anastasia to high society. My niece will be brought out in true Colby style, with all the grace and distinction Henry would have wanted."

Anastasia started. This was the *last* thing she'd expected, especially knowing her uncle as she did. His mind was preoccupied with business, not parties, and his motives were never selfless—even if he was using her father's money to pay for all this. The bottom line was, what possible benefit could holding an event of this magnitude have for him?

"Uncle George," she responded carefully. "That's really not necessary. I appreciate your sentiments, but I don't think Papa expected . . ."

"Nonsense." George waved away her protest. "You're the only daughter of my only brother. I insist." He turned to Damen Lockewood, who was watching him with an unreadable expression on his face. "What do you think of the idea, Sheldrake?"

The marquess cleared his throat. "I think it has merit. After all, Henry set aside ten thousand pounds for this occasion. So there are more than enough funds available, as I'm sure you know." A pointed pause ensued— enough to make Anastasia wonder if Lord Sheldrake was thinking along exactly the same lines as she was. "When did you want to hold this party?"

George shifted in his chair, noticeably flustered by the marquess's reference to his source of capital. "As soon as possible. In a week, perhaps. I'll send out the invitations this very day."

"A week?" Anastasia echoed. "Isn't that a little ambitious? From what I recall, Mama and Papa used to receive invitations to parties of this size at least a fortnight in advance. That was the only way to ensure none of the balls would conflict."

"During the Season, that's true," her uncle returned. "But the Season is long past. So we don't run the risk of such conflicts."

"Yes," Damen agreed. "Which brings up a different problem. Much of the *ton* is either in Brighton, Bath, or traveling abroad. Why not wait for the fall when everyone is back?"

"Because by then, Anastasia will have endured two months of loneliness and grief," George replied with a generosity of spirit that nearly made Anastasia gag. "This way, she'll remember her first summer here as a joyous one, filled with laughter and festivities." He gave a careless shrug. "The majority of those I know have remained in England for the summer. As for Brighton and Bath—neither are too far from here to travel."

"I suppose not." Lord Sheldrake brought his wineglass to his lips, savoring the final drops. "Fine. A house party it is."

"Excellent." George sank back in his chair. "I'd appreciate your advice with regard to the guest list. I want the most influential members of society here."

"Influential—does that include businessmen?" Anastasia came abruptly to life.

"Yes." Her uncle shot her an odd look. "Of course. Businessmen, nobles, landed gentry. Everyone worth meeting."

"It sounds wonderful," she declared, interlacing her fingers in her lap to curb her excitement. "Thank you, Uncle George."

Lord Sheldrake coughed—a cough that sounded suspiciously like smothered laughter. "Of course, Medford. I'd be glad to advise you on your guest list. We'll include prominent noblemen, respected gentry . . . oh, and affluent businessmen, of course." He tossed Anastasia a quick, wry grin—one she pretended not to notice.

"Good." Uncle George was oblivious to the exchange. Instead, he was scrutinizing his knife and fork, visibly preoccupied by another detail yet to be addressed.

Anastasia soon found out what that other detail was.

"Ah, Sheldrake." George abandoned his silverware, casually refolding his napkin. "You will do me the honor of escorting Breanna to the ball."

"Father." Hot color rushed to Breanna's cheeks, and she lowered her eyes, torn between embarrassment and fear of defying her father. "I don't think . . ."

"It would be my pleasure to escort Breanna to this grand ball of yours," Lord Sheldrake interrupted, giving Breanna a warm smile. "Together, she and I will see to it that Lady Anastasia enjoys her first taste of English society." He slanted a look at Anastasia, a decided twinkle in his eye. "In fact, I personally vow that between her own efforts and ours, your niece won't be bored for a moment."

"What did Lord Sheldrake mean by that last comment of his?" Breanna demanded as she and Anastasia enjoyed a late afternoon stroll through the gardens.

"H-m-m-m?" Anastasia shaded her eyes from the sun, drinking in the vibrant colors and intoxicating scents of Medford's flowers. The goldenrod, the honeysuckle, the wild roses—she'd missed this most of all. England's glorious countryside, unhurried and unrivaled. The beauty of nature, the freedom to walk for hours and never reach a destination, the sense of peace and adventure all rolled into one.

Lord, it was good to be home.

"Stacie?" Breanna prompted.

Smiling, Anastasia paused at a massive oak, whose profusion of branches overhung the lawns and headed up a grove of now-blossoming trees that lined the estate's south gardens.

"Remember this tree?" she asked Breanna, caressing the trunk. "It's the one I climbed when we were four. I wanted to be taller than anything else, so that nothing could impede my view of the grounds."

"I remember," Breanna returned dryly, folding her arms across her chest. "You fell out, caught your gown on one of the branches, and slashed the top of your thigh. You bled for half an hour—it took three of Grandfather's handkerchiefs to stop the bleeding."

Anastasia chuckled. "I still have the scar." Her smile

faded. "I remember how frightened you were, and how much the gash hurt. I even cried—no, I sobbed—and you know how seldom I do that. But I also remember how incredible it felt, for one fleeting instant, to stand on top of the world. And do you know what? It was worth it. Tears, pain, scar and all. It was worth it."

"Stacie, are you going to tell me what Lord Sheldrake was alluding to or aren't you?" Breanna interrupted her cousin's reminiscing. "For that matter, are you going to fill me in on what happened at your meeting this morning? Whatever it was, it couldn't have been *too* dire. You and the marquess seemed to be getting along reasonably well at lunch; certainly better than you were yesterday."

Anastasia wasn't sure why, but she had the sudden urge to sidestep her cousin's question—at least that part which dealt with her attitude toward Lord Sheldrake.

"That's probably because I was too taken aback by Uncle George's surprising announcement about his ball in my honor," she replied instead. "A costly frivolity like a party? Hardly typical of your father."

"I agree," Breanna said. "It stunned me, as well. And then to insist that Lord Sheldrake escort me . . ." She flushed. "I'm sure that was part of Father's plan. I assume he wants to make a grand display of some kind, to show the *ton* that the Colbys are still every bit as influential as they ever were—despite Grandfather's death, and now Uncle Henry's."

"You have a point." Anastasia tucked her gown around her and lowered herself to the grass. "Either that, or perhaps he's in the midst of a business deal he feels will progress faster in a social setting." She patted the large, flat stone embedded in the earth beside her. "Let's sit for a while, savor the sunshine. You can use this as your chair. That way, you won't get grass stains." A mischievous twinkle. "I assume soiled garments still enrage Uncle George."

Breanna's lips curved at the memories Anastasia's comment elicited, but there was a kind of sad resignation in her eyes. "Everything enrages Father," she replied. "Some things more than others—such as soiled gowns." Gingerly, she gathered up her skirts and perched at the edge of the stone's clean surface.

That all-too-familiar fist of worry knotted Anastasia's gut, worry she'd known since childhood but had been too afraid to address.

Now she did.

"Breanna—he doesn't hurt you, does he? Physically, I mean."

Her cousin stared out across the grounds. Then, she slowly shook her head—a half-hearted gesture that looked suspiciously like she was shading the truth, trying to keep Anastasia from worrying. "No. Not really. Not yet." A pause. "He's always been volatile. You know that. But most of the time he expends his anger by lashing out verbally. Once or twice it's gone beyond that—usually when I question his decisions at the wrong times. I usually know when those times are, and I make myself scarce. But sometimes I approach him before I have time to recognize the signs."

"What signs?"

"Long, bitter silences. Excessive drinking and brooding—usually following tense business meetings behind closed doors. You know how preoccupied Father is with making money. When things don't go right, he explodes."

"And he strikes you?"

"Sometimes. Nothing I can't bear."

"You said *yet*. What does that mean?"

Breanna plucked a blade of grass and rubbed it between her fingers. "I don't know. Lately, his moods seem more intense than they've ever been. It's like he's seething beneath the surface, fighting the need to erupt. The way he used to act when your mother was in the room."

"I remember." Anastasia fell silent, reminding herself that there were pieces to this puzzle Breanna still didn't know—pieces she herself would supply when the time was right.

"I didn't mean to worry you, Stacie. I'm probably overreacting. It's just that this situation with Lord Sheldrake is causing an inordinate amount of friction. My misgivings are infuriating Father. When the marquess is here, I'm embarrassed, ill at ease—and, yes, dubious. I know what Father expects of me. But I can't promise him I can supply it."

"Of course not," Anastasia proclaimed, feeling faintly guilty, and unwilling to ponder why. "You can't force affection the way you can obedience. Surely Uncle George realizes . . ."

"He doesn't. Nor am I apt to convince him." Breanna propped her chin on her hand, angling her face toward her cousin's. "I'm not a coward, Stacie," she said quietly. "It's important to me that you know that. I'm also not the same frightened little girl I was ten years ago. When I feel strongly enough about a situation, I do challenge Father, regardless of how angry he gets. If Lord Sheldrake turns out to be one of those situations, so be it. The point is, I just don't defy my father often or without good cause. Frankly, given the outcome, it isn't worth it."

"I never thought of you as a coward." Anastasia took

her cousin's hand and squeezed it. "You're a survivor. We both are. Sometimes survival means holding one's tongue—a feat you're far better at than I. That doesn't make you fainthearted. It makes you wise. I'd be wise to learn some of your self-restraint. And to use it—such as earlier today." A sigh. "Ah well. This time survival will have to mean deviating from my original plan."

Breanna's expression turned quizzical. "What on earth are you talking about?"

Another sigh, and Anastasia leaned back on her hands, letting her palms sink into the plush green bed of grass. "We're talking about me and my grand scheme to leave the Colby mark—*my* mark—on the world. A scheme that now needs to be modified, thanks to Lord Sheldrake."

"You've lost me."

"I wanted to use my inheritance to open a bank in Philadelphia—one that would grow and expand and eventually offer all the resources and stability to Americans that the House of Lockewood offers to the Continent and to England. I announced my intentions to Lord Sheldrake, asked him to share in this venture as my partner. He refused. He also refused to let me use Papa's funds to pursue this investment on my own, either now or for the duration of time in which he's in control of my inheritance. So I told him I'd seek backing elsewhere, from other prominent businessmen willing to take a chance on something new. He was amused, but dubious. He also realized—right after Uncle George's announcement—exactly where I meant to begin my campaign for capital: at this gala house party. Thus, his taunt about my never being bored at the ball."

Breanna's jaw had dropped a bit farther with each word. "Stacie, you spent your meeting with Lord Sheldrake informing *him* how *you* intend to invest your money?"

"Yes. For all the good it did me. Not that I plan to be dissuaded. I don't. I'll simply find another way."

"A bank. You mean to open a bank—in Philadelphia." A disturbing possibility, secondary or not, struck Breanna—hard. "Does this mean you'll be going back to the States?"

"Only to visit," Anastasia assured her. "England is my home. Breanna, I don't mean to build the bank's walls with my bare hands or count out each shilling that's dispersed. Between the relationships Papa formed and Lord Sheldrake's contacts and experience, that won't be necessary. I'm supplying the idea. Now all I need is the capital to get things started. It would succeed. I *know* it would. But the marquess is so damned stubborn . . ."

"Stacie, he's a financial genius. Surely he knows better than you what would make a profitable investment."

"I'm sure he does—or would, if he were willing to listen. But he's not. He's convinced that Europe is a sure thing and America an uncertainty. Well, vast empires were founded on risk. Ventures require nothing less. And if Damen Lockewood is too pigheaded to see that, I'll simply go elsewhere."

"Seeking funds from whomever you meet at the ball."

An anticipatory grin lit Anastasia's face. "Exactly. Which is where you come in. I'll ask Uncle George for an advance copy of the guest list. Don't worry," she added, seeing the anxious pucker form between Breanna's brows. "I'll use the excuse that I want to review the names in advance so I don't embarrass him by mispronouncing anyone's title. That's just the type of dutiful gesture Uncle George would applaud."

"That's true," Breanna concurred. "But where do I come in?"

"You'll study the list with me, and tell me who's who. I need you to distinguish which guests could be potential backers." Anastasia waved away Breanna's anticipated protest. "I realize you don't involve yourself in Uncle George's business, but surely you know who his colleagues are, and who are the most successful of the bunch. Then, on the night of the ball, you'll point those particular gentlemen out to me, and make the proper introductions. I'll do the rest. By the time my coming-out is complete, my venture will be fully funded."

Breanna couldn't help but chuckle at her cousin's enthusiasm. "Tell me, are you going to enjoy a single hour of this party? In the traditional sense, that is. You know—chatting, meeting interesting people, even dancing. Or are you going to spend the entire time doing business?"

Anastasia's grin widened. "That depends on how quickly I accomplish my goal."

Accomplishing his goal, George reflected bitterly one short week later, was a damned, bloody nuisance—one he resented with every fiber of his being.

Fixing a polished smile on his face, he assessed the grand ballroom, which, a mere hour ago, had been empty. Now, it was bursting at the seams, a profusion of color and movement as streams of arriving guests made their entrance, while those already in attendance whirled about the dance floor, chatted in ever-growing groups, or made their way over to the refreshments.

The typical onset to an extravagant house party.

Clasping his hands behind his back, George resumed

his role as host. He milled about, dropping a smile to his left and a greeting to his right, all the while mentally tabulating how much this wretched affair had wound up costing. Oh, he'd padded the receipts as best he could, adding fifty pounds here and a hundred pounds there. But he hadn't dared get too carried away. Not with Sheldrake's watchful eye overseeing every pence of Henry's money. As a result, George had scarcely been able to squeeze out enough profit to make this whole bloody affair worth his while. In fact, he'd be willing to bet that, once the final numbers were tallied up, he'd be lucky to come out a thousand pounds ahead.

And what would a thousand pounds buy him? A two- or three-week reprieve, perhaps. No more. It certainly wouldn't restore his business to its necessary peak.

Dammit.

George paused as he heard Wells announce Lord and Lady Dutton, and cursed under his breath as he watched them make their entrance. So, the pompous windbag had convinced his tyrant of a wife to leave Bath for the occasion after all. That was hardly an inspiring discovery. It wasn't as if he and Dutton were doing business at the moment. The problem was, that could change at any time. The man was too damned influential to snub, and he had enough money to keep himself that way. Fine, George decided. He'd go over there and do his duty. Then, he'd take a moment or two to find the man he needed to see and set his own dealings back on track.

Resignedly, George headed for the doorway, raising his chin in greeting, and steeling himself for a quarter hour of annoying chatter.

"Good evening, Lady Dutton." George bowed, kissing her gloved hand and wondering idly how her husband's protruding belly was going to allow room for the other two hundred guests. "Dutton," he added, stepping back to welcome the man without slamming into his stomach.

"Medford. Good evening. This is a splendid party," Dutton proclaimed, nodding his approval as he assessed the other attendees. "I give you credit. You've managed a fine gathering on very short notice. And at a very inconvenient time of year. As you know, Penelope here had to be coaxed away from Bath. I'm relieved to see it was worth my efforts in doing so . . ." A swift man-to-man look together with a subtle roll of the eyes. ". . . or she'd never let me forget it."

Ignoring the poisonous glare Lady Dutton threw at her husband, George nodded his understanding. "I'm delighted you could both come." He gestured for them to enter, half-hoping he could cut the conversation short. "Please, enjoy yourselves."

"Which young lady is your niece?" Dutton pressed, dashing George's hopes of an abbreviated chat by remaining where he was, peering over as many heads as his stubby height would allow. "Ah," he interrupted himself. "I see a familiar face: your Breanna. She's over there by the French doors—alone, surprisingly. It's been quite some time, but I'd know her anywhere. Although I do believe she's grown even lovelier; she's a veritable vision in yellow."

Tensing, George pivoted, followed Dutton's line of vision, and visibly relaxed. "You're mistaken, Dutton. My daughter is among the crowd enjoying the strings." He waved his arm in the direction of the musicians. "Her gown is blue, not yellow. And she's dancing with Sheldrake. The young lady you spied is my niece, Anastasia."

Dutton's jaw dropped, and he stared from one girl to

the other. "My goodness, they could be sisters. Twins, actually."

"They've been mistaken as such." George was in no mood to pursue this particular line of conversation. In fact, he'd had about all he could stand of Dutton. Having made the requisite amount of small talk, and having assured himself that Breanna was, indeed, where she was supposed to be—at Sheldrake's side—he had more important business to attend to than answering this buffoon's nosy questions. "I'll be officially presenting Anastasia to everyone once the majority of guests have arrived. In the interim, if you'll both excuse me, I have a few matters to attend to. Please—partake. My home is yours."

"Yes. Most gracious of you, Medford." Dutton licked his chops, easing his wife—and his belly—farther into the room, doubtless toward the refreshments, George thought in disgust.

"Hello, Medford."

George had scarcely taken a step when Lyman appeared at his elbow, nursing a cup of Regent's punch and speaking in an undertone. "This ball is elegant—*and* expensive. I'm relieved to see that your financial reverses have righted themselves."

George stiffened. "Not now," he muttered under his breath. Without sparing Lyman another look, he moved deeper into the crowd.

He was more determined than ever to conduct his business.

Just inside the double doors leading onto the balcony, Anastasia watched the short, chunky man leave Uncle George's side and steer his wife into the room. Impatiently, she shifted from one foot to the other, willing the minuet to end so Breanna could perform the introductions. From the description her cousin had provided, Anastasia was almost certain that the new arrival was Lord Dutton. Based on what Breanna had said, Lord Dutton was an affluent nobleman who owned several enormous estates, a shipbuilding company, and a string of smaller businesses. And *that* made him an ideal candidate to finance her bank.

She frowned, her gaze—with a will all its own—shifting back to the same place it had traveled a dozen times: to the dance floor where Lord Sheldrake was gliding Breanna about. Not for any personal reason, she assured herself hastily. Only to see if they were concluding their dance so she could proceed with her plan.

Even as she assured herself of that fact, she knew it was a lie.

The truth was, she couldn't stop staring at Damen Lockewood. He was easily the most compelling man in the room, his dynamic presence seeming to overshadow everyone around him. He looked devastating in his formal evening clothes, a fact that was evidenced by all the admiring glances cast his way by women of all ages.

Breanna looked breathtaking at his side. She was poised, graceful, incredibly beautiful; her upswept hair— a shimmering crown of auburn laced with pearls—as perfectly in place as if she were reposing rather than dancing. She was refined, captivating, the consummate lady, and Anastasia felt incredibly proud of her.

Ruefully, she tucked a stray tendril of her own hair behind her ear, almost laughing aloud at the realization that, in this one way, little had changed since their childhood. She was still the hoyden, Breanna the lady.

And while Breanna might admire her for her forthright-ness, Anastasia was in perpetual awe of Breanna's natural grace and composure.

Still, Anastasia knew her cousin better than anyone. And, composed or not, Breanna looked very strained at the moment, almost as if she were silently willing the minuet to end.

Or was that only wishful thinking on her own part?

Stop it, Anastasia admonished herself. *Whatever you think happened last week in the yellow salon was all in your mind. Lord Sheldrake is the overseer of your inheritance—and the main obstacle in your path. He's fervent in his beliefs, which explains the intensity you felt during those unexpected final moments of your meeting. Stop reading anything more into it.*

As if on cue, Damen Lockewood raised his head, his gaze spanning the ballroom and finding hers.

Their eyes met—and held.

Feeling that same warmth shimmer through her, Ana-stasia jerked her gaze away. This reaction was unaccepta-ble, for many reasons. Least of all was the role the marquess had been assigned to play in her life. Most of all was the role he'd been assigned by Uncle George to play in Breanna's.

Anastasia sucked in her breath. She had to stop staring. The last thing she needed was for Lord Sheldrake to think she was assessing his and Breanna's suitability. She had enough to handle, just trying to line up her backers—and holding Lord Sheldrake to his vow not to undermine her attempts to do so. Provoking him would hardly serve her best interests. Besides, his relationship—or lack there-of—with Breanna was their concern, not hers.

With staunch determination, Anastasia shifted her attention to locating Lord Dutton, who'd disappeared somewhere in the crowd. Not that his girth would allow him to remain unnoticeable for long, she reminded herself with a grin. On impulse, she turned toward the refreshment table, her lips curving as she saw that her instincts had been correct. The rotund fellow was in the process of gobbling down a large pastry, simultaneously inching away from his wife and her gossiping circle of friends.

Perhaps it was time to take matters into her own hands . . .

"It would be far easier if I supplied the introduction."

The sound of Lord Sheldrake's amused baritone from directly behind her made Anastasia start.

"Pardon me?" She whipped about to face him, spotting Breanna by his side and wondering when the two of them had finished their dance and made their way over.

"Lord Dutton," Sheldrake supplied, tipping his head in that direction. "I assume you're about to ask him for money. If you stroll up to him alone, I doubt he'll make the connection between a beautiful woman and a business deal. Shall I pave the way, or would you prefer to ask your uncle to do the honors?"

Anastasia sucked in her breath. "Tell me, my lord, how do you read minds and execute a minuet at the same time, without missing a step? Or is that similar to conducting two business meetings simultaneously?"

The marquess's teeth gleamed. "I'm flattered you were watching. As for my mind-reading abilities, they're uncanny—whether or not I'm otherwise occupied. However, in your case, they're hardly necessary. You're eyeing Dutton like a wolf circling a sheep. And given that the gentleman in question is married, over fifty and wider than he is tall, I ruled out any romantic interest on your part."

An impish grin curved Anastasia's lips. "Perhaps I prefer fat, married men. Have you considered that?"

All humor vanished from Lord Sheldrake's eyes. "No," he replied quietly. "I haven't. That would be too great a waste to consider."

Anastasia's breath lodged in her throat, the marquess's words burning through her like a kindled flame. She searched his face, his expression no longer teasing but probing, intense.

Tearing her gaze away was even more difficult this time.

"I—I'd appreciate the introduction," she managed, struggling to regain her composure. "Plus any others you'd care to provide. I had asked Breanna to present me, but I'd be a fool not to realize that they'd take me far more seriously if the introductions came from you."

"Consider it done." Lord Sheldrake took her arm, arching a questioning brow at Breanna. "You're sure you don't mind?"

Breanna shook her head. "As I told you on the dance floor, I'd be thrilled to be relieved of the awkward duty. Approaching a dozen overbearing men is hardly my idea of an enjoyable evening." She gestured gratefully at a cluster of young women who were chattering in the far corner of the room. "Besides, Margaret Warner has been trying to catch my eye for the past hour. She and her friends want to hear all about my long-lost cousin who's finally returned from America."

Anastasia wrinkled up her nose. "Why would they want to know about me?"

Breanna's sigh was the essence of exasperation. "Because while you're preoccupied with business, most women are not. My guess is that Lady Margaret and her chums want to assess their competition. You're far too pretty to suit the unmarried ones." A flash of recall flickered in her eyes and, without thinking, she muttered, "Don't forget, I did experience one London Season. And I learned that although the men might be lechers, the women are lethal."

Laughter rumbled in Lord Sheldrake's chest. "I'll refrain from comment."

"Oh—" Breanna flushed, looking startled by her own uncharacteristic frankness. "I suppose that was incredibly rude."

"No, it was merely accurate." Anastasia grinned. "I encountered similar types of women in Philadelphia. In my case, I avoided them. Otherwise, I shudder to think what trouble my quick tongue would have gotten me into. But with your inherent gift of tact, you won't run that risk. Lethal or not, those girls will be charmed by you. Everyone is."

That comment made Breanna smile—a fleeting smile that tugged at her lips, then vanished—almost as if she'd enjoyed a private joke she alone was privy to. "If you say so." She gathered up her skirts. "Anyway, if you'll both excuse me, I'll head over to the ladies' corner. It will be entertaining to hear the latest gossip." She paused, squeezing Anastasia's arm. "Good luck finding investors, Stacie. My fingers are crossed."

Anastasia watched her cousin weave her way across the room. "Sometimes I forget how much Breanna is deprived of," she murmured to herself. "So much so that a chat with a group of women is like an extraordinary gift. How in God's name can Uncle George . . ." She broke off, realizing she'd spoken her thoughts aloud.

"I don't know," Lord Sheldrake surprised her by answering. "But it can't stay that way. Nor will it, now that you're home. You're very good for Breanna. I've never heard her speak her mind before. It's a healthy sign."

Before Anastasia could respond or even contemplate the marquess's words, he dropped the subject. Turning on his heel, he tightened his grasp on her arm and began drawing her toward the refreshment table. "Come. It's time to accost Lord Dutton."

Anastasia complied, although Lord Sheldrake's subtle taunt was not lost on her. In response, she tossed him a saucy look. "I'm not going to accost him," she retorted. "I'm going to offer him the chance of a lifetime."

5

*U*nfortunately, Lord Dutton didn't seem to share Anastasia's opinion. Oh, he gleefully acknowledged Lord Sheldrake's introduction, swaggered his fat little body when he heard she wanted to speak with him alone, then gobbled her up with his eyes when the marquess walked away. But when he heard the nature of her business—or rather, that all she wanted to discuss was business—his entire demeanor changed. He looked shocked, then offended, and finally scornful, not even waiting to hear the details before he brought the conversation to a rapid close and made his way back to the desserts.

She received similar responses from the other eleven businessmen she approached—from Edgar Lyman, the shipbuilder, to Arthur Landow, the wealthy manufacturer, to Viscount Crompton, a retired military general who invested his inherited fortune just for diversion, even to William Bates, a London magistrate who received huge stipends for keeping dangerous criminals off the streets and who reputedly had a knack for making large amounts of money through various business ventures—to every other prospective investor on her list.

No one was interested in conducting business with a woman, much less investing their funds in an American bank.

An hour later, Anastasia was more discouraged than she could bear.

Easing her way through the throng of intoxicated guests, she slipped out onto the balcony, hoping to have a few minutes to herself. She needed to collect her thoughts before her uncle summoned her for the inevitable formal introduction to the room at large—an introduction that would be happening at any moment, given that almost all the guests had now arrived.

The night sky was clear, and filled with stars. Anastasia leaned against the railing, gazing up at the bright specks of light and remembering when she and Breanna used to count them, trying to get closer to the heavens by climbing that favorite oak of theirs.

Somehow Anastasia never felt she'd climbed high enough.

But Grandfather always believed she would someday, that both she and Breanna would reach their own symbolic peak.

With a wistful smile, Anastasia gazed off to the right, fond memories of her grandfather and her childhood surging to the forefront of her mind.

It was too dark to make out the outlines of specific buildings, but she knew the stables were in the direction she was facing. She remembered the dawn when she and Grandfather had walked there to see a new foal being born. Life, Grandfather had explained to her, was the most precious gift God offered. And the ties born of that life were equally precious. Even animals knew that, he'd explained. Even they possessed that unique, priceless instinct to love those who belonged to them.

He'd shown her the natural affinity between mare and foal, a bond that was only a fraction of what human beings felt toward their young.

Family. That was even more important than personal accomplishments—not only to Grandfather, but to her. But what if one was integrally tied to the other? What if accomplishing a feat was the first step in carrying on a lineage, perhaps even in restoring ties that should never have been broken?

Anastasia massaged her temples, contemplating not only her immediate goals—to pay tribute to her father and unite and expand Colby and Sons—but the enormous sum of money Grandfather had left her and Breanna. How would they put that money to work in order to do their grandfather justice, to reap the rewards he was determined that they reap, not only for themselves, but for their children, their future?

If tonight was any indication, then Anastasia feared Grandfather's hopes and dreams would fall by the wayside.

Dear God, what if she let him down?

"Here you are."

Damen Lockewood strolled out onto the balcony, coming up to stand beside her. He leaned his elbow on the railing and angled himself to face her. "You're discouraged. After twelve fruitless efforts, I can't blame you."

Anastasia continued to stare off into space, hovering somewhere between dejection and nostalgia. "Have you come out here to gloat?"

"Hardly." He fell silent for a moment, studying her

profile intently as he chose his next words. "Tell me something, my lady. Is your original offer still open—the one regarding a potential partnership between us?"

Whatever Anastasia had been expecting, it hadn't been this.

She whirled about, her eyes wide. "What did you say?"

"I asked if your original offer still stands. Because if it does, if you're still interested in having me co-finance this venture of yours, I'd like to accept."

Pensively, she studied the marquess's face, puzzled and curious all at once. What had prompted this total turnaround? she wondered. Certainly not some absurd sense of gallantry. Not with a man like Damen Lockewood, who regarded business above all else.

Except perhaps loyalty. Was that it? Did the marquess feel a sense of commitment to her father, a responsibility not to let Henry's daughter falter?

If that was the case, she wanted no part of his charity.

"Why?" she demanded, giving voice to her thoughts. "Why would you change your mind so suddenly and completely? Out of duty? Pity?"

One dark brow shot up. "Neither. To begin with, I don't pity you. Doing business means experiencing disappointment, sometimes even coping with failure. What's more, even if I did feel sorry for what you're going through, I don't allow emotions to dictate my business decisions. And that includes loyalty to fine men like your father. Henry would laugh in my face if he heard me suggest investing in something I didn't believe in just out of respect for him. So, no, put those foolish notions out of your mind. I'm reversing my decision because it's prudent to do so."

Sheldrake lifted one shoulder in a careless shrug. "As it turns out, I spent the better part of last week researching your ideas. I made some inquiries, pored over long columns of numbers. And I discovered that you were right. I didn't give your proposal a fair chance. Well, now I'm ready to. If you're still interested."

Anastasia eyed him skeptically. "Why didn't you mention this change of heart before an hour ago when I went on my futile crusade to solicit backers?"

"Because I wanted you to explore all your options before I made my offer. After all, there was every chance you'd reject it at this point, given my initial response. Especially if you'd found someone else to finance your venture."

"Which I didn't." Anastasia frowned, contemplating another, equally important, question. "Let me ask you this: what if I say no? Will that preclude me from using my own funds to finance the bank? Will I have to wait until October, when you're no longer managing my inheritance, to get started?"

Lord Sheldrake's jaw tightened fractionally. "What you're effectively asking is whether or not I'd resort to blackmail. The answer is no. I don't do business that way. You'll have access to your funds immediately, whether or not we form a partnership. I'll sign the necessary documents at my bank on the morning after this party ends. No strings attached."

"I see." Anastasia wet her lips with the tip of her tongue. "Forgive me if I insulted you. But I had to be sure."

"No insult taken—this time. However, I don't expect my integrity to be questioned again."

"Fair enough." The first ray of hope she'd experienced all evening dawned inside her. "You really believe in my bank?"

"*Our* bank," Sheldrake corrected with a cocky grin. "At least if you accept my offer. And, yes, I do."

With visible relief and excitement, Anastasia extended her hand. "Then consider us partners."

"Splendid." Solemnly, he shook her hand, his fingers lingering far longer than necessary. "Tell me, now that we're partners, do you think we might dispense with the formalities?"

Anastasia swallowed, her pulse picking up speed. "Which formalities in particular, my lord?"

"The ones you just employed." His gaze held hers. "I believe it's fitting for partners to call each other by their given names."

"I suppose that makes sense."

"Good." Abruptly, his grip tightened, refusing to let go, and his stare delved deep inside of her. "When I first walked out here, you weren't only thinking about the bank, were you? There was far more on your mind."

Anastasia blinked—startled by the abrupt change of subject, taken aback by the marquess's boldness and his insight. She had no idea what prompted her to answer. Perhaps it was the camaraderie of the past few minutes; perhaps it was the vulnerable state in which he'd found her or the compassion she heard in his voice.

Or perhaps it was the heat that emanated from their joined hands.

In any case, she stared at his strong fingers wrapped around her slender ones and replied, "Yes, I was pondering far more than the bank. I was thinking about many things—my grandfather, my father, how much I missed

Medford Manor while I was away, how much I still . . ." She bit her lip, then blurted out, "Is it possible to miss home even when you're right there in it?"

"Yes," the marquess responded without pause. "When that home is no longer the same as the one you remember. And the one you remember is the one you miss."

Slowly, Anastasia tilted her face up to his. "You're a very perceptive man, Lord Sheldrake."

"Damen," he corrected. "And you're a very intriguing woman, Anastasia."

Without any warning, he stepped closer, caught her chin between his fingers, and lowered his mouth to hers.

Anastasia had no time to think, no time to prepare.

She only had time to feel.

Damen's lips brushed hers in a whisper of sensation, a warm, fleeting caress that sent tiny shivers up her spine. He repeated the motion, and Anastasia caught her breath, her eyes sliding shut as she reeled with newfound awareness.

She'd been kissed before—on the hand, an occasional peck on the cheek, even one tentative sampling of her mouth, given by a brazen though unimpressive suitor. But never before had she felt this tingling sensation, this quivering that rippled from her head to her toes.

The odd thing was that Damen's kiss was no less chaste than those that had preceded it. It was a mere grazing of the lips—the only difference being that it lingered, its motion retraced in slow reversal—first right to left, then left to right.

And then it ended.

Damen raised his head, his eyes smoky as he gazed down at her. His knuckles brushed her cheeks—first one, then the other—before gliding down to skim the side of her neck. Then, he framed her face between his palms and bent to take her mouth again.

This time his lips settled more fully on hers, moving back and forth in a purposeful dance of discovery, and Anastasia leaned closer, instinctively seeking a closer contact.

His mouth was warm, firm, as intense and insistent as he, and equally as restrained. There was fire burning beneath the surface, fire she could sense, but he kept it carefully in check, smoldering beneath the surface.

When finally they eased apart, it was gradual, their lips brushing softly—once, twice—before relinquishing contact altogether. Anastasia's lashes lifted as the night air fluttered across her damp mouth, gently prodding her back to reality.

Damen was watching her, his stare intense, his steel-gray eyes alive with sparks. Still cupping her face, he murmured, "If I apologize for doing that, will you stay out here a while longer?"

"No. But I'll stay out here a while longer if you don't apologize."

He chuckled, lifted a few loose strands of burnished hair off her face. "Fair enough. Also far more honest. The truth is, I'm not sorry. I've been wanting to do that all night." He took a reluctant step backward, dropped his arms to his sides. "But I won't press my luck. If we stay out here, it's to talk."

"About our bank?"

"About whatever it is you'd like to talk about."

Anastasia nodded, still somewhat off-balance, besieged by too many emotions to ponder. "Tonight is certainly a night of surprises," she managed.

Damen's stare was deep, contemplative. "Is it?" he asked huskily. "Odd, it doesn't feel that way to me."

Inside the ballroom, George greeted the last of his arriving guests, then moved briefly into the hallway, standing alone to ponder the evening's accomplishments.

All in all, things were moving along nicely. Breanna was dutifully stationed at Sheldrake's side, Lyman and his curiosity had been deferred to a more appropriate place and time, and his own business discussion—handled earlier as planned—had yielded the necessary results.

Silently, George congratulated himself on the excellent argument he'd presented. The necessary party now understood what needed to be done in order to ensure the highest profits were reaped and maintained. Not only understood the situation, but intended to act upon it.

Yes, the response had been gratifying, and as a result, more attention would now be paid to the details. With that extra supervision, the quality of their next shipment would be better, the quantity greater. And the profits, higher. Hopefully, much higher.

Now, if Sheldrake would only propose to Breanna, and he himself could somehow gain access to Anastasia's inheritance . . .

"Medford." Lyman joined him outside the doorway, glancing about to ensure that no one could hear them. "I've been looking for you. You were swallowed up by the crowd before we could finish talking."

"We *were* finished talking," George replied tersely. "As for where I was, I was greeting my guests—and solidifying our future success. That was part of my reason for holding this ball. From now on, we can expect our shipments to be more substantial, and our merchandise of finer quality."

"Ah. Excellent. And imperative." Lyman took a step closer, and George could see the beads of perspiration on his brow. Clearly, the man was even more rattled than he'd realized. But why?

"Imperative?" he repeated carefully. "That sounds rather ominous."

Lyman's tongue wet his lips. "It is. That's what I was trying to tell you earlier. I'm glad you've corrected your business reverses, and equally glad our shipments will be improved. Because our costs have just gone up. Significantly. Fifty percent, to be exact. Effective immediately."

George's brows drew together in a scowl. "Where did this information come from?"

"From Meade. He's flatly refused to work another day without getting paid—in full. He won't accept your credit any longer, not for past shipments and definitely not for future ones. There have been too many late payments. He insists on your debt to him being satisfied immediately— in pound notes. As for upcoming deals, he wants his money up front and with a fifty percent increase. He says the risks are just too great, and your ability to pay too uncertain. I tried everything to convince him to reconsider, to bend a bit, but to no avail." Lyman whipped out a handkerchief, dabbed at his face. "So I'm glad we can meet his demands. Otherwise . . ."

Anger surged through George's veins. "Are you telling me Meade is blackmailing us?"

"I'm telling you he wants his money. He's not going to be deterred, not this time."

"Oh, yes he is." George drew himself up, his mind

already racing over possible solutions, and settling on a logical one. "I'm tired of Meade and his threats. It's time I eliminated them."

"You're going to confront him?"

"In effect. Nothing *too* uncivilized." George's jaw set. "Let's just say I'm going to see that the wind is knocked out of his sails." His hand sketched a dismissive wave, as Lyman began asking another question. "It's no longer your problem. I'll attend to it."

"Very well." Lyman appeared to be relieved. Still, he hesitated, lingering in the hallway as if he had something more to say.

"Is there something else?" George snapped, eager to bring this conversation to a close.

"Frankly, yes." A frown creased Lyman's forehead, and he blurted out, "Do you actually approve of your niece's behavior—involving herself in business, investing in, of all things, an American bank, seeking backers right here at her own coming-out party?"

The questions struck George like a series of blows.

"What in the name of heaven are you babbling about?" he demanded.

"Your niece. Anastasia. You mean you don't know? She's intent on starting a bank in the colonies. And she's asking Lord knows how many of your guests to finance this venture."

Silence.

"I didn't think you'd approve of it," Lyman concluded, seeing George's livid expression. "Not only Anastasia's choice of ventures, but the very idea of her being actively involved in business. And using this ball to acquire her . . ."

"Are you certain about this?" George interrupted.

"Of course I am. She approached me directly, requested my backing. She also approached Landow, Crompton, Bates . . ."

"Where is she?" George broke into Lyman's explanation, whipping about to scrutinize the ballroom from the entranceway door, only to find his niece was nowhere in sight. "Where's Anastasia now?"

"With Sheldrake. I assume she's soliciting his help as well."

"That's impossible. Sheldrake is with . . ." George's mouth snapped shut as he spied Breanna, chatting with a group of girls near the punch. "Dammit," he muttered. He turned to glare at Lyman. "You say Anastasia is with Sheldrake?"

"Yes. On the balcony. They've been out there for quite some time. Then again, as I understand it, the man is her financial overseer. Perhaps he's trying to talk some sense into her. I hope he succeeds."

George's hands balled into fists at his sides. Bad enough that Sheldrake wasn't with Breanna, as planned. But this? This was disastrous. It had never occurred to him that Anastasia might have made plans with regard to her father's money. But he'd obviously underestimated her. And if she squandered that inheritance before he got his hands on it . . .

Slowly, he sucked in his breath. Ludicrous. In order to spend her money, Anastasia needed Sheldrake's permission, something the marquess would never provide, not for a stupid venture such as this. And as far as getting other backers to finance her endeavor, that was equally preposterous. Not one man in this room, even the most outlandish of gamblers, would agree to do business with a woman. On the contrary, the stupid chit had probably succeeded in alienating every member of the peerage, a likelihood that posed an entirely different set of problems.

It was time to contain the damage.

"Excuse me, Lyman," George told his colleague. "All the guests have now arrived. I'm going to summon Anastasia and make her formal introduction."

"A wise idea."

George wasn't interested in Lyman's blessing. He weaved his way through the ballroom, forcibly restraining himself from plowing his way to the balcony. He had to look unconcerned, to avoid arousing suspicions. No one must think anything was amiss, that he was at all distressed by his niece's outrageous behavior. Oh, he didn't doubt the room was abuzz with gossip. But he'd deal with that later, address the comments, one by one. As for now, as host of an elaborate party, all that mattered was saving face.

Schooling his features, he edged closer to the open French doors, mentally rehearsing how he'd introduce Anastasia, diffuse the gossip, and find a way to stifle his niece's campaign for funds long enough to get through this house party, after which he'd deal with her privately.

He paused and, in a tone that echoed loud and clear, ordered the footmen to refill everyone's glasses. He was well aware that by doing so he was alerting the whole ballroom to the fact that an announcement was about to be made.

Satisfied, he strolled out onto the balcony.

Anastasia and Sheldrake stood near the railing, engaged in heated debate. George couldn't hear their actual words, but it was obvious his niece was uttering something decisive, her gloved hand slicing the air in emphasis. Sheldrake responded with an adamant shake of his head, refuting her position in no uncertain terms, his arms folded tightly across his chest, his baritone firm, uncompromising.

Thank goodness.

George could actually feel a bit of the tension drain from his body. But only a bit. Because he had an excellent memory. And if his now-grown niece bore any similarity to the willful child she'd once been, it would take sheer wizardry to alter her intentions.

Wizardry or a heavy hand.

He'd decide later which of the two to employ.

"Anastasia." George bore down on her, determined to aid Sheldrake's efforts and divert Anastasia's attentions—at least temporarily—before she decided to seek support elsewhere in the room. "I've been looking for you. It's time for your formal presentation."

Anastasia inclined her head and blinked, looking as if she had forgotten the whole purpose of this bloody ball. "Oh—yes. Of course. I'm coming, Uncle George." She gathered up her skirts, giving the marquess a measured look. "You'll have to excuse me."

Sheldrake gestured for her to join her uncle, then followed politely behind. "By all means. We'll continue this discussion later."

"My announcement will only take a minute, Sheldrake," George informed him. "After which I'm going to ask the musicians to strike up a waltz to commemorate the occasion. I'm sure Breanna would enjoy dancing with you. So feel free to interrupt and ask her."

With that, he guided Anastasia into the room, well aware that hundreds of eyes were upon them.

"Ladies and gentlemen," he began, a polished smile on his face. "It's no secret why I've invited you all here. My niece, Anastasia, who's been living abroad for the past ten years, has returned to England. It was my late brother Henry's fondest wish that his only daughter be properly brought out and introduced to English society—a society that Henry so deeply missed and that Anastasia has yet to experience. Tonight is her first foray into that society, and she's eager to embrace it, to leave the colonies and all they represent behind." A pointed pause. "I'd appreciate your joining me in helping her do that, and in welcoming her back home to England. Everyone—my lovely niece, Anastasia."

There was a round of applause, accompanied by some heated whispers among the ladies and a healthy number of fervent nods among the gentlemen—gentlemen who were openly proclaiming their approval of George's tacit message; that is, relegating Anastasia to her proper place.

In response, Anastasia smiled and thanked her uncle, although she nearly had to bite off her tongue to manage it, so great was her outrage. She recognized only too well the less-than-subtle admonishment she'd just received, and she harbored no illusions as to why it had been given. Obviously, one or more of the gentlemen she'd approached with her business offer had gone to her uncle to complain. And Uncle George was furious at what he'd perceive as nothing short of flagrant disrespect and indignity.

Inwardly, Anastasia frowned, realizing that, in her haste to acquire financial backing, she hadn't fully considered this. Oh, she'd expected her uncle to be annoyed when he learned of her behavior. But after a ten-year separation, she'd forgotten just how severe his reaction could be.

In any case, she'd have to deal with this later.

The musicians struck up the promised waltz, and Anastasia found herself automatically glancing about for Damen. She spotted him without too much trouble, across the ballroom, watching her with an enigmatic expression.

"Well, Anastasia." Her uncle's voice cut into her thoughts. "I see you already have a captive audience." He drew her attention back to him—and away from Damen—gesturing toward the opposite wall. "There are three gentlemen on their way toward us, all arguing over who will have the honor of dancing with you first. I'll let you decide. It will keep that active mind of yours occupied with something useful."

Anastasia didn't pretend to misunderstand. Nor did she flinch. She simply nodded, seeing beyond her uncle's practiced smile, noting that his eyes were icy chips of jade. "I'm sure it will," she replied.

Fortunately, the three eager suitors reached her side at that moment—bickering among themselves about the order in which they'd dance with her ladyship—so Anastasia wasn't forced to contend with her uncle's antagonism any longer, at least for the time being.

She turned away from him, as one simpering fellow, Edward something-or-other, claimed her, bowing and grasping her gloved hand simultaneously, leading her onto the dance floor and into the waltz.

The second young man, fair-haired and thickset, whose name she didn't catch nor cared to, hovered nearby like a hungry lion, whisking her away the instant the waltz ended and a minuet began. And the third chap, Lord Percy Gilbert, a handsome, ebony-haired fellow whose opinion of himself had to exceed any plausible reality, swept her into a reel, his dark eyes glued to her, rife with promise.

Somehow, Anastasia managed to enjoy herself, more as a consequence of the dancing than the company. She did, however, find herself glancing about the room, involuntarily seeking out Damen, only to spy him dancing with Breanna.

She forced herself to look away, and to stifle the unwelcome surge of envy that welled up inside her.

"You dance magnificently, my lady," Lord Percy informed her as the music stopped.

"Thank you." Anastasia smiled. "I've always loved to dance. Then again, I love any kind of activity that involves physical exertion: climbing trees, racing horses. But dancing is a pleasure unto itself."

He gave a warm chuckle. "You must have learned to dance at the same time as you learned to climb trees—as a child."

A puzzled tilt of her head. "No. I learned at the customary age of thirteen or fourteen. Why would you think otherwise?"

Lord Percy looked utterly taken aback. "But you were in the colonies at that time. Do they actually teach English dances there?"

Anastasia wasn't sure whether to laugh aloud or shout in frustration. "The dances we're enjoying tonight weren't English inventions, my lord," she reminded him, rectifying his ignorance in as gentle a tone as she could muster. "That particular reel was Scottish, the minuet came to us from France, and the waltz originated in

Vienna. We simply borrowed them. As did the States. Might I also remind you that America, too, is not an extension of the Crown. It's a country all its own now."

Gilbert stared at her, astonishment reflected on his chiseled features. "I stand corrected." He cleared his throat, a gleam of anticipation lighting his eyes. "You're a very frank and knowledgeable young woman, my lady. Also refreshingly unconventional. I hope to sample more of your free-spiritedness—and of you."

Before Anastasia could open her mouth to reply, a hard hand closed about her forearm. "Here you are, Lady Anastasia." Damen's deep baritone sliced the air. "That waltz you promised me is about to begin." He guided her firmly away from her companion. "Excuse us, Gilbert."

Whether or not Gilbert excused them was irrelevant, since they were already halfway across the floor. Damen signaled the musicians with a purposeful lift of his brows. In response, they commenced playing.

Anastasia began waltzing before her mind fully grasped what had just occurred.

When her thoughts finally caught up with her feet, she began to smile. "Why don't I recall discussing this particular dance?" she inquired. "In fact, why don't I think this waltz was planned at all, but, rather, was requested at the last minute—by you?"

"Because it was." Damen's expression was hard, and a muscle flexed at his jaw. "Your earlier scrutiny of the guest list might have told you who the investors were, but they didn't shed much light on the lechers. Gilbert is one of the latter."

Anastasia felt an irrational rush of pleasure. Was Damen being protective? Or was it just possible he was jealous? "Thank you for disclosing that bit of information. However, I'd already guessed as much."

"Really? Did you also guess that what he just suggested sampling wasn't another reel?"

"Indeed I did." Anastasia bit back her laughter. "I'm not stupid, my lord. I know when I'm being approached for an immoral liaison. Just as I know when I'm being rescued. Speaking of which, now that you've accomplished your valiant rescue, could you stop looking so fierce? People will think I'm an excruciating dancer, too trying to endure."

Damen's lips twitched. "We can't have that now, can we?" He whirled her about. "Very well. I'll try to look as if I'm having a wonderful time."

"And is that so difficult to manage?"

His smile faded. "The only difficulty tonight will be my keeping the proper distance from you. That, and restraining myself from breaking Gilbert's nose."

Anastasia's heart gave a tiny leap, and she studied Damen's face, wondering at the precise meaning of his comment. Was he referring to retaining the immediate physical distance between them, or to a far more significant, long-term distance?

Their gazes locked.

"Are you all right?" Damen asked quietly. "Your uncle's announcement obviously upset you."

She gave a small shrug. "Not upset me, angered me. The reasons why have nothing to do with the announcement itself, but with its underlying meaning. I'm not sure I can explain."

"You don't have to."

Taking in Damen's hard tone, the grim lines about his

mouth, Anastasia tried to figure out whether he was alluding to the fact that he didn't want to pry or to the fact that he already knew what she was feeling.

Either way, his compassion warranted some sort of response.

"Perhaps not," she conceded. "But I'll try just the same. You see, Uncle George made that pointed reference to my severing all ties with the States for a reason. He was blatantly condemning the idea of my starting a bank there. Knowing my uncle, I suppose I should have been prepared for his reaction to my plan. But after ten years, it seems I'm out of practice."

Memories flickered to the surface and brought a wave of sadness to Anastasia's eyes. "Once upon a time I was accustomed to Uncle George's rules, especially with regard to anything that might undermine him or cause him embarrassment. Both of which would definitely result from a Colby pursuing a business venture that not only excludes him but that puts a woman—his niece, no less—at the helm." She stared at the wool of Damen's coat, reflecting on how foolish she'd been to forget her uncle's rigid beliefs. "It was naive of me not to realize he'd feel that way. And it was equally naive not to realize that one of his colleagues would tell him what I'd been up to. In any case, that announcement was Uncle George's way of putting me in my place."

"I wonder if he has any idea what your place is."

Anastasia blinked, her gaze darting back to Damen's. She was taken aback by the fervor of his statement, and its remarkable accuracy. "I doubt it, Lord Sheldrake," she replied softly.

"Damen."

"Damen," she corrected herself, with a small smile.

Abruptly, that smile vanished. "Something else just occurred to me, something I should have thought of before now. Will the outcome of my actions tonight—namely, our partnership—jeopardize your business relationship with Uncle George?"

The severe lines on Damen's face softened, and a hint of satisfaction glinted in his eyes. "I like the sound of my name on your lips," he murmured. "And, no, your uncle won't let his disapproval of our partnership interfere with his dealings with my bank or me."

Anastasia pursed her lips, still unconvinced. Given Damen's role in Uncle George's life and the powerful position he held on the board of Colby and Sons, it was doubtful he'd even seen the dark side of Uncle George, much less dealt with it. But Anastasia had. And she didn't want to be responsible for Damen's encountering it now. "Perhaps I shouldn't mention the partnership to him."

"If you don't, I will. And not only because the man is your guardian." Damen's fingers tightened around hers. "Anastasia, I'm not in the habit of explaining or defending my investment decisions, not unless those decisions involve my clients' funds. But when the funds in question are my own, I answer to no one but myself. If your uncle is uncomfortable about the partnership you and I struck, that's his problem, not mine. And definitely not yours. All right?"

A hesitant nod. "All right."

"There's still something troubling you," he pressed.

Anastasia quirked a brow. "You really do read minds."

"Um-hum." Damen shot her a broad grin. "Even while I'm dancing. As you yourself said, without missing a step."

His teasing relaxed her into her customary candor.

"Very well, then. It's Breanna. I feel guilty. You should be dancing with her, not me."

Damen frowned, although he didn't look startled by her admission. "You worry about your cousin a great deal, don't you?"

"Yes. I did, even as a child. Probably because I had reason to."

"Well, you don't now; not at this particular minute. Breanna is surrounded by a large crowd of admirers. You can see for yourself after we round the next corner of the dance floor. Just look over my shoulder, to the left of the musicians." So saying, Damen whisked Anastasia about, angling her so she could see her cousin, who was, indeed, chatting with three or four gentlemen, obviously having a wonderful time.

"If you ask me, she's catching up on the Seasons she never had," Damen continued quietly. "She's enjoying all the newfound attention. Which is why it's too soon for her to be dancing with the same partner all night, and far too soon for her to be tied down to just one suitor. She knows I'm dancing with you. In fact, she urged me to go. Especially when she saw the predicament you were in. She was nearly as eager as I to rescue you from Percy Gilbert's lascivious hands."

Anastasia's eyes twinkled. "You just got to me first."

"Exactly."

"Tell me, Damen, how is it you know so much about Breanna and me? According to her, you've spent little time in her company. And I met you less than a fortnight ago. So where do these accurate perceptions come from?"

He drew her a tad closer. "Come riding with me and I'll tell you."

"What?" Anastasia was so surprised that she missed a step.

"Tomorrow. Before breakfast." Damen's grip about her waist tightened, steadying her on her feet. "I heard you tell Gilbert that you love to race. As it happens, so do I. We can take Medford's course at a rushing gallop. The winner gets to decide the order of surnames in our new partnership: Lockewood and Colby, or Colby and Lockewood. He or she also gets to choose the name of our new bank. Remember? That was what we were arguing about on the balcony when your uncle interrupted us."

"I remember." Anastasia wondered if she'd ever breathe again. This man affected her more powerfully than she ever would have believed possible. She was actually trembling, and she wasn't even sure why. "You have yourself a deal, my lord. We'll race at dawn. And *when* you lose," her eyes sparkled, "I want to hear how you come upon your insights into my cousin and me. *Then* I'll name our bank."

"Agreed." Damen's eyes were smoldering clouds of smoke. "I look forward to it—to the ride, to the conversation, and to whatever follows."

Across the room, Lord Dutton finished his fourth pastry and tapped George on the shoulder.

"Your niece and Sheldrake appear to be getting on famously," he noted, dabbing at his mouth with a napkin and pointing. "It seems that he's spent half the evening with her and the other half with Breanna." A chuckle. "Then again, perhaps he's lost track of which one is which."

"Yes. Perhaps," George muttered, watching intently as

Sheldrake swept Anastasia about the room. They were too far away to make out their expressions, and he found himself fervently hoping that Sheldrake's sole purpose in sharing this prolonged waltz with Anastasia was to shake some sense into the outspoken chit.

Because if not . . .

"Pardon me, sir."

Wells came up behind him, and cleared his throat before continuing. "I apologize for interrupting, but this message just arrived from the Continent. It's marked urgent."

George pivoted, glancing down at the envelope and recognizing the familiar hand. "Thank you, Wells," he said, taking the message and giving Dutton a terse nod. "Pardon me, Dutton. There's some business I must attend to."

"Of course, of course." Dutton waved him away, hungrily eyeing the new platter of food that had just been carried in. "Business first."

"Right." George weaved his way through the room, again reminding himself to behave calmly, not to alert anyone to the urgency that was swelling inside him with each passing step.

He made his way to the hall, veering left, then striding purposefully down the corridor.

At last, he crossed the threshold to his study, shutting the door behind him.

Swiftly, he tore open the envelope, palms sweating with anticipation as he extracted the single sheet of paper and unfolded it.

It was inside the note.

George scanned the draft, then swore under his breath.

The payment might have been anticipated, but the amount was not.

Determined to find answers, he turned his attention to the note.

Your last shipment was of poor quality and insufficient quantity, it read. *As a result, the agreed upon price of three thousand pounds is reduced to fifteen hundred pounds. Draft enclosed. Next shipment best arrive in a fortnight, prompt and up to previous standards, or no payment will be made and our association will be terminated.—M. Rouge*

"Goddammit." George crumpled the note into a ball and flung it into the fireplace. Broodingly, he watched it fray, then burn, turning to ashes before his eyes.

Raking a hand through his hair, he began pacing the room, sweat beading on his brow.

This was the last complication he'd expected. First Lyman, then Meade, now Rouge. The obstacles were closing in on him like steel walls.

He'd be damned if he'd get crushed.

He *had* to regain control. And to do so, he had to get his hands on some money. Now.

Time was running out.

6

*D*awn was slicing the sky in wide streaks of orange and yellow when Anastasia made her way down to the stables the next morning.

She wasn't sure what to expect. Damen hadn't specified a time, and she hadn't had the opportunity to ask. In fact, they hadn't had a minute alone after their waltz together had ended. Immediately after the strings fell silent, a group of businessmen had cornered Damen, and Lord Percy Gilbert had whisked Anastasia into the next dance. After that, Gilbert had monopolized her attention, relinquishing her only when one of his persistent friends wedged his way between them, demanding a dance.

Breanna had eventually saved her, tactfully summoning her over to where the young women were clustered. According to her, the ladies were eager to make Lady Anastasia's acquaintance.

Anastasia didn't care whether that were true or not. She was thrilled to escape Gilbert's bold innuendos and wanton stares.

But as it turned out, it was true, and Anastasia had

found herself the center of a hundred questions about life in the States, the gentlemen she'd met there, and the parties she'd attended.

Sometime after midnight, Damen had wandered over, politely interrupting only to bid both Colby girls good night.

Now it was morning—barely—and Anastasia wondered if Damen was even awake to keep their scheduled appointment. And if so, was he alert enough to race?

She rounded the path leading to the stables and got her answer.

There, leaning against the stable door, clad in a brown riding coat, beige breeches and black Hessian boots, arms folded across his chest as he awaited her arrival, was Damen.

He straightened when he saw her, his lips curving with pleasure, and a touch of surprise.

"I wasn't sure whether or not to expect you," he stated bluntly, walking toward her. "When I said good night, you were still very involved with your guests. I had visions of you dancing till dawn."

"No, only till one," Anastasia assured him, smoothing the folds of her bottle-green riding dress. "And I must admit, I, too, wasn't sure I'd find you here this morning. I thought you might be exhausted from hours of dancing and dispensing business advice."

Damen chuckled. "I don't tire that easily." He stopped, mere inches away from where she stood, his gaze sweeping over her appreciatively. "You look beautiful this morning. As you did last night, by the way. I never had the chance to tell you so. Not one man in your uncle's ballroom could tear his eyes away from you."

"Including you?" Anastasia asked boldly.

"Yes," Damen replied without the slightest hesitation. "Including me." With that, he gestured toward the stable door. "I took the liberty of having two horses saddled, in the event that you did arrive as planned."

"Really?" Anastasia baited. "And are they equally matched? Or can I expect you to be riding Uncle George's swiftest stallion while I'm on a sweet old nag?"

"Now how did I know you'd ask that?" he questioned with a wry grin. "Don't worry. I specifically asked the head groom to choose two well-matched, exceedingly swift mounts for our race." A grand sweep of his arm. "You're welcome to verify it for yourself."

"That won't be necessary." Anastasia tucked a strand of hair behind her ear, studying Damen as she spoke. "Any man who's as honorable in business as you wouldn't resort to cheating in a race. Besides, if you recall, I did promise never to question your integrity again."

"So you did." Damen glanced up as a leathery-faced groom led two horses out—both alert, both sleekly beautiful, their tails flicking in anticipation.

"This here is Sable, on account of her being all black." The groom indicated the first horse. "She's yours, m'lord. And this is Whisper, 'cause she's real quiet, likes to keep her ears up and listen to the other horses. She's for Miss Stacie here. Both these mares can run like the wind."

Anastasia looked at Whisper and frowned.

"What is it?" Damen asked.

"I intend to win this race. And I won't do that if I ride sidesaddle." She inclined her head at the groom. "Hughes, would you mind very much switching saddles for me? I'm going to race astride."

Hughes's gaze widened, but he nodded, dragging a

forearm across his brow. "Whatever you say, Miss Stacie." He led Whisper back into the stable.

A corner of Damen's mouth lifted. "A wise decision."

"One that might cost you the race."

"I'll take my chances, and I'll take them with fair odds." His gaze narrowed quizzically. "I notice people call you Stacie."

"Only those who have known me since I was a child." A fond smile touched her lips. "When we were little, Breanna couldn't pronounce my name. Not that I blame her. It was hard enough for *me* to pronounce. Anyway, she shortened it to Stacie when we were three. The staff seemed to like it, so the name stuck. Those household members who are still here now—Wells, Hughes, Mrs. Rhodes, and a handful of others—seem to have reverted back to it since I returned. It makes me feel a little more at home." Anastasia's smile faded, and a wistful look crossed her face. "Grandfather called me Stacie. He said it suited me because I never stood still long enough for anyone to say Anastasia."

"An astute observation," Damen replied, his tone curiously gentle. "Then again, your grandfather was an astute man."

"Yes. He was."

"Here you are, Miss Stacie." Hughes led Whisper out, a standard saddle strapped on her back. "Just make sure to tuck those fancy skirts of yours out of the way," he advised, averting his face, which had gone beet red.

Anastasia's smile returned. "Don't worry. I will." She tossed Damen a challenging look. "Ready?"

"Ready."

They led the horses down the path to the open, grassy

fields where the Medford horses were exercised. There, they stopped.

"You choose our course," Damen offered, gripping Sable's reins and squinting to assess the area. "Since you obviously know Medford Manor better than I do."

"Do I? You've probably spent more hours here than I have."

"That might be true, but my hours here have been spent in your uncle's library and study, while yours were spent racing horses and climbing trees. So you're far more familiar with the grounds than I."

"Agreed." Anastasia blew yet another loose strand of hair off her cheek, considering Damen's words. "In which case, I'll not only lay out our course, I'll deliberately alter it from the one I used to take as a child. That way, you won't be at a disadvantage." A sparkle danced in her eyes. "You see, my lord, you're not the only fair and ethical adventurer."

"So I see."

Giving up on her stubborn wisps of hair, Anastasia pointed across the field. "Do you see that fence? The one way down near the stream? We'll ride from here to there. Then, we'll veer left and make our way across to that line of hedges over there." She pivoted, drawing an imaginary line with her forefinger. "From that point, we'll race back to our starting point. How would that be?"

"Excellent. We'll use my coat as our makeshift finish line." Damen shrugged out of his coat and lay it on the ground, stretching the sleeves out to reach their maximum span. He gazed across the field intently, visually reviewing their path. Then, he turned and eyed Anastasia with a hint of a grin. "Can I offer you my assistance in mounting? You're going to have your hands full tucking those skirts out of the way."

She conceded, reluctantly, turning toward Whisper and frowning at the notable distance between the ground and the saddle. "This is not going to be one of my more graceful maneuvers."

"It won't be so bad. Watch." Damen came up behind her, his hands anchoring her waist. "Go ahead and put your left foot in the stirrup." The instant she complied, he lifted her off the grass, gently rotating her frontward as he did. "Now swing your right leg over. Gather up your skirts first. You'll worry about rearranging them once you're settled." A teasing note crept into his voice. "I won't peek. I promise."

Anastasia was laughing as she followed his instructions—a fact that slowed down the process considerably.

At last, she sank into the saddle, taking the handfuls of muslin she'd gathered up and shoving them beneath her.

"You don't look particularly comfortable," Damen noted, his gaze traveling up her bare legs and settling on the bulky cushion that separated her and the saddle.

"I thought you weren't going to peek."

His teeth gleamed. "That was when you were mounting. I couldn't resist watching this preparation ritual of yours."

Anastasia tossed him a saucy look. "Fine. Then, to answer your question—I don't feel particularly comfortable. However, I do intend to win."

"That remains to be seen." Damen walked around to Sable's left and mounted her in one smooth motion. "Shall I act as starter or would you like to?"

"By all means, my lord, you do the honors." Anastasia

gathered up her reins. "I trust in your integrity." She leaned forward, her eyes straight ahead, her heels pressed close to Whisper's sides.

"Very well." Damen followed suit, a fine tension permeating his body as he leveled his stare at the fence. "On your mark . . . get set . . . go!"

The two horses took off like bullets, tearing down the path, Sable just a neck ahead of Whisper.

Sable reached the fence with two seconds to spare, then veered to the left, heading toward the line of hedges. Anastasia picked up speed, and she and Whisper caught up just as Damen rounded the hedges, prepared to make a break for their goal.

They galloped the last lap neck-and-neck.

Itching to glance over and see Damen's expression, Anastasia fought the impulse to do so. Even a small gesture like that would break her concentration and cost her precious seconds. And *that* could cost her the race.

Blood thrummed through her veins as she urged Whisper on, feeling the mare's instantaneous response. Her gallop increased, her legs literally flying off the ground, propelling her forward.

The problem was, Damen had the same idea.

Crouching low and forward, he and Sable moved as one, tearing toward the finish line, undaunted by Anastasia and Whisper's remarkable show of horsemanship.

Two pairs of front hooves struck the jacket simultaneously, one pair on the left sleeve, one pair on the right.

"Well, what do you know—a tie," Damen observed, his breath coming rapidly as he brought Sable around.

"Yes. It was." Anastasia sounded not only winded, but positively stunned. Patting Whisper's neck, she gave

Damen a look of grudging respect. "You're a splendid rider, my lord. I didn't expect such fine competition."

Damen chuckled, gripping the front of the saddle as he dismounted. "What you really mean is, you expected to win." He walked over, inclined his head. "Right?"

Anastasia didn't hesitate. "You're right."

Laughter rumbled from Damen's chest. "Candid, if not modest. Then again, given your skill in the saddle, modesty would be misplaced." Idly, he stroked Whisper's muzzle, his brow creased in thought. "You do realize that our dilemma remains: the christening of our partnership and our bank."

"No," Anastasia corrected at once. "Only half our dilemma remains. With regard to our partnership, it will be Lockewood and Colby, just as I would have declared it had I won."

Damen looked startled. "But I thought . . ."

"You thought wrong. You assumed that, like most women, I'd be swayed by emotion. I'm not. The truth is, your family name carries a great deal more weight in the financial community than mine does. Colby and Sons is a trading company. The House of Lockewood is the most influential merchant bank in England, if not the world. The power of its name is invaluable. I'd be stupid not to use it to promote our bank. And, just as you claimed about yourself, I'll echo about me: I'm *never* stupid." An impish smile curved her lips. "However, I'm not entirely magnanimous either. I do demand equal say in naming our bank—just as a tie commands."

Rather than bantering back, Damen sobered, an odd expression flitting across his face—one that made Anastasia's own banter fade and caused her throat to tighten. "You're astonishing," he murmured.

"Is that a compliment?" she managed to ask.

"Yes." His gaze intensified, and he reached up, indicating his desire to help her dismount. "May I?"

Nodding, Anastasia leaned toward him, her breath catching as he lifted her up and out of the saddle.

She swung her right leg over to join her left, letting the damp folds of her gown flow free as Damen lowered her to the ground.

Their gazes caught—and held.

His hands lingered, and she could feel the pressure of his gloves, generating a heat that seeped through her clothes and into her skin, which was moist from the exertion of the race.

"Your riding is extraordinary," he told her. "As is your candor, your determination—and you."

"I'm also a mess." Anastasia couldn't believe those words had just popped out of her mouth. When had she ever been preoccupied with her appearance? When had it ever mattered to her how she'd looked after a wild dash on horseback?

Only now.

Tearing her gaze from Damen's, Anastasia regarded herself; the ruined gown flowing around dirt-stained stockings, not to mention her hair, which now tumbled free, cascading over her shoulders and back and sticking to her perspired neck and cheeks. She considered trying to rearrange it, then gave up the idea as hopeless. "It seems to me I'm in a perpetually rumpled state."

Damen shook his head slowly from side to side. "Not rumpled. Genuine. Uninhibited. Free-spirited. There's a big difference." He tugged off one of his gloves, capturing a strand of her hair and rubbing it between his fingers.

"You embrace life, live it to its fullest. Never make light of that. It's a great blessing."

Anastasia's heart began hammering against her ribs. "You're speaking from experience."

"Um-hum." His knuckles caressed her cheek, his forefinger slipping beneath her chin to tilt it upward. "I'm much the same way. I seize life with both hands, savor every opportunity it hands me." His gaze fell to her lips. "Every one."

He lowered his head, capturing her mouth beneath his.

This kiss was nothing like the one he'd given her last night; nothing like anything she'd ever experienced. It was intense, commanding, his lips molding and shaping hers, urging them apart, his hands gripping her shoulders, gliding down the sleeves of her gown, then settling on her waist, tugging her closer as he deepened the kiss.

Anastasia shivered as his tongue touched hers, then claimed it in a slow, purposeful melding she felt down to the soles of her feet.

She moaned, torn between dizziness and drowning, and clutched at Damen's waistcoat, much more for balance than resistance. The truth was, resistance was the farthest thing from her mind. Not when what was happening was so unbearably exquisite.

"Put your arms around me," Damen instructed hoarsely, seizing her arms and bringing them up and around his neck. "Yes. Like that." His own grasp tightened, one arm anchoring her at the waist, the other tangling in her already disheveled hair. "Now give me your mouth."

"Damen, I . . ."

"Kiss me." He gave her no time to reply before swallowing her words, tasting and awakening her in a way that made her entire body start to tremble.

She sank into the kiss, her fingertips feathering over the nape of his neck, discovering the damp strands of hair that lay against his cravat, and exploring their silky texture. In contrast, his body was hard and powerful, his muscles flexing beneath her touch, his entire frame taut even through the confines of his shirt and waistcoat.

As if sensing her thoughts, Damen sharpened her awareness of him, drawing her closer, then crushing her fully against the unyielding wall of his chest. Anastasia's breath expelled in a rush, her breasts tingling beneath the onslaught, her entire body shimmering to life.

The kiss burned on and on.

When they finally broke apart, it was long minutes later, and they stared at each other in mutual astonishment, their breath coming in harsh rasps.

"God," Damen muttered, half to himself. His fingers, of their own volition, continued sifting through her hair, letting damp strands trail across his palm, between his fingers, then watching as they feathered slowly to her shoulders. "I expected fireworks. But *that*—that was . . ." He shook his head, as if words escaped him.

Anastasia licked her lips, trying desperately to gain control of herself. She felt wobbly, as if she'd run a great distance, and her heart was racing its accord. Her skin felt hot and shivery all at once, and there was a dull ache inside her—one that made her feel strangely empty and yet simultaneously full. Worst of all was her reeling mind, which seemed unable to grasp even a thought, or much of anything else for that matter.

Damen framed her face between his palms, his expression still reflecting amazement, his tone husky. "Are you all right?"

Reflexively, she nodded, although she doubted it was true. "I . . . yes."

A corner of his mouth lifted. "I'm not either."

"I'm not sure what just happened," Anastasia blurted out. A bright flush stained her cheeks. "I mean, I realize what happened, I just don't . . ."

"I understood what you meant." Damen's thumbs stroked her cheeks. "And I felt it, too."

Swallowing, Anastasia tried once again to collect herself, to right her upended emotions. "Our bank," she said, grabbing hold of the first coherent thought that flitted through her brain. "We should name it."

"Coward," Damen teased gently. But he followed her lead, letting his arms drop to his sides and taking a deliberate step away. "Very well, do you have a suggestion?"

"Yes." Anastasia was glad she'd mulled this over last night. There was no earthly way she could conjure up something profound in her current dazed state. "I think we should call it by the terms through which it was formed: Fidelity Union and Trust."

Damen's nod was almost instantaneous. "I agree. Lockewood and Colby. Fidelity Union and Trust. Fitting. Consider it done. I'll issue instructions to my assistant, have him draw up the papers with Fenshaw this very day. I'll look them over when I return to London tomorrow night. And you and I can sign them the next morning in my office."

"Wonderful." Anastasia averted her gaze, gripped Whisper's reins securely in her hand. "I think we should bring back the horses. It's nearly time for breakfast."

Silently, Damen studied her, and she could feel his steel-gray stare bore through her, even without turning her head for firsthand confirmation. "Fine," he said at length. "But we *will* talk about what happened here, Anastasia. Count on it."

George rose from behind his study desk, scanning the note he'd just penned.

Rouge, it read, *Received your meager draft. Consider it an installment on our agreed-upon sum. Be advised that, as my costs have risen, so have yours. Therefore, the shipment you received was fair and adequate. Nonetheless, you'll be pleased to learn that I've found a new source of supply which will improve both the quality and the quantity. To demonstrate my good faith, a more extensive lot will be leaving in two to three weeks. The cost of that shipment is seven thousand five hundred pounds, including the fifteen hundred pounds due on the previous shipment. I'll advise you when the cargo is ready to sail. Rest assured, if you don't want the merchandise, another buyer will.—Medford*

That said it all. Clear, direct, and without revealing any of the worry that gripped his gut.

With a terse nod, George folded the note in two, slipping it into the envelope he'd addressed beforehand and sealing it.

Two could play this game of threats.

Unfortunately, only one could win.

Pressing his lips tightly together, George yanked open his drawer and returned his writing paper to its proper home. He hated leaving things out of place. In fact, he hated disorder of any kind.

In the process of shutting the drawer, he paused, extracting the miniature portrait he kept hidden in back.

Staring at the delicate features and flawless skin, captured so perfectly on the tiny canvas, he scowled, the familiar rage starting to churn in his blood. Damn her. Damn them both. Things could have been so different. If only this part of his life had fallen neatly into line, everything else would have followed suit. His life, his family, his business—everything would have been in perfect order.

Well, it hadn't. And now chaos was everywhere.

With that, he shoved away the picture, shut and locked the drawer, and snatched up his letter. There was no time for brooding. He had work to do.

Purposefully, he strode down to the entranceway door, signaling for Wells as he did.

"I need this delivered immediately for dispatch to the Continent," he instructed the butler.

"Of course, sir." Wells glanced at the envelope as he took it. "Is it going to the customary address in London?"

"Yes."

"I'll see to it at once, my lord."

"Good." George glanced at the grandfather clock in the hallway. "It's after ten. Have the first guests awakened yet?"

"A few have made their way in for breakfast. A dozen or so of the gentlemen went out early, some to fish, others to hunt. All the ladies are still abed." A tender smile. "With the exception of Miss Stacie, of course."

"Anastasia? Is she in the dining room?"

"No, my lord. Although I should think she'd be ravenous. She was up and out before the sun, and returned to the manor, along with Lord Sheldrake, before eight."

"Returned?" That brought George up short. "Returned from where?"

"Why, from their ride, sir."

George stiffened. "You're sure it was Anastasia and not Breanna who went with Sheldrake?"

"Quite sure, sir. According to Miss Stacie, she and the marquess had some business to discuss."

"They left together?"

"No. Lord Sheldrake left the manor first, Miss Stacie about a quarter hour later." Wells frowned. "They were only gone a few hours, my lord."

"And then what?"

Wells's frown deepened. "Then they returned, each requesting that hot water be sent up to their respective bedchambers. After that, they went their separate ways. Lord Sheldrake came downstairs for breakfast and left the manor again about a half hour ago. And Miss Stacie is upstairs, waiting for Miss Breanna to awaken. She wants to have breakfast with her cousin."

"Did the marquess mention where he was going?"

"No, he didn't, my lord. He sent a message off to Mr. Cunnings at the bank, then headed out. I didn't get the impression he'd be gone long. Perhaps he joined the other gentlemen at the stream."

"Perhaps," George muttered, his lips thinning into a tight line of disapproval. "Then again, perhaps not."

Upstairs in her bedchamber, Anastasia paced restlessly about. She'd been unable to sit still—with the exception of her long soak in the tub—since she'd returned from the stables. And she knew exactly why.

It was that kiss she'd shared with Damen. Not only the kiss, but its significance—*and* its complications.

A deluge of guilt crashed down upon her shoulders, shattering the last vestiges of her earlier daze and bringing to light an issue she'd been evading since last night's ball.

Breanna. Or rather, Damen and Breanna.

Last night the prospect had hovered on the periphery of her consciousness, but had been eclipsed by her quest for financial backing, and later by her fascination for Damen. But there was no longer any excuse for dodging the all-too-crucial questions that today's kiss had accentuated.

Could a relationship between her cousin and Damen ever exist—not now, but in the future? True, they were merely acquaintances now, but might that change? Might they develop feelings for each other—feelings stemming from mutual respect and compatibility? After all, Breanna was changing, coming into her own. Damen himself had noticed that. Was it possible her feelings for him might change, too—or, if not change, grow? She *had* said she found the marquess charming, handsome, and intelligent. And as for Damen . . .

Almost against her will, Anastasia remembered Damen's observation of Breanna last night, what he'd said as they'd waltzed by.

She's enjoying all the newfound attention. Which is why it's too soon for her to be dancing with the same partner all night, and far too soon for her to be tied down to just one suitor.

By one suitor, had he meant himself? And if so, had he meant it as a response to Uncle George's obvious attempts to push him in Breanna's direction, or as a response to his own inclinations? Could Damen's comments be an indication, inadvertent or otherwise, that he intended to wait for Breanna, to indulge her until she came into her own? Was he destined to be the partner who ultimately stood at Breanna's side?

If so, Anastasia thought wildly, *then what happened this morning could completely undermine Breanna's future.*

She chewed her lip, her mind racing. Whatever had occurred between her and Damen, it had been based on passion, attraction, fascination; call it what you will. But it wasn't the kind of emotion that futures are based on. And if he and Breanna were meant to share a future—not one inspired by Uncle George's selfish whims, but one rooted in devotion—then what had she been doing, kissing Damen, losing herself in his arms and wanting never to stop?

Dejectedly, Anastasia dropped onto the edge of her bed, wondering how in the name of heaven she was going to deal with this. She couldn't speak to Breanna about it. She knew her cousin only too well. Breanna would always place her cousin's happiness above her own. If Anastasia so much as hinted at her attraction to Damen, Breanna would immediately squelch any feelings she might be developing just so as not to stand in Anastasia's way.

My way to what? Anastasia questioned herself. *There's no reason to assume Damen thinks of me as anything more than an exciting diversion.*

But if he did . . .

If he did, then there was something else to consider, something just as critical as Breanna's feelings, and perhaps a great deal more dangerous.

Uncle George. Uncle George and *his* reaction if a relationship were to develop between his niece and the man he intended to be his daughter's husband. Lord only knew how angry he'd get—and how he would vent that anger.

Or on whom.

Anastasia's jaw tightened. That settled it. She couldn't let this flirtation between Damen and her continue. She'd have to put an end to it—now—before it really began.

George was in a foul mood.

He continued to trudge across the eastern portion of the grounds, having already covered the western and northern sections, searching for any sign of Damen Lockewood. The marquess hadn't been in the expected locations: the stream, the hunting or riding areas, as the other guests had been. In fact, wherever he was, it was becoming increasingly apparent that he was alone. Because the only guest who, according to the others, was out and about and who George had yet to come upon during this unwelcome excursion about Medford's grounds, was Viscount Crompton.

Predictably, the viscount had left the group he'd been hunting with to engage in target shooting on his own. As a retired military general, he prided himself on his superior skill with both rifles and pistols—a passion the other guests soon grew tired of hearing about and being forced to watch. And, as far as George knew, Damen had no particular affinity for the viscount and no interest in marksmanship. So, unless the two men were chatting about business, Sheldrake was alone.

The question was, why? Had Anastasia said or done something to give the marquess food for thought? Because Lord help her if she had. She'd already caused more trouble than she was worth, standing between him and Henry's assets, then embarrassing the hell out of him by approaching his guests for money to pour into some idiotic venture in the States. And now, this unexpected affinity between her and Sheldrake. It was trouble, any way you viewed it. Either the marquess was intrigued by her business ideas—or worse, by her.

Neither was acceptable.

But he'd find out exactly what was going on.

Then, he'd stop it.

7

*T*he crack of a pistol brought George's head up.

Crompton, he thought, turning in the direction of the sound. He must be nearby.

Striding forward, he found himself hoping that the viscount might at least have spied Sheldrake. Hell, who was he kidding? That self-absorbed loon probably hadn't noticed a bloody thing. No doubt he was too caught up praising himself over his incomparable aim.

At that moment, he spied Crompton, standing in a clearing and reloading his pistol, his stance every bit as arrogant as he.

George approached quietly, coming up behind the viscount as he raised his head and surveyed a line of trees.

"Do you see that cluster of oaks over there?" Crompton inquired conversationally, never turning around. He smoothed his gloves more snugly into place, then gripped the handle of the pistol and raised it. "I'd judge them to be about a hundred feet away. See that center oak—the short one that's dwarfed by the others? There's a good-sized knot about halfway down. You can see it if you look closely. I'm going to hit that knot directly in the center." So saying, he aimed and fired, striking the knot dead-center.

"Excellent," George commended, wondering if Crompton was talking to himself or if he actually knew someone was behind him, given that he'd yet to look. And, once he realized he had company, did he plan on launching into an endless lecture on the fine art of marksmanship; or worse, recounting long-winded stories of his years in the infantry, fighting the French, the Americans, and whoever the hell else he'd fought?

"Thank you." The viscount turned, his lean, tanned face relaxing into a smile. "Ah, Medford. I thought you might show up, acting as a good host and checking to see if I'm enjoying myself. Well, I am. And I must say, it's nice to have an appreciative audience." He sighed, waving his arm, presumably in the direction of the gentlemen who were out hunting. "I grew tired of shooting pheasants with amateurs. Anyone can strike a fat, slow-moving bird. It's mastering difficult targets that makes one feel truly accomplished."

George was in no mood for small talk, and less in the mood for Crompton's eccentric babbling. "I'm sure that's true. Actually, I can't stay and join you, much as I'd like to. I need to find Sheldrake. You haven't seen him, have you?"

"As a matter of fact, I have." Crompton flexed his shoulder, relaxing his lanky but well-muscled build for a moment. Despite the fact that youth had long since passed him by, extensive military training had left him as fit as a man twenty years his junior. "Sheldrake stopped by here a short while ago, said he was taking a walk." A knowing gleam. "And this time he was actually alone—not with that beautiful niece of yours."

A knot formed in George's stomach. "Why would you comment on that?"

"Oh, come now. Surely you saw the amount of time Sheldrake spent dancing with Anastasia last night. And they went riding early this morning. I saw them on their way back. They were laughing and joking like old friends. At first I thought it might be Breanna—I've heard rumors that you were encouraging a match between those two. But then I overheard snippets of their chatter: financing, business endeavors, and the like. Not to mention the woman's less clipped articulation. And I realized it was Anastasia."

In one smooth motion, Crompton reloaded his weapon. "Maybe she managed to convince Sheldrake to invest in that bank of hers. She certainly tried to convince me." A definite shake of his head. "But I have other ideas for how to increase my assets—ideas that can be furthered right here in England. And once those assets are mine, I'll deposit them in the bank of the very man you're looking for. He went in that direction, by the way." Crompton pointed toward the gardens on the south side of the estate. "He's a shrewd man, that Sheldrake. Smart as a whip."

"I agree." George was already walking. "That's why I need to find him. I'll catch up with you later, Crompton."

"Fine." The viscount adjusted his gloves, raised his pistol, and resumed his target practice.

Unaware he was being discussed, Damen continued along the path that led through the southern gardens.

Hands clasped behind his back, he was lost in thought, scarcely noticing the colorful array of flowers at his feet.

His rule about never allowing anyone to surprise him more than once had long since fallen by the wayside. And the person responsible was the same person he couldn't seem to get out of his mind—not for a minute, not since she'd first confronted him in Fenshaw's office, fire burning in those beautiful jade-green eyes as she'd battled her resentment over finding out that he'd been appointed her financial administrator.

Anastasia.

Damen paused, staring out across the manicured lawns beyond the garden, marveling at the unprecedented effect this one woman had on him. While he was definitely a man of passionate views and commitments—and an equally passionate sense of adventure—he was not a man given to sentiment, nor was he particularly romantic in nature. He enjoyed women, their company and their charms, as they enjoyed his. But as for anything deeper, more significant—no woman had ever inspired that sort of response from him.

Then again, Anastasia was nothing like any other woman he'd ever known.

She was beautiful, yes, but her beauty was just the outermost layer of something far more compelling. It was like the sugar drizzled over a tantalizing confection: initially, it lured you over, made you want a taste. And yet, having sampled one, you suddenly realized that the icing was but the finishing touch on a cake that was distinctively luscious unto itself.

God, he was thinking like either a starving man or a romantic. And since he'd already eaten, that left the latter alternative.

So much for his lack of sentiment.

Damen stopped, leaning against a tree and contemplating the facts, if not the emotions, of the situation, with the careful deliberation he applied to investment matters.

Anastasia was drawn to him. She was too open to hide that. She was also enthralled by his knowledge, his contacts, and his influence in the financial community. She enjoyed his company, whether on the dance floor or on horseback, and she especially enjoyed matching wits with him, a fact that kept both their conversations and their arguments vibrant and interesting.

He, for his part, was fascinated by her quick mind, her untainted spirit, and her determination to overcome impossible odds—namely, becoming a successful businesswoman in a world dominated by men. He was impressed as hell by her intelligence and insight; it had been her absolute belief in their banking venture that had provoked him into doing additional research and, ultimately, into reversing his decision.

On a more intimate level, he was aroused by her boldness and her fire—aroused, he reminded himself ruefully, to the point of behaving like a rash schoolboy. Bad enough that he'd overstepped his bounds with last night's kiss. This morning, he'd all but devoured her—and that was nothing compared to what he'd wanted to do.

She hadn't pulled away, he reminded himself. Quite the opposite, in fact. She'd come alive in his arms, responded to his kiss—no, *shared* his kiss—with an intensity that had nearly brought him to his knees. And the bewilderment he'd seen in her eyes afterward: awe and pleasure combined with reluctance at having to stop, that only served to heighten the already unbearable ache in his loins.

He'd known her less than a fortnight, yet he wanted her to the point of distraction. He wanted her ardor, her innocence, the wealth of untapped passion he yearned to ignite, then go up in smoke with.

On a completely different note, he was also touched by the tender-hearted side of her; the side that wanted to shield Breanna, to recapture the past, to change and shape the future. He was moved by her unwavering loyalty and commitment to her cousin; to the entire Colby family, actually. He'd seen the sadness in her eyes that first day in Fenshaw's office, watched her reaction during her father's will reading. She'd been heartbroken by the loss of her parents—something that no inheritance could abate.

And she'd adored her grandfather.

Figuring out what made people tick was one of Damen's finest abilities—an ability that made him damned good at his profession. He'd watched Anastasia carefully as Fenshaw told her about the six hundred thousand pounds; first noting her zealous refusal to produce her coin, then perceiving her inner turmoil as she struggled to understand just what her grandfather had wanted of her and Breanna, what he'd hoped to accomplish with his elaborate provisions.

And last night, when he'd come upon her on the balcony, when she'd spoken of a Medford Manor that no longer was—the late viscount was the person she'd been speaking of, the person she'd been missing.

Obviously, Anastasia's grandfather had been very close to his granddaughters—far closer than he'd been to his sons.

But George and Henry Colby were very different people, not only from their father, but from each other. And given George's unfeeling nature—well, there was no doubt in Damen's mind that Anastasia saw herself as Breanna's protector.

The question was, did Breanna need a protector?

"Sheldrake. At last."

The very man Damen was about to ponder headed toward him.

"Hello, George." Damen turned, arched a quizzical brow. "I assume you were looking for me."

"Indeed I was." George stopped alongside the tree where Damen was lounging, mopping his brow after the exertion of his walk. "I was beginning to fear you'd left Medford Manor entirely."

"Why would I do that?"

A stiff shrug. "It's just that no one knew your whereabouts. Wells said only that you'd taken a stroll, and it became clear to me that you did so alone. Is everything all right?"

Damen's eyes narrowed. "Of course. Why wouldn't it be?"

George hesitated, as if he were trying to decide how to phrase his answer. "I was concerned that someone might have offended you."

"Anyone in particular?"

"To be blunt, yes. My niece."

"Anastasia?" Damen feigned surprise, although he'd been expecting something like this. "Why would you think that?" A flicker of supposed realization—and a chuckle. "Do you mean because of her preoccupation with business? You know me better than that, George. I'm not bound to convention. Your niece is a very bright young woman."

"But she *is* a woman," George returned, his tone crisp. "And many of my guests were put off by her inane chatter about investing in an American bank."

Damen smiled, idly adjusting his cuffs. "Then your guests are fools. Because the notion is an excellent one. I've looked into it and I fully support Anastasia's efforts."

George's jaw looked as if it might drop into the peonies at his feet. "Are you saying you're allowing my niece to squander away a portion of Henry's money on a bank? In the States?"

"It's Anastasia's money now, George," Damen reminded him. "*All* of it. And, yes, I'll be authorizing the release of the necessary funds. In fact, I'll be doing more than that."

His complexion turning a sickly shade, George wet his lips with the tip of his tongue. His heart raced frantically as he tried to fathom just how much of Anastasia's inheritance was about to be lost to him forever. "You aren't suggesting . . ." He broke off, falling deadly silent as the final part of Damen's statement sank in.

Abruptly, the knot in his gut tightened to the point where he could barely speak. "More than that?" he repeated woodenly. "Are you suggesting that, on top of wasting Henry's funds, you're considering aiding Anastasia, acting as her backer in this absurd venture?"

"Her backer? No, I'm not considering that."

A tinge of relief crept into George's veins. "Thank goodness. You had me worried for a minute. I actually thought you were going to allow her to commit a large chunk of her inheritance to this, then make up the difference by loaning her your own funds . . ."

"I'm her partner," Damen interrupted. "We'll be investing equally in our new bank."

Another lethal silence.

Then: "You aren't serious."

"Oh, I'm very serious. The papers are being drawn up as we speak."

Unable to hide his outrage, George straightened, his eyes green chips of ice. "Why wasn't I consulted on this matter?"

Damen tensed ever so fractionally. "Because it wasn't necessary. If you recall, your guardianship doesn't extend to Anastasia's finances."

A flinch, the anger wavering a bit. "How much will each of you be investing?"

"That's not your concern either. Not unless Anastasia wants to share that information with you. The choice is hers." Damen's eyes narrowed on George's face. "Why does this bother you so much, George? It's not as if it's *your* money Anastasia is committing."

Sucking in his breath, George brought himself under rigid control. "You're right. It's not. But she is my niece; Henry's only child. And I worry that she'll squander the funds he provided for her future. Surely you can understand that?"

"Oh, I understand perfectly." A meaningful pause. "But don't lose a moment's sleep over Anastasia's financial security. I take my role as her administrator very seriously, just as Henry intended. I'd never allow her to compromise her inheritance."

"Of course you wouldn't." Damen's pointed tone found its mark, and George flushed, cleared his throat. "Why don't we just drop the entire matter? I spoke without thinking. Of course my concerns are unfounded.

With you managing Anastasia's assets, she'll never want for anything. I'm just glad you weren't offended by her rather forthright nature."

"I wasn't."

"Then why are you out here alone?" George forced a smile to his lips. "Or is that because you're passing time waiting for my lovely daughter to awaken from her long night of dancing?"

"Actually, there are several matters at the bank weighing heavily on my mind," Damen replied, choosing his words with purposeful care. "I only wish it *had* been Breanna I was contemplating. Your daughter has been one of the bright spots in my week. It occurred to me last night just how drab the past Seasons' balls have been without her there to light up the room."

This time there was a genuine, if still weak, quality to George's smile. "I'm pleased to hear that." He clapped Damen on the shoulder in an awkward gesture of friendship. "Then why don't we stop talking about finances and return to the manor? I'm sure Breanna is awake by now."

"A fine idea."

Breanna and Anastasia had just finished breakfast and were descending the stairs when the two men entered the manor.

"Ah, Breanna." George took a step forward, then paused, glancing uncertainly from one girl to the other.

"Yes, Father?" Breanna gathered up her skirts and moved forward, automatically touching her smooth knot of upswept hair to ensure it was in place.

"Lord Sheldrake was wondering where you were," George responded, totally ignoring his niece. "I assured him you'd be awake by now."

"We were experimenting with Stacie's hair," Breanna responded, glancing proudly at Anastasia, whose hair had been arranged in much the same fashion as hers. "Doesn't it look lovely?"

"H-m-m-m?" George gave his niece a perfunctory look. "Oh. Yes, yes, of course."

A grin curved Anastasia's lips. "It's stayed put for nearly ten minutes now. That's a record, at least for me." Her laughing eyes met Damen's, and instantly she averted her gaze. "If you'll excuse me, I promised Mrs. Rhodes I'd give her Mama's recipe for glazed cross-buns. They were the talk of Philadelphia."

"I'm sure they were." George gave a dismissive wave. "By all means, go." He waited until she'd complied, then turned to Damen. "I'd best check on the rest of my guests. I'll leave Breanna in your capable hands."

"My pleasure." Damen gave a half-bow, smiling at Breanna as George turned and walked off.

But once George was gone, and for the briefest of instances, Damen's gaze flickered toward the kitchen, watching as Anastasia disappeared from view.

Dammit, George thought, hovering on the threshold of the billiards room, observing his guests as they played. What else could go wrong at this bloody party? First the news about Meade and his threats, then Rouge trying to renegotiate their deal, and now Sheldrake and his unexpected affinity for Anastasia.

Bad enough that Sheldrake was actually condoning the chit's squandering away funds that by all rights should have been his—and believing in her enough to invest his own money, to actually form a partnership. But the amount of time the marquess was spending with her—

the waltzes, the early morning rides—how much of that was business and how much personal interest?

George had taken steps to find out how much money was being invested in that partnership—the right steps. It had been a stupid blunder on his part to ask Sheldrake outright how much of Anastasia's inheritance she was committing. With any luck, he'd withdrawn the question in time to avoid permanent damage. He'd find out in his usual fashion, from his usual source, who'd be receiving his instructions within the hour. As for the personal aspect of Sheldrake and Anastasia's relationship, he'd take care of that himself.

He needed Sheldrake. He needed more and better quality merchandise. He needed the money both would yield. And he needed time to get them—time he didn't have.

Only ten weeks until Anastasia's twenty-first birthday. If he didn't get his hands on Henry's money by then, it would slip through his fingers. Anastasia would be an independent woman, no longer under his guardianship; free to go where she pleased, live where she pleased, marry whomever she pleased.

And take her bloody inheritance with her.

Damn. He *had* to get Henry's money while Anastasia was still living at Medford Manor, under his roof and his guidance. He had to eliminate all the obstacles. They were cluttering his path. Especially Anastasia.

First things first. One obstacle at a time.

Shifting his weight, George peered into the billiards room, waiting for just the right moment to catch Bates's eye.

The magistrate must have sensed something because he missed his shot, then glanced up to find George studying him from the doorway. Ever so slightly, George angled his head in the direction of the French doors, indicating to Bates that he wanted to see him alone.

Bates gave an almost imperceptible nod.

"That's enough for me," he announced, tugging his waistcoat down over his portly belly and backing away from the table. "My luck is definitely not here today. Perhaps I'll do better at the gaming table."

A few grumbling retorts followed, but on the whole the men accepted Bates's quitting without question and resumed their play.

Bates checked the doorway again, noticed that it was now empty. Confirming that everyone's attention was no longer on him, he ambled toward the rear of the billiards room and strolled through the French doors. There, he paused, whistling as he idly surveyed the grounds.

As if by chance, George joined him, coming around the side of the manor and greeting his guest.

The two men walked off, chatting amiably.

"What's wrong?" Bates murmured when they were beyond hearing range. "I thought we'd taken care of your problem when we spoke last night. I told you I'd find you a new source. And I will."

"There's another problem I need to discuss with you—one I couldn't get into at the ball," George replied.

"Which is?"

"Meade."

A sigh. "Is he giving you trouble again? What is it this time—stealing the goods or tampering with them?"

"Worse. He's refusing to deliver my merchandise without a hefty pay increase. He's also making some threatening noises that sound disturbingly like blackmail. And *that* is something I will not tolerate."

No, but you'll inflict it, Bates thought bitterly. Aloud, all he said was, "What do you need?"

"An arrest warrant." George pursed his lips. "I need something to hold over Meade's head. A warrant would do the trick nicely. The charges are certainly real enough. The bastard is guilty of smuggling, privateering, maybe worse. You've conveniently overlooked all that to suit our purposes. Well, now our purposes have changed. And, as we both know, Meade is terrified of being sent to the gallows."

"So if you remind him that we can send him there, you ensure his cooperation." Bates nodded his balding head. "A sound idea. Consider it done."

George came to a halt. "When can you get it to me?"

"Is tomorrow soon enough? I can have my messenger deliver it by nightfall."

"Tomorrow is fine. I'll pay Meade a visit the next morning, wave the warrant in his face." A bitter smile. "That will do a great deal toward ensuring his cooperation, and his flexibility about payment."

"Then it's settled." Bates relaxed, as he always did when he'd satisfied Medford's demands. In truth, he hated dealing with the man. It made him jittery every time the viscount sent for him. But he owed Medford, and would continue to owe him as long as he wanted to keep his position of power.

How many times had he berated himself for accepting Medford's first offer, thus allowing the snake to have this much control over his life? But it was too late now. Medford's support, his connections, were what had ensured that Bates received—and kept—his appointment as magistrate of, not one, but three thriving districts, including this one in Kent. Undermining Medford would cost him everything: his reputation, his appointment, and, knowing Medford, perhaps even more.

The prospects were chilling.

"Your party is a rousing success," Bates commented, switching to the safer ground of casual conversation. "Your niece was welcomed with open arms by nearly every unattached man, as well as many of the attached ones. And the added attraction of having Breanna among us again—" A chuckle. "If I weren't so old, I'd give Sheldrake some competition myself. I'd happily choose either of the women he's pursuing."

George's head snapped up. "Either of the women he's pursuing?"

Instantly, Bates realized his error. "Not to worry. He spent most of the evening with Breanna."

"And the rest of it with Anastasia," George amended bitterly.

"I'm sure he was just being cordial. I wouldn't give it a thought."

"I have to give it a thought. More than a thought, in fact." George's hands balled into fists at his sides, his mutterings only half audible. "If she does anything else to ruin my life . . ." He stopped, sucked in his breath. "Just take care of the warrant," he snapped at Bates. "I'll deal with Anastasia."

8

*T*he House of Lockewood was even more impressive than Anastasia had imagined. Running almost the full length of Bishopsgate Street, it was a veritable world unto itself—a dignified world, with high, molded ceilings, polished marble floors and, at the head of the room, a bronze plaque of a coin bearing the Lockewood family crest, set on a pedestal and flanked by twin columns. One side of the bank boasted a triple set of doors that admitted patrons, and between the doors were rows of floor-to-ceiling windows, adorned by deep-green velvet drapes.

The uniformed staff, properly spaced along the entire periphery of the room, stood behind walnut gates, ready to assist the bank's clientele. In the rear of the room were small, private cubicles, where bank officers could meet with customers on matters that required additional attention. Behind the cubicles stood a towering walnut door bearing a bronze plaque etched with the word PRIVATE—a clear divider between the main room and whatever lay beyond.

Anastasia wandered farther into the bank, her gaze

shifting to the bustle of activity taking place around her. How many dozens of people must come and go from here over the course of a day, contributing to the aura of importance that permeated the House of Lockewood? How many of those people had Damen Lockewood advised, turned profits for, vitally impacted with respect to their financial success?

"My lady." A reedy gentleman, whose sleek top hat and dark green uniform heralded him as an employee of the House of Lockewood, hurried forward, bowing the instant Anastasia entered the bank. "We've been expecting you."

As he spoke, the bank's clock chimed eleven, precisely the hour Anastasia had told Damen she'd be arriving.

Curiously, she inclined her head. "Forgive me, sir, but how do you know who I am?"

A polite smile curved his lips. "I'm the head gatekeeper here. It's my job to recognize all our clients. Lord Medford visits our bank often, sometimes with Lady Breanna. And Lord Sheldrake told me how much alike you and your cousin look."

Anastasia smiled back. "I'm impressed, Mr. . . . ?"

"Graff," he supplied. Another bow. "And it's my pleasure to assist you, my lady." He stepped back, making a grand sweep with his arm. "If you're ready, I'll show you to Lord Sheldrake's office. Mr. Fenshaw is expected shortly."

"Thank you, Mr. Graff." Anastasia cast another awed look around, then gathered up her skirts and followed him across the marble floors, past the individual cubicles, and through the massive walnut door.

A semicircular expanse of imposing offices loomed before her.

"This way, my lady." Graff gestured toward the farthest—and, clearly, the grandest—office; the one nestled in the corner by itself. He paused, knocking briskly on the gleaming door.

"Yes?" Damen's deep baritone rumbled from within.

"Lady Anastasia is here, my lord."

"Show her in, Graff."

"Yes, sir." Graff turned the handle and eased open the door. "Go right in, my lady," he instructed, carefully remaining outside.

"Thank you." Wondering what on earth to expect, Anastasia gripped the folds of her lilac gown, and crossed the threshold.

Instantly, the door shut behind her—so firmly that she jumped.

Chuckling, Damen rose from behind his desk, smoothing his striped silk waistcoat as he walked around to greet her. "Alone in the lion's den," he teased, taking her gloved hand and kissing it.

"That's a bit what I feel like." Anastasia studied her surroundings, taking in the walnut furnishings and green velvet drapes, similar to the ones that accented the rest of the bank, along with a few personal touches: stacks of leather-bound books on the desk and shelves, an Oriental carpet atop the polished floor, and two magnificent landscape paintings adorning the walls.

"Are you pleased with what you see; actually, with everything you've seen throughout the bank thus far?"

Anastasia nodded in amazement, her gaze returning to his. "I'm astounded. In fact, it's good I met you elsewhere first, or I'd probably be very intimidated."

Laughter rumbled from Damen's chest. "I can't imagine anyone or anything intimidating you."

"You're right." An impish grin. "Then let's just say I wouldn't have been nearly as relaxed around you as I have been." A bright flush stained her cheeks. "By relaxed, I didn't mean . . ."

"I know what you meant." He was still holding her hand, brushing her gloved fingers against his lips. "I also know that something's going on in that beautiful head of yours, something that's making you keep your distance from me. You barely spoke a word to me at the party—*after* our ride, that is. Those few minutes following the race, when we were together—did I offend you?"

She didn't pretend to misunderstand. "You know you didn't."

"Good. I didn't think so." Without warning, Damen tugged her closer, brought her arms around his neck. "In that case we'll discuss your misconceptions later, whatever they might be. Because Fenshaw's due here soon with our papers, after which we won't be alone. And since I've been unable to stop thinking about you—the feel of you in my arms, the taste of your mouth under mine—and since I can't seem to act rationally around you, I need to do this." His palms slid down the length of her arms, capturing her face and angling it toward his.

Anastasia's breath caught, but she had no time to react before Damen's mouth swooped down, seized hers in a hot, bone-melting kiss. Demonstrating none of the other morning's gradual onset, he let the powerful pull between them take over, his lips moving purposefully over hers, his arms rigid as they shifted to her waist, bringing her against him.

"Anastasia." He said her name, and the sound made shivers go through her. She opened her mouth to respond, and his tongue slid inside, teasing and caressing hers until a low moan escaped her.

Damen tightened his grip, drawing her closer still, kissing her more deeply, his hands moving restlessly up and down her spine.

For a moment, Anastasia gave in, her eyes sliding shut as she sank into the kiss, pleasure drenching her senses as she felt Damen's warmth, his incredible power, engulf her. She pressed against the solid wall of his chest, felt the silk of his waistcoat against her cheek, the crisp muslin of his shirt collar beneath her fingertips. It was exquisite, this intoxicating feeling that flowed through her, making her limbs go weak and her heart pound like a drum. The sensations were just as they had been two days ago, only stronger, more potent. She could drown in this feeling, her body too alive to protest, her mind too dizzy, too clouded . . .

Much too clouded.

That triggered a warning bell—one that screamed its reminder about her decision—and its basis.

Abruptly, Anastasia tensed, planting her hands firmly on Damen's shoulders and wrenching herself away. "Don't," she managed, her breathing shallow. "Please."

Damen caught at her elbows, his tone and expression raw. "What is it? Why are you pulling away?" He frowned. "Dammit, Anastasia, answer me. Are you upset with me?"

Resolutely, she stepped backward, folding her arms across her breasts—whether for emphasis or emotional support, she wasn't certain. "I'm not upset with you. I'm upset with me. With us. With the situation." She inhaled slowly, determined to stand her ground. "Why don't we pretend this never happened, and just get to the purpose of my visit: signing our partnership papers?''

His eyes narrowed on her face. "I can't do that. Neither, for that matter, can you. As for the papers, we can't sign them until Fenshaw gets here. And he's not due for twenty minutes.''

Anastasia blinked. "Your note said the appointment was at eleven.''

"It said *your* appointment was at eleven. Fenshaw's is at half after. I wanted some time alone with you.''

Why did that notion elicit a rush of pleasure she couldn't squelch? "Damen, this is a bad idea,'' she informed him, knowing how unconvincing she sounded.

"On the contrary, it's the best idea I've had in ages.'' He moved closer again, threaded his fingers through her hair. "What happened to the new style you were trying?'' he murmured, sifting strands of burnished copper off her shoulders.

"It failed miserably. By last night I gave it up. I simply can't keep my hair from toppling to my shoulders, no matter how hard I try.''

"Stop trying.'' Damen brought one tress to his lips, savoring its texture. "You weren't meant to look prim. You were meant to look unaffected, sometimes disheveled, always beautiful—and always unique, the way you looked on horseback.'' His forefinger slid beneath her chin, raised it until their gazes locked. "The way you look now, with your lips still moist from mine and your eyes asking me to kiss you again.''

"Damen . . .'' Anastasia had no idea what she was going to say. Her palms were on his lapels, smoothing up the cloth of his blue tailcoat.

"H-m-m?" His lips brushed hers, once, twice, then hovered as he awaited her consent. "One more kiss," he said, his breath teasing her mouth. "Just one. Then we'll talk."

She took an unconscious step closer. "And this kiss will be the last?"

"If you want it to be."

Her eyes searched his face. "You know I don't want it to be."

"Um-hum. And I also know why you believe it should be." His knuckles caressed her cheek, the side of her neck, the curve of her shoulder, absorbing the tiny shivers his touch elicited. "What you're thinking—it's not true, Anastasia," he said huskily. "I promise you, it's not. Now stop fighting the inevitable and kiss me."

"You don't understand . . ."

"Yes I do. Now kiss me."

She gave up. She didn't have the strength not to. Not when she wanted more than anything to feel the incredible pleasure of his mouth on hers again.

With a breathy sigh, she leaned up, closing the distance between their lips and giving him exactly what they both wanted.

Damen took over, penetrating and devouring her mouth in hungry, relentless possession. His arms locked around her like steel bands, and he drew her up on tiptoe, crushing her body to his in a way that made her blatantly aware of his hardening contours.

"Don't pull away," he muttered against her lips. "Just lose yourself. For a minute. That's all I ask."

Ask? He didn't need to ask. Anastasia was already complying, molding her body instinctively to his, twining her arms about his neck as their tongues melded, parted, melded again.

With a rough, appreciative sound, Damen relinquished another modicum of control, his hand gliding around to find and cup her breast. His thumb found her already hardened nipple, rubbing it sensuously through her gown, sending skyrockets of sensation shooting through her.

"Damen . . ." She gasped his name, every nerve ending in her body centered beneath this new, incredibly spectacular sensation. His only answer was a harsh groan, a tremor racking his body as he pressed more urgently against her, his thumb continuing its motion—faster, more voracious.

Long minutes passed, time and the world held at bay, the kiss, the embrace, blazing hotter, growing more abandoned.

Abruptly, with what was clearly a herculean effort, Damen yanked up his head, dragged his hand away from Anastasia's breast. He planted both hands on the safety of her waist, gripping her tightly as if to anchor not only her but himself. Neither of them spoke, just stared at each other, their breathing labored, uneven.

"Anastasia," Damen managed at last, her name a hoarse, awed caress. "Ending that was the hardest thing I've ever had to do." His gaze sharpened, delved inside her. "But the kiss is all I ended. Make sure you understand that. Everything else between us is just beginning."

Pangs of guilt and worry intruded on the moment. "It can't."

An astute look. "Because of Breanna. Or rather, Breanna and me. And whatever it is you perceive about us."

She started. "You *do* know."

"I told you I knew. I also told you you're wrong."

"If you'd already guessed the reason for my aloofness, why did you question me?"

"Because I wanted to make sure there wasn't something else bothering you—something more than the foolish conclusions you'd jumped to. I saw my answer in your eyes."

Anastasia sighed, still reeling from the impact of their embrace. "What you saw there was real; I'm not denying that. I wanted you to kiss me. But that does nothing to change what can and cannot be."

Damen's jaw set. "Don't you think *I* should have some input into that decision? Or have you already sent me marching down the aisle with your cousin?"

Confusion knotted Anastasia's stomach, and she broke Damen's grasp, turned away. "I'm not planning your life, Damen. That was done before I arrived."

"By your uncle," he supplied.

"Or by fate."

"Fate?" Damen made a frustrated sound, gripping Anastasia's shoulders and whirling her around to face him. "I'd say fate is playing a much bigger hand in fanning the flames that burn between you and me, than in pushing me toward Breanna."

That Anastasia couldn't deny. "I'm not saying you're in love with Breanna. Nor, for that matter, is she in love with you. But you do enjoy being in each other's company. That was obvious at the ball. And given time . . ."

"Given time, she and I would be nothing more than good acquaintances who like and respect each other," Damen finished. "Just as we are now. And, before you ask, that would have been the case whether or not you returned to England."

"How can you be so sure?"

A wry grin tugged at Damen's lips. "If you'd given me the chance to tell you about my insights into you and your cousin, you'd know why. That was one of the unfulfilled terms of our racing bet, remember?"

Anastasia felt her lips curve in return. "I remember." She inclined her head, studying Damen's expression. "Very well. Share your insights with me."

"All right. I'll begin with my assessment of you." Damen's fingers caressed her shoulders, his touch warming her skin through the fine muslin of her gown. "You, Lady Anastasia Colby, are a strong-willed, intelligent, spirited nonconformist. You're always the leader, never the follower. You believe in yourself, in your ideas and your principles, and you believe life was meant to be savored, not nibbled at. You have keen instincts, a quick mind, and an independent nature. You also—as you're first discovering—have a rush of untapped passion just waiting to burst free." Damen's gaze fell to her mouth. "And I unlock that rush of passion in you. Just as you do in me."

Anastasia swallowed. "I think I've just been called a bluestocking," she managed weakly. "A bluestocking and a wanton."

"I think you've just been called breathtaking," Damen replied. "Breathtaking, enticing, and so beautiful you bring a man to his knees." He lowered his head, brushed her lips with his. "All of which you are." Another whisper of a kiss. "Shall I continue?"

A heartbeat of a pause.

"With my insights," Damen clarified.

"Oh." Why did she have to sound so disappointed? Probably because she was. "Yes—go on."

The glitter in Damen's eyes said he knew precisely what she was thinking, and that he shared her hunger. "Now for Breanna," he said, his lips hovering just above hers. "Breanna is like a beautiful flower: sweet, vivid, always pleasing to the eye, every petal perfectly in place. She's delicate, yes, but she's stronger than she appears to be—*if* she's cared for. *When* she's cared for," Damen amended. "Which she will be—by the right man." He framed Anastasia's face between his palms. "I'm not that man, Anastasia. I never will be. Breanna and I just aren't right for each other—not now, not ever."

Anastasia wet her lips with the tip of her tongue. "Does Uncle George know that?"

"No. He doesn't *want* to know that. And I've been reluctant to tell him—probably for the same reason you are."

She hesitated, then blurted out, "How well do you know my uncle—on a personal basis?"

Damen considered the question. "Not well. But the way a man conducts himself in business tells you a lot about the way he conducts his life."

"Business *is* Uncle George's life," Anastasia replied bitterly. "Business and the money it generates."

"I'd be a nice source of income, wouldn't I?" Seeing the startled look on Anastasia's face, Damen quirked a brow. "Did you think I was so arrogant—and naive—as to believe your uncle wanted me for his son-in-law because of my outstanding character and kind heart?"

Anastasia's lips twitched. "I suppose not."

"My suspicions are that he's not faring as well financially as he would have liked. Frankly, he just doesn't have either your grandfather's business acumen or your father's innovativeness and flair with people."

"Are you saying he's having monetary problems?"

Damen shrugged. "I only know as much as George lets me know. Colby and Sons is doing fine. But as for your uncle's private investments—those he doesn't conduct through me—I have no idea. Still, it would certainly explain his eagerness for Breanna and I to wed."

Anastasia's laugh was humorless. "You don't know my uncle. He doesn't need a reason to crave money and power. He could be the second richest man on earth, and he'd still battle for first place. And you: the head of the House of Lockewood, rich, titled, renowned everywhere and by everyone; you're an asset that's far too desirable to let slip through his fingers—whether or not he's short of funds." She averted her gaze, her expression drawn with worry. "Uncle George is such a cold, hard man. My only fear is that . . ."

"You think he'll take out his anger on Breanna? That he'll blame her for not winning me over, so to speak?"

A chill permeated Anastasia's heart. "I don't know. Nor do I know just how severe a form that anger might take. But I don't want to find out."

"At some point, we'll have to."

"Perhaps by then, Breanna will have met someone else—someone even wealthier and more influential than you." Anastasia sighed. "I don't suppose your scores of contacts could arrange that, could they?"

Damen gave a rueful chuckle. "They could summon extraordinary gentlemen from all four corners of the globe. But they couldn't ensure that one of those men would be right for Breanna."

"No, I suppose not."

Gently, Damen tilted up her chin. "Would you feel better if I spoke to your uncle? I could take full responsibility for not pursuing Breanna."

Anastasia's inner chill intensified. "And then do what, pursue me instead?" A hard shake of her head. "That would be the worst possible course to take. Rejecting Uncle George's daughter, then showing an interest in his brother's? You have no idea of the reaction you'd trigger. I shudder to think." She chewed her lip, chose her next words carefully. "The resentment Uncle George feels for Papa—for all three of us: Papa, Mama, and me—runs deep."

Again, Damen's eyes narrowed. "And you don't want to discuss why."

"No. I don't. But please, Damen, I need your word that you won't say anything to my uncle—not about what you don't feel for Breanna or what you might be feeling for me."

"I can't do that. Not when I fully intend to see you again. Not just once, but over and over." Damen's voice grew husky, and he threaded his fingers through her hair, that hot light flaring in his eyes. "We can't ignore what's happening between us. I *won't* ignore it."

A shiver ran through her. "Nor can I. But we'll have to be discreet about seeing each other. We'll have to say we're meeting just to discuss my inheritance."

"And our partnership," Damen reminded her.

She frowned. "I have to ask again, are you sure you want Uncle George to know about that?"

"He already does. I told him the morning of our race."

"You did?" Anastasia's eyes widened. "He hasn't said a word." She contemplated that fact. "Then again, I haven't seen him alone for a minute. He was with his guests until the final ones took their leave late last night. And this morning, he left right after breakfast." An uncertain look. "How did he react?"

Damen shrugged. "Much as you'd expect. He wasn't happy—not with the partnership, nor with the fact that a portion of your inheritance will be leaving the country. But he'll get over it. He'll have to. He has no choice." A quick glance at the clock. "Speaking of our partnership, Fenshaw is due here any minute. I'm afraid our private moments together are running out, for now."

That brought a sparkle to Anastasia's eyes. "Tell me, Lord Sheldrake, now that we've enjoyed this half hour alone, what would you have done if I'd brought my lady's maid with me? May I remind you that most women don't travel to London alone?"

"True. Most women don't, but you do." Damen's teeth gleamed. "You would never allow a chaperon to attend this meeting, or any other business meeting that involved you, for that matter. Even if your uncle insisted, you'd have asked your maid to wait in the carriage." A cocky look. "Another splendid insight?"

"Definitely."

Damen snapped open his gold pocket watch and realized Fenshaw's arrival was imminent. "We'll decide later how to handle your uncle—and what the best strategy is for seeing each other. In the meantime . . ." He buried his lips in hers for a brief, heated kiss that singed her down to her toes. "As I said before—only the beginning," he muttered as Graff's knock sounded. "Remember that, Anastasia. We're going to find out where this fire blazing between us is going to lead. Soon."

* * *

Forty-five minutes later, Damen sat back in his chair, nodding as he scanned the final page of the document he held. "Excellent," he praised Fenshaw. "You've put in all the terms we discussed."

"I'm glad you're pleased." Mr. Fenshaw, seated on the other side of the massive desk, pushed his spectacles higher onto the bridge of his nose, and gestured at Damen's quill. "Shall we summon Cunnings and you can begin signing . . . ?"

"Not yet." Damen held up his palm, glancing at Anastasia, who sat beside Fenshaw. "There are two of us involved in this partnership. I have yet to hear Lady Anastasia's final word on these papers."

Fenshaw's red cheeks grew redder. "Forgive me. I'm just not used to . . . I'm not in the habit of . . ."

"I understand, Mr. Fenshaw," Anastasia soothed him. With a twinkle, she turned back to Damen, sliding her copy of the document onto his desk. "The terms are not only fair, they're even readable to those of us who are new to the world of finance. I thank both you and Mr. Fenshaw for being so considerate." She inclined her head. "One question: once we sign, what's the procedure?"

"Before we sign, John Cunnings will be joining us. He's my senior officer, and my right-hand man. He's also in charge of the House of Lockewood's overseas investments. He'll be joined by another officer of the bank. Together with Mr. Fenshaw, those gentlemen will witness our signatures. Graff will then see to it that one copy of the sealed document is sent by courier to Mr. Carter in Philadelphia. Authorized funds from both my account and yours will be transferred to the States, after which, the building of our new bank will commence." A corner of Damen's mouth lifted. "Any other questions?"

"Not for now." Anastasia folded her hands primly in her lap. "I'll let you know if that situation should change."

"I'm sure you will." Damen rang for Graff, who hurried in, the essence of professionalism.

"Yes, my lord?"

"Tell Cunnings we're ready for him. Ask Booth to join him."

"Right away." Graff rushed off, leaving the door ajar.

Not a minute later, two men entered; one an older fellow with a round face and a full head of white hair, the other—who led the way—younger, in his mid thirties perhaps, tall and broad, with dark, close-cropped hair, a square jaw, and intelligent blue eyes.

"You're ready for us?" the younger man asked Damen, waiting respectfully just inside the office.

"Yes. Come in." Damen rose to his feet. "You both know Mr. Fenshaw, of course. And this is Lady Anastasia Colby, my partner in the business venture we're consummating today. Anastasia, may I present John Cunnings and William Booth."

"A pleasure, my lady." Mr. Cunnings bowed, kissing Anastasia's hand and clearly trying not to stare.

"Yes, she is beautiful and yes, she does bear a remarkable resemblance to Lady Breanna," Damen supplied, as if Cunnings had spoken.

"She certainly does." If Cunnings was embarrassed by Damen's remark, he gave no indication of such.

"It's uncanny." Mr. Booth—who upon closer inspection was not old as Anastasia had first thought, but rather prematurely white-haired—shook his head in amazement, assessing her thoroughly as he bowed, brought her hand to his lips. "Are people actually able to tell you apart?"

"Not most people, no." Anastasia fought the urge to look at Damen who, thus far, was one of the few people who seemed never to confuse her and Breanna. "Often not even our parents."

"I'm not surprised." Booth made another sound of disbelief, then recovered himself. "Forgive me for staring. I've seen your cousin only twice, but she has such vivid coloring, such striking beauty—suffice it to say she's not easy to forget. And the resemblance between you two is staggering." Roughly, he cleared his throat. "I apologize for rambling on like that. I hope I haven't embarrassed you."

"Not at all," Anastasia assured him. "Actually, your compliment was lovely; sincere enough to be appreciated, yet indirect enough to avoid making me feel self-conscious." A smile. "After all, it was Breanna you were describing, not me."

Damen interrupted the exchange with a purposeful rustle of the papers that were the subject of today's meeting. "Now that we've completed the introductions, let's get our signatures on these, shall we?" He produced a second quill from his desk drawer, handed it to Anastasia. "Ready?"

A definite nod. "Ready."

Ten minutes later, the papers were ready to dispatch.

"Do you miss America?" Cunnings asked conversationally as they awaited Graff's return.

"Some aspects of living there, yes," Anastasia replied with total candor. "I miss the people; they were lovely. I miss some of the freedom I had in Philadelphia that isn't possible now that I'm home. But most of all, I miss the essence of my life in the States: my parents." A reflective pause. "Actually, that's not a fair statement. I'd miss Mama and Papa no matter where I lived, possibly more so if I'd stayed on in America without them."

She dispelled the sober mood with a dismissive wave. "On the other hand, it's wonderful to be back in England. I longed for so many aspects of home; the bustle of London, the beauty of the countryside and, of course, Medford Manor and Breanna. It means the world to me that I'm with my cousin again. Breanna and I have always been more sisters than cousins."

"That's true." A half-smile touched Fenshaw's lips. "I remember the stories your grandfather used to regale me with—tales of your antics, of your deep attachment to each other. Even as tots, you girls were inseparable, whenever you had the opportunity, that is . . ." Fenshaw broke off, gave an uneasy cough, as if he realized he'd said too much. Frowning, he removed his spectacles, began polishing them furiously. "It would do the late viscount's heart good to see you and Breanna reunited after all these years. As for the ties you and your parents forged with the States, those will be sustained through the opening of this bank."

"I agree." Cunnings rubbed his palms together. "What's more, I think that launching an American bank will prove beneficial, not only on a personal level, but on a financial one, as well. Like Lord Sheldrake, I believe this investment is going to be a lucrative one."

"As do I," Booth concurred. His gaze flickered from Anastasia to Damen and back again. "It's also gratifying to see how amenable a partnership you're forming. Too many business associations are clouded by emotion. Clearly, you and Lord Sheldrake don't suffer from that problem—which is good, since it only gets in the way. Personal feelings of any kind have no place in business."

Anastasia squirmed in her seat, made distinctly uneasy by Booth's assessment. Why would he make such an odd, extraneous comment about her partnership with Damen?

Maybe it hadn't been extraneous. Maybe it had been deliberate. Maybe Booth sensed the attraction between her and Damen and was tactfully chiding her for it.

Or was she being overly sensitive, projecting her own feelings onto others since she herself was so vitally aware of the pull that existed between her and Damen?

She studied Booth carefully—a tactic that yielded no results. He was simply gazing at her politely, his hands clasped behind his back. Damen, for his part, seemed oblivious to the remarks, his attention focused on Graff, who now hovered in the doorway.

He signaled for the gatekeeper to enter. "You know what to do with these."

"Yes, sir." Graff collected both sets of documents. "One envelope will be secured right here in the bank. The other will be on its way to the States before nightfall."

"Excellent." Damen rose to his feet, nodding to each man in turn. "Thank you all. That completes everything we came here to do." He extended his hand to Fenshaw. "Thank you for your time and attention in preparing the documents."

"Not at all." Fenshaw clasped Damen's hand. "I'm glad things went so smoothly. If there's anything else I can do, just let me know."

"I will." Damen frowned as he saw Anastasia rise, shake out her skirts. "We have more business to discuss," he reminded her.

"I know, my lord."

Anastasia felt Damen's brooding stare, knew he wanted to continue their private talk, to work out how they should handle her uncle. But now was not the time, for a variety of reasons. First, she'd told Breanna she'd be away only a few hours; and second, she didn't want to arouse suspicions about the nature of her relationship with Damen—suspicions that, judging from Mr. Booth's reaction, might already have been kindled.

"I realize we still have some unfinished business," she said, meeting and holding Damen's gaze. "But it will have to wait. I must get home. As it is, I've been away far longer than I expected. I don't want Breanna to worry." *Or to get in trouble with my uncle,* she added silently.

As if reading her mind, Damen relented. "Very well. I'll drop by tomorrow then. Right after breakfast."

"That would be fine."

"I'll escort Lady Anastasia to her carriage," Booth offered, taking a step toward her.

"There's no need for you to inconvenience yourself," Fenshaw said, waving away Booth's offer before Anastasia could respond. "I'll be leaving now anyway, to return to my office. I'll personally escort Lady Anastasia to her carriage." He offered Anastasia his arm. "My lady."

"Thank you, Mr. Fenshaw." Anastasia complied, wondering why Booth was so eager to get rid of her. Was he anxious to get back to his work, or was he just trying to prevent her from being alone with Damen?

"It was a pleasure meeting you, my lady." John Cunnings interrupted her thoughts, bowed as he moved toward the doorway.

"I return the compliment, sir," she replied. "And I

appreciate your belief in our venture." She turned to Damen, gave him a cordial, businesslike smile. "Lord Sheldrake—I look forward to a profitable association."

"As do I." Damen came around the front of his desk and kissed her gloved hand, his silver-gray gaze boring inside her, telling her he was far from happy with this abrupt departure. "I'll see you first thing tomorrow morning."

The noon hour came and went.

The skies remained gloomy, a fine drizzle dampening the London docks, turning the bank of the Thames to mud.

Still, activity was at a peak. Crewmen yelled back and forth to each other as they readied ships about to set sail. Cranes hoisted cargo from arriving vessels. Porters stood at wharfside, ready to unload incoming coal, and watermen adeptly rowed passengers out to catch departing ships they'd missed. Dock workers, their skin glistening with raindrops, strained as they jumped on and off ships, some loading, others unloading cargo. This all-important hustle and bustle dominated the wharf, and warehouse doors were flung wide as able-bodied men carried thick bags of cargo in for storage.

Meade made his way up the path leading to the warehouses, two heavy sacks pitched on his back, their cumbersome weight doubling him over until his chin could practically touch his protruding belly. He entered the warehouse, falling to his knees and letting the bags drop to the rotted wooden floor beside him.

The relief was blessed.

He rose up, shaking strands of unkempt hair out of his face and dragging a sleeve across his sweaty forehead.

Sugar. Pounds and pounds of wretched sugar.

What a waste. Granules—useful only to make cake. Pretty poor chance of making any real money out of that.

Then again, there hadn't been much money made out of anything else lately either. At least not for him. And his belly was the only one he cared about feeding.

Well, all that was about to change. After his talk with Lyman, everything would change.

The warehouse door flung wide, striking the wall with a thud.

Meade whipped around to see who had joined him, automatically stooping to snatch his knife from his boot.

He straightened, the blade glinting in the dimly lit warehouse.

Faint or not, the lighting was good enough. He recognized Medford right away by his haughty air and deceptively hunched shoulders.

"Put the knife away, Meade." The viscount advanced toward him in slow, predatory steps. "I think it's time we had a talk."

Meade wasn't alarmed. He'd expected a visit like this the minute he made his demands. Of course Lyman would go straight to Medford. He was the one who paid their wages. As for Medford's anger, well, he'd expected that, too. The son of a bitch didn't take threats lightly. He liked being in control. That suited Meade just fine. He didn't want control. He wanted money. Which, after this little talk, was just what he'd get. Because Medford needed him. They both knew that.

Steeling himself, Meade ignored Medford's command. How the hell did he know the bastard wasn't armed? He couldn't take that chance. No, he'd keep his blade right where it was—clutched and ready.

"I don't wanna talk." The privateer's eyes glinted, his

whiskered jaw tightly set. "I want me money. *All* me money. And more of it from now on."

"So I heard. Fifty percent more." Undeterred by Meade's weapon, Medford never paused, walking forward until he could almost touch the gleaming blade—then halting. "The fact is, you won't be getting your money. Not yet. I don't have it. And your generous wage increase? *That* you won't be getting at all."

"Then I won't be deliverin' yer merchandise."

"Ah, but you're wrong. You *will* be delivering my merchandise—willingly and without further threats." Medford slipped his hand into his pocket, and Meade tensed, his fingers tightening about the handle of his blade.

"I told you to put that away, Meade," the viscount commanded.

"And let ye shoot me? Not a chance."

"I don't plan to shoot you." George withdrew his hand and flourished a sheet of paper. "I won't have to. That task will be taken care of for me."

Meade's eyes narrowed. "What are ye talkin' about?"

A tight smile. "If you'll hold this up to the light, you'll see it's an arrest warrant. It was issued by the magistrate himself. You're a wanted man, Meade—a renowned privateer and smuggler. Why, if I turn you in, you'll be in the gallows before you know it, hanging by the neck at the end of a very short, tight rope. How does that sound?"

Lowering his blade, Meade snatched the page, brought it over to the window. He swore at the official-looking seal at the bottom of the document, knowing right away what it meant.

"Now, can we renegotiate our terms?" George inquired. "Instead of your demands for an increase and your threats to expose me, why don't we settle for keeping things just as they are? In return, I'll pretend I never heard of you, should I be asked. I'll simply ignore the dictates of my conscience, refrain from turning you in. I think that's a fair arrangement, don't you?"

Silence.

"Good. Then we understand each other. Right, Meade?"

Another long silence, during which Meade felt his heart drumming wildly in his chest. Hanging. Dying. Feeling his neck crack in two.

Nothing was worth that.

Resignation sank deep in his gut, and he saw his fortune go up in smoke. "Yeah, Medford," he muttered bitterly. "Right."

Triumph glittered in the viscount's eyes. "Excellent. The next shipment will be ready in ten days. Be prepared to deliver it on time. And Meade? Don't *ever* blackmail me again."

9

The victory was little cause for celebration.

George leaned back in his carriage, his teeth gritting as he assessed the situation.

All well and good that Meade would deliver the shipment as planned. First, the damned merchandise had to be secured, a reality that Bates was supposedly seeing to. And even if both tasks went smoothly, George had to pray that his note to Rouge had been convincing enough to inspire a modicum of patience; that, as a result of George's threat to take his business elsewhere, Rouge would adhere to the specified terms and pay the full amount due.

And if that happened?

Even the full amount was a mere drop in the bucket compared to George's ocean of debt.

His colleagues, his creditors, his informants.

The very thought of how many thousands and thousands of pounds he owed made him ill.

And then there was Anastasia.

Just pondering his niece, the fact that she held his fate

in the palm of her hand, made his skull pound with rage. Oh, Henry's precious brat had no idea of the power she wielded. But George did. And he loathed her for it.

What had his contact found out? he wondered bitterly. How much of Henry's money had been committed to this wretched bank Anastasia hoped to open? And what were the details of her partnership with Sheldrake—and any other unwelcome bond that might be developing between them?

George wasn't stupid. He knew only too well that business associations often led to personal ones. And given that it was a man and a woman who were involved in this particular partnership—well, suddenly the word *personal* took on a whole new meaning. If Anastasia and Sheldrake were to spend any substantial amount of time together . . . George's hands balled into fists at his sides. Damn her. She would not rob him of that, too.

He'd have another talk with Breanna—immediately— and make his intentions for her future unmistakably clear. Then he'd find ways to throw her and Sheldrake together, and ways to keep the marquess and Anastasia apart. He needed Sheldrake in the family, not only to provide money and status, but to shed a favorable light on George's reputation, and to ensure his silence if he were to learn anything damning about his new father-in-law.

Perhaps there was something to say for family after all.

A humorless smile twisted George's lips. Family hadn't been enough motivation for Henry, not when it came to including his brother as a beneficiary to his estate. Well, with the right manipulation, Henry's funds would find their way into the right hands after all.

Whatever was left of those funds, that is.

George stared out the window, watched as the gates of Medford Manor came into view.

He had to find out how much of Henry's inheritance had been allocated to that bloody bank. And he had to find out *now*.

He was in trouble. Big trouble. His options were vanishing before his very eyes. With Anastasia controlling half of Colby and Sons, and Sheldrake acting as her trusty administrator, there was little hope of doctoring receipts to Lyman or any other supplier without getting caught. As for a more readily available source, there were only a few thousand pounds left to drain of the funds Henry had set aside for Anastasia's coming-out.

He needed that inheritance.

Ten weeks. After which, it would be too late. Everything would blow up in his face. Rouge would find another supplier, the creditors would close in, and Anastasia would walk away with her inheritance, her half of Colby and Sons, and—Lord help her—Damen Lockewood.

No. George sat upright, his fingers reflexively gripping the door handle, ready to twist it the instant the carriage came to a halt. He wouldn't allow it. He'd talk to Breanna right now. Then, he'd summon his contact, learn the details of that bloody partnership.

And then, he'd do whatever he must to save his neck.

Wells stood in the open doorway, his expression nondescript as he watched the viscount stalk up the stairs and into the manor.

"Where's Breanna?" George bit out, glaring at his butler.

"In the library, my lord. Shall I summon her?"

"No. I'll do my own summoning. Besides, the library is as good a place as any."

Wells stiffened a bit. "For what, sir?"

"Nothing that concerns you." George strode down the hall, jerking open the library door and stepping inside.

"Father." Breanna started, as she looked up from the settee upon which she was curled, thumbing through a novel. She studied her father's expression, a certain wariness coming over her. Slowly, she shut the book. "Did you wish to see me?"

"Indeed I did." George shut the door firmly behind him. He crossed over to the sideboard, poured himself a drink. Tossing it down in three gulps, he slammed the goblet onto an end table and walked across the room until he loomed directly over his daughter. "You and I are going to talk. Or rather, *I'm* going to talk. *You're* going to listen. And then, you're going to do as I say."

Instinctively, Breanna scooted to the far corner of the settee. "What is it we're talking about?"

"You and Lord Sheldrake." George pressed his palms together, studying his hands as if that act could help him maintain his self-restraint. "It's time we took definite steps to ensure your future as Mrs. Damen Lockewood."

Color suffused Breanna's cheeks, and she lowered her lashes, contemplating the cover of her book. "I think any steps we take would be futile," she said at last. "In fact, I think we should both accept the fact that I don't have a future with Lord Sheldrake."

Her breath lodged in her throat, as George swooped down, gripping her shoulders and nearly lifting her off the settee. "I don't think you understand. So let me make it clear. Giving up is not an option. Not in this case." His eyes blazed with jade fire, his fingers bit into her flesh.

"You *will* marry Lord Sheldrake. Soon. What I'm here to discuss is how best to speed up this courtship."

Breanna's eyes widened in fear, but she didn't retreat. "What courtship, Father? There is none."

"Then there will be one as of now." George lowered Breanna back to the settee, his forefinger jerking up her chin to meet his gaze. "Besides, you underestimate yourself. The marquess was very attentive at the ball. He danced with you for most of the evening. Afterward, he spoke highly of you. I think all he needs is a little encouragement—not from me, from you. And you're going to give him that encouragement."

"Why? Why is it so important to you that I marry Lord Sheldrake? Are you hoping he'll offer you money for my hand?"

A flicker of astonishment, after which George's lips thinned into an angry line. "Where is this newfound impertinence coming from—having Anastasia living with us?"

Breanna swallowed. "I apologize if I sounded rude. But it's only natural for me to have questions. After all, it is *my* life we're discussing. And I'd like to understand what you hope to gain by wedding me to Lord Sheldrake. I know how much wealth and position mean to you. We wouldn't be having this conversation if the marquess were poor and unrenowned. Is it that you hope to gain access to his fortune? If so, I don't think that's an unspoken certainty—not unless Lord Sheldrake chooses it to be. And, to be honest, I don't think he's so enchanted with me that he'd pay handsomely just to give me his name."

George twisted Breanna's chin until she whimpered, then shoved her away. "My motives, daughter, are my own. Your job is to make them a reality. Now, I'm going to invite the marquess to breakfast tomorrow. Once the meal is over, I'll suggest that you two take a private stroll. During that time, I expect you to make it blatantly clear that you enjoy his attentions, and that you'd welcome his affections. Is that understood?"

Silence.

Renewed anger flared in George's eyes, and he leaned menacingly over her. "*Is that understood?*"

Breanna nodded, but didn't flinch. "Yes, Father. You've made your expectations perfectly clear."

"Good." George backed away, walked over to freshen his drink. "Where is Anastasia—in her room?"

Steeling herself for the inevitable explosion, Breanna shook her head. "No, she went out several hours ago. She should be back any minute."

Something about Breanna's tone must have aroused George's suspicions, or perhaps it was the fact that Anastasia rarely went out alone that made him leery.

He turned, goblet in hand. "Where did she go?"

"To the House of Lockewood." Breanna tried not to react to the fury that twisted her father's features. "She said something about a meeting."

"Dammit." George raised his arm over his head, and Breanna braced herself for the crash of the goblet striking the floor.

The crash never came.

Slowly, George lowered his arm, visibly trying to control his wrath.

"Send her to my study," he ground out between clenched teeth, "the minute she returns. It's time your cousin and I had a little talk, as well."

"She's only gone to finish settling Uncle Henry's affairs," Breanna defended at once, trying to ward off whatever confrontation her father had in mind. "I'm sure she would have told you about this meeting herself, but you'd already left the estate."

"I'm sure she is and I'm sure she would have." George's words were as caustic as his smile. "But the fact remains that I'm her guardian. And, as such, I can't have her gallivanting about without permission or, knowing Anastasia, without a proper chaperon. I'm concerned for her safety, and for her reputation. After all, this is England, not America."

"Still, I don't think . . ."

"Stop shielding her, Breanna. Just send her to my study. Immediately." George's eyes narrowed into glittering jade chips. "And remember what I said. I expect to be announcing your betrothal to Lord Sheldrake in a matter of weeks."

Anastasia sensed something was wrong the minute she saw Wells's drawn expression.

Glancing about, she noted the empty hall, felt the tension permeating it.

"Wells?" she murmured, inclining her head. "What is it?"

The butler didn't mince words. "Your uncle arrived home an hour ago. He was unusually distressed."

"Distressed," Anastasia repeated. "You mean angry. Especially when he learned I wasn't here—and probably where I was." Another swift glance down the hall. "Is he with Breanna now?"

"Not anymore. He was with your cousin in the library for about twenty minutes. Then, he emerged rather briskly, and disappeared into his study."

Anastasia's uneasiness intensified. "What about Breanna? Is she still in the library?"

"Yes, Miss Stacie. She's come out twice asking if you were home yet. I promised to send you down the moment you arrived."

"I'm on my way." Anastasia hurried down the hall, tiptoeing past her uncle's study, and made her way to the library.

She pushed open the door and stepped inside.

Breanna was pacing in front of the windows.

"Stacie. Thank goodness." She motioned for her to enter and shut the door behind her.

Anastasia complied, frowning as she studied her cousin. Breanna was noticeably upset, just as she always was after dealing with her father. But this time she was more; this time she was totally distraught.

"What happened?" Anastasia didn't mince words. She crossed over, seized Breanna's hands.

And went utterly cold inside when she saw the bruise on her cousin's chin—a bruise that could have been caused by nothing but the punishing grip of a thumb and forefinger.

"Oh, no." She reached out, touched the mark ever so gently.

"It doesn't hurt." Breanna waved away her cousin's concern. "Honestly, Stacie. I don't even think Father knew he was doing it. He was desperate to make his point, to push me into doing his bidding. And when I balked . . . well, I truly think he lost his reason."

"You're defending him?" Anastasia asked incredulously.

"No, of course not. All I'm saying is, he didn't beat me.

He didn't even shout. It's as if he's desperate—desperate enough to be even more callous than usual."

"But it's *me* he's angry at, not you."

"Actually, it's both of us." Breanna smoothed a shaky hand over her upswept hair. "You, for going to Lord Sheldrake's bank; me, for not yet wearing his wedding ring." She dismissed Anastasia's onslaught of questions with a firm shake of her head. "Listen to me, Stacie. You and I can discuss this in detail tonight after Father's gone to bed and we're alone. Right now, he's awaiting your arrival like a hungry lion awaits its dinner. He's angry, he's unnerved, and he's determined to have his say. All that's important is for you to know what you're in for. Father feels threatened by your relationship with Lord Sheldrake—both personally and financially. He has his own plans for the marquess's fortune—and his future. Father wants me to marry Lord Sheldrake. You and I both know that. We also know it's never going to happen, and why. How we get Father to accept it is another matter entirely. I tried, and failed. It's your turn. But tread carefully. This is not going to be a pleasant meeting."

Anastasia listened closely, appreciating Breanna's worry, at the same time captured by her cousin's adamant statement: *We also know it's never going to happen, and why.*

The way Breanna said that—with the certainty of one who knew rather than surmised—clearly, she was referring to something more concrete than the fact that she and Damen were mere acquaintances. And, given how finely attuned she and Anastasia were, given that they'd always been able to read each other's thoughts, it didn't take a genius to figure out that Breanna had sensed the attraction between her cousin and Damen.

A dozen questions hovered on Anastasia's tongue, and

were silenced as she stared at the bruise on Breanna's chin.

At the moment, none of her questions mattered; not those concerning Breanna's underlying meaning, nor those pertaining to how much of the truth she'd guessed. What mattered was Uncle George—Uncle George and his violent determination to shape the future his way.

Anastasia clenched the folds of her gown, her resolve strengthening twofold. She knew how she must handle this impending confrontation, and it included keeping her bloody tongue in check. Otherwise, it wouldn't be she who would suffer. It would be Breanna.

"Don't worry," she said lightly, squeezing her cousin's arm. "You've prepared me. I can handle Uncle George. Who knows? Maybe I can even mollify him a bit."

Breanna gave her a small smile. "I wouldn't count on it. He's incensed. And he'll be more incensed once you've spoken your piece."

The girls' eyes met.

"Tell him, Stacie," Breanna said quietly. "He'll find out anyway."

Anastasia was still puzzling over her cousin's words as she approached Uncle George's study. What exactly had Breanna been urging her to disclose? That she'd opted to invest in an American bank? That she'd formed a partnership with Damen Lockewood?

Or was it more?

Sucking in her breath, Anastasia paused at the study door. She'd get her answer later. Whatever it was, it wouldn't affect her decision.

She raised her hand, rapped on the door.

"Who is it?" her uncle barked.

"Anastasia."

A dozen purposeful strides sounded from within, after which the door was yanked open, and her uncle stood before her, his expression taut, his eyes burning with suppressed ire.

"You wanted to see me?" Anastasia asked, as nonprovokingly as she could.

"Indeed I did. Come in." He snapped out the words, gesturing for her to enter, then shutting the door firmly in her wake. He stared at the carpet for a moment—doubtless trying to curb his anger—then jerked up his head to meet her gaze. "You went to the House of Lockewood this morning while I was out. You traveled alone, unchaperoned, and you never mentioned to me that you had an appointment. Why is that?"

Anastasia forced what she hoped was an apologetic look on her face. "I'm not accustomed to taking a chaperon with me when I go out for a simple ride. I realize that's inappropriate now that I'm home, and I'll try to be mindful of that in the future. As for my appointment, I intended to tell you about it. But you'd already left. So I asked Breanna to do it for me."

"And what was your business at the bank?"

He's testing me, Anastasia thought. *He's trying to catch me in the act of lying; or rather, of hiding the truth. Well, I'm about to surprise him.*

"I had business with the marquess," she answered, looking her uncle squarely in the eye. "Regarding an investment I'm about to make. I want to use a portion of Papa's inheritance to invest in an American bank."

A flicker of surprise—one that was quickly replaced by a dark scowl. "An American bank," he repeated icily. "I heard that you approached a number of my guests about financing that ludicrous venture. But I assumed that, once you saw their aversion to the notion—and to the notion of even discussing business with a woman—you'd been wise enough to abandon the idea. Really, Anastasia, isn't it enough that you offended a roomful of prominent noblemen with your unprecedented audacity? Did you then have to force your ideas on Lord Sheldrake?"

"I didn't force my ideas on Lord Sheldrake," Anastasia replied, fighting to keep her temper in check. "I merely presented them."

"Call it what you will." Her uncle's steely tone told her he was unwilling to be deterred. "It still adds up to one thing: you've forgotten who and where you are. You're my niece. You're also no longer in America. Perhaps there it's common for women to take an active role in financial matters, but . . ."

"It's not," Anastasia interrupted. "I was bolder than American women, too."

George's mouth thinned into a grim line. "I don't find your cheekiness amusing. Need I remind you that this is my home? Therefore, you will abide by my rules. And one thing I will not permit is impertinence."

Silently, Anastasia counted to ten. "I didn't intend to be impertinent," she said at last. "Just honest."

"I don't require honesty, not unless I specifically demand it by way of a direct question. What I do require is obedience. Further, I won't tolerate having my guests insulted."

This was becoming more difficult by the minute.

"Insulting your guests was never my intention, Uncle George. My intention was to gain support for my bank." Anastasia made a wide sweep with her hands. "In any event, I was unsuccessful. Obviously, your guests feel as you do about women in business. So I won't try that tactic again." She literally forced out her next words. "I apologize for any embarrassment I caused you."

"Fine." A terse nod. "Then, let's return to today's meeting at the bank. What is it you hoped to accomplish?"

You already know, Uncle George, she reflected. *What you don't know is that I'm aware of that. Very well. There's no harm in reiterating what Damen already told you.*

"As that was a direct question, I have to assume you're expecting honesty," she responded, rubbing her skirts between her fingers in a seemingly nervous gesture. "Therefore, I'll provide it. The purpose for my meeting this morning was to sign a partnership agreement with Lord Sheldrake. He's joining me in this banking venture—not as a backer, but as an equal partner."

George started—his surprise prompted not by her news, she fully recognized, but by her unanticipated frankness. It was plain that this was one time he *had* expected her to lie, after which he'd planned to throw that lie in her face.

"I see." He scowled, clasping his hands behind his back and regrouping his thoughts. "I'm astounded that Lord Sheldrake would agree to involve himself in this pointless endeavor."

"He doesn't expect it to be pointless. He expects it to be profitable. As do I." Anastasia raised her chin a notch. "I realize you and I have differing opinions on this subject, Uncle George. However, with all due respect, you're not my financial guardian. Lord Sheldrake is. So while I'll abide by your rules of behavior, I won't seek your approval on how I invest my money. Fortunately, Lord

Sheldrake and I are of the same mind with regard to that."

"You and Sheldrake seem to be of the same mind with regard to many things," George bit out, a vein throbbing at his temple.

Anastasia's brows lifted. "I don't understand."

"Oh, I think you do. Especially given the amount of time you and he spent together at your coming-out party."

"He's the administrator of my inheritance, and now my business partner. Of course we spent time together."

"And that's all there is to it?"

"What else could there be?"

Thunderclouds erupted on George's face, and he sliced the air with his palm. "Don't be coy with me, Anastasia. I'm not stupid. Nor are you. So I'll spell out the situation for you. I intend for Lord Sheldrake to marry Breanna. In fact, I expect to be announcing their betrothal any day now. Your cousin will have a wonderful life with the marquess. He'll give her everything she could ever want or need. And I don't plan to let anything, or any *one*, stand between them. Am I making myself clear?"

Anastasia swallowed—hard—keeping her expression as nondescript as possible. "Perfectly clear."

"Good. I'll hold you to that. One, because I know how much Breanna's happiness means to you, and two, because I know you'd never purposely undermine me. Not when you know how dire the consequences could be. And I *do* mean dire."

A chill ran up Anastasia's spine at the biting intensity of her uncle's words. She stared at him, trying to decipher his precise state of mind. She saw bitterness and anger in his eyes, as well as a dislike and resentment that was far older than she. But she also saw desperation—a desperation she couldn't quite fathom.

What was prompting it? Was it simply a grasping desire for Damen's money and power—greed combined with a need for retribution? Or was it more? Just how depleted were Uncle George's personal funds? Colby and Sons might be flourishing, but that told her nothing about what her uncle did with his portion of the profits, nor about how he handled any of his personal investments. Damen himself had bluntly told her he didn't have much faith in her uncle's business acumen, adding that he suspected her uncle might be struggling financially. Just how badly *was* he struggling? Enough to breed this level of desperation?

A sixth sense told Anastasia there was more here than met the eye.

"I take your silence to signify agreement." Her uncle interrupted her thoughts, his gaze narrowed on her face. "Am I correct?"

Careful, Anastasia. Don't provoke him. Not until you have all the facts. He'll only take it out on Breanna.

"You know how deeply I care for Breanna." She lowered her chin in a gesture of compliance. "I'd never do anything to stand in the way of her happiness. Never."

"Fine. Then we understand each other."

Anastasia nodded, still staring at the carpet. "Yes, Uncle George. We understand each other very well."

"Was it as bad as I expected?" Breanna asked the minute Stacie slipped into her room that night. Anxiously, she scrutinized her cousin, returning the porcelain figurine she'd been holding to the top of her nightstand.

Anastasia shrugged, tying her wrapper more firmly about her waist and pacing restlessly about. "Let's say there were no surprises."

She headed toward a chair, pausing to glance at her cousin's nightstand. A reminiscent smile touched her lips, and she walked over, gingerly touching the porcelain horse that had always been Breanna's favorite. "Every one of them, just as I remembered," she murmured, her gaze shifting to the bureau where rows of delicate figurines stood—tiny statues depicting everything from children to animals to vases with flowers. "The entire collection, as if time stood still. Then again, I suppose for these beautiful statues, it does."

"There are a few you haven't seen. I added them over the years." Breanna pointed out the new additions, including one of two little girls, laughing and picking flowers. "This one reminded me of us," she said, lifting it up and cradling it tenderly in her hands. "I first saw it about a year after you left England. I admired it in the shop window for months. I fully intended to save my pence, one at a time, until I could buy it. But Wells—dear man that he is—surprised me instead. He bought it for me that Christmas. It's the most precious figure in my collection. If you look closely, you'll see why."

Quizzically, Anastasia inclined her head, taking the porcelain object and inspecting it up close. Two little girls, their bright heads bent over the row of flowers they were picking.

A glistening object caught Anastasia's eye, and she peered closer, spotting the sliver of metal wedged between the flowers and the children.

The silver coin.

She reached out, touched it ever so gently. "So this is

where you kept it. I thought it was under the base of your porcelain horse."

"It was. Until Wells bought me this. It reminded me so much of us, I couldn't help but feel the coin belonged here."

A tender nod. "The gold coin is still in my jewel box—the one Mama got me when I was four. It was supposed to hold my hairpins and ribbons, so I'd find them in time to make my hair look presentable when need be. Of course, I lost every ribbon and hairpin I ever owned, so the box was never used for that. Instead, I kept my treasures in it: that wonderful multicolored stone you and I found near Medford Manor's pond, that odd-shaped leaf I plucked off our oak—things like that. Years later, I added new, equally precious treasures: every letter I received from you when I was in America, special mementos of Mama and Papa. The gold coin has never left that box. Except when I needed to see it, touch it, hold it to feel closer to Grandfather—and to believe that you and I really would be reunited one day."

"Well, now we are." Breanna's voice was choked, and Anastasia felt her own heart constrict with emotion.

Her gaze returned to the exquisite figure in her hands, and she studied the tiny glazed sculpture. Two girls, sharing laughter and confidences, and an absolute trust that not even distance could sever.

A trust as precious as the gold and silver coins themselves—and all they represented.

"Breanna, we need to talk." On that thought, Anastasia acted, setting down the delicate statue and marching over to the bed. She perched at the edge, her expression determined.

Nodding, Breanna gathered up the folds of her night

robe, tucking them around her as she lowered herself to the armchair alongside the bed. "Tell me what Father said," she urged, her green eyes searching Anastasia's face.

"He lectured me about approaching his guests on such a scandalous matter as business. He interrogated me about my partnership with Lord Sheldrake. And he warned me not to come between you and the marquess." Anastasia dispensed with the facts as quickly as possible, sensitive to Breanna's concern, yet focused on getting at the more significant matter of Damen, and how Breanna perceived—or *didn't* perceive—her future with him.

"I see," Breanna reflected aloud. "And did you set Father straight about Lord Sheldrake?"

There it was again. That feeling that Breanna was referring to something far deeper than that which they'd already discussed.

"That depends on what you mean by setting Uncle George straight," Anastasia replied, carefully gauging her cousin's reaction. "I apologized for upsetting his guests. With regard to Damen, I told him the truth about our partnership . . ."

"And about your feelings for each other? Did you tell him about those, as well?"

Anastasia caught her lower lip between her teeth, taken aback—not by Breanna's insight, but about the forthright way she gave voice to it. It was unlike her cousin to be so direct. Then again, it was better that she'd chosen this opportunity to be as such. This issue needed to be resolved—now.

"No," Anastasia responded, equally blunt. "I said nothing about my feelings. For many reasons." She scrutinized Breanna's expression, looking for some sign—any sign—that her cousin was upset. But all she saw there was curiosity; curiosity and a touch of confusion. "Breanna," she blurted, leaning forward and clutching the folds of her robe. "I'd rather die than hurt you. I wish you hadn't guessed my feelings, because I'm determined to know yours before I even allow myself to contemplate mine. If you love this man, if you *could* love this man, if you can even imagine—by some remote chance—that you might be happy with him . . ."

"Stop right there," Breanna interrupted, holding up a deterring palm. "Is that what's holding you back? *My* feelings?" Shaking her head, she reached over, took Anastasia's hand in hers. "I already told you there's nothing between the marquess and me. He's a charming, charismatic man. He's been very kind about diffusing Father's anger—pretending to be captivated by me, spending hours at my side. But, Stacie, I have no romantic interest in Lord Sheldrake." An impish grin. "*You*, on the other hand, do. And as for the marquess, he's so smitten, he can scarcely tear himself from your side."

"Did he actually tell you that?" Anastasia heard herself ask.

Breanna's eyes twinkled. "No. But he stepped on my feet four times when you were dancing with Lord Percy. Also, twice he mistakenly called me by your name—and not because he didn't know who he was dancing with."

Despite her best intentions, Anastasia couldn't deny the rush of pleasure that revelation brought. Still . . .

"I wouldn't lie to you, Stacie," Breanna assured her softly. "Not about something as important as this. I'd sooner challenge you for the marquess's affections—*if* I had feelings for him. Not because I'd place my needs above yours, but because I know you'd forever blame yourself if I forfeited a man I cared for just to ensure your happiness. But that's not the case. So put the notion out of your head." Her grip tightened, her cheeks glowing with excitement. "Instead, tell me what it feels like. Has he kissed you yet?"

Anastasia's lips curved as relief swept through her—relief more powerful than even she'd anticipated. "Yes. I thought my knees were going to buckle." She eased back, tugged her hand free to run it through her tumbled waves of hair. "It's all happening so fast—and I'm not even sure what *it* is."

A dubious glance. "Aren't you?"

"No. All I know is that I want to find out." Abruptly, Anastasia's smile faded. "But I can't. Not with Uncle George as vehement as he is."

"Don't be a fool, Stacie. You never let Father stop you before. You certainly can't start now, not when your whole future could be at stake."

"It's *your* future I'm worrying about—and what will happen to it if your father discovers the truth."

Breanna's jaw set in that rare but unyielding way of hers. "He'll get over it. He'll have to."

"I doubt it will be as simple as that. Not given all the instigating factors involved." Anastasia paused, knowing it was time to fill Breanna in on the pieces of the past she'd never been told, praying it wouldn't cause her cousin too much distress. "This adamancy of Uncle George's is prompted by more than just his plans for you, even more than his plans for himself. It's prompted by feelings of bitterness and resentment that began over two decades ago and have sprouted like ugly weeds ever since."

"You're talking about our fathers' hostility for each

other," Breanna murmured. Her forehead creased with puzzlement. "You think Father wants to wed me to Lord Sheldrake just to outdo Uncle Henry?"

"Not to outdo him—to punish him. More specifically, to punish him through me."

"Now you've lost me. How would my marrying Lord Sheldrake punish Uncle Henry? It might satisfy some warped need on Father's part to attain a higher level of power and position than Uncle Henry ever did. But that's all."

"No, that's not all." Slowly, Anastasia rose to her feet, gripping the bedpost and turning to face her cousin. "Uncle George hated Papa for more than just their differing principles. He hated him for marrying Mama."

A baffled pucker formed between Breanna's brows. "It's no secret that Father disliked Aunt Anne. You and I both sensed that, even as children. But how does his dislike for her . . ." Abruptly, her eyes widened. "You know the reason for that animosity, don't you?"

"Yes," Anastasia confirmed. She paused, wet her lips with the tip of her tongue, and provided the truth. "It was because Uncle George wanted—no, expected—that it would be *he* who wed Mama."

Breanna started. "What?"

"Mama told me the whole story several years ago." Anastasia leaned her head against the bedpost. "Evidently, she was introduced to Uncle George during her very first London Season. He began courting her, intent on winning her hand. A month later she and Papa met. It was by sheer chance. She was coming out of a shop on Bond Street when she saw a man—whom she presumed to be Uncle George—leap from the path of a speeding carriage. He fell against a lamppost, twisting his ankle in the process, after which he crept to a nearby bench to nurse the swelling. Naturally, Mama hurried over to help—only to discover that the victim was not Uncle George, but his twin brother. They fell in love during that first chance encounter. Papa tried everything to make Uncle George understand, but to no avail. He never forgave either of my parents."

"Nevertheless, they married," Breanna murmured, the pieces falling rapidly into place. "And Father's hatred festered. That explains so much: why he always acted so strained around Aunt Anne; why he never stayed in the room with her unless he had to." A quizzical tilt of her head. "Did he love my mother? Or did he marry her as a substitute for Aunt Anne?"

Anastasia chewed her lip. "I honestly don't know. Your parents got married a few months after Mama wed Papa."

"Our mothers were sisters. They looked so much alike. They were only a year apart. And Father married my mother right after he lost Aunt Anne to Uncle Henry. Surely that can't all have been a coincidence."

"Knowing Uncle George, I'd have to agree." Anastasia frowned, intent on clarifying what she *did* know. "I've hesitated telling you this because I didn't want to upset you. But, Breanna, please believe this: you *were* wanted. Quite fiercely, from what Mama told me. Aunt Dorothy was a gentle, caring person. She yearned with all her heart for a child—possibly so she could share her love with someone who craved it, given that her husband undoubtedly didn't. If she were still alive, I'm sure . . ."

"Stacie, don't." Breanna waved away her cousin's assurances. "I don't doubt that my mother wanted me. Aunt Anne told me stories about her, too—as did Wells. Enough so that I know what kind of a person she was, and how eagerly she awaited my birth. As for my father, I also recognize what kind of a person he is. Still, it's crucial that I know all the details of the past so I can comprehend why Father hated—*hates* . . ." she corrected herself. ". . . Uncle Henry so vehemently. What you just divulged saddens me, but it doesn't shock or wound me."

"I'm glad." Anastasia felt as if a great weight had been lifted from her shoulders, until she remembered why she'd told Breanna the truth in the first place. "Surely now you realize why Uncle George is so hellbent on winning this battle to see you become Mrs. Damen Lockewood. It's not just about ensuring that you end up with Damen, but about ensuring that *I* don't. I shudder to think how he'd react if the reverse were to occur. Couple that with the fact that he seems to need Damen's wealth and influence so badly . . ." Anastasia gave a hard shake of her head. ". . . and the thought of telling him the truth becomes untenable. I refuse to put you in that position."

"*You're* not putting me in that position. *I* am. And since it's my fate in question, I'm the one to decide whether or not I'll walk into the lion's den . . ." Abruptly, Breanna broke off, a sudden, reminiscent spark lighting her eyes. "Let me amend that," she murmured, the spark igniting to a full-fledged glow as her idea took hold. "There is a way for you to explore this fascination between you and Lord Sheldrake without arousing my father's wrath."

"And just how am I going to accomplish that? It's you Uncle George wants to see with Damen."

"Then that's precisely what he'll see. Beginning tomorrow morning, when Lord Sheldrake comes for breakfast, as per Father's invitation." Breanna stood, reaching up to pull the pins from her hair, shaking the tresses free. "You said once that a day might come when you'd need to be me. Well, that day has arrived." She smiled triumphantly. "Come, *Breanna*. It's time to tousle my hair and restore your accent to its former clipped tones. Tomorrow morning we reinstate our pact."

The pub was small, dark, almost unnoticeable from the main road. Its walls were chipped and peeling, but the ale was cheap—a factor that was most crucial to those who frequented the establishment. And nobody asked questions, not if your money was good.

Which made it the perfect place for these meetings.

George rubbed his palms distastefully down the front of his coat, as if by doing so he could dispel the odious feel of the room. He hovered in the entranceway, wincing at the filth and clutter, and trying to ignore the raucous laughter that exploded as drunken sailors sank deeper into their cups. It took every ounce of his self-control not to gag at the offensive smells accosting his nose.

But right now he had more important things on his mind.

Swiftly, he perused the room, eager to conduct his business and be gone.

At last, he spied the telltale flare of light from the pub's far corner.

He crossed over, slipped into his seat.

"What did you find out?" he demanded.

His companion lit a cheroot, gazed calmly back at him. "The partnership's real. The terms are standard. They each invested twenty-five thousand pounds."

"Twenty-five thousand . . . dammit!" George nearly forgot himself and slammed his fist to the table.

"Easy, Medford. That's going to get you noticed. Which is the one thing you don't want."

A terse nod. "What about my niece and Sheldrake? What can you tell me?"

"Your niece is beautiful. Every bit as beautiful as your daughter."

"I didn't ask for your opinion. I asked you what was going on between her and Sheldrake."

"Nothing I could see. Then again, they were alone in his office for about a half hour. I have no idea what went on during that time. But otherwise, it was only business."

"Make sure it stays that way," George hissed. "And if it changes, let me know. Immediately." He scowled. "Any word on that damned trust fund my father set up?"

"I had the terms checked into. They're solid as steel. Forget that money, Medford. You won't be touching it— ever."

A bitter laugh. "All the more reason why I've got to get my hands on the rest of that inheritance. Before my bloody niece squanders away every last pence." He leaned forward, glared at his companion. "Did you get that message off to the Continent?"

"The very night I got it."

"Good. Now keep your eyes on Sheldrake. And make sure he keeps his eyes off Anastasia."

10

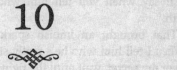

By half after nine that morning, the girls were—even to the most discerning observer—each other.

The transformation took a surprisingly short time to complete: a swap of gowns, a few quick pointers on how to keep Anastasia's hair from tumbling free, some powder on Breanna's bruise, and a few practice sessions— Anastasia on the proper articulation of words, and Breanna on the fundamental points underlying Anastasia and Damen's partnership.

"I'd forgotten how much I enjoy being assertive," Breanna teased, parading around the bedchamber in Anastasia's bolder, more confident stride. "I'll be sure to voice all my opinions between mouthfuls."

"I wouldn't," Anastasia cautioned dryly, holding her perfectly coiffed head at just the right angle. "Uncle George made it clear to me he doesn't welcome honesty. He's also not too thrilled with me right now. So I would curb my forthrightness, if I were you."

"But you *are* me." Breanna grinned. "Remember?"

Anastasia couldn't stifle a smile. "You're really enjoying this, aren't you?"

"Absolutely. I'll enjoy it even more when I see you and Lord Sheldrake go off for a private stroll. I wonder what he'll say when you tell him who he's really strolling with."

That brought an impish spark to Anastasia's eyes. "*When* I tell him who he's really strolling with. I plan to savor my secret, wait until the right moment to disclose it. I'm looking forward to outwitting Damen Lockewood. So far, I've managed only to equal him—in intelligence, in inventiveness, even on horseback. It's time I won at something."

Breanna rolled her eyes. "You're impossible. I hope the marquess is up for the challenge he's about to face. He might be a financial genius, but no transaction he's concluded has prepared him for you. Of that, I'm certain."

A knock at the door interrupted their chatter.

"Yes?" Anastasia called out, given that it was Breanna's room—supposedly *her* room—in which they were dressing.

Lizzy poked her head in. "Pardon me, m'lady," she said, her gaze fixed on Anastasia. "But your father asked me to tell you that the marquess has arrived. They're awaiting you and Lady Anastasia in the dining room."

"Thank you, Lizzy," Anastasia replied serenely. "We'll be down in a moment."

"Very good, m'lady." The door shut behind her.

"Now *that* was a good start," Anastasia commented. She gathered up her skirts in Breanna's customary graceful manner.

"Indeed," Breanna agreed. She tied her hair back with

a ribbon, making sure to let one or two burnished strands tumble onto her cheeks. "Come, Breanna," she urged with a twinkle. "Your suitor awaits."

Damen rose the minute the girls entered the room, his keen silver gaze shifting from Breanna to Anastasia and back again. "Good morning, ladies. It's a pleasure to see you both."

"And you, my lord," Breanna returned immediately. She smiled, then walked over to Anastasia's seat, giving her father a measured look. "Good morning, Uncle George."

George's nod was customarily aloof. "Anastasia." He turned to the girl he presumed to be his daughter. "Breanna." With that, he reseated himself, signaling for the footmen to serve their meal.

"Anastasia, I was just telling your uncle about our meeting yesterday," Damen said, sipping at his tea. "But it seems you'd already spoken to him about it."

"Yes, I did," Breanna replied, choosing the strawberry jelly rather than her customary apple, just as Anastasia would have. "Right after I returned. Actually, I should have told him about my plans before I left Medford Manor. As it was, he was terribly worried about me. I'm going to have to learn to curb my independent streak. As Uncle George rightfully pointed out, this is England, not the States."

"True." Damen bit into a biscuit, chewing it thoroughly, then swallowing before he spoke. "But you were hardly in danger. The viscount's carriage took you directly to my bank, where my entire staff had been alerted to your arrival." A pointed look at George. "Your niece was in good hands."

"I'm sure she was." George's jaw tightened as he spoke. "Nevertheless, we have her reputation to consider—even though her business with you was just that—*business*. She still should have secured my permission and taken her lady's maid with her." He dismissed the matter with an adamant flourish, his shoulders stiff as he commenced eating his meal.

Anastasia and Breanna exchanged glances.

Silence descended, punctuated only by the clinking of china and crystal—and a few undisguised, meaningful glares by George, aimed at the girl he thought to be Breanna.

Anastasia shifted uncomfortably in her chair, fully aware what she was being ordered to do—what *Breanna* was being ordered to do. But how did one initiate a courtship? More important, how would her cousin do so?

The truth was, she wouldn't.

Weighing that knowledge against the unspoken command in her uncle's eyes, Anastasia wracked her brain for a solution. Deliberately, she avoided her uncle's blistering stare, choosing instead to toy with her breakfast as she pondered how on earth to approach Damen in a manner that even remotely fit her cousin's more reserved demeanor.

"Breanna, what did you do yesterday while your cousin and I were hard at work?" Damen inquired, breaking the silence and providing just the opening Anastasia needed.

Nearly sagging with relief, she folded her napkin neatly in her lap. "I have to admit, I was lonely." *Good start, Anastasia,* she commended herself. *It makes you sound wistful. Keep it up and Damen will have no choice but to gallantly offer you some time in his company.* "The truth is, I've grown accustomed to having Stacie home," she confessed in Breanna's quiet, vulnerable tone. "I never realized until now how seldom I'm among people, and how much I enjoy sharing my thoughts with a sympathetic listener."

Self-consciously, she broke off, pausing to sip at her tea. "In any case, that's not what you asked. Let's see. I took an early morning walk, before it became too hot. Then I went to the library and read. That helped the morning pass. And Stacie returned before lunch."

Damen nodded, giving her a warm smile. "After which, I'm sure you spent the afternoon together."

"We usually do." Anastasia smiled back, responsively but demurely. "Stacie and I have a lot of years to catch up on, my lord."

"And you've come alive since she returned," he noted, polishing off the last bite of his breakfast. "You're like another woman these days. It's wonderful to see—a beautiful butterfly emerging from its cocoon."

"Goodness, I hope that doesn't mean I was a caterpillar before."

"Not at all." Damen chuckled. "Just a shyer butterfly."

George shoved away his plate—his food only half-eaten. "I have a splendid idea," he declared, looking decidedly more cheerful than he had a few minutes earlier. "Breanna, I recall your mentioning something about wanting to seek Lord Sheldrake's advice on that trust fund your grandfather left you. Why not do so now, right after you finish breakfast? I have some papers to go through before I'm ready to meet with the marquess. And it's a shame for him to sit here idle, especially given that it's such a beautiful day. Why don't you walk down to the stream, stroll through the gardens?"

Anastasia gave her uncle an obedient smile. "Of course,

Father. That's a good idea." She inclined her head uncertainly at Damen. "If Lord Sheldrake wouldn't mind, that is."

"Mind? I'd enjoy the company." Abandoning his own meal, Damen pushed back his chair and stood. "I'm ready whenever you are."

Gracefully, Anastasia rose, resisting the urge to do her usual bolting to her feet. "Would you excuse us, Father?"

"Of course. Anastasia and I still have to finish our meal. So take your time."

The real Anastasia shot her cousin a questioning look. "You don't mind, do you, Stacie?"

"Of course not," Breanna retorted in her cousin's bold tone. "You two go and enjoy yourselves."

It took all Anastasia's restraint not to succumb to laughter. Instead, she took Damen's arm and let him lead her from the dining room through the hallway, toward the entranceway door.

From his post, Wells watched their approach, straightening in surprise. "Miss Breanna. Are you leaving?"

"No, Wells. Lord Sheldrake and I are just going for a walk. We'll be back soon."

"I see." The butler frowned. "Your father knows this?"

"Of course."

"Very well then." He opened the door. "Don't wander far."

Anastasia stifled another grin. "We won't."

"Your butler is very protective," Damen commented, tucking Anastasia's arm through his as they headed away from the manor.

"Yes, he is." She kept her stare fixed on the path. "I don't often leave the manor—certainly not unchaperoned and escorted by a gentleman."

"I suppose not." A corner of his mouth lifted. "So, where is it George ordered us to go—to the stream?"

"Yes." She sighed. "It's on one of the more remote sections of the estate."

"Giving us the maximum amount of time alone." Damen chuckled. "Why am I not surprised? And why don't I believe you had any plans of asking my advice about your inheritance?"

"Because I didn't." Anastasia peeked up at him through the fringe of her lashes. "Although perhaps I should. You know how little I understand about money or how to invest it."

"Would you like to learn?"

She pretended to consider the notion. "I don't think I'd enjoy it very much. Nor would my father approve. Business is a man's forte."

"Anastasia would disagree."

"You're right. Then again, Stacie's not a typical woman."

"I can't argue with you there." Damen fell silent, and Anastasia would have given anything to be able to read his thoughts.

They continued walking, and when Anastasia couldn't bear the silence for another instant, she blurted out, "Have I offended you?"

"No, of course not. Why would you think so?"

"I don't know. Maybe because I'm not enthused by business. Or maybe it's because I said what I did about Stacie," she added, unable to resist the urge to probe.

"Ah. That." He gave an offhanded shrug. "Well, neither comment offended me. I don't expect everyone to share my fascination for investments. As for Anastasia, she *is* different. *Very* different."

"Is that approval or disapproval I hear?"

"Neither. It's captivation. Anastasia intrigues me in a way no other woman ever has." He shot her a questioning look. "Now I hope *I* haven't offended *you.*"

"H-m-m? No, not at all." Anastasia had to firmly remind herself that it was Breanna he was addressing, not she. Therefore, emitting a gleeful shout would be totally out of place.

"Are we headed in the right direction?" Damen asked, slowing his steps as their path wound its way into a thick grove of trees.

"Yes."

"Good." He guided her through the profusion of oaks, walking steadily until the sun and the grounds were eclipsed by greenery.

Abruptly, he stopped, lush branches enveloping them as he tugged her around to face him.

Anastasia blinked in the filtered daylight. "Is something wrong?"

"Wrong? No."

She looked puzzled, studying his nondescript expression, cast in the shadows of the encompassing trees. "Then why are we stopping?"

"To talk." He brushed a leaf off the top of her smoothly coiffed hair. "You did say you were lonely, didn't you?"

Anastasia didn't have to feign the astonishment that flashed across her face. "Well, yes. But . . ."

"I'd like to eliminate that loneliness."

"By talking?" she asked cautiously.

"Among other things." He traced the delicate curve of her jaw with his fingertips. "You're incredibly beautiful."

"*That's* what you want to talk about?" Anastasia's surprise rapidly transformed to anger. "My beauty?"

"Um-hum." He caressed her cheek, her chin. "That, and everything else about you."

"Such as?"

"Such as—you said Anastasia's forte was business. What are *your* interests?"

Retreating from his touch, Anastasia rubbed the folds of her gown between her fingers, frantically trying to sort out what was happening here.

The problem was, she knew *exactly* what was happening. There was no mistaking this flagrant a seduction.

But Damen Lockewood—the *principled* Damen Lockewood—was not only trying to seduce an innocent woman, but trying to seduce Breanna. *Breanna.* After promising Anastasia he felt nothing for her cousin but friendship; after, just moments ago, proclaiming how captivated with Anastasia he was.

She didn't know whether to strike him or scream.

"Tell me," he coaxed, clasping his hands behind his back—as if he were exercising great restraint—"what is it *you* like to do?"

Slap you, she thought furiously. "My interests?" she repeated instead. "Reading. Drawing. Ah, and collecting porcelain figures. Nothing you'd find exciting."

"Never make assumptions." His tone was as intimate as a caress. "What type of porcelain figures?"

"All types—people, animals, flowers, objects. I began my collection when I was a child. It's grown to be quite extensive at this point."

"Really? You'll have to show it to me sometime."

When? she wanted to blurt out. *When you carry me—*

rather, Breanna—*off to your bed?* "Don't tell me you're actually interested in examining little statues."

A quizzical lift of his brows. "You sound surprised."

"I am. I never imagined a man like you would enjoy such a thing. Then again, I never imagined a man like you would stoop to . . ." She snapped her mouth shut before she said something that would give her away.

"Would stoop to what?" Damen inquired. Undeterred by her obvious distress, he stepped closer—much closer—reaching out to capture her hands in his. "And a man like me—tell me, what type of man is that?"

"An honorable one. One who's absorbed in investments rather than . . ." Her breath caught as he brought her hands to his lips, and simultaneously eased her deeper into the shelter of the trees.

"Rather than . . . ?" he prompted, tugging off one of her gloves and pressing his open mouth into her palm.

"What are you doing?"

"What does it look like I'm doing?" Damen tugged off the other glove, tossed them both aside. Then, he drew her closer, and planted his hands firmly on her waist.

"Lord Sheldrake, really." Anastasia twisted free, her fury as genuine as if she were truly being violated. How *dare* he? Given what was supposedly happening between him and Anastasia, how dare he make blatant advances toward Breanna? "I think you'd better take me back to the manor," she instructed sharply.

"I'd rather not."

"Fine. Then I'll take myself." She attempted to walk around him.

"No—you won't." His arm snaked out, caught her around the waist, and dragged her back to him. "Not when I've sat through an entire breakfast in order to get you alone."

That did it.

"Release me this instant." She slapped at his arms, stiffening as he lowered his head, brushed the curve of her shoulder with his lips. "Stop," she commanded, an inadvertent quiver rippling through her. "Let me go. Before I . . ."

"If I'm to be honest, I prefer your hair down," he murmured, kissing the pulse at her neck, working his way down the column of her throat. "But it does look more convincing this way. And I wouldn't want to upset your brilliant plan. So I'll restrain myself from pulling out all the pins." His thumb tilted up her chin, and he lowered his mouth to hers. "Instead, I'll concentrate on doing this." His lips brushed hers. "Kiss me."

Something in his husky mutterings struck her as significant, but she was too besieged by conflicting feelings to determine what that something was.

Her hands balled into fists, shoved against his chest, even as the warmth of his kiss surged through her. "I don't want . . ."

"Kiss me, Anastasia."

Realization struck her like a tidal wave.

Her eyes snapped open, peered directly into his, and she saw the utter awareness in his gaze. "You . . . knew?" she managed.

"From the instant I saw you." He silenced her protest with a heated nudge of his mouth against hers. "Berate me later. For now, just kiss me."

Whatever indignation Anastasia felt was dwarfed by the hypnotic effect of being in Damen's arms. Without another word, she relented, stepping closer and angling her mouth to his.

Damen made a rough sound of approval, capturing her arms and bringing them high around his neck, then pulling her against him, covering her lips with his.

Fire ignited Anastasia's mouth, spread through her like a rampaging blaze. She flung herself into the kiss, parting her lips to Damen's seeking tongue, meeting his sensual strokes with her own.

Growling her name, Damen lifted her from the ground, carrying her backward three steps until she felt the cool bark of a tree behind her. Using that as an anchor, he crushed her body to his, devouring her mouth and letting his hands roam over her soft curves, awakening her through the confines of her gown.

He cupped her breast, molded it to his palm, and Anastasia moaned aloud, shifted restlessly to afford him greater access.

He took it.

Slipping his hand inside her bodice, he worked his way beneath her chemise to the warm, responsive flesh that craved his touch. His thumb found her nipple, already hardened with desire, and circled it, teasing the aching peak with unrelenting strokes.

The fire inside Anastasia grew.

Shuddering from the intensity of sensation, she heard herself whimper, arch instinctively closer. Damen's breath rasped at her lips, and he tore his mouth away only long enough to drag in air. Then, he buried his lips in hers again, consuming her mouth with an intensity that jolted through her like bolts of lightning.

"Damen . . ." Her arms twined more tightly around his

neck, and she clung to him, succumbing more deeply to the flames scorching her from the inside out.

With a muffled oath, Damen dragged down her bodice, and tugged open her chemise.

There was a brief rush of cool air as her breasts sprang free, and then it was gone, as Damen lowered his head, captured her nipple between his lips.

This time she sobbed aloud, unable to stifle the unbearable pleasure screaming through her veins. She clutched at his head, cradled it closer, silently urging him to take more and more of her.

Damen indulged her—and himself.

He shifted, his lips closing around her other nipple, his tongue lashing across it as his thumb stroked its already dampened mate in slow, arousing circles.

A twig snapped just beyond where they stood.

Damen's head shot up, and he surveyed the area, instinctively shielding Anastasia's body with his.

The culprit scooted into view: a red squirrel who, startled by Damen's sudden motion, dropped his acorn and darted off.

Slowly, Damen lowered his head, staring down at Anastasia, his normally silvery gaze almost black with passion. Sanity warred with desire as his hot stare moved restlessly from her face down to her naked breasts, then back up again.

"You're so bloody beautiful," he muttered, his breath coming in hard, uneven rasps. "And all I want to do is . . ." He bit off his remaining words, his jaw working as he brought himself under control. In a few taut motions, he lowered her feet to the ground and tugged up her bodice. "Anastasia . . ." He cupped her hot face between his palms, uttered her name in a husky whisper. "I never meant to let it go this far. I'm sorry."

"No, you're not," she managed in a shattered voice that bore no resemblance to her own. "And neither am I." She leaned her head weakly against his chest, willing her trembling limbs and wildly pounding heart to calm.

Damen seemed to understand, because he gathered her closer, enfolding her against him and resting his chin atop her head. He was as affected as she, his arms shaking with reaction, his heart thundering against her ear. "You're right," he said hoarsely. "I'm not sorry. What's more, if that damned squirrel hadn't interrupted . . ."

Anastasia nodded, still trying to regain her wits and her thoughts.

"Are you all right?" Damen's breath ruffled her hair.

That question jogged the memory of what had preceded these erotic moments.

"You knew." Anastasia's pronouncement was weak, more a statement than an accusation, her words muffled by Damen's waistcoat. "All the time—you knew."

She felt him smile against her hair. "From the instant you walked into that dining room—yes, I knew."

Her hand balled into a fist, struck ineffectually at his shoulder. "Damn you, Damen Lockewood. Can't you *ever* be outdone?"

His smile vanished. "I just was," he confessed raggedly. "Not just outdone, but brought to my knees."

Anastasia leaned back, watching him solemnly as she shook her head. "That's not what I meant."

"I know. But it's true nonetheless."

"For me, as well." She swallowed. "How long were you going to play your little game of cat and mouse with me?"

Again, his lips twitched. "I could ask you the same

question. How long did you want me to think you were Breanna?"

An impish grin. "Until I told you otherwise."

Damen chuckled. "Honest to a fault." His thumbs caressed her cheeks. "Let's get this straight here and now. I'm never going to confuse you and Breanna. So you might as well give it up. Although I am curious as to why you're carrying out this little masquerade. I suspect it has more to do with your uncle than with your desire to outwit me."

Anastasia sighed. "You're right. Uncle George has all but forbidden me to see you. He's planning on announcing your betrothal to Breanna in a matter of weeks. And he's warned me not to do anything to jeopardize that announcement, or Breanna's future."

Glints of anger flared in Damen's eyes. "This delusion of his is going too far."

"I agree. But the situation is more complicated than that." Anastasia disengaged herself from Damen's arms, stooping to pick up her gloves. She tugged them on, then tucked her stray tendrils of hair back in the smooth knot atop her head. "We'd best keep walking," she advised, indicating the path. "I don't want to have to lie to Uncle George about where you and I went for our stroll. As you yourself pointed out, I'm not a terribly convincing liar."

"True." Damen caught her arm, tucked it through his. "But let's take advantage of the fact that you're supposed to be Breanna. After all, nothing would please George more than if he peered out the window and saw his daughter and I walking arm in arm."

"Nothing except if he saw his daughter and you walking arm and arm down the aisle as man and wife," Anastasia amended dryly.

Damen's lips thinned into a grim line. "Tell me what happened," he commanded as they resumed their walk. "What took place after you returned from the bank yesterday?"

Omitting nothing, Anastasia relayed the details of her conversation with her uncle, and those of the lecture Breanna had endured from him earlier. Having done that, she told Damen her theories on the reasons for her uncle's extreme behavior.

"I understand your concern," Damen said thoughtfully when she'd finished. "And I agree that George must be deeper in debt than we know. But how will this pretense of yours make things better? Sooner or later, he'll have to be told there's no future for Breanna and me."

"We'll deal with that if it becomes necessary."

"*If?*" Damen stopped, caught her shoulders in his hands. "It's already necessary," he stated flatly, his gaze boring into hers. "As I told you, what's happening between you and me is not going to go away. It's only going to grow stronger, more consuming. So if you're waiting for it to end . . ."

"I'm not," Anastasia interrupted. She pressed her lips together, trying to decide how much to say. "Damen, I'm afraid he'll hurt her."

His eyes narrowed. "Does he strike her?"

"Sometimes. I don't know how hard or how often. But I suspect it's a lot more frequent and more severe than Breanna will admit—even to me. She's very close-mouthed about that part of her life. But she did say her father has been unusually short-tempered these days, even for him. He's been tense, brooding, ready to explode at the slightest provocation. When I came home yesterday, she had a bruise on her chin—a bruise bad enough to need a half hour of powdering in order to conceal, especially given she was supposed to be me. And that was only as a result of his wanting to stress a point. What would he do if she failed to give him the prize he wants— you?"

Damen's breath expelled in a hiss. "And how do we protect her from that?"

"By continuing this charade. By my pretending to be Breanna whenever you visit—unless that visit pertains to our partnership. Then, I'll be me."

"Until when?"

"Until I figure out just how heavily in debt Uncle George is, and how violent he'd become if he were crossed. And until I think of a way to protect Breanna from that violence. Damen, I'm all Breanna has, at least until she meets the right man. I can't turn my back on her."

"I wouldn't expect you to." Damen guided her into the clearing, then toward the glistening stream across the way. "That's one of the traits you and Breanna do have in common," he remarked. "You're both soft-hearted." He paused as they reached the stream, tipped up her chin. "Although you're the true romantic. I didn't miss your pointed 'until she meets the right man.'" A smile. "Forward-thinking or not, you believe in the age-old sentiment of one man for one woman."

"So do you," Anastasia reminded him. "I distinctly recall your assuring me that Breanna would flourish once she met the right man."

"So I did." A corner of Damen's mouth lifted. "I never thought of myself as a romantic. But damned if I'm not finding out that I am one."

"Romantic about love, but pragmatic about business."

A reminiscent light dawned in Anastasia's eyes. "That's the way my father was. Practical in his work, emotional about Mama and me." She sighed. "If I'm a romantic, it's not a surprise, nor an accident. My parents were deeply in love. I grew up seeing that, knowing that love was a rare, priceless treasure—one to be fervently sought and captured as a prerequisite to marriage. Breanna never had the chance to learn that firsthand. Her mother died when she was born."

"I remember how much Henry adored your mother," Damen reflected. "He couldn't take his eyes off her when they were together, and he spoke of her often when they were apart. As for Breanna's parents, I was a boy when her mother died. Tell me, did your uncle feel the same way about his wife as your father did about his?"

Anastasia lowered her lashes. "I was only a few months old when Aunt Dorothy died in childbirth. I never knew her."

"Surely your mother spoke of her. She was her sister, after all."

"Her younger sister, yes." Anastasia had no desire to pursue this subject—not again. Telling Breanna was one thing; she had a right to the truth. But opening up to Damen was another matter entirely. His role in her life was too new, too fragile, to share the sordid details behind her uncle's hatred for her father. Perhaps someday . . . but not yet.

"Mama and Aunt Dorothy looked very much alike," she offered instead. "Between that and the fact that our fathers are twins, it's no wonder Breanna and I are identical."

"You're not identical. And you're changing the subject, just as you did in my office when we touched on your uncle's resentment toward you and your parents. It's obvious these two subjects are related. It's also obvious you're not ready to discuss either one with me."

"For now—no, I'm not. Please understand, this is all very personal."

"All right." Damen nodded slowly, his eyes hooded. "I won't push you."

"I appreciate that." Anastasia cleared her throat. "You said that soft-heartedness was one of the traits Breanna and I have in common. What other ones do you perceive?"

"Loyalty." Damen followed her lead, abandoning the prior topic and picking up the current one. "Loyalty and love—especially for each other. And, I suspect, for your grandfather."

Anastasia blinked, taken aback, yet again, by the depth of Damen's insight. "I'll repeat what I said to you that night on the balcony: you're a very perceptive man, Lord Sheldrake."

"And I'll repeat what I answered you then: you're a very intriguing woman, Anastasia." He caressed her cheek, let his fingers trail down the side of her neck. "Intriguing and intoxicating. So intoxicating that I can't keep my mind—or my hands—off of you." He wrapped an insistent arm around her waist, pulled her against him. Then, he lowered his head, buried his lips in hers for a long, dizzying minute. "Tell me you feel the same way," he murmured, ending the kiss with the greatest reluctance. "Tell me."

"I do," she replied breathlessly.

Abruptly, his mood altered, and he gripped her arms, searching her face with those smoky, compelling eyes. "Then let me help you. Let me help unravel this puzzle."

"How?"

"I have many contacts. I'll make some inquiries, find out just what George's financial situation is. The sooner we know what we're up against, the sooner we can set things right."

A surge of relief flooded through her, and for the first time she realized how alone she'd felt in this dilemma. Her parents were gone, her uncle was suspect, and Breanna was too much at risk to call upon for help. She'd had no one to turn to, no one to ask for help.

Until now.

"Stacie," Damen said softly, mistaking her silence for refusal. "You sought me out as a partner for your bank. This is no different. I know you value your independence. But sometimes success requires drawing upon additional resources in order to achieve the most profitable outcome. This is one of those times."

Anastasia arched a teasing brow. "Spoken like a true investment adviser. Tell me, Lord Sheldrake, are you proposing yet another partnership between us?"

He grinned. "Um-hum. And I'd jump at this one if I were you. I'm a damned good risk."

"Yes," she agreed. "You are." This time it was she who initiated things, reaching up to tug Damen's mouth down to hers. "Consider this my signature."

He made a rough sound against her lips, his arms tightening, drawing her closer. "Much better than a quill," he muttered.

"And far more binding."

Slowly, Damen raised his head, stared deeply into her eyes. "Binding. I like the sound of that." He smoothed his fingers over the shining crown of her hair. "And speaking of binding, I hope that soon you'll decide to tell me the details of whatever caused George's hostility toward you and your parents. And after that . . ." His thumb caressed her soft lower lip. ". . . I want to hear all about the special tie you shared with your grandfather."

An ardent sparkle lit her eyes, and she kissed his fingertips. "That will take long hours in private, my lord. Do you think you can arrange that?"

"Oh, yes. I can definitely arrange that." On the heels of his vow, all teasing vanished, and Damen's expression grew intense. "But, Stacie, if I do—I'm not sure I can promise to display that honorable quality you obviously believe I possess."

Anastasia's heated gaze met his. "Good. Because I'm not sure I want you to."

The next few weeks were torture.

None of it was internal turmoil; deep within Anastasia's heart, she was buoyed by the thought that she and Damen were forging a life that Damen visited Medford Manor. Despite the sheer joy that pretending to be become entailed her—time she spent, if along, hours alone with Damen—Anastasia couldn't escape the worry that her uncle would discover the truth; that his rush to shore Damen to Medford and Anastasia was forced to factor and that he was being milked and duped by his nephew and his niece. And if he were to discover that truth, Anastasia knew very well who would bear the brunt of his rage: Breanna.

Until this discovery at that she sensed that the tension was leaving her, and to whatever extent concern was own personal apprehension. She just didn't know what that secondaries was.

But she knew very well who would be most hurt—and Breanna knew that and it was. Something and threatening, something of everyone rushing at the suspects that perhaps

11

The next few weeks were fraught with tension.

Some of it was internal, coiled deep within Anastasia's gut—tension incited by the deception she and Breanna were fostering each time Damen visited Medford Manor. Despite the sheer joy that pretending to be Breanna afforded her—namely, spending long hours alone with Damen—Anastasia couldn't escape the worry that her uncle would discover the truth: that his plan to snare Damen Lockewood as a son-in-law was doomed to failure *and* that he was being tricked and defied by his daughter and his niece. And if he were to uncover that truth, Anastasia knew very well who would bear the brunt of his rage: Breanna.

Still, regardless of all that, she sensed that the tension was being triggered by something far more vast than her own personal apprehension. She just didn't know what that something was.

But she knew very well who was at its center: her uncle.

George was drawn taut as a bowstring these days, barking at everyone, snapping at the servants, and generally slamming about the manor as if nursing a barely controllable rage. Every day, he'd closet himself in his study for hours, muttering loudly to himself—loud enough for his voice, if not his words, to be heard in the hallway. That only served to arouse Anastasia's curiosity, compelling her to try to decipher the muffled sounds. Several times a day, when no one else was about, she'd hover outside the locked study door and eavesdrop intently, pressing her ear to the doorway and straining to listen. But the wood was thick, and all she could make out was her uncle's tone, which was undeniably agitated, vacillating from bitter to apprehensive to sullen.

To make matters worse, he'd been drinking heavily, commencing each day with a full goblet of brandy, then steadily increasing his intake until, by midafternoon, he was actually slurring his words, so deep in his cups was he.

Clearly, it wasn't Breanna's relationship with Damen that was instigating these drinking bouts. In fact, quite the opposite was true. Given Damen's seemingly avid courtship of Breanna, George had ceased pressuring Breanna, and appeared to be satisfied with the way things were going—at least on that score.

No, it was something else that was tormenting her uncle, something that eclipsed even acquiring Damen as a son-in-law.

One thing was certain. Whatever was plaguing him, he was like a cannon waiting to explode.

Tucking her legs beneath her, Anastasia settled herself more comfortably on the sitting room window ledge and gazed across the grounds. The head gardener was manicuring the shrubs that lined the length of the drive, but she scarcely noticed him, so preoccupied was she with pondering her uncle's state of mind.

Especially after hearing all that Damen had relayed to her yesterday during their meeting at the House of Lockewood.

She'd gone there—presumably—just for business purposes: to receive an update on the status of their joint venture. But only a portion of their conversation had been allocated to Damen's recounting of how things in America were progressing, including an estimated forecast on when the doors of Fidelity Union and Trust would open for the first time. By mid fall, he speculated. Excellent timing indeed.

The rest of their meeting had been about George, as Damen told Anastasia about what his contacts had unearthed and just how deep a financial hole her uncle had dug himself.

That hole was pretty damned deep.

George owed thousands of pounds to his creditors. On top of that, he'd invested thousands more in foolish, unsuccessful ventures and, in the process, had lost every last shilling. In short, he was a man facing monetary ruin. The only thing in his favor was the continued success of Colby and Sons. But even that success he seemed to be destroying, in Damen's judgment.

"I don't understand. Aren't the profits of the business enough to sustain him?" Anastasia had asked.

"They might be, *if* he managed them wisely," was Damen's reply. "The problem is that all signs indicate he hasn't. He certainly never deposited any recent profits at the House of Lockewood, which is where he keeps the bulk of his savings, or whatever's left. Nor have those profits turned up at any other reputable institution, according to my contacts. In my mind, that means George probably squandered them away. What's more, he probably did so carelessly, based on his original expectation that your father would bequeath his half of the business to him, rather than to you."

"Yes," Anastasia had agreed dryly. "Uncle George didn't exactly hide his indignation at Papa's will reading, did he?"

"He wanted Henry's half of the business—badly," Damen responded. "In that way, he would have had a greater amount of profits to gamble with, and would hopefully have recouped some of his losses."

"Only to lose them again," Anastasia had pointed out.

Damen had given her a terse nod.

Well, that explained why George was so desperate for Breanna and Damen to wed. He was frantic to get his hands on Damen's wealth. But it didn't explain the magnitude of his growing anxiety—given the fact that, in his mind, Breanna's relationship with Damen was secure. Based on the frequency of Damen's visits and the obvious attraction that existed between him and the woman George thought to be Breanna, their union was on the verge of becoming a reality. But instead of the relief Anastasia expected her uncle to display, it was almost as if he were waiting for something pivotal to occur—something that could either restore or destroy him.

What was it?

Or was she just dramatizing things in her mind? Was her uncle's strain simply the cumulative effects of a downward monetary spiral?

Somehow she didn't think so.

A flash of motion from outside caught her eye, and Anastasia sat up straighter, peering more closely at the drive just in time to see a carriage come to a screeching halt.

A familiar-looking man—middle-aged, stocky, with a square jaw—emerged, speaking sharply to his driver and eyeing the house nervously before sucking in his breath and hastening up the steps.

Anastasia watched him, racking her brain as she tried to put a name to the familiar face. She'd met hundreds of people at her coming-out party, but this one she recalled. He was one of the gentlemen she'd approached with her business proposition, one of the men who'd turned her down. He was an affluent businessman, not titled, but prominent nonetheless. He owned a shipping company, she remembered in a rush. Lyman. That was it. Mr. Edgar Lyman.

Obviously, he was here to see Uncle George.

And judging from his agitated stance, whatever news he brought, he wasn't looking forward to sharing it.

Squirming to the edge of the window seat, Anastasia waited, poised like a cat ready to spring. Not yet, she cautioned herself. Wait. Five, maybe ten minutes. After that, she'd casually meander down the hall and hover near Uncle George's study. Perhaps she'd overhear something that would shed a ray of light on whatever was at the root of his agitation.

Down the hall in his study, George tossed off his goblet of brandy and ordered Wells to show Lyman in.

"What are you doing here?" he demanded the instant they were alone. "I told you I'd contact you as soon as I got word from our envoy that the shipment had reached port."

"You won't be hearing from him." Lyman's forehead

was dotted with sweat, his palms trembling as he rubbed them together. "The ship isn't going to reach port."

George started. "What are you talking about?"

"I'm talking about that horrible storm we had two nights ago." Lyman wasn't mincing words. "My ship was caught right in the middle of it. Lightning struck the main mast. The ship went down."

All the color drained from George's face. "It went down? What about the cargo?" he demanded. "Surely the crew was able to save . . ." His voice drifted off as he watched Lyman's adamant shake of the head.

"No, Medford. No one was saved. It happened in the dead of night. Everyone was probably asleep. I assume that by the time they realized what was happening, it was too late." He clutched his head in a helpless gesture. "What point is there in speculating? The fact is that no one survived. No one and nothing. Oh, except Meade. He took the one bloody longboat that wasn't destroyed or lost and rowed to shore. Isn't that ironic? He's the one who came and told me about all this. And don't bother asking me if he's lying. He's not. I had it checked out. Our entire shipment is lost." A tremor quivered through his voice. "And I needn't tell you there was no insurance. How could there be, in this case? So it's gone. All the merchandise, all the profit. Gone."

George swore viciously, sweeping his arm across his desk in one violent motion and sending everything on it crashing to the floor. "No. Goddammit, *no.*" He snatched the bottle of brandy off the side table and refilled his goblet with shaking hands. "We'll sail out there ourselves, comb the waters. Surely some part of the cargo can be rescued . . ."

"No. It can't. Four of my best men have already done

what you just described. Other than the wreckage, there's no sign of anything, except a few dead bodies floating in the water."

"Dead bodies?" George bellowed. "Dead bodies don't do me a damned bit of good." He tossed back three healthy gulps of brandy. "What the hell am I going to do? That merchandise was worth a fortune—you saw the quality Bates came up with. We would have gotten thousands for it. *Thousands*. And Lyman, it was our last chance. *Our last bloody chance!*" George flung his glass against the wall, where it shattered into a dozen fragments. "Damn Meade to hell! The son of a bitch should have saved the most valuable cargo and pulled it into the longboat. Instead, he sacrificed the whole shipment just to save his own miserable neck—a neck we could well do without."

In the hallway just outside the study, Anastasia pressed herself against the wall, her eyes wide with shock as she struggled to assimilate all the information that had just been hurled in her face—and the resulting unanswered questions.

Who was this stranger she called her uncle—a man who would place cargo above human life? And what kind of cargo could be so important as to cause such a frenzy at its loss?

Illegal cargo. *That* much was a certainty. It was the only explanation for Uncle George and Mr. Lyman's drastic reaction, and the only explanation as to why no insurance had been obtained before the merchandise was shipped.

But what kind of illegal cargo?

What in God's name was her uncle involved in?

She had little time to contemplate the possibilities. A

thud of approaching footsteps from inside the study crossed toward her, separated only by the still-locked door.

Panic gripped her. She couldn't let her uncle find her standing here. Lord only knew what his reaction would be—and how severe a form it would take.

She had to get away.

Squelching her panic, Anastasia took off at a run, rounding the corner of the hallway and darting up the stairs. She didn't pause until she'd crossed the threshold of her bedchamber and shut the door. Her heart slamming against her ribs, she pressed her ear to the door, listening intently to see if she'd been followed.

Silence.

Her shoulders sagged with relief. No one was coming after her. Whatever she'd learned was her secret.

For now.

Damen. She had to get to Damen.

But how? What excuse could she use to go to the House of Lockewood when she'd just been there yesterday and, upon returning, had made no mention of a subsequent meeting scheduled for today?

She'd have to elicit help—not from Breanna, because involving her cousin would be too dangerous.

Then from whom?

From Wells. Yes, Wells held a special, affectionate place in his heart for her and Breanna. He might be willing to help—if she managed to convince him how vital his part in her plan might be. Of course, she'd have to accomplish that without revealing too much or betraying her uncle— both of which would compromise Wells's integrity and perhaps even threaten his position in the household.

She'd simply ask him straight out—without providing any details.

That decided, Anastasia walked over to the window, shifting the curtain just enough so she could peek out without being seen. Her guess—if the purposeful footsteps she'd heard within her uncle's study had been any indication—was that Mr. Lyman would be making his exit any moment now.

Sure enough, the door opened and their agitated visitor hurried down the steps and into his waiting carriage.

The carriage rounded the drive and sped off.

For a long minute Anastasia waited, peering outside to see if any further activity would ensue.

She was greeted with nothing but stillness.

Stepping away from the window, she rubbed her temples, trying to imagine what her uncle was doing right now—or more importantly, where he was. Clearly, he wasn't rushing off to meet anyone. What that suggested, given his recent behavior, was that he'd bid Mr. Lyman good-bye, then retreated back into the refuge of his study, where he'd promptly drowned himself in more brandy.

On the other hand, he could be making provisions to go out, perhaps getting some papers in order or composing himself enough to ride off and deal with this Meade person he blamed for the loss of his cargo.

If that was the case, Anastasia could very well come face-to-face with her uncle in the entranceway door. Fine. That was a chance she'd have to take. And if it happened, she'd have to pray that Wells would sense her dilemma and choose to follow her lead.

Sucking in her breath, Anastasia smoothed her gown, tucked a few loose tendrils of hair behind her ear, and left her bedchamber. She paused outside Breanna's door, wondering if her cousin was inside. Her fingers automatically reached for the door handle, then, just as quickly, fell away. It didn't matter whether or not Breanna was in her room. She couldn't be involved in this. In fact, the less she knew of Anastasia's intentions, the less vulnerable she'd be to Uncle George's outrage. That way, when interrogated by her father, Breanna could honestly declare she'd been totally unaware of her cousin's last-minute decision to travel to Town.

Staunchly, Anastasia continued on her way, descending the stairs while forcing herself to appear as casual as possible.

The ground floor was deserted.

Slowly, nonchalantly, Anastasia headed toward the entranceway door, half expecting her uncle to spring out at her and demand to know where she was going and why.

No such confrontation occurred.

Wells looked up as she approached, inclining his head in question. "Miss Stacie." He determined her identity upon seeing the loose waves of hair that tumbled about her shoulders. "Are you going out?"

"Yes, Wells, I am." Stacie glanced about quickly, ensuring that they were alone. "I need your help," she confessed in a whisper. "And, unfortunately, in this case that means lying to Uncle George. I wouldn't ask it of you unless the matter was critical."

The butler cleared his throat, appearing less surprised by her request than she'd expected. "What sort of lie is it you require?"

"A minor one," Anastasia assured him. "It's crucial that I speak with Lord Sheldrake—at once. And since the marquess isn't due here today, I need a reason to go to the

House of Lockewood. I'd like you to advise Uncle George that the marquess contacted me with regard to our investment; that his message said something had come up—something that required my immediate attention—and my immediate presence at his bank. Can you do that without feeling disloyal?"

"Crucial, you said." Wells's gaze remained steady. "May I assume you're choosing me to provide this lie in order to protect Miss Breanna?"

"You may."

A flicker of resolve. "In that case, I can manage to live with my guilt. Consider your favor granted." He pivoted, tugging open the door. "Go. If your uncle asks, Lord Sheldrake summoned you to his bank. You left immediately thereafter. We won't expect you back until late this afternoon." The barest hint of a smile. "In fact, you were in so much of a hurry that you dashed off without your lady's maid."

Anastasia's head snapped up, and she studied Wells's face, wondering if the astute butler understood even more than she'd suspected. "Thank you," she murmured, recognizing that now was not the time for questions. "That explanation would be ideal."

"You're quite welcome, Miss Stacie." Wells's expression turned sober, and a note of concern crept into his voice. "Good luck. And be careful."

Solemnly, Anastasia nodded. "I will."

The House of Lockewood was buzzing with activity when she burst in several hours later.

Graff spotted her immediately, and strode rapidly to her side. "Lady Breanna," he greeted her. A quick scan of the doorway told him that she was unaccompanied by the

Viscount Medford. "Or is it Lady Anastasia?" he amended, with a questioning lift of his brows. "Forgive me, but I still can't seem to tell you two apart."

Anastasia grinned. "And since you saw I was unchaperoned, you made an educated guess as to which cousin I was—a correct guess, I might add. Very good, Graff. Lord Sheldrake is lucky to have you in his employ."

A bow. "Thank you, my lady." He pursed his lips. "Is the marquess expecting you?"

"No, but it's imperative that I see him." For the first time, the untenable possibility that Damen might not be at the bank occurred to her. "Is he available?"

"He's in his office, meeting with a client. But let me tell him you're here. I'm sure he'll make time to see you."

With a crisp bow, he headed off toward the private section of offices.

Anastasia paced about the lobby of the bank, plucking at her gloves as she awaited Graff's return. She hoped he'd be persistent enough to yank Damen off to a side, at least long enough to tell him not only who was here, but how anxious she was to see him.

"Why, hello."

A masculine voice, faintly familiar, brought her head around, and Anastasia found herself looking up into Mr. Booth's round face and thoroughly pleased expression.

"My lady." He bowed, lifting her hand to his lips. "I had no idea you and your father were expected today. It's a pleasure to see you."

"Good afternoon, Mr. Booth." Anastasia shifted a bit, thinking there was something about this man that made her feel vaguely uneasy. Perhaps it was his obvious captivation with Breanna, and now with her. "It's no surprise you weren't expecting me," she added. "My visit to your bank wasn't planned. It just came up. By the way, I think you've confused me with my cousin."

Booth had clearly come to that conclusion on his own, given Anastasia's easily detected, diminished accent. "Lady Anastasia," he corrected himself. "Forgive my error." He offered her a small, apologetic smile. "It's hard to believe that two such lovely young women exist, much less how identical in appearance they are."

"I . . . thank you for the compliment," she replied, more self-conscious than flattered. "But I assure you, Breanna and I are anything but identical, other than in our appearance."

"Anastasia."

Before she could elaborate—in whatever as-of-yet undetermined manner she intended to do that—Damen came up behind her, his tone clearly commanding her full attention. "Is everything all right?"

She whipped about, met his penetrating gaze, and nodded. "Yes. I apologize for interrupting your meeting. But I needed to see you right away."

He scrutinized her for another long, probing minute, then nodded, lifting his head and fixing his hard stare on Booth. "Crompton's in my office. You'll have to take over for me—at least until John gets back from his meeting at Lloyds."

"I'm here, Damen." As luck would have it, John Cunnings happened back at that moment, reaching his employer's side in ample time to deduce what was going on. "I'll handle Crompton. The investment he's contemplating extends to several European countries as well as to Singapore. I'm familiar with the risks and rewards of the transaction."

"Excellent. I'll send him to your office." Having resolved the matter to his satisfaction, Damen gestured to Anastasia, careful to maintain the aloof, professional air they'd established between them in public. "Come, my lady."

Anastasia preceded Damen to his office, pausing only to greet Mr. Crompton as he gathered up his portfolio, nodding his agreement to join John Cunnings.

"I see you found a backer," Crompton noted in that crisp, military way he had. "Good for you, dear girl."

"Thank you." Anastasia didn't bother correcting him about Damen's role in her venture. She was far too preoccupied to concern herself with how Lord Crompton perceived her business acumen. "I'm grateful to be working with the marquess."

"As well you should be. He and his officers are among England's finest." Crompton smoothed his waistcoat, then tugged each finger of his gloves snugly into place. "Sheldrake," he continued, snapping his lean body into formal erectness. "I appreciate your preliminary advice. Cunnings can handle things from here. I'll stop by your office after he and I have conducted our business. I assume by then you and Lady Anastasia will have completed yours."

"That will be fine." Damen held the door ajar, waiting politely until the older man had left. Then, he shut the door and turned the key in the lock.

An instant later, he was across the room, gripping Anastasia's shoulders, his eyes boring into hers. "What's wrong? You're white as a sheet."

She swallowed, realizing for the first time how unnerving this day had been. "I overheard something. A conversation. Frankly, I don't know what to make of it."

"What kind of conversation? Between whom?"

Carefully, Anastasia recounted whatever snatches she could recall of her uncle's discussion with Edgar Lyman.

"Dammit," Damen hissed when she'd finished. "I was afraid something like this might be going on." His grip on her shoulders tightened. "You're sure neither of them saw you? That they had no idea you were there?"

"I'm sure. I was gone before they opened the study door." She made a helpless gesture. "Damen, obviously whatever my uncle is involved in is illegal. The question is, what? And who else—besides Mr. Lyman—is involved in this sordid scheme?"

"This Meade person, for one." Damen frowned. "But my guess is he's just some unsavory seaman who works for Lyman. He might not even know what the hell it is he's carrying aboard his ship. If we go to the trouble of finding and confronting him, it's very likely we'll learn nothing, and risk exposing ourselves in the process."

Anastasia nodded. "Meade would doubtless tell Mr. Lyman about our visit. And he, in turn, would tell Uncle George. After all, that's where Meade's loyalties—and his wages—lie."

"Exactly." Damen pressed his lips together. "Did your uncle or Lyman mention any other names?"

"I'm not sure. It's possible." Anastasia squeezed her eyes shut, trying to recall every word of the conversation. A nagging feeling plagued her, the vague awareness that she was forgetting something—something important. Whatever it was, it hovered just beyond the periphery of her memory—tangible, but out of reach. "I was so overwhelmed by what my uncle is doing—not to mention his cold-blooded attitude about the loss of all those lives—that I had trouble focusing on the rest of what he and Mr. Lyman were saying. Also, their voices were muffled. The study door is thick."

Damen nodded his understanding. "If there's something more, you'll remember it. In the meantime, whatever goods George is transporting, they're obviously damned valuable. Otherwise, he'd never take this kind of risk. Then again, I don't know how desperate he is. Maybe his finances have deteriorated to the point where he'll do anything just to recoup a portion of his losses."

Anastasia inhaled sharply, then blew out her breath. "We need answers. And to get them, we need proof. Without it, there's nothing we can do, except put ourselves—and most of all, Breanna—at risk."

"I have scores of contacts, Stacie. But even my resources can reach just so far, especially when it comes to unethical dealings. I'm not exactly an expert on those."

"I know."

With an exasperated sound, Damen scowled, racking his brain as he sought the right avenue to pursue. "Meade is inconsequential. For that matter, so is Lyman. He'd never tell us a thing, not when talking would incriminate him as much as it would your uncle. No, what we need is someone who can get us concrete evidence. Someone who can gain access to actual records—written documentation of these dealings your uncle is involved in. Those records have got to exist, even if they're disguised as innocent exchanges of money for merchandise. If I could get my hands on them, I could figure out what George's arrangement is, and with whom—possibly even what they're transporting. But who's close enough to your uncle to gain that sort of access? Wells?"

Anastasia gave a definitive shake of her head. "No.

Asking Wells to betray Uncle George would be dangerous and unfair. Besides, Wells knows the household like the back of his hand, but he hasn't an inkling how Uncle George conducts his business. Nor would my uncle agree to share that sort of information with a servant. No, whoever does this bit of detective work has to delve beyond whatever sketchy records Uncle George most likely keeps in his study. They have to have access to . . ."

Breaking off, Anastasia met Damen's gaze, the obvious choice exploding in her mind like fireworks. "Me." She gripped the lapels of Damen's coat. "Why didn't I think of it before? I've been so fixed on the fact that our answers lie at Medford Manor, that I overlooked the obvious—the place where records could more easily be hidden: Colby and Sons."

A dark scowl blackened Damen's face. "I don't like the sound of this."

"I'm sure you don't." She chewed her lip, her mind racing as she followed her idea through to completion. "But it's the logical choice—the only choice. Damen, you yourself said that Uncle George's sole source of income seems to be coming from the profits of Colby and Sons. Couple that with what we've just learned, and the fact that no one else has the key to his private office." A smug smile. "*Yet,*" she amended. "All that's about to change. I now own all Papa's shares of Colby and Sons. It's only natural that I show an interest in the running of our family business. I'll tell Uncle George I want to visit the offices, to see the ledgers, the receipts, all the records of our recent profits. I'll ask to meet our suppliers—*all* of them—one of which you and I know to be Mr. Lyman. Uncle George will have no choice but to comply. Not unless he wants me to discuss his lack of cooperation with Mr. Fenshaw."

Damen's jaw had dropped, a look of disbelief slashing his features. "You must be joking. Do you honestly believe your uncle would willingly, and without suspicion, share the details of his business operations with you?"

"It's not *his* business. It's our family's. He won't have a choice. And, knowing me as he does, he won't suspect anything but that I'm being my usual audacious, bluestocking self. It would never occur to him that I'm actually searching for something incriminating, nor that I'm clever enough to find it. I am a woman, after all." She shot Damen an impish grin. "I assume you noticed."

"Oh, I noticed, all right." Damen's scowl deepened. "I also noticed you're reckless and over-confident. What you're planning—it could be incredibly dangerous."

"Or incredibly informative." Anastasia's resolve was strengthening more with each passing instant. "Damen, my uncle is bitter and greedy. As we've just learned, he's also unlawful. My worry is that he's dangerous, as well. Any man who would do what he's doing, speak as he spoke . . ." A distasteful shudder. "My concern is Breanna."

"It should also be you." Damen dragged her against him, tucking her head beneath his chin and stroking the tumbled waves of her hair. "Stacie, if your uncle is the criminal we suspect, you represent a major obstacle in his path. If he should suspect . . ."

"He won't." Anastasia drew back, offered Damen an appealing look. "Give me a few days. That's all I ask. Let me poke around the offices at Colby and Sons. If I don't stumble on anything, or if I sense I'm walking into any sort of danger, I'll stop. You have my word. I'll come straight to you, and we'll think up another tactic. Agreed?''

"Two days," Damen clarified. "Beginning tomorrow. And at the end of each of those two days, I'll be riding to Medford Manor for dinner. To call on Breanna," he added with a meaningful look. "She and I will take two very long walks on those nights. After which, we'll determine our next step. *Now* are we agreed?''

Something warm and wonderful unfurled in Anastasia's chest. "Yes," she murmured, reaching up to kiss his chin. "Agreed."

Damen tugged back her head, lifted her face to his for a profound, lingering kiss. "You and I have things to discuss," he muttered against her lips. "You know that, don't you?"

She nodded, not daring to allow herself the sheer joy of contemplating what those things might be.

"We've put off this conversation far longer than I care to contemplate—*weeks* longer." He drew back, threaded his fingers through her hair. "But no more. These feelings between us—feelings that started that first day in Fenshaw's office and have intensified every moment since— they're very real. Very real and *very* permanent. And the instant this dilemma with your uncle is resolved . . ."

"Yes. That instant." Anastasia pressed her fingertips to his lips, silencing his declaration. "But until then . . ." She shivered, her eyes sliding shut as Damen drew her fingers into his mouth, caressed them with his tongue.

"Until then?" he prompted.

"Oh, Damen, I'm falling in love with you," she confessed breathlessly. "Surely you know that."

He pulled her against him, covered her mouth with his.

"Yes, I know that," he murmured huskily. "But I had to hear it. Because I'm so in love with you I can hardly think."

He sealed his vow with a kiss that both cherished and consumed her, wrapped itself around her heart with a force that nearly made her legs give out.

A knock sounded at the door, interrupting their precious moments of discovery, and Damen gave a disgusted grunt deep in his throat. "We could ignore it," he said, his voice rumbling against her lips as he continued to kiss her.

"We could." Anastasia sighed. "But we'd only arouse suspicions. And that's the last thing we want."

"Is it?"

Their gazes met—and held.

"A few days, Damen," she said in a pleading whisper. "Just to ensure Breanna's safety. Remember, I can challenge Uncle George's guardianship any time I please, request that Mr. Fenshaw find a more appropriate person to oversee my well-being. But Breanna doesn't have that option. She's completely at his mercy. Please—a few days is all I ask."

"A few days," Damen agreed. "No more. After that, I'll break into Colby and Sons myself if I have to, find the bloody evidence we need to put your uncle in prison. And once Breanna is safe, nothing is going to stop me from making you mine. Nothing, Anastasia."

Another knock.

Muttering a curse, Damen walked over and turned the key, flinging the door open to admit a startled Cunnings. "What can I do for you?"

One of Cunnings's dark brows arched. "Have I interrupted something?"

Damen pivoted, stalking over to his desk. "I'm trying to review some details with Lady Anastasia. Which I can't do if I'm interrupted." His head came up, and he met Cunnings's curious gaze. "I repeat, what can I do for you?"

Cunnings took a few tentative steps into the office. "I just wanted to see if Lord Crompton's portfolio was in here. He seems to have misplaced it."

"Here it is, Cunnings." Booth stood in the doorway, waving the portfolio in the air. "Evidently, Crompton left it in the waiting area. Graff retrieved it and brought it directly to your office."

"Ah. Good." Cunnings smiled, heading for the door and pausing only to shoot Damen an odd look. "I apologize for interrupting your meeting. Lady Anastasia . . ." He bowed. "Good day." His heels echoed down the corridor.

Booth hovered in the doorway for a minute, staring at Anastasia as if she were a priceless painting.

"Yes, Booth?" Damen prompted.

"H-m-m? Oh, nothing, sir. If you'll excuse me . . ." One last reverent glance, and he left, shutting the door behind him.

"That man makes me very uncomfortable," Anastasia declared. "He gapes at me as if I were a valuable jewel of some kind."

"You are." Damen's tone was fervent.

"Thank you." Anastasia smiled. "Coming from you, that's a lovely compliment. Mr. Booth, however, is another story entirely. He's not my suitor, Damen, he's your employee. And he ogles me every time I walk through those doors."

"It's not ogling, it's admiration. He does the same to Breanna." Damen shrugged carelessly. "Booth is a shy man who doesn't spend much time with women. My guess is he's lonely. But he's harmless, believe me."

"If you say so." She sounded dubious.

"I do." Damen walked over, brushed his knuckles across her cheek. "I'll see you tomorrow night."

A faint smile. "No, you'll see Breanna."

"Everyone else might see Breanna. I see you."

Anastasia leaned reflexively closer, half-wishing she could just fling herself into Damen's arms and let the rest of the world take care of itself.

"Two days," he reiterated quietly, as if reading her mind. "Two risky days in which I'll probably worry myself sick. After that, we're taking whatever steps are necessary to bring down your uncle and end this ridiculous charade."

Today had been a nightmare, George reflected bleakly. Hovering inside the dingy pub, he peered about through bloodshot eyes, trying to clear his muddled brain. The room swam around him, and he wobbled a bit, then glared at the buxom barmaid who shot him a curious look. *Cast your wretched gaze in a different direction*, his icy stare seemed to command.

That did the trick.

She hurried off, and George leaned against a pillar so as not to make the same mistake again. The last thing he needed was to call attention to himself. Or maybe it didn't matter. Maybe nothing mattered anymore.

Brushing droplets of rain off his coat, he blinked, trying to focus on the rear of the tavern where his contact doubtless awaited him. He was rankled that he'd been summoned in the first place—today of all days. After Lyman's devastating news and all the havoc it prophesied, he had enough to contend with without traveling to this filthy hovel for yet another meeting.

He'd spent the entire afternoon and evening closeted in his study, buried in his brandy as he desperately tried to conjure up a solution to his crumpling life. Rouge wouldn't be assuaged or bullied, not this time. No, this time all George could expect was fury, condemnation, and a complete severing of business ties between himself and his Paris buyer. And then what would he do? How would he find another interested party? He couldn't exactly advertise for one in the newspaper. Further, how would he recoup his staggering losses? He'd invested nearly every last pence in this final shipment—a shipment whose exceptional quality Rouge would never see, nor believe existed.

Perhaps that's what this late-night meeting was about, he thought with a surge of panic. Perhaps Rouge had already sent him a message terminating their association, and he was about to receive it. But no, he decided, commanding his frayed nerves to quiet. His contact never accepted or delivered messages in person. He hired a courier to do that, for the obvious purpose of protecting his own identity.

Then what the hell was tonight about?

The note had said it was important.

What could possibly be important when his entire life was falling apart?

Damn Meade. Damn the storm. And damn the fates for once again shattering his life.

The fates—and Anne. Nothing had been right since she betrayed him.

Squelching that unwelcome thought, he straightened, sharpening his search of the darkened pub.

From the far corner, a telltale flicker of light caught his eye, and he strode toward it.

"I'm not in good humor," he bit out, dragging out his chair and dropping heavily into it. "So make this brief."

"Fine." His contact lit his customary cheroot, assessing George curiously as he blew out a ring of smoke. "Are you all right?"

"I didn't hire you to inquire about my health," George snapped back. "Just tell me why the hell you needed to see me so I can go home."

An offhanded shrug. "Very well. I thought you should know that your niece was at the House of Lockewood today. It was a most unexpected visit."

"*That's* what you dragged me out here for—to talk about my wretched niece?" George shoved back his chair, ready to stagger to his feet and leave. "The only good news you could give me about Anastasia is that she'd been struck by a carriage and killed."

"I was under the impression you wanted me to keep an eye on her, at least with regard to Sheldrake."

"I did." George gave a dismissive wave. "But a visit to the bank hardly constitutes a tryst. Besides, I already knew about her little excursion. My butler gave me the message right after she left Medford Manor. He said Sheldrake sent for her about some nonsensical matter. I think he needed to review some details of that contemptible venture of theirs."

"Did he?" Another slow draw of the cheroot. "That's

not the way it seemed to me. To me, it seemed like Sheldrake was as surprised by Lady Anastasia's visit as I was—and even more pleased than he was surprised."

George went still. "You're saying this visit wasn't at Sheldrake's initiation?"

"It certainly didn't look that way. What's more, they were in his office for nearly an hour, with the door locked. After which, their physical appearance was . . . shall we say, distinctly mussed."

"Mussed." George scowled. "You're crazy. Sheldrake's been at the manor three or four times a week, hovering at Breanna's side like a hawk circling its prey. There's nothing between him and my niece. He scarcely acknowledges her, except for some polite conversation over dinner."

"Whatever you say. But when that office door opened it didn't look to me as if he and Lady Anastasia had been discussing business of any kind. Sheldrake was brusque and out of sorts, while your niece's hair was tousled, her cheeks flushed . . ."

George gave a derisive laugh. "Anastasia is perpetually disheveled. She has been since childhood. If looking rumpled was deemed grounds for punishment, she would have been thrown in prison long ago." A pause. "Did you actually *see* the two of them in a compromising state?"

"No. As I said, the door was locked. And in public, well, in public they behave like business associates."

"Then there you have it." A worried frown creased George's brow as a sudden, untenable thought struck. "This business meeting—Anastasia isn't planning on squandering any more of Henry's inheritance, is she?"

"I've seen no papers to indicate that. So far, it's been only the American bank."

"Good." George felt only a minor surge of relief, the most current dilemma still weighing heavily on his mind. "And your courier's brought you no messages for me from the Continent?"

"If so, you'd already have received them."

"I suppose I would have." A wave of futility swept over George. "It doesn't matter. It's inevitable anyway. Damned, bloody inevitable. All of it. Except Sheldrake. He's my last hope. He—and whatever I can recover of my brother's funds before that miserable bitch invests it all away." George teetered to his feet. "In any case, this whole meeting's been a waste of time. I'm going home for a brandy."

The other man studied George thoughtfully, simultaneously grinding out his cheroot. "You can get a drink here."

George eyed him as if he were insane. "I don't drink the swill they serve in this place." He buttoned his coat, missing the second buttonhole twice. "Good night." He paused, blinking to make the room right itself, reflecting on what he'd just said. An inner voice penetrated his foggy state, warning him that he couldn't afford to be too lax, too sure of himself, when it came to Sheldrake. Marrying the marquess off to Breanna might very well turn out to be his last hope, his last chance of survival.

"Whether or not you're imagining things, I want you to continue as you were," he instructed his contact. "Keep your eye on these meetings between my niece and Sheldrake. Make sure all they share is that bank. Because if it's more . . ." Rage momentarily twisted his features. "Just make sure it's not."

12

George's late-night brandy was just burning its way down to his stomach when a knock sounded on the study door.

He scowled, staring down at the miniature portrait of Anne and willing whoever was summoning him to go away.

His wishes went unheeded.

A second knock sounded, this time more firmly.

"What is it?" he barked, carefully replacing the portrait and rearranging the drawer before sliding it shut.

The study door opened and a young woman who was either Breanna or Anastasia stepped inside. The girl's hair tumbled about her shoulders, and her bold gaze flickered from the near-empty goblet to the neatly stacked desk to George's bloodshot eyes, blatant disapproval registering in her own.

Anastasia.

"What do you want?" George snarled.

"I need to speak with you, Uncle George."

"Not tonight." He waved her away, fuming at the

intrusion. The last thing he wanted to deal with tonight was this outspoken bitch—a bitch who was the living embodiment of Anne's betrayal. "I'm too tired. Whatever it is can wait."

"No, it can't." Anastasia walked toward him, her unwavering stare meeting his head-on. "Uncle George, it occurs to me that I'm neglecting my role as Papa's heir. I've been so caught up with my own coming-out party and my reunion with Breanna, that I've completely overlooked my responsibility to Colby and Sons."

George went rigid. "What are you talking about?"

"Our company. I own half of it now. In America, Papa spent long years teaching me about the family business. He'd want me to continue with my education, to share with you the full responsibility of running Colby and Sons. I intend to do that. Starting tomorrow."

Bile rose in George's throat, and he quickly washed it down with another gulp of brandy. "I must be misunderstanding you."

"I don't think so," she countered brightly. "What I've planned is to visit our London offices tomorrow. I'll go through our current list of business associates, our suppliers, our contacts throughout the Continent. I'm sure most of those names will be familiar to me—after all, we dealt with them from our American offices, too." She inclined her head quizzically. "Would you like to join me? Or shall I just take the plunge on my own?"

George felt as if his head was about to split in two. How dare this impertinent little bitch walk in here and announce that she was assuming a role in his company? How dare she presume she had the right?

His knuckles whitened around the periphery of his glass.

The trouble was, she *did* have the right.

"Uncle George?" she pressed. "Shall I tell Wells that I'll be traveling to London alone, or . . ."

"No," he ground out, fighting the vise of panic that gripped him at the thought of Anastasia having access to his doctored receipts, his veiled correspondence. *Stop it,* he commanded himself. *She'll never see through it—not if you don't condemn yourself by acting guilty.* "I'll go with you," he continued, in as calm a voice as he could muster. "I'll show you around the office. I'll ask my carriage driver to wait, so you can run along home immediately thereafter."

"Oh, I don't want to run along," Anastasia declined with a reassuring smile. "I want to stay—to read through the ledgers, the ongoing contracts, everything." Her smile faded, and she gave him an apologetic look. "I know you find the prospect of a woman in business outrageous. But I think you'll be surprised to see how quick my mind actually is. I suppose I take after Papa. I find the import–export business fascinating." With that, she glanced at her uncle's half-empty brandy bottle, and backed away. "Anyway, I won't keep you. You mentioned you were tired. And I, too, had best get a good night's rest. I want to be especially alert tomorrow."

George stared after her as she left, watching blindly as the door shut in her wake. A fury like he'd never known surged inside him, pulsed through his veins. Violently, he seized his bottle of brandy, hurling it at the now-closed door, staring at the dark splotches of color that splattered the walls, stained the carpet.

If only it was Anastasia he'd shattered, her blood he'd spilled.

Then maybe retribution could blot out adversity.

It was just past dawn when Breanna knocked on her cousin's bedchamber door.

"Stacie, are you awake?"

Anastasia opened the door, a surprised expression crossing her face. "Awake and dressed," she assured her cousin. "Is everything all right?"

"You tell me." Breanna walked into the room, shutting the door and leaning back against it. "I tossed and turned all night. I couldn't shake the feeling that you're in some kind of trouble. Are you?"

Rubbing her palms together, Anastasia contemplated how to answer that. It didn't surprise her that Breanna sensed her turmoil, not given the uncanny connection that existed between them. But what could she possibly say to ease her cousin's mind?

"Don't skirt the issue or try lying to me," Breanna second-guessed her to warn. "You're terrible at hedging and even worse at lying."

A grin. "That certainly limits my options, now doesn't it?" Her smile faded. "Breanna, I'm not trying to hide things from you. I'm only trying to protect you."

"From my father," Breanna concluded.

"Yes. From your father."

A contemplative pause, during which time Breanna studied her cousin, tapping her chin thoughtfully. "But you *have* shared this dilemma of yours with someone. And I'd be willing to bet that someone is Damen Locke-wood."

"You'd be right." This, at least, was something Anastasia could share with Breanna—something she was aching to share with her. "I'm in love with him," she admitted, gauging her cousin's reaction. "And what's even more wonderful, he's in love with me."

Genuine joy erupted on Breanna's face, and she rushed over, hugged Anastasia tightly. "I'm so happy for you—for you both." She drew back, teasing laughter dancing in her eyes. "Of course, *I've* known this for weeks. I was wondering how long it would take the two of you to figure it out. You're both so miserably stubborn."

"You're right." Anastasia smiled. "But we finally declared our feelings aloud."

"When?"

"Yesterday. At the House of Lockewood."

That elicited an entirely different reaction, worry clouding Breanna's face. "You didn't mention to me that you were going to the bank."

"The visit wasn't planned." Anastasia fell silent, torn between the attempt to protect her cousin and the realization that Breanna had a right to the truth—especially if that truth turned out to be a dangerous one. "Breanna, I overheard something yesterday, something terribly unnerving. I went to Damen for advice, and perhaps for help."

"And that something involves Father."

"Yes."

"Tell me what it is. I deserve to know." Breanna's jaw set as if to steel her for what was to come. "Even if I won't like what I hear."

"All right." Anastasia sank down on the bed, relaying the entire conversation she'd overheard, ending with her talk with Damen and her subsequent decision to visit the offices of Colby and Sons. "If there's anything incriminating to be found, I'm sure that's where it will be. It's the only place Uncle George would feel secure about leaving such records."

"God." Breanna sank down beside her cousin. "This is even worse than I suspected." She massaged her temples, then abruptly stopped. Twisting about, she faced Anastasia. "But if my father is involved in something ugly, you could be endangering yourself by going there and trying to uncover evidence."

"That was Damen's argument. It didn't deter me. Nor will it now."

"Fine. Then I'm going with you."

"No." Anastasia leapt to her feet. "You're not."

"Stacie, he's *my* father. You're not putting yourself at risk alone."

Anastasia gave a hard shake of her head. "Breanna, listen to me. I'm not trying to be heroic. I'm trying to find answers. Thus far, I've succeeded in arranging all this without arousing Uncle George's suspicions. But if you suddenly appear by my side, insisting on learning a business you've never before expressed any interest in, all that will change. Your father's not a stupid man." Anastasia took Breanna's hand in hers. "I have to do this alone—for all our sakes, to get at the truth as soon as possible. And if our worst suspicions are confirmed, if Uncle George is indeed dangerous . . ." A swallow. "Then he must be dealt with before he can harm anyone."

"Anyone—meaning me."

"Yes, meaning you." Anastasia never diverted her gaze. "I asked you this once before, in a less than straightforward fashion. Now I'm asking you directly: does Uncle George strike you?"

"Strike me, yes. Beat me senseless, no. Do I sense an element of cruelty in him? Of course. But can I say I've ever feared for my safety? I . . . I don't think so."

"You've never given him reason to threaten your safety, or to become truly enraged, for that matter. But if you did, especially now, when he's constantly drinking, when his humor is as black as night and his temper so short that everyone cringes the minute he enters the room . . ." Anastasia's voice trailed off. "I can't vouch for what he might do. Nor can I vouch for his stability. The bottom line is, he's your father. That's not something you can undo. You're his responsibility until your twenty-first birthday. I can sever ties with him if need be. You can't. And I won't leave you here at his mercy." A pause. "Can you shoot a pistol?"

Breanna sucked in her breath. "What?"

"Humor me. Can you shoot?"

A nod. "At targets and pigeons, yes. But not at people." Breanna gave her cousin an incredulous look. "Do you honestly believe I'll need to defend myself to that degree?"

"I don't know what to believe. And I'm not thinking only of the possible danger Uncle George represents. If he's involved in something illegal, who knows what type of people he consorts with? Or how many of those unsavory contacts won't get paid—and, as a result, will become very agitated—because that shipment of Uncle George's went down?" Anastasia counted off on her fingers. "There are those who supplied the illegal cargo, those who awaited its arrival, investors—the possibilities are too vast too contemplate. Will any of those lowlifes show up here to retaliate? I'm not going to speculate. But I have a very uneasy feeling about all this. And I'd feel better if you kept a pistol nearby, just in case."

Breanna frowned, unable to dispute her cousin's reasoning. "Very well. As I recall, Father keeps an extra pistol in the library, to have on hand in case of a burglary. Since he never uses it, he wouldn't notice if it were to disappear, at least not for a few days. I'll go downstairs and get it after you and he leave for the office. I'll hide it in my bureau drawer." Her frown deepened. "What about you? How will you protect yourself?"

"If I sense anything out of the ordinary today, I'll slip off and go straight to the House of Lockewood. If need be, I'll borrow a pistol from Damen. But Uncle George wouldn't dare harm me in public—especially not once I casually mention that I informed Damen during yesterday's meeting that I'd be going to Colby and Sons today."

"I see your point. My father would never want to tarnish his image—not in the eyes of Lord Sheldrake." Breanna captured both Anastasia's hands, squeezed them tightly. "Please. Be careful. And try not to act too cheeky. Things will go much better with Father if you don't challenge his opinions or his authority."

A rueful smile tugged at Anastasia's lips. "I hear the message you're giving me loud and clear. I promise to do my best to keep my place and not antagonize Uncle George."

That promise wasn't going to be easy to keep, she fumed silently, after traipsing along behind her uncle for an hour, exploring the wonders of the outer office at Colby and Sons. The sum total of the room was a desk, occupied by their mild-mannered clerk Mr. Roberts, a row of chairs and a file cabinet against one wall and, against the wall adjacent to George's private offices, a settee and two end tables, before which rested a long, rectangular table. Not a sheet of paper lay exposed upon the desk or any of the tables, nor was there visible evidence of any other business-oriented material.

Did her uncle actually think she'd be content with this inane tour and then run along home like a good little girl?

If so, he had quite a surprise in store.

She'd begin with the obvious file cabinet.

"Uncle George, if it's all right with you, I'd like to start familiarizing myself with the company." She gestured toward the cabinet. "What if I begin by glancing through the files so I can acquaint myself with our current transactions, as well as the names of those suppliers we deal with most frequently."

Her uncle bristled and Mr. Roberts's head shot up as he awaited his employer's reply.

"Fine," George bit out, practically choking on his words. "I have some papers to sort through in my office." He turned to his clerk. "Roberts, give Lady Anastasia whatever she needs."

"Certainly, my lord." The poor little man whipped off his spectacles, wiping at an imaginary speck of dust before shoving the spectacles back on his nose and rising to his feet. "Why don't you have a seat, my lady? I'll bring the files to you."

"Thank you, Mr. Roberts. That would be very kind." Anastasia settled herself on the settee. Surreptitiously, she peeked at her uncle from the corner of her eye, watching him approach his private office, then extract a key from his pocket, which he used to unlock the door. That done, he pushed open the door and stepped inside.

It took all her self-restraint not to dash in after him.

Leaning forward, she peered around the open doorway and caught a glimpse of a tidy room with a walnut desk and sideboard. Ledgers were neatly stacked on the far left-hand corner of the desk alongside a tray of papers—correspondence, perhaps—and what looked to be an appointment book. The sideboard was uncluttered, although she'd bet her last pound that it was stocked with liquor.

She was dying to go through those ledgers and that appointment book. But she'd have to wait, bide her time, until she could find the means to get in.

The door slammed shut.

Sighing, Anastasia resettled herself on the settee, awaiting Mr. Roberts, who was gathering files for her from the cabinet. Instinct told her she'd find nothing incriminating in what she was about to be given. Whatever her uncle was involved in, he certainly wouldn't want Roberts having access to those records. Still, she had to be sure. She also had to start somewhere.

Two hours later, she had three stacks of files piled up on the long table before her, and she'd learned nothing other than the fact that Colby and Sons had a healthy clientele and a substantial number of ongoing transactions. The only curious detail that struck her was the high prices charged by several of their shippers. If all the shipping companies' fees had been uniformly higher, she would have assumed that shipping costs in England simply exceeded those in America. But that didn't seem to be the case, not when most of the companies appeared to be charging fees that were comparable to what she was accustomed to seeing in her father's records. Further, of those few shippers who commanded a higher price, one was Mr. Lyman, whose very name sent off warning bells in Anastasia's head. This she'd have to investigate further.

She was just about to plow through yet another pile of receipts when the entrance to Colby and Sons was flung open.

"Roberts, I need to see Lord Medford right away." A stout man who looked distinctly familiar burst into the room, his pudgy cheeks bright red, whether from the exertion of hurrying or something more, Anastasia couldn't determine. But he certainly seemed agitated, and urgent about his demand to see her uncle.

Before Roberts could respond, the inner office door nearly flew off its hinges, and Uncle George stalked out, brushing by the settee where Anastasia sat, and crossing over to join his caller. "I didn't expect you today," he greeted, his entire demeanor strained as he backed the other man toward the entranceway. "Roberts, you may go to the bank for me now," he instructed brusquely over his shoulder.

The nervous clerk jumped to his feet, and George waited, keeping his back to Anastasia and remaining silent until Roberts had excused himself and left. Then, he continued speaking to his guest, his voice, and that of his companion, scarcely audible.

Casually, Anastasia rose, twisting about to eye her uncle's now-vacant office longingly. She turned back, studying the two men and grappling over which to do: Should she sidle closer to them, try to eavesdrop on the conversation, and learn what this visit was all about? Or should she use this time to try to slip into her uncle's private domain and glance at his personal records?

Since the men's voices were so quiet that eavesdropping was a virtual impossibility, and coupled with the fact that she might never have another chance, she opted for the latter.

Slowly, she edged toward the inner office, never looking away from her uncle and his visitor. They were engrossed in heated discussion, their agitated tones escalating into hisses, both men totally unaware of her presence.

At the precise moment, Anastasia eased inside, then halted, deciding quickly where to spend the few seconds she had. Scrutinizing the room, she made an impulsive decision, and acted upon it. She rushed to the desk, snatched up the appointment book, and tucked it in the pocket beneath her skirts. Holding her breath, she inched back to the threshold, peeking outside and feeling a surge of relief when she saw the two men still talking. She slipped out, sidled over to the settee, and resumed her position.

"Uncle George, may I help myself to the next drawer of files?" she inquired brightly.

"What?" Just the sound of her voice made George's shoulders go positively rigid. "Oh, yes, yes. Mister . . . my guest and I will be going out for a few minutes." He turned, hurried over to lock his office door. Pausing beside Anastasia, he glanced down at what she was perusing, and looked subtly but discernibly relieved at whatever he saw. "Browse through the files as you please," he forced himself to offer. "Save any questions you have for Roberts. He'll be back within the half hour."

"Thank you. I will." She smiled, holding her breath until her uncle and his portly guest—who had retreated into the hallway to wait—had left.

She heard their footsteps fade away, and waited an extra moment to be safe.

Then, she whisked the appointment book out from under her skirts, and began scanning the entries.

Rather than starting at the beginning, she focused on the 7th of August, about one week ago, hoping to see a name that would leap out at her and correspond with the timing of the shipment of that questionable cargo.

Lyman's name appeared several times, but that was no surprise. So did a few other names. Curiously, they were all the shippers whose rates were higher than their competitors.

A rather clipped entry dated two days ago caught her eye: *Rouge—receive Paris shipment.*

No further details were provided, an oddity, given that the other entries in the book were thorough, described in full.

And neat.

That was another thing. Unlike George's other entries, which were precisely penned, as fastidious as he, this one was uneven, its awkwardly scrawled letters crammed in the corner, almost as if he wanted them hidden.

Which he probably did.

The date on the entry was August 12th—just one day after the shipment had gone down.

Paris. Was that where that illegal cargo had been headed? And, if so, who was Rouge?

Quickly, Anastasia flipped through the appointment book, noticing two additional, equally obscured entries that indicated other occasions when this Rouge was expecting something from Uncle George—something to be delivered to Paris.

But what?

A noise in the hallway caught Anastasia's ear, and

swiftly she slipped the appointment book back into its hiding place beneath her skirts. When Mr. Roberts entered an instant later, she was calmly leafing through a stack of receipts.

"Have you everything you need, my lady?" he asked timidly.

"Yes." Anastasia gave him a grateful smile. "Thank you, Mr. Roberts. Oh, Uncle George said he'd be back shortly. He went for a stroll with Mr. . . . Mr. . . ." She screwed up her face, seemingly searching for the name of their visitor. "I'm sorry. I've received so many introductions since I returned to England. I completely forgot the surname of that pleasant gentleman who was just here."

"Bates," Roberts supplied, nodding his understanding as he resumed his place at his desk. "Mr. Bates. The magistrate."

"Yes, that's right. Mr. Bates." Anastasia nearly leaped out of her seat as the name fell into place. Of course. Bates—the magistrate. No wonder Uncle George hadn't wanted her to get too good a look at him. He knew that if she saw him up close she'd recognize him, and wonder why a magistrate was visiting the offices of an import–export company.

Mr. Bates. *Now* she remembered. He'd been one of the potential backers she'd approached at her coming-out party. He was financially secure and well-connected.

And his was the name she'd overheard her uncle speak to Mr. Lyman in their meeting yesterday.

Anastasia had to keep herself from shouting aloud as that snippet of memory fell into place, and she recalled her uncle's words.

That merchandise was worth a fortune—you saw the quality

Bates came up with. We would have gotten thousands for it.
Thousands. And Lyman—it was our last chance. Our last
bloody chance!

Bates. *That* had been the name that had hovered out of
reach when she'd recounted the conversation to Damen.

And now that she did recall it, a whole new set of
questions emerged. Why in the name of heaven was a
magistrate involved in supplying goods? What stolen or
illegal merchandise had he gotten his hands on that
Uncle George had shipped to someone named Rouge in
Paris? Valuable jewels? Opium?

She'd be willing to bet that the sunken cargo was the
reason for Bates's visit today—*and* the reason for his
unsettled state of mind. He'd probably just found out that
whatever he'd provided to Uncle George was never going
to reach its destination.

Anastasia massaged her temples. She had to assimilate
all this information, to review it with someone she
trusted—the same someone who could help her make
sense of all she'd gleaned today.

Damen.

Half tempted to make some excuse and head out, she
suddenly remembered the appointment book. If she left
the office without returning it, her uncle would undoubtedly come back and discover it missing. Then he'd know
she was up to something, which would arouse his suspicions and, consequently, undo everything she'd accomplished thus far.

She eased back on the settee. She had to have patience,
to find a way to replace the appointment book before
leaving the office.

How was another matter entirely—one she wished
she'd given some thought to before she'd snatched the

bloody thing. Then again, there hadn't been time. If she'd taken one extra minute to think things through, her opportunity to seize the book would have vanished and she never would have had the chance to read those potentially incriminating entries.

Somehow, some way, she had to await her uncle's return and accompany him into his office, then find a way to slip the appointment book back onto his desk—before he noticed it was missing.

Lord only knew what she was letting herself in for, especially given the wretched mood her uncle would doubtless be in after his heated discussion with Bates.

Well, she'd just have to contend with that, as well.

She lowered her head, resuming her perusal of the files. Being she was stuck here, she might as well make the most of it. She'd pore over as many receipts as time permitted.

Twenty minutes later, George stalked into the office, a black scowl darkening his face. His breath was coming quickly—as if he'd been running or, perhaps, arguing strenuously. He barely glanced at Roberts or Anastasia, but headed straight for his office door. His hand shook as he fitted the key into the lock, and it took him three attempts to get the door open.

Either he's been drinking or, more likely, he craves a drink, Anastasia mused silently.

Just the thing she needed to save her.

Moving to the edge of the settee, she waited until her uncle had taken a few steps inside his office. Then, she shot to her feet, following him in as quietly as she could.

Sure enough, he had crossed the room and was pouring himself a generous helping of brandy.

Without pause, Anastasia yanked the appointment

book from beneath her skirts and placed it silently on the desk where she'd found it.

"Uncle George?" she said, pretending she'd just entered the room. "I want to thank you for giving me free rein to explore. It's been exciting to learn just how vast our company has become."

George's head jerked around, and he stared at Anastasia as if she were a loathsome insect. "I'm glad your morning was exciting. Mine wasn't." He drowned his bitterness in two deep swallows of brandy, clearly trying to squelch his obvious hostility toward his niece— hostility rooted in something far harsher, more deep-seated than mere disapproval over her business acumen. "Have you seen enough for one day, or are you intent on further upsetting my filing system and my schedule?"

Anastasia chewed her lip in apparent distress. "I didn't mean to be disruptive. But perhaps you're right. Perhaps I did overstay my welcome a bit, especially in the case of poor Mr. Roberts. He's been waiting on me all morning, probably to the exclusion of his other work." She glanced over her shoulder at the outer office, a rueful expression on her face. "The more I think about it, the more I think I'll be going."

A spark of relief flickered in George's eyes. "I'm sure Roberts would appreciate that. We still have quite a bit of paperwork to review today."

"Then I'll be on my way."

"Fine. Take the carriage."

"But how will you get home?"

"I'll find a way," George snapped. "Just go."

"All right." Anastasia wasn't waiting for her uncle to change his mind. "I'll thank Mr. Roberts and be off."

* * *

A half hour later she walked into the House of Lockewood.

Impatiently, she looked around for Graff, eager to have him announce her to Damen.

She needn't have bothered.

Damen himself was pacing about the bank, his gaze flickering from his customers to the entranceway and back.

The instant he saw Anastasia, he broke away from the crowd, making his way to her side.

"Are you all right?"

"Fine. May we talk?"

"Right now." He gripped her arm, led her across the floor, through the rear door, and directly into his office.

He shut and locked the door.

"What happened?" he demanded, turning to face her. "I've been watching the clock and worrying since I got up this morning. Actually, I worried all night, too. I didn't shut an eye. I never should have agreed to this. The risk is too great."

"But well worth it." Anastasia rushed forward, clutched his forearms. "Damen, I got results. At least I think I did." She blurted out everything she'd discovered, from the odd discrepancy in the receipts to the entries in her uncle's appointment book, to the most damning information of all: Bates's visit and the fact that it had been his name she'd overheard in her uncle's conversation with Lyman yesterday—all of which added up to the fact that the magistrate was somehow involved in these shady dealings.

Damen's scowl deepened with each passing word. "That's it," he declared the minute she was finished. "Your part in this is officially over. Whatever your uncle is involved in is more serious than I thought, and even more dangerous. Magistrates and affluent businessmen who risk their positions in society are desperate men. When they're backed into corners, they react like trapped animals. They attack when threatened. As do unscrupulous viscounts who already despise their nieces and find out those nieces have played a major role in bringing them down. I'll take it from here, Stacie. I mean it."

Anastasia sucked in her breath. "What will you do?"

"I'll have Bates investigated. It should be easy enough to find out if George is compensating him in some way. My guess is it's with power, not money—being that your uncle has none of the latter to offer. But he does have influence, or at least his title does. I wouldn't be surprised if he's had a hand in broadening Bates's area of jurisdiction."

"That makes sense," Anastasia concurred. "What about Rouge? How do we get information on him?"

"I'll notify one of my contacts in Paris, see what they can dig up. Whoever this Rouge is, he can't be too hard to find, especially if he doesn't know we're looking for him." Damen considered the rest of what she'd told him, and his lips thinned into a grim line. "As for the companies you mentioned—the ones whose prices were higher than the others—my guess is that either your uncle's cohorts padded those receipts and split the difference with him, or that the companies in question have investments in his seedy operation, in which case, he's giving them a percentage of what he's making by paying their inflated bills."

"In other words, he's embezzling from Colby and Sons—my grandfather's company." Anger flared deep within Anastasia's gut.

"Yes. He's nothing but a common criminal—he and his despicable partners. A common criminal, *and* a dangerous one."

The anxiety in Damen's voice dispelled Anastasia's ire, supplanted it with concern. "You're worrying about me," she stated quietly.

"I bloody well am. As your grandfather would be if he were alive. Funds can be recouped. People can't. Besides, I know firsthand that Colby and Sons is in no financial danger. You, on the other hand, are another matter entirely. As of this moment, you're to stay as far away from your uncle as the walls of Medford Manor permit. I'd recommend the same for Breanna—although I doubt George would be suspicious of her. Just steer clear of him. Live there, eat there, but keep your distance. No more visits to Colby and Sons, no more inflammatory confrontations. And no more deceptions."

That brought Anastasia's head up. "If you're referring to Breanna and me switching places, the only way we can end that deception is if you stop visiting me. Is that what you want?"

A muscle worked in his jaw. "You know it isn't." He dragged her against him, buried his lips in her hair. "I can't—*won't*—stay away from you."

"Nor I from you." She rested her forehead against his chest. "We'll just have to make sure Uncle George doesn't figure us out. Because until you gather enough evidence to have him thrown into jail, he's a threat to Breanna. Especially now, when your supposed preoccupation with her is my uncle's main source of hope. If he were to discover there's to be no future between Breanna and you . . ." Anastasia sighed. "I shudder to think what he'd do."

"And if he discovered the lengths you and she are going to to deceive him into believing that lie? What would he do to her then?"

Silence.

Damen's embrace tightened. "I've got to get that evidence—fast. It's the only way to ensure your and Breanna's safety, and allow us the future I intend us to have."

Anastasia inhaled sharply and broke away, crossed over toward the desk.

Her abrupt movement startled the shadowy figure that hovered outside the office door.

Tension rippling through him, he pressed close to the wall, waiting to see if bolting would become a necessity. It didn't. The office door remained shut. Better still, the voices from inside, until now too muffled to discern, loomed within clear, distinguishable range.

"Stacie? What is it?" Unaware he was being eavesdropped upon, Damen walked over, turned Anastasia about to face him.

She squeezed her eyes shut, wishing she could explain how badly she needed the balm Damen's words provided, how impossibly thrilling a future with him sounded. "Tell me about our future together."

He seemed to understand, because his hand stroked her hair, moved it out of the way so he could caress the nape of her neck. "Later. For now, I'd rather show you."

"That would be heaven," she breathed, feeling shivers go up her spine. "Far more wonderful than telling me. Certainly better than talking about my uncle and whatever criminal activities he's involved in. And much, much better than your lecturing me about the dangers Breanna and I are flirting with by switching places."

Damen tilted back her head, his hot gaze probing hers with burning intensity. "I wish I didn't want you so damned much," he muttered. "Because, despite your insistence to the contrary, my every instinct is screaming that I should continue lecturing you. It's time for you and Breanna to stop this insanity, to stop pretending to be each other during my visits. Sweetheart, you're playing with fire."

"M-m-m," Anastasia murmured, only half-listening to Damen's words. She was still contemplating his vow to show her what was in store for them. She turned her head, brushed her lips against his throat. "Playing with fire—well, maybe I am. Fortunately, I only burn when I'm with you."

Damen's muscles went rigid. "You're trying to distract me."

"And if I am?" She slipped her fingers into the knot of his cravat, untied it. "It's working, isn't it?"

"Yes, it's working. Too damned well."

"Good," she breathed, kissing the strong column of his throat. "Because I don't want to talk about my uncle anymore, at least not now. In fact, I don't want to talk at all."

With a rough groan, Damen tugged back her head, lowering his mouth to hers. "You make me crazy," he muttered against her lips. "I want to protect you and throttle you all at once. And I want to strip away every last barrier between us and make love to you until neither of us can breathe."

"Um-m-m, the last sounds spectacular," Anastasia murmured, sliding her hands beneath his waistcoat, gliding them up the fine linen of his shirt. "Terribly improper, but spectacular."

"This discussion is not over," he warned, his fingers automatically reaching around, dispensing with the buttons of her gown. Hungrily, he tugged the bodice down to expose the upper slope of her breasts. "Understood?" His lips blazed a path to her chemise, dipping lower as he untied the ribbons, one by one. "We have to come up with a different plan for us to be together—one I can live with."

Anastasia urged him closer, welcoming his caresses, the all-encompassing surge of heat that claimed her, obliterated all else from her mind. "Understood," she managed. "We'll fight this battle out—later." She shifted restlessly, eager to free herself from the confinement of her chemise. "Much later."

Outside the door, the eavesdropper straightened, stepped away. He'd learned all he had to. He didn't need to tarry any longer—not when every moment meant risking discovery. Besides, it didn't take a scholar to guess what was about to take place behind that door.

Glancing around to confirm he'd remained undetected, he made his way toward the privacy he sought. His mind was racing, reminding him that time was of the essence. He'd send a message off right away, arrange for a meeting tonight.

What he'd just heard explained everything. He was pleased to discover his instincts hadn't failed him, contrary to what Medford claimed. He'd been right about Lady Anastasia and Lord Sheldrake.

As for Medford—well, the viscount certainly wasn't going to be happy with the news he was about to receive. Especially since the courier was already en route to his lordship's residence with that letter from the Continent he'd been dreading.

Two pieces of bad news in one night.

The man scowled. Ah, well. Making the viscount smile wasn't his job. Giving him information was.

With that, he stepped into the empty room and quietly shut the door.

Inside Damen's office, Anastasia, oblivious to anything but what was happening between them, lost patience. She reached around, untying the final ribbon of her chemise and shrugging the garment off her shoulders.

Damen drank in her beauty, his eyes darkening to that smoky gray that made her heart pound. "You're pushing me to a dangerous brink," he whispered roughly, bending his head to draw one aching nipple into his mouth. "Perhaps *too* dangerous."

"I don't care." She arched, offering him more of herself, quivering as he took it. "For once, I don't want to think. I want to go wherever this takes us. And when we get there—I don't want you to stop."

With a harsh shudder, Damen caught her about the waist, backing her up until she collided with the edge of his desk, then lifting her onto it. Urgently, he pushed up her skirts and wedged himself in the cradle of her thighs. "I won't stop," he vowed huskily. "I can't." His forefinger lifted her chin, and he lowered his head again, sealing their lips in a kiss that was slow and hot and deep. His tongue slid across hers, taking it in blatant possession, and his fingers tangled in her hair, cradling her head so she couldn't move away.

Moving away was the farthest thing from Anastasia's mind.

She moaned softly, wriggling closer to the warmth of Damen's body, knowing she was testing his control and half-hoping it would shatter.

It nearly did.

He gripped the bunched muslin layers of her gown, pushing them higher, gliding his palm up her stocking-clad inner thighs. He kept kissing her, his mouth eating at hers, devouring her with an intensity he'd never before allowed. He muttered her name, his fingers shifting higher, finding the spot where her stockings left off and her bare skin began.

"Damen." Anastasia clutched at him, sensing what he was about to do, frantic for him to do it.

"Do you want this?" he rasped against her mouth.

"Yes. Please. Yes." She nodded wildly, her hips lifting instinctively toward him, silently begging for his touch.

His palm climbed that last tantalizing inch, grazed the burnished nest between her thighs. Then, his fingers parted her, stroked the delicate flesh that screamed for his touch.

Anastasia's breath lodged in her throat. Time seemed to stand still, all sensation concentrated beneath Damen's heated caress. She heard him groan, felt the tremor that racked his body. But all she knew was the unbearable stirring inside her, the rush of wet warmth that surged through her core, the tight knot of need that coiled inside her, an awakening and an emptiness all at once.

"Silk," Damen breathed into her lips. "Hot, flawless silk. God, I want to be inside you." His fingers responded to his command, gliding into her warm wetness, caressing and exploring her, only to emerge, circle the tight bud that throbbed with yearning.

Anastasia whimpered into Damen's open mouth, parting her thighs shamelessly and moving against his hand, unable to get close enough, to deepen his presence in her body fully enough.

Somehow he understood.

His fingers withdrew, then entered her again, only this time they began an unbearable rhythm of plunge and retreat, moving faster and deeper, reaching high inside her, pushing toward that unendurable tightness curled in her very center. At the same time, his thumb found that tight little bud, circled it enticingly, first once, then again and again and again.

Abruptly, bright colors exploded inside Anastasia's head, and her entire body clenched and convulsed, shimmering and shattering into a million fragments of sensation. She tore her mouth from Damen's, burying her face against his shoulder as spasms racked her body. She cried out, the sound muffled by Damen's woolen coat, and he held her as she came apart in his arms, his fingers heightening her pleasure until the final spasm had subsided and she sagged against him, everything inside her melting and sliding away into nothingness.

From a distance, the faint sounds of the bank trickled back into consciousness, and gradually, Anastasia became aware of her surroundings again. Damen was holding her, stroking her back in slow, soothing motions, gently kissing the crown of her hair, his own breath emerging in harsh, shallow rasps.

With a herculean effort, Anastasia raised her head, gazed into the blazing inferno of Damen's eyes. "God," she whispered, her voice as unsteady as her heartbeat. "That was . . ."

"Inconceivable," Damen supplied, smoothing damp tendrils of hair off her cheeks. "It defied words, surpassed even my wildest fantasies. And it was only the beginning, Stacie. There's more—so much more."

Anastasia heard the strain in his voice and her gaze fell

reflexively to his trousers, noting the obviously rigid contours of his body and, despite her innocence, realizing precisely what they meant. "But you . . ."

". . . will survive—at least for the time being." Damen smiled at the stricken expression on her face. "I'm not being selfless, sweetheart. Trust me. I intend to succumb to this relentless craving inside me, to pour myself into you until every last drop of me is spent. But I want more than a few stolen minutes in my office. Once I make you mine . . ." A profound light flickered in his eyes. "I don't intend to let you go. Not ever. You asked me to tell you about our future. Well, now I will. I'm going to marry you, Anastasia. I'm going to place my ring on your finger and declare my love for you before God and all mankind. And I'm going to do it the instant this insanity is behind us— after which, nothing and no one is going to stop me."

Tears glistened on Anastasia's lashes. "Have I any say in this new partnership you're describing?" she asked in a small, quavery voice.

"One word. That's all the say you have."

A tremulous smile. "Very well. Then here's that word: yes. Yes to everything you just described. Yes to everything you want but have yet to describe. Yes."

13

*I*t was the first time George had ever arrived at this filthy establishment before his contact. Then again, he was early. Ordinarily, he kept a close eye on his pocket watch, never riding off to their meeting place one moment sooner than was necessary. But tonight, he hadn't so much as glanced at his timepiece. He'd been too preoccupied with Rouge's message.

It couldn't have come at a better time.

The day had been nerve-racking. After a sleepless night—filled with dark dreams of Anastasia discovering his doctored receipts, then flourishing them before the authorities—he'd been forced to escort her into London, through the doors of Colby and Sons, all the while treating her as if she belonged there. And then, as if that hadn't been enough, he'd been forced to watch the bitch tear his office apart file by file as she immersed herself in *his* company.

On the heels of that, Bates had arrived.

Of all the days for the fool to find out about the lost cargo, it had to be today. Calming him down, assuring him his identity had been kept secret, never mentioned in the records of the lost shipment, had taken the better part of an hour.

But dealing with Bates had been more aggravating and time-consuming than it had been alarming. George knew the magistrate would never betray him. He enjoyed his position too much. As long as his name stayed unsullied, he'd be cooperative and keep his mouth shut.

What had been alarming was the prospect of Anastasia recognizing Bates, wondering what a magistrate was doing bursting into the office of an import–export company, sputtering on as if he'd lost his last dollar here.

The very thought of the interrogation that would have followed made George's insides clench.

Thankfully, he'd kept Bates well-concealed, and too far away from Anastasia for her to recognize him, especially given the fact that they'd only been introduced once, at Anastasia's coming-out ball, where they'd chatted only long enough for Anastasia to seek the magistrate's financial support in her banking venture.

Still, it was hardly time for self-congratulations. Who knew how many more trips that miserable wretch intended to make to Colby and Sons, how many more visitors she'd glimpse that would give her pause, would make questions crowd her head?

How long would it be before she discovered just a little too much?

Damn, how he wished he could snuff her out like an unwanted candle.

He'd arrived home, waved away dinner, and gone straight to his study and his brandy. He'd yanked out Anne's miniature portrait, gripped it so tightly his knuckles had turned white, and sworn at her as he drank himself into oblivion.

That's when the courier had arrived.

He'd nearly thrown the man out, weaving back to his desk and ripping open the envelope with enough venom to tear it in two.

Fortunately, the message had remained intact. Because it had been anything but the terse rending of ties he'd expected.

He'd read it through five times, and was almost totally sober by the time the second message came.

Its urgency had been palpable, unable to be ignored. It demanded that he be at the customary location at one A.M. sharp, to discuss information that would alter his plans, his perspective, his life.

And so he'd come, arriving at half after twelve so he could read and ponder Rouge's message once again before the arrival of his contact.

Resettling himself on the hard, rotting chair at the pub's far corner table, George unfolded the letter again, reread the unexpected contents.

Ordinarily, I'd be severing our association at this time, as this extraordinary shipment you promised never arrived. However, circumstances allow me to give you one last chance. As luck would have it, I've been approached by a wealthy client with very specific tastes and an unreasonable sense of urgency. Nothing in your previous supply would have suited him, extraordinary or not. To be brief, he requires a specimen of rare beauty and breeding—a specimen as untouched as she is well-bred. A lady in speech, manner, and upbringing. And he requires her within one week's time, after which he'll be taking her and sailing for India. To this end, he is willing to pay an enormous sum. Your compensation would be fifty thousand pounds and a resumption of our business alliance—ONLY *if your shipment meets my client's needs. Don't even consider sending that gutter trash you've shipped in the past. If you do, it will be discarded, no payment made, and our business together permanently terminated.*

I'll expect your shipment within the week. Otherwise, consider this to be my final communication.—M. Rouge

George stared broodingly off into space, contemplating this unforeseen opportunity he was being handed. Fifty thousand pounds—an astounding amount of money. Certainly enough to pay off some of his debts, to keep his life from crumbling into bits.

And all in exchange for one girl.

But where could he get such a girl—a lady rather than a common wench? Oh, Bates's latest crop had been exceptional—clean, attractive, a bit more refined and less dissipated than the previous ones. But they were still a workhouse crop—poor, uneducated, of questionable origins.

A well-bred young lady . . . that was another matter entirely. Where would he find someone of that caliber, someone who was not only polished, beautiful, and untouched, but who also came without the ties that would cause her to be missed if she were to disappear—permanently?

His mouth twisted into a bitter smile as, for the dozenth time, the ideal candidate sprang to mind—or if not ideal, at least the one young woman he *really* wanted to send.

Anastasia.

Every time he remembered the way he'd had to bow and scrape before her this morning, offer her unrestricted access to those files when all he'd really wanted to do was to choke her with his bare hands . . . the very memory sickened him. She was everything ugly and painful in his life—the embodiment of Anne's union to Henry, the usurper of Henry's inheritance, the intruder in his business.

The only thing she hadn't been able to take away from him was Sheldrake. The marquess was clearly enamored with Breanna. Lucky for Anastasia, or with God as his witness, she'd be on that ship to Paris right now.

How delightful it would be to send her off to become some rich man's whore—to reap that ultimate revenge and, in the process, earn a hefty sum *and* regain Henry's estate.

Reason intruded. Tempting as that prospect was, there would be too many unanswered questions, too many tracks to cover. And too little time to get it all done.

Still, the notion was enticing . . .

"Medford. You're unusually prompt tonight."

George's thoughts were interrupted by the arrival of his contact, who slid into the chair opposite his.

"Yes, well, I was preoccupied by the correspondence your courier delivered earlier. In fact, I brought it with me. I had to reread it."

"That bad?"

"Let's say it wasn't what I expected." George folded the letter and slipped it back into its envelope. "In any case, *your* message was extremely urgent, more so than ever before. What's happened?"

"Quite a bit." The other man leaned forward, not even taking the time to light his customary cheroot. "Your niece was at the bank again today."

George stiffened. "That's impossible. She spent the whole morning at . . ." His voice trailed off. "What time did she arrive?"

"Around noon. And to answer your unfinished bit of reasoning, she came directly from Colby and Sons. She made that clear during her meeting with Sheldrake."

"They met?"

"Oh, very much so." An uneasy cough. "Sheldrake was waiting for her. More than waiting. He was pacing. He'd canceled all his afternoon meetings so he'd be free whenever she arrived. The moment she did, he whisked her away to his office."

"And?" George could feel his stomach knot.

"And I went after them as soon as the area was deserted. I missed the first part of their conversation between the noise of the bank and the thickness of the door. But I sure as hell heard the last part."

"Stop playing cat and mouse games with me," George snapped. "Tell me what you heard."

"Two people making plans to spend the rest of their lives together, for starters."

Dead silence. Then: "You'd better explain."

"Your niece and Sheldrake are all but at the altar taking their vows. Your whole plan to see him married to your daughter is never going to happen."

"But his visits to my home . . . their walks . . . the way he looks at her . . ."

"That's Anastasia he's looking at, not Breanna." Suddenly realizing the magnitude of the fury he was about to incite, George's contact opted to have a cheroot after all. He shoved it between his lips, lit it with unsteady hands. "Your daughter and niece have been playing games with you," he continued, keeping his tone as light as he could. "Whenever Sheldrake visits, they change places, each one pretending to be the other. That way, Anastasia can spend time with the marquess without any interference from you—given that you believe it's Breanna he's out strolling with."

"*What?*" Rage contorted George's features. "You're saying . . ."

"There's more." The other man stabbed out his cheroot, lit another. "Evidently, Anastasia has some suspicions about you. She said something about your being involved in something illegal. I'm not sure what, only that it's criminal. Whatever it is has her all agitated."

George could feel the room spinning. "And she told this to Sheldrake?"

"I don't know what she told him. As I said, I couldn't hear the beginning of their conversation. And at the end . . . well, at the end they weren't doing very much talking. They were . . . absorbed in doing other things, shall we say."

"I don't believe this." George dragged a hand over his face, his heart pounding like a drum. "They were carrying on in Sheldrake's office?" His mind wouldn't stay still long enough to wait for a reply. "And Sheldrake—what did he say about Anastasia's suspicions? Did he believe her?"

A shrug. "He seemed more worried about what would happen to her if you found out what she and Breanna were up to. He knew you'd be furious."

George wet his lips, panic washing over him like an icy wave. It dragged him under, and mentally he thrashed about, desperately seeking a buoy to cling to. His wild gaze darted about the room, seeing nothing but the undoing of his life.

Questions erupted, screaming over the roaring in his head in their efforts to be heard. What part of this madness should he focus on first? What should he *do* first?

How much did Anastasia know? What had she discovered in his office? It had to have been in his office—didn't it? Had she recognized Bates? Found something in the files? And how much had she told Sheldrake? Enough to convince him? Had her visit to his bank been to report on the embezzling going on at Colby and Sons, or had it been a prearranged tryst between her and Sheldrake?

The last made uncontrollable rage explode inside George's head, supplanting panic with fury.

The little trollop. All this time. Luring Sheldrake into private alcoves on the grounds of Medford Manor. Convincing Breanna to help her. Wresting away the final chance George had to restore himself and his fortune.

Henry's fortune . . . their father's fortune . . . the company . . . now Sheldrake . . .

Hatred, absolute and consuming, boiled up inside him, spilling over rather than abating. It extinguished all traces of panic and fear, permeated his very being with its intensity.

And in that frozen moment, George made his decision.

He'd see the bitch in hell.

"Medford, I'm getting you a drink." Observing the play of emotions on George's face, his mottled color, the other man signaled to a barmaid, gestured for her to bring two ales to the table.

Dutifully, she complied.

"Down that," the other man instructed, shoving the mug toward George. "I don't care what it tastes like. You need a drink."

"You're right," George replied in an odd, tight voice, staring at the mug for a long unseeing moment before grasping its handle, tossing down the entire contents in a few gulps. "I need a drink—and a great deal more. She thinks she's won, the wanton bitch, that she's taken it all. Well, she's about to learn otherwise. I'll see her dead before I let her destroy my life. *Dead.*" He slammed the mug to the table, undeterred by the few nearby sailors who turned to gape. At this point he didn't give a damn if he were noticed or not.

"Is there something I can do to help?" his contact asked carefully.

The question echoed eerily in George's head. Help? No, he didn't need help. He needed Anastasia to die—to die and take the threats and memories with her. Then, it would finally be over.

"Medford?" the other man pressed.

"No," George bit out. "You can't help. Not unless killing people is also your forte. Because my survival is contingent upon Anastasia's untimely death. Interested?" he added scornfully.

A heavy silence descended, during which his companion traced the rim of his mug thoughtfully.

"Actually, I might be able to help you," he offered in a low, intense tone. "I know someone who does just what you require. He's very proficient at it, and very much in demand."

George felt the ale burn its way to his stomach. It was potent, yes, but it hadn't dulled his senses *that* much. "You know an assassin?"

"As luck would have it—yes."

"How?"

"That doesn't matter. The point is, I can contact him, if you're serious about wanting your niece dead, that is."

"Serious?" Pure venom glittered in George's eyes. "I've never been more serious in my life. She should never have been born in the first place. I want nothing more than to

erase her very existence, to make her vanish . . ." He
broke off, his own words triggering the ultimate solution
to his problem. Swiftly, he yanked out Rouge's letter,
scanning the already memorized words. "I can," he
muttered aloud. "I can make her vanish, rid myself of her
forever—*and* get rich in the process. It'll be tricky, given
the limited amount of time I have, and the number of
people I'll have to convince—most especially Sheldrake—but I'll find a way. I have to." A triumphant
laugh. "It's the ultimate vengeance."

His contact frowned. "What are you talking about?
What do you intend to do?"

A brittle smile lingered on George's lips. "I intend to
take care of everything in one fell swoop—to recoup my
losses, to regain my company, my brother's inheritance,
and Breanna's position in Sheldrake's life . . . and to
condemn my niece to the very hell she deserves."

"It sounds complicated. A lot more complicated than
my suggestion."

"But a lot more rewarding." George shoved back his
chair and rose, stuffing Rouge's letter back into its envelope. "Thank you for the information. I'll be in touch."

Slowly, his contact came to his feet, eyeing George as if
he were unsure whether or not he was in his right mind.
"I assume you know what you're doing," he said at last.
"But if you should change your mind . . ."

"I'll advise you immediately." Folding the envelope in
half, George tucked it into his coat pocket. "Good night."

It was the ideal plan.

Unfortunately, there were obstacles mocking him at
every turn.

Closeted in his study, George paced away the long

hours of night, alternately drinking and swearing at the portrait of Anne.

It had seemed so simple when he thought it up in the pub—ship Anastasia off, claim what was his, and savor the revenge of a lifetime.

Since then, however, he'd examined the plan from every angle, pondered it when he was sober, then again and again as he sank deeper into his cups. It didn't matter whether he was drunk or clearheaded. There was no resolution that covered everything, made all the pieces fit.

Originally, George had intended to announce that Anastasia had grown restless here in England, sailed off to see more of the world. The problem was, he'd never convince Breanna and Sheldrake that she'd leave so abruptly, and without a word of good-bye. To further complicate the matter, even if Fenshaw were more easily convinced than they, even if he believed that Anastasia had just up and gone, the solicitor's hands would still be tied about transferring Henry's inheritance to George. That would only be possible if Anastasia was dead.

Had it not been for Rouge's offer, George would have been thrilled to make that happen.

But not now.

If he hired that assassin, arranged to have him kill Anastasia, that would eliminate any chance of fulfilling Rouge's request—an idea that was equally as untenable as forfeiting Henry's money. And not only because of the fifty thousand pounds he'd earn or his renewed association with Rouge.

But because of what it would do to Anastasia.

For the umpteenth time, George grasped Anne's portrait, stared bitterly at the beautiful features that gazed back at him. How fitting that Anne's daughter should become a whore. Just like her mother—the woman who'd claimed to care for him, then left him for his brother. Well, history was about to repeat itself. In more ways than one. Because just as he'd had to settle for Dorothy—the lesser sister, the one he didn't want—so Sheldrake would do the same with Breanna. Once Anastasia was gone, he'd turn to her cousin for comfort and, ultimately, for marriage.

Sheldrake.

George slammed down the portrait, dragged a hand through his hair. How much did the marquess know? More important, how much did he believe of what Anastasia had said?

Nothing, he assured himself for the dozenth time. If Sheldrake knew the truth, or even a portion of the truth, he'd be breaking down the doors with the authorities in tow. Whatever Anastasia suspected, it had to be a vague hunch only, something she couldn't substantiate with proof.

Still, the sooner he shipped her off, the better. Because knowing Anastasia, she wouldn't rest until she found that proof.

There *had* to be a way to reap the benefits of her death without killing her.

There was, George determined abruptly. He had to stage her death, convince everyone she was dead when she'd really be very much alive, warming the bed of Rouge's client, while he'd be reaping the rewards.

Poor Anastasia. She wouldn't *really* be dead—but she'd sure as hell wish she was.

An ugly laugh escaped George's lips, all the effects of the brandy vanishing as the pieces of his plan fell into place.

Bates. He'd begin with Bates. From there, the rest would be easy . . .

Just before dawn, George emerged from his study, feeling more in control than he had in months. He went directly to the entranceway, summoning Wells with a wave of his hand.

"Yes, my lord?" the butler said politely, trying not to stare at Lord Medford's disheveled state.

"Wells, I need you to do something for me." He stuffed a note in the butler's hand. "Have this delivered to Bates immediately. I want him here in one hour. When he arrives, show him directly to my study." A meaningful pause. "No one else is to know about the magistrate's visit. In fact . . ." He stroked his chin thoughtfully. "Arrange for Breanna and Anastasia to be at the stables, or in the far gardens, or somewhere equally remote when Bates arrives. Have their breakfast served there, if need be. I don't want them in this manor during Bates's visit. Is that clear?"

For a moment, Wells said nothing. Then, he nodded. "Quite clear, sir."

Anastasia hadn't slept a wink all night.

She and Breanna had talked until half after three, analyzing what Anastasia had found in that appointment book, trying to fit it together with Bates's visit and this mysterious Rouge. They were both frustrated by their lack of ability to do anything, although they saw the wisdom of leaving things in Damen's hands—for now. Still, they couldn't stop their minds from racing as they discussed the possibilities, the options, the dangers. Nor could they shake the feeling that they were hovering on the brink of something explosive, and that it was up to them to keep their eyes and ears open in order to prevent it. After all, Damen might be the wiser and safer choice to actively investigate matters, but *they* were the ones who were living here.

They'd retired to their separate chambers a few hours before dawn, agreeing to try to get some rest, then resume their discussion at dawn while taking a long walk through the gardens.

For Anastasia, sleep hadn't come.

She'd finally given up, climbing out of bed and taking her small, ornate strongbox out of the nightstand drawer. Opening it, she'd smiled fondly as she sifted through the mementos of her parents and the ten years of correspondence with Breanna, reaching beneath them to extract the precious gold coin her grandfather had bequeathed her a veritable lifetime ago.

What should I do, Grandfather? she pondered silently, leaving her bed and crossing over to the window, staring out across the grounds and clutching the coin in her hand. *I know you perceived Papa and Uncle George's animosity, but did you ever have any idea it would come to this?*

She glanced down at the coin, tracing the beloved imprint of Medford Manor, then flipping the coin over to caress the elegant seal that signified the Colby family name.

A name her uncle was bent on destroying.

"I see you couldn't sleep either." Breanna came up behind her cousin, sighing as she saw what Anastasia clutched in her hand. "I was cradling my coin for the longest time, too, hoping it would help supply the answers."

"And did it?" Stacie asked softly.

"I think we're going to have to do that on our own."

"I agree." Anastasia continued staring off into the distance, studying all the beloved places where she and Breanna had played as girls, then raising her eyes up to the heavens. "He's counting on us, Breanna," she murmured. "Somewhere up there, Grandfather is watching and counting on us to set things right."

"And we will." Breanna followed Anastasia's gaze. "He has faith in us, Stacie. Giving us the coins, leaving us that trust fund—those were his ways of making sure we'd always recall how deeply he believes in us. Just as he believes we'd never let him down."

"I know that," Anastasia replied. "I just wish . . ." She broke off, a fragment of memory from so long ago flashing through her mind.

You're extraordinarily special. I don't doubt you'll accomplish all your fathers didn't and more. Anastasia could hear her grandfather's voice as if he were standing there beside her, having just presented her and Breanna with their coins. *I only wish I could make your paths home easier . . .*

" 'I only wish I could make your paths home easier,' " she repeated aloud. "That's what Grandfather said when he gave us our coins. It's as if he had a sixth sense of how complex the situation would become—even if he was spared having to live through it firsthand."

"It wouldn't surprise me if he realized how deep my father's hatred ran—*and* what he was capable of," Breanna murmured in agreement, as Anastasia's memory triggered her own. "Grandfather was an extraordinary man. He seemed to know us better than we knew ourselves."

"Indeed he did. Our faults, our virtues, even our dreams."

Hearing the tremor in Anastasia's voice, Breanna intentionally lightened the mood. "Speaking of our dreams, one thing I'm sure Grandfather is extremely pleased about is you and Damen. I don't think he could have picked a more perfect man for you—someone who might actually manage to keep you in line. Occasionally."

That elicited a grin. "When *I'm* not keeping *him* in line. But you're right. Grandfather would be pleased. He and Papa both had great respect for Damen. I'm sure they'd applaud the idea of us sharing our lives." Anastasia hesitated a moment, then turned to meet her cousin's gaze. "Breanna, I didn't mention this last night because of the gravity of our discussion. Still, I want you to be the first to know—Damen's asked me to marry him. Not now, of course," she added quickly. "Not until this nightmare is behind us."

Breanna was already hugging her. "That's just the news I wanted to hear. And it's all the more reason for us to resolve things quickly. What a beautiful bride you're going to make," she added, drawing back to dab at her eyes. "Although I do wonder if you'll be able to make it through an entire ceremony *and* a wedding breakfast without tearing your dress or tousling your hair."

"I doubt it," Anastasia returned, squeezing Breanna's hands fiercely. "My saving grace will be having you as my bridal attendant—which you will be, right?"

"Just try and stop me." Breanna drew a calming breath. "We have lots of planning to do. First, we've got to think up a way to help Damen find out what Father is up to. After that, we have a wedding to arrange." Her fingertips grazed Anastasia's coin. "Put that treasure away. It's time to get dressed and go for our stroll. I have a feeling we're about to come up with something."

Savoring the coin's comforting shape, Anastasia could

actually sense her grandfather's presence, as if he were gifting them with his love and his strength. "You know what, Breanna? I have the same feeling."

Wells was fidgeting.

Anastasia noticed it as soon as she and Breanna caught sight of him from the other end of the hallway.

Breanna noticed it, too, for she cast a swift, curious glance at her cousin, who shrugged in reply.

Something was definitely amiss.

Wells never fidgeted.

"Wells? Are you feeling all right?" Anastasia asked as they approached the entranceway door.

The butler started, his brows drawing together as he turned to study them. "I? Yes, Miss Stacie, I'm fine. I was actually just contemplating the two of you, wondering if I'd be overstepping my bounds if I were to awaken you."

"You could never overstep your bounds with us. But was there some reason you needed to awaken us; something in particular you wanted?"

"No, no. It's just that it's such a lovely day, I thought you might prefer having a private breakfast served to you in the east gardens. Right now—while the sun is still making its glorious assent."

"I see." Breanna was openly regarding him as if trying to decipher the cause of his odd behavior. "Ironically, Stacie and I were just headed to that very place for a stroll. Breakfast there would be lovely. Wells, are you *sure* you're feeling all right?"

Pressing his lips together, the butler nodded. "Quite all right, Miss Breanna, thank you." A distinct pause. "However, I *am* concerned about the two of you. You look peaked."

"I suppose we are. We've been up most of the night."
Breanna hesitated, shot her cousin a sidelong look.

"We have a great deal on our minds," Anastasia added.
She had the oddest feeling Wells was steering the conversation in a specific direction.

"Then a walk will do you good," the butler declared,
adjusting his spectacles and peering intently at a stray
thread on his sleeve. "And it all works out quite well—
the timing, that is. You'll be gone for several hours, which
should give the gentlemen ample time to conclude their
meeting."

"What gentlemen?" Anastasia jumped on the butler's
words at once. "What meeting?"

Slowly, Wells raised his head, met Anastasia's gaze
head-on. "I really can't say, Miss Stacie. No one is to
know who our guest is or when he arrives. My job is to
maintain my silence, and to assure your uncle the privacy
he's requested. You're both to remain absent from the
manor, starting from about a half hour from now." With
that, Wells clasped his hands behind his back, all traces of
fidgeting gone. "I've done as I was asked. How you two
respond is entirely up to you."

Anastasia's eyes had grown round as saucers. "You're
advising us to stay here," she breathed. "You think we
should know who Uncle George is meeting with—and
what they're meeting about."

"Your grandfather did so enjoy the earliest hours of
morning," Wells declared. "He always claimed he made
his best discoveries then, before the world was awake to
clutter his thinking."

"That *is* what you're saying," Breanna concurred.

Wells's glance flickered over them, and his voice quavered ever so slightly. "You two were the light of your grandfather's life. Nothing would mean more to him than ensuring your safety. Not duty, not faithfulness, not even loyalty. Nothing."

On impulse, Anastasia stepped forward, reaching up and kissing the butler's cheek. "Thank you, Wells. Grandfather was lucky to have you. And so are we."

A hard swallow. "Be careful," he cautioned. "Both of you."

"Don't worry. We will."

Tender amusement softened Wells's features. "You two were always the very finest of eavesdroppers. I suspect you still are."

The quality of Anastasia and Breanna's eavesdropping was never in question, at least not in their minds.

Still, certain precautions had to be taken before they could begin doing what they did so well.

To protect Wells and ensure things proceeded as planned, the girls left the manor that very instant, walking off in the direction of the east gardens as if they intended to spend the morning there, milling about and having breakfast.

But the minute they were far enough away from George's study window to avoid detection, they darted back toward the manor. Except that instead of retracing their steps to the front door, they headed for the rear, slipping in through the servants' entrance.

From there, they crept down the hall and into the alcove nestled just off the main hallway. Waiting, they listened intently until they heard two sets of footsteps—one belonging to Wells, the other to their surprise guest—along with Wells's clear, polite voice instructing their visitor to follow him. Clearly, the butler was ushering someone in the direction of George's study, and alerting them to that very fact.

The footsteps faded. Minutes later, Wells's resumed, this time alone. He paused mere feet from where they stood, and pulled out his handkerchief. Folding it in two, he blew his nose loudly—once, twice—then continued on his way.

Despite the tension permeating her body, Anastasia had to bite her lip to keep from laughing. "I believe that was our signal," she hissed.

Breanna nodded, her own lips twitching. "Let's wait another minute, make sure we've given Wells enough time to get back to his post. If anything should go wrong, I don't want him in trouble."

"Agreed."

They held their breath, counted slowly to sixty. Then, they tiptoed down the hall, rounding the corridor that led to George's study.

Outside, they halted, ears pressed close to the tightly shut door.

"No, I don't want a drink," a muffled voice was refusing. "I want an answer to my question. What in God's name possessed you to drag me here at six A.M.?"

"I know that voice," Anastasia muttered. "I've heard it recently."

"I dragged you here because I've thought up the solution to all our problems," George was replying. "With a little work on both our parts, our circumstances will be better than ever in one week's time."

"How can that be? Just yesterday you told me that the entire shipment I supplied you with is lost, with no chance for recovery."

"Bates," Anastasia determined in a low voice. "The magistrate. That's who Uncle George is talking to."

"I know what I told you, Bates," George confirmed with his next words. "But things have changed since then. Everything's changed."

"I don't care. I'm finished worrying myself to sleep every night, finished praying I'll have a job rather than a cell to go to in the morning. Whatever it is, Medford, count me out."

Footsteps, as Bates veered away, marched toward the door.

The girls tensed, preparing to bolt.

"I can't do that." George's icy statement halted the magistrate in his tracks. "And I wouldn't suggest you walk out of this study. Because if you do, I'll be forced to uncover records tying you to that final shipment, and all the others that preceded it." A pause. "Ah, I see I have your attention. Does that mean you'll be staying?"

"What choice do I have?" was the bitter response. "Tell me what you want of me. And it better not be another lot; I've exhausted my contacts."

"No, no, this time I've got my own merchandise to provide. As luck would have it, only one girl is required, not an entire crop. And I've got the perfect one picked out."

"Then why do you need me?" Bates sounded as puzzled as he did unnerved.

"Because this is going to take some creativity to pull off. And I need your cooperation to do that." The clinking of a glass . . . no, a cup and saucer. George wasn't drinking spirits, not this time. "As you know, I've recently ensured our friend Meade's continuing services. We'll need him for this particular assignment. He'll be our captain. Lyman will supply the ship, and the falsified records as to its destination. And I'll supply the passenger."

"What the hell are you talking about? What false destination? And where do I come in?"

"I'm just getting to that part. Unfortunately, soon after leaving England for America—which, in answer to your question, is our false destination—our ship will encounter some turbulent seas. Sadly, our homesick passenger, who will be strolling on deck when the harsh seas strike, will topple overboard and drown, despite Meade's frantic attempts to save her. Terribly upset, Meade will steer the ship back to London, bringing with him our passenger's personal effects—personal effects I can easily supply. At which point you will declare her legally dead. And the sun will, once again, shine."

"America." A nervous cough. "Where will this ship really have gone?"

"To Paris, as usual. To deliver the merchandise to Rouge."

"The merchandise. In other words, this girl isn't really going to drown. She's going to . . ." A long, uneasy pause—as if Bates had already guessed the answer to his question. "Who is it you're sending to Paris?"

"Why, Bates. I'm surprised you have to ask."

"My God, Medford. You wouldn't."

"Wouldn't I?" A biting laugh. "I'll get Henry's inheritance, Rouge's generous payment, and the perfect son-in-law from one swift, ingenious transaction. Who am I sending? Why, my niece, Anastasia, of course."

14

*A*ll the color drained from Anastasia's face, as she clapped a hand over her mouth to keep from crying out.

Uncle George was selling women. And *she* was next.

"Oh my God," she heard Breanna gasp. An instant later, distraught hands grasped her arms, and Breanna gave her a hard, insistent shake. "Stacie, come on. We've got to get out of here. We've got to go—*now*."

Anastasia turned her head, stared blankly at Breanna as shock continued to ripple through her.

Abruptly, her cousin's words sank in and she sprang to life.

Gathering up her skirts so as not to make a sound, she slipped past Breanna to lead the way. They tiptoed halfway down the hall, then abandoned precautions and dashed the remaining distance to the stairway, tearing up the steps and down the corridor to Anastasia's room.

Breanna shut the door firmly behind them, turning to gape at her cousin.

"Do you realize what's been happening? Worse, what's

going to happen?" She pressed her fingertips to her temples. "I can't believe what I just heard, what my father is capable of."

Now that the shock of discovery was fading, Anastasia felt reason seep back into her brain. "Even I never suspected . . ." She sucked in her breath. "Women. The man is actually peddling women, selling them as possessions." She shot her cousin a look of utter revulsion. "I shudder to think how many unsuspecting girls he's done this to."

"Obviously many. At least according to what Bates said."

"Bates," Anastasia echoed in disgust. "Well, he should certainly know. He's been supplying them. It's barbaric." With an appalled shiver, she wrapped her arms about herself, as if to ward off her uncle's vile intentions. "And lucrative," she continued bitterly. "And, in my case, the perfect way to even a long-unsettled score."

"Oh, Stacie." Breanna looked as if she were going to be sick. "I'm so sorry. I don't know what to say."

"Don't you dare apologize. You and I have always known that all you and Uncle George share is blood. You're *nothing* like him. And the onus of who he is, what he does—that's his alone to bear." Anastasia laced her fingers together, contemplating the current dilemma. "We could analyze this for hours, and we'd probably come up with all the missing details. Unfortunately, I seem to have run out of time. I suspect that Meade and his ship will be leaving soon—with me on it, if Uncle George has his way."

"Well, he won't." Breanna dashed across the room, pulling out Anastasia's bags and tugging her gowns from her wardrobe, one by one. "You're leaving Medford Manor. Today. Right away."

Anastasia frowned, stayed Breanna with her hand. "And do what—run away? I won't do that. Nor will I leave you here alone with that monster."

Breanna straightened, facing Anastasia, hands on hips, in that rare but unyielding stance she used when her mind was utterly made up. "I won't be alone. I'll have Wells— who is clearly more than a little suspicious of Father— and a houseful of servants, any of whom would come to my aid if need be. As for you, I think the more distance you put between yourself and Father, the safer you'll be. Go to Mr. Fenshaw, ask him to put you up at a local inn . . ." She broke off, seeing the insightful spark that lit Anastasia's eyes. "You have a plan," she realized aloud. "What is it?"

"I need a quill and some paper." Anastasia marched over to the desk, extracting both. "I'm going to write your father a note. Then, I'm going to help you pack my things. I'll be gone within the hour."

"A note? Saying what?"

"That I'm off to supervise the opening of my new bank."

Breanna started. "In Philadelphia?"

"Exactly." A hint of a smile. "Every new business needs overseeing in order to ensure a smooth onset. And if *I* know that, your father will, too. Actually," she added thoughtfully, beginning to write, "I have him to thank for my plan. After all, it was he who first came up with the idea that I should return to America—*allegedly*."

"Allegedly." Brows drawn, Breanna studied her cousin's face. "So you won't really be leaving England."

"No. Definitely not." Anastasia tossed her cousin a

sideways look. "Did you actually think I'd leave you, leave all Grandfather wanted for us—especially now, when everything is about to explode in our faces?"

"Truthfully? No." A quizzical glance. "Where do you intend to go—or need I ask?"

"I doubt you need to ask. But I'll answer anyway. I'm going to Damen."

"So I assumed." Breanna peered over her cousin's shoulder, read her words. "Ah, you're telling Father that you're traveling to Philadelphia at Damen's request. That sounds believable. After all, half that investment money is his."

"Exactly." Anastasia paused, frowning. "I'll have to reach Damen right away, not only so he can make provisions to hide me, but so he'll know what I've told Uncle George and can play along."

"So you're going straight to the bank."

A hard shake of the head. "That would be too easy for Uncle George to trace, in the event he decides to verify my story. He could simply ask his driver, who'd say he drove me to the House of Lockewood. And why would I be going there if I'm leaving the country? No, I'll send Damen a note, asking him to meet me at the docks. I'll have Uncle George's driver deliver me there. That way, everything will appear legitimate."

"Fine. *I'll* find a way to get the message to Damen."

"Oh, no you won't. Getting you involved is the last thing we need. Wells will take care of it for me, quickly and discreetly. I'll pen the note to Damen as soon as I'm finished writing the one to your father. I'll give both notes to Wells as I leave the manor, ask him to dispatch Damen's right away, then wait a bit before handing Uncle George his. Damen will be at the docks before I know it."

"Not soon enough." Breanna frowned. "Those docks aren't safe."

"It's broad daylight. The warehouses will be swarming with activity."

"They'll also be swarming with lowlifes like that Meade person," Breanna countered. "Face it, Stacie—you're female, you're pretty, and you're alone." She leaned forward, snatching up another sheet of paper and motioning for Anastasia to make room for her at the desk. "You finish the note to my father. I'll write the message to Damen. Then, I'll give it to Wells while you pack the rest of your things. Wells will make sure the letter is on its way to London before you climb into that carriage. With any luck, Damen will be waiting for you when you get to the docks."

Reluctantly, Anastasia nodded. "You're right." She hesitated a minute, chewing her lip as she studied her cousin, contemplated Breanna's status in all this. "You *did* fetch that pistol from the library, didn't you?"

Breanna nodded, pivoting slowly to meet her cousin's gaze. "It's in my nightstand."

"Good. Keep it close by at all times."

"Stacie . . ."

Anastasia waved away whatever protest Breanna was about to make. "Your father is unstable. He must be, to actually sell women for profit. We don't know how he'll react to my bolting like this. He might panic at the thought of losing out on his profit, or explode at the realization that I've eluded his sick attempt at revenge. In either case, he'll probably vent his emotion at you or, if he decides to try to stop me from leaving, he might try forcing you to tell him details of my departure—details you're going to claim not to know. I'm not sure what tactic he'll take. But, servants or not, you must keep up your guard. Promise me."

"All right. I promise." Breanna swallowed. "How will I contact you? How will I know you're all right? When will I see you?"

Anastasia squeezed her hand. "Damen is courting you, remember? He'll be sure to take you for many carriage rides. Well, I'll be the destination of those rides." Her jaw set. "It will be a matter of days, Breanna, not weeks. With what we overheard in that study, I have more than enough incriminating information to pass along to Damen. He'll use it to dig up whatever evidence we need." A frustrated sigh. "If we only had that evidence now, I'd go straight to the authorities, rather than dropping out of sight. But all we have is a conversation we'd attest to having heard. Your father would, of course, deny everything."

Pondering her own words, Anastasia gave an ironic laugh. "Not only would he deny everything, he'd probably arrange for his friend Bates to hear our charges. And we both know how that would turn out. Uncle George would walk out of that courtroom a free man, and you and I would bear the brunt of his rage. No, when we confront your father, I want to be sure we have all the evidence we need to send him to Newgate for a long, long time."

"I agree." Breanna dipped her quill into the inkwell, gesturing for Anastasia to do the same. "And speaking of time, let's not waste it. You have to leave Medford Manor—before it's too late."

Damen's carriage sped to a stop.

Leaping out, he stalked down to the wharf, peering

between the masts of ships and rows of warehouses, pushing his way through the crowds of workers and searching for Anastasia.

Where the hell was she?

What was going on?

Why did she have to meet him here, now, without a single word of explanation?

And why had the note he received been written by Breanna rather than by Anastasia herself? What in the name of heaven had happened?

"Damen."

As if in answer to his fears, Anastasia called out to him, her voice shaky, barely audible above the surrounding din.

But Damen heard it.

He swerved, watching as she stepped out of a warehouse doorway and beckoned to him, her cheeks flushed, her entire body sagging with relief as he strode to her side. "I'm so glad you're here."

"Stacie." His own relief was absolute, and he gathered her against him, savoring the sheer joy of holding her, knowing she was safe. "Are you all right?"

"I am now."

"How long have you been waiting here alone?"

"Only a quarter hour or so. Breanna rushed the note off to you to avoid my having to linger here for an extended length of time."

Damen's sigh ruffled her hair. "Thank God for your cousin's cautious nature. I left my office the minute Graff brought me her message." His gaze fell to Anastasia's bags, which were hidden behind the open warehouse door. "Why are you packed? Where are you going?"

"With you." Reluctantly, she eased out of his embrace,

gave an uneasy glance around. "Is your carriage nearby? I'd prefer if we talked there."

His jaw set, but he didn't press her. "It's just beyond these buildings, off to a side. I came alone, just as Breanna asked. Let's go." Without another word, he picked up her bags and led the way, weaving through the crowd until he reached his waiting phaeton. He tossed the bags inside, helped Anastasia into her seat, and climbed into his own. Then, he turned, gripped Anastasia's shoulders. "Now— tell me what's happened."

Anastasia drew a slow, shuddering breath. "I don't know where to begin. Yes I do. Damen, I'm in danger. I need somewhere to hide, somewhere Uncle George can't find me."

Thunderclouds erupted on Damen's face. "What has that bastard done to you?"

"Nothing—yet. Please, I'll explain everything. But first I need to know if you'll . . ."

"There's nothing to discuss on that score. You'll stay with me."

Another surge of relief shot through her. "Thank you."

Damen tipped up her chin, his silver-gray gaze scrutinizing her. "Why did we meet here? Are you being followed?"

Reflexively, Anastasia looked around. "No. Uncle George is probably first finding out I've gone. I asked Wells to wait as long as he could before giving him my note. We're meeting here to substantiate the story I made up."

"Which is?"

"In my note, I told Uncle George I was leaving England immediately. I said I was on my way to Philadelphia, that you'd foreseen some problems with the completion of our bank and that you'd advised me to sail home and oversee things." She clutched Damen's arms. "If he should come to see you at the House of Lockewood, if he should ask you any questions . . ."

"I'll confirm your story. You're on your way to the States." Damen's knuckles caressed her cheek, his insides growing colder by the minute. Medford must have done something brutal to incite this type of fear in a woman like Anastasia—a woman who'd never cowered in her life. "What did your uncle do? How did he frighten you like this?"

Anastasia wet her lips with the tip of her tongue, clearly still battling major shock.

"Stacie—did he hurt you?" Damen demanded, fear knotting his gut.

"No. Not yet. But he will. Rouge will. Rouge and whoever the man is who's paying him."

"Paying him? Paying him for what?"

"For me." Anastasia's shaken gaze met Damen's. "Uncle George intends to sell me. To an affluent bidder. In Paris. Through this Rouge. Just like the other women he's sold . . . that Bates has gotten him . . . like that illegal cargo that went down . . . we thought it was opium, or jewels—but it was women. And now I'm scheduled to be next . . ." Her voice broke, and her entire body began to shake. "My God, Damen. My own uncle . . ."

Damen swore under his breath, his fingers unconsciously biting into Anastasia's shoulders.

Women. The merchandise Medford had been selling, shipping to Paris, was women.

Bile rose in his throat.

Abruptly, urgency supplanted worry, and a self-imposed calm settled over Damen—a calm born of necessity.

"Stacie, listen to me." His palms framed her face. "Nothing is going to happen to you. I won't let it. Your uncle won't get close enough to touch you, much less ship you to Paris. I want to hear every bloody detail of what you and Breanna heard, to understand *exactly* what your uncle's been doing and with whom. But later. Right now, all I want is to get you to my Town house where you'll be safe. I don't want to give George one extra second to realize you're gone. All right?"

She gave a definitive nod.

"Good. Let's go."

With that, Damen released her, slapped the reins, and urged the horses forward.

The phaeton sped toward London's west end.

Damen's home was masculine and spacious, its heavy walnut furnishings richly appointed and refined, the rooms commanding yet unpretentious—much like Damen himself. His staff was small but incredibly effective, every one of them the essence of discretion. Not a question was asked when he ushered her inside, announced that Lady Anastasia would be staying here for a few days, and instructed them that no one outside the house was to learn a word about this arrangement.

Within minutes, Damen's housekeeper had arranged a bedchamber for Anastasia's use, his cook had begun preparations for dinner, and his butler had sent a footman up with Anastasia's bags and a serving girl to bring tea to the sitting room. Once that had been done, all the servants tactfully disappeared—including the marquess's valet—having assessed the situation with the realization that Lord Sheldrake's guest was far more than just a casual acquaintance.

"Your servants must think I'm a harlot," Anastasia noted, settling herself on the settee and sipping at the welcome cup of tea. "A harlot," she repeated in a hollow voice, staring into the delicate china. "How ironic. I almost was one."

Damen muttered an oath under his breath, began pacing about the room. "Don't talk that way. Don't even think that way." He stopped, slamming his fist against the sideboard. "Tell me everything you and Breanna overheard—slowly, word for word. We're going to assemble all the pieces. And then we're going to see your uncle rot in prison."

Anastasia placed her cup and saucer on the table, then folded her hands rigidly in her lap. "Bates was at the manor this morning. He and Uncle George had a conversation—one Breanna and I weren't supposed to overhear."

"But you did."

"Yes. We made sure of it, thanks to a few subtle hints from Wells. And it's a good thing we did, or I shudder to think what my fate would be."

A muscle in Damen's jaw began to work. "How did George intend to manage this . . . this . . . atrocity of his?"

Thoroughly, in as much detail as possible, Anastasia recounted the plan her uncle had shared with Bates. "He was going to stage my death—doubtless, so he could get his hands on Papa's inheritance—while actually selling me as a whore, earning a hefty profit from Rouge. Oh, and getting you in the bargain."

"Pardon me?" Damen's voice became deadly quiet.

Anastasia never averted her gaze. "Uncle George was quite clear on that point. He obviously assumed that whatever threat I represent to Breanna's and your future would be eliminated at the same time as I. His exact words were: 'I'll get Henry's inheritance, Rouge's generous payment, and the perfect son-in-law from one swift, ingenious transaction.'"

Fury slashed Damen's features. "The deluded son of a bitch actually thought I'd just accept your disappearance without question?"

"I assume so. Remember, he has no idea how much we mean to each other."

"I don't give a damn. Even if our relationship was strictly business, I'd never believe you'd run away like that. Certainly not after just having been reunited with Breanna after ten long years. And not with your grandfather having placed so much faith in yours and Breanna's ability to rebuild your family ties . . ." Damen made a harsh sound, dragged a hand through his hair. "What am I rambling on about? George is clearly unbalanced—unbalanced, immoral, and corrupt. Why would I expect him to think rationally?" A probing look. "How deep is Bates's involvement? From what I managed to dig up yesterday, his jurisdiction was definitely expanded as a result of your uncle's influence. And, just as I thought, his financial situation is moderate at best. So increased power was the bait George used to lure him in."

"And blackmail is what he's using to keep him there," Anastasia added. "Uncle George was quite clear in his threats this morning. Which is what kept Bates from walking out the door. As for the depth of his involvement, I'm not sure. Truthfully, I didn't stay to hear the rest of their conversation. I bolted as soon as I realized what Uncle George intended to do to me. But obviously Bates supplies the women—from where, I don't know. And Rouge, well, he's at the other end to receive them."

"And I'd be willing to bet that Lyman supplies the ships, and maybe even lowlifes like Meade to captain them. That would explain the inflated receipts you found."

Anastasia considered that, and nodded. "That makes sense. But it's all supposition. I don't know who else is involved, or how the payments are divided up. We'll need proof to determine that, and to guarantee they're all locked up, especially my uncle. What I do know is that in Uncle George's mind this is about more than money. He wants to punish me, to punish my parents."

"For what?" Damen approached the settee, dropped down on the cushion beside Anastasia, and angled her face toward his. "Isn't it time you told me what caused this deep-seated grudge your uncle bears?"

"It's not that big a mystery," Anastasia replied softly. "In fact, I'm sure you've guessed what it concerns."

"I suspect it has something to do with your parents, with how deeply they loved each other," Damen replied, not even feigning ignorance. "I sensed that the day I asked you about them, and about George's feelings for your aunt."

"He wanted my mother. She fell in love with my father instead. Uncle George never forgave either of them. His hatred festered over the years, turned into an obsession. After Grandfather died, Papa decided that putting distance between himself and his brother would be for the best. Perhaps he even hoped Uncle George would soften with time. He never did."

"I see." Damen pursed his lips, contemplating Anastasia's revelation. He wasn't shocked. He'd guessed that something like this was at the root of George's bitterness. But to carry it to this extreme?

"I'm sure this factored into your grandfather's decision," he murmured. "Since I imagine he was privy to all the reasons behind George's animosity—not only his greed and thirst for power, but his antagonism over losing Anne to Henry. That's why your grandfather was so adamant about leaving the coins—and the inheritance that was tied to them—only to you and Breanna."

"Yes." A fond smile touched Anastasia's lips—the same fond smile that always accompanied mention of her grandfather. "Grandfather knew the facts. He also knew his sons. Thus, he concluded that any chance of seeing them bury the past and act like brothers was hopeless." Her smile faded, and that stunned disbelief returned to her eyes. "But I doubt he ever imagined Uncle George would stoop to the abduction and selling of women—including his niece."

With a rough sound, Damen drew her against him, buried his lips in her hair. "That's not going to happen. You're with me, and you're safe. I'll kill him before I let him near you." As he spoke, a fierce rush of protectiveness surged through his blood, heightened the all-encompassing emotion he already felt for this woman. "Marry me, Anastasia. Now. Today."

Anastasia started, leaning back to gaze up at him. "I can't," she whispered. "My birthday's still nearly two months away. I'd need Uncle George's permission—or Mr. Fenshaw's agreement to assign me another guardian, after which I'd need *that* guardian's permission."

"We'll ride to Gretna Green. We can be married in a matter of days." Damen's fingers tangled in her hair. "Dammit, Stacie, don't you see it's the only way I can protect you?"

"What I see is that you love me." She reached up, caressing his jaw with her palm. "Oh, Damen, I wish it were that simple. I want to be your wife. I want that more than you can imagine. But not under these circumstances." Her eyes begged for his understanding. "You said I was a romantic. Well, when it comes to marriage, I am. When you and I take our vows, I want it to be the most wonderful moment of our lives, not a rushed ceremony cluttered by worry and fear. Think about it. If we gallop off to Gretna Green, we'll be gone for nearly a week, leaving Breanna alone with that monster. I was reluctant to abandon her even for today, and I did so only after she promised to keep her pistol nearby. Lord only knows what Uncle George will do when he realizes I've gone. But whatever he does, he'll do it to Breanna. We've got to stay in London, find the proof we need, and bring this madness to an end. We've got to."

Jaw clenched, Damen struggled for reason. "Yes, and I'm going to get that proof. Hopefully, it's already on its way. I sent an urgent letter to the head of my Paris branch yesterday, seeking information on this mysterious Rouge. With any luck, what I find out will tie Rouge to George, and to the women they're transporting. Hell, I'd break into Colby and Sons and steal George's damned appointment book and private ledgers if I thought they'd give us what we need. But your uncle isn't stupid enough to actually pen the word 'women' under the heading 'merchandise being shipped.' He probably uses some code word. It doesn't matter. I'll get him. That bastard will soon be in Newgate, along with all his colleagues. I promise you that."

Anastasia sank gratefully into Damen's strength, rested her cheek against his waistcoat. "I believe you."

He heard the exhaustion in her voice, and frowned. "How much sleep have you gotten this week? Next to none," he answered for her. "Come." He drew her to her feet. "There's nothing more we can do right now. You're going upstairs and getting some rest."

"Rest? It's still afternoon."

"Then you'll be awake in plenty of time for dinner." Gently, Damen guided her across the sitting room and into the hallway, which was still deserted. "I'll take you up," he announced, looking unsurprised by the utter lack of activity.

"Where is everyone?" Anastasia asked. Her attention diverted, she glanced about as they ascended the stairway, curious over the odd, absolute silence.

"Occupied elsewhere, if they're smart."

Anastasia blinked, shot him a quizzical look. "Did you tell your staff we wanted privacy?"

"I didn't have to. They're very astute."

"I see." Anastasia was starting to become irritated by Damen's glib responses, and their implications. She frowned as they rounded the second-floor landing and headed down the hall. "Are you in the habit of entertaining women here?"

A corner of Damen's mouth lifted, and he came to a halt outside the bedchamber his housekeeper had prepared for Anastasia. "No," he replied, a self-satisfied gleam lighting his eyes. "Although I'm delighted by the fact that you're jealous."

"I'm not jealous. I'm . . ."

"Jealous," he supplied. His knuckles caressed her cheek, and he moved closer, stopping only when mere inches separated them. "You have no cause to be." He traced the bridge of her nose, his voice husky. "I've never brought a woman here before. As for my staff's perceptiveness, it isn't coincidental. It's based on the fact that I called them together last night to say there would be some changes occurring here soon."

"Changes?" Anastasia sounded breathless.

"Um-hum." Damen's thumb grazed her lips. "I told them that this manor would, within the month, be acquiring a mistress. And that that mistress would be Lady Anastasia Colby, who would, by then, be the Marchioness of Sheldrake . . ." He lowered his head, his lips brushing hers. "Mrs. Damen Lockewood," he clarified, kissing her again. "My wife."

"Oh," Anastasia managed.

Damen smiled at the wonder in her voice, her eyes. "Any further questions?"

Mutely, she shook her head.

"Good." He turned the handle and pushed open the door, gesturing for her to enter. "I hope you'll be comfortable here." He watched her cross the threshold; then, after a heartbeat of a pause, he followed her in. "At least for now. These quarters are only temporary. After we're married, your chambers will be adjoining mine."

"I can't wait." Anastasia turned to face him, never even glancing about to view her surroundings. Her gaze—a luminous jade green—was fixed on him. "Although I can't imagine I'll be using my bedchamber much, not with yours right next door."

The tension that had permeated the day intensified,

shifting its focus to something equally powerful, but far more inspiring.

"Shall I send up a maid?" Damen inquired, hearing the jagged edge to his tone.

"Definitely not." Anastasia reached up, tugged out the few hairpins she wore. "I'm very efficient at dressing and undressing myself. I lived in America, remember?"

"I remember."

"Still," she added with a siren's smile. "I suppose some assistance would be nice." She shook out her auburn tresses, making no attempt to disguise her growing anticipation. "Better than nice—wonderful. But not from a maid. A maid is the last person I need—or want—right now."

Blood pulsed through Damen's veins, pounded at his loins. "And the first person you need—and want—right now?"

"You."

He shut the door, threw the bolt before he could stop himself. "I should leave—now, while I'm still able." Even as he spoke, he was disregarding his own words, walking toward her. He reached her side, taking over her task and freeing her hair until burnished waves tumbled over his hands. "Beautiful," he murmured, caressing the silken strands. "So impossibly beautiful." He brought a handful to his lips, savored it, as his other arm clamped about her waist. "Send me away."

"No." Anastasia stepped closer, gliding her hands beneath his coat, unbuttoning his waistcoat with trembling fingers. "I can't do that."

"Stacie . . ." Damen's fingers were already dispensing with the buttons of her gown. "I didn't intend . . ."

"I know." She stood on tiptoe, kissed the strong

column of his throat as she untied his cravat. "Neither of us did. But it's so right." She sighed, opening his shirt and pressing her lips to his chest. "Don't leave me—not now."

"Leave you?" He gave a hoarse laugh, dragging her gown off her shoulders, letting it drop to her feet. "There's not a prayer of that. I'll never leave you. Not now. Not ever."

His mouth found hers, covering it, his lips parting hers with a hunger that was too powerful to stave off with light, teasing kisses. He grasped handfuls of her hair, angling her face closer to his, possessing her with his tongue, his breath, devouring her mouth totally, voraciously—again and again. Anastasia moaned, leaning into him to give him better access, clutching at his shirt and returning his hot, open-mouthed kisses with her own. Their tongues intertwined, melded and caressed with dizzying sensuality.

They broke apart only to gasp in air, and Damen's gaze burned into hers, his fingers shifting to the ribbons of her chemise, yanking them free until the scanty garment joined her gown on the carpet.

He paused then, his ravenous stare raking her from head to toe, lingering on the burnished nest between her thighs, his fists clenching and unclenching at his sides as he struggled for control.

Anastasia wrested it away.

Boldly, she shoved off Damen's open coat, waistcoat and shirt, letting them drop to the floor. Her palms smoothed up the hard planes of his bare chest, exploring the hair-roughened texture, the solid muscle beneath. Then, she reversed her motion, her palms traveling down to his waist, lingering at the buttons of his trousers.

With a wonder and curiosity too arousing to bear, she descended lower, her fingers brushing the rigid length of him, reveling in discovery, then shifting impatiently to the buttons that separated her from her goal.

It was too much.

With a strangled groan, Damen shoved away her hands and dragged her against him. He lifted her in his arms, nuzzling the warm valley between her breasts as he carried her to the bed.

In one unsteady motion, he yanked back the bedcovers, lay her on the sheet, and stepped away only long enough to finish the task she'd begun, kicking free of his remaining clothes. He was literally shaking with need, his hands trembling so badly he could hardly believe this was he.

Naked, he loomed over her, slipping her stockings down her legs and off, already making love to her in a way that made her breath come in shallow pants.

"You're exquisite," he muttered in a raw voice. "My fantasies pale in comparison."

"And you're magnificent." She scrutinized his body with open fascination, shivering as he reached down, cupped her breast, his thumb rasping over the taut nipple.

"Damen." His name was a wisp of sound, a glimmer of heated longing. "Please." She opened her arms to him.

Another filament of control snapped.

"God, I want you," Damen ground out, coming down beside her, watching her breasts swell to his touch, unable to tear his eyes away. "There aren't words . . ."

"Then don't search for any." Anastasia stroked his shoulders, the muscled planes of his back. "Just make love to me."

A hoarse sound vibrated through him, and Damen covered her body with his, tangling his hands in her hair and lifting her mouth to receive his kiss. His mouth ate at hers, and his chest rubbed across her breasts, teasing her already hardened nipples with slow, tantalizing strokes.

Anastasia whimpered, shifted restlessly beneath him, her thighs instinctively parting to make room for him.

He nudged his hips into place, nestling within the cradle of her thighs and continuing to kiss her, fighting the urge to relinquish the next glorious minutes and just plunge into her, join himself to her in the most fundamental way possible.

This was one fight he intended to win.

Not only to avoid causing her pain—although he was determined to eclipse whatever pain was unavoidable with a deluge of pleasure so acute she'd remember nothing else—but to prolong what he inherently knew would be the most breathtaking of preludes.

One that would lead to the most breathtaking of joinings.

"Not yet," he murmured, shifting his weight to his elbows, staring into her beautiful flushed face.

Anastasia's eyes flew open, her expression rife with confused disbelief.

"Soon," Damen promised, answering her unspoken question, kissing her hot cheeks as he continued to fight the instinctive motion of his hips. "Very soon." He kissed a slow path to her breasts, drawing first one nipple into his mouth, then turning his attentions to the other, teasing each with whisper-light strokes of his tongue.

He was rewarded with a shuddering moan.

Easing himself upward, he covered her mouth with his and kissed her—slow and deep—his tongue gliding forward to entwine with hers. Simultaneously, his palm drifted over her breast, his thumb circling the nipple, still damp from his mouth, then dropping lower, defining the curve of her waist, her hip, finally slipping between her thighs to claim the moist haven he craved above all else.

Anastasia's grip on his shoulders tightened and, reflexively, her back arched, her hips lifting to receive his caress.

Damen's thighs pushed hers farther apart, opening her completely to the heated stroke of his fingertips.

Too far gone to withstand tentative explorations, he slid two fingers inside her, nearly wild with his need to feel her softness close around him. "Yes," he muttered thickly, savoring her warmth, her wetness, her quivering welcome to his penetration. He stroked softly, his thumb teasing the tiny bud that cried out for his touch.

Abruptly he needed more.

He tore himself away, shoving himself downward on the bed. He felt her start of surprise, but he didn't—couldn't—pause to explain. In a few jerky motions, he raised her legs, draped them over his shoulders.

And buried his mouth in her sweetness.

Anastasia stifled a scream, nearly coming up off the bed as sensation slammed through her. Her fingers laced through Damen's hair, and her head tossed from side to side on the pillow, her hips arching wildly, lifting her closer to Damen's mouth, his seeking tongue.

Damen's own need surged inside him like a drowning wave. He gripped Anastasia's bottom, hauling her upward, anchoring her so she couldn't escape a fraction of the havoc he was lavishing on her senses. Her scent, her taste, were driving him insane, taking him so close to the edge, he wondered if he'd survive. He deepened his caresses, felt her body grow taut, tauter still, clenching and tightening as he drove her to the brink of climax.

"Damen . . . no . . ."

It took him a full minute to realize she was struggling, her hands shoving at his shoulders as if to push him away.

He raised his head, passion pounding through his brain, and stared at her in stunned noncomprehension.

"Not alone," she whispered, her entire body trembling with a need she refused to give in to. "Please . . . not this time, this first time. I want us together."

Damen sucked in his breath, blind desire transforming to comprehension.

"Stacie . . ." Rasping her name, he capitulated, crawling over her and hooking his elbows beneath her legs. With unerring precision, his throbbing shaft found the welcoming entrance to her body.

Slowly, erotically, he pushed into her.

"Oh . . . yes." Half-whimpering, half-sighing, Anastasia wound her arms and legs around him, undeterred by the pain she knew must follow, focused on nothing but the need to be one. "This way. It's perfect."

"Sweetheart, I . . ." Damen had no idea what he intended to say. His body was inadvertently thrusting, urging him into her, crowding him into her snug, clinging passage. His eyes slid shut, all his energies concentrated on the incomparable feeling of making this woman his. "Anastasia." Her name was a love word, uttered over the roaring in his head, the pounding in his loins. She was so incredibly tight, quivering, poised on the brink of climax. And he wanted to share that climax, to meld his fire with hers, to feel her pulse and shatter all around him while he poured his entire soul into hers.

He reached the barrier of her innocence, and reality intruded in a jarring blow.

Damen froze, his fists clenching on either side of

Anastasia's head, leaving deep impressions in the soft pillow below. Every muscle in his body went rigid, tremors of restraint quivering through him as his body screamed its protest.

God, he wasn't sure he could stop.

"Damen."

Anastasia whispered his name—a frantic whisper— and his eyes snapped open. Their gazes met and locked— hers wild, pleading; his hot, frantic.

"Don't stop." Her fingers, which had been clenched in the damp strands of hair at the nape of his neck, moved down his spine, clutched at his buttocks with an urgency as palpable as his own. "Please." She swallowed, clearly at the edge of her control, scarcely able to speak much less express her desperation. "I need you." Her hips undulated, wordlessly beckoning him deeper. "I ache. I can't . . . bear it . . ."

Damen groaned, gave in to the inevitable. Framing her face between his palms, he stared deeply into her eyes, his own glittering with emotion. "I love you," he said fiercely. His hands shifted to her hips, gripped them tightly. "I love you, and you're mine."

He thrust forward; she arched to meet him.

The delicate barrier gave, and Damen couldn't stifle his exultant shout as he buried himself to the hilt, stretching and filling her entirely. At the same time, he was acutely aware of the pain he must be causing her, and he forced himself to still, not daring to move until he was sure she was all right.

Her body gave him his answer.

For the briefest second, she tensed, her body recoiling from the sharp, first-time intrusion. Then, the pleasure took over. She emitted a wondrous sigh, softening and melting, wrapping herself around him and sheathing him in liquid fire.

"Damen." She undulated her hips to feel him deeper inside her, then moaned as the frantic need for completion screamed to life, this time unwilling to tolerate delay. "I'm . . . dying . . ." she gasped, her nails digging into his back. "Damen . . . please."

It was all the encouragement he needed.

Withdrawing slowly, he watched her face, memorizing her expression as he surged forward, pushed even higher inside her, then repeated the motion, penetrating her in one deep, inexorable stroke. He heard her sob, felt her clench all around him, and he thrust forward again, angling his body so he could caress her inside and out, take her over the edge.

She screamed, her entire body dissolving into wrenching spasms of completion, and Damen pushed deeper into her, matching the rhythm of her climax even as his own built to excruciating heights, clawed at his loins until holding back became an impossibility.

He erupted, hot bursts of seed exploding from inside him, gushing into her in torrents. He threw back his head, shouted her name again and again, every fiber of his being focused beneath the onslaught of sensation. Her climax retriggered his, and spasm after hot spasm wrenched at his loins, shuddered through his body.

Finally, they both collapsed, sinking deep into the bed, too weak to move or speak, too sated to try.

Inhaling the scent of their lovemaking, Damen drifted, savoring the tiny aftershocks of pleasure that rippled through him. He cradled Anastasia in his arms, marveling at the extraordinary sense of peace and contentment that pervaded him.

It was ironic. He'd spent his life making investments—for himself, for others—embarking on ventures that altered circumstances, lives. And yet, despite the magnitude of these investments, he'd just discovered one that was far more vast, one that required all one's resources but yielded immeasurable riches in return.

Love, he mused in wonder. The greatest venture of a lifetime. And it's made without forethought, without reason, and without a whit of control—all of which he prided himself on displaying.

Clearly, he wasn't quite the genius everyone believed him to be.

But, damn, he was lucky.

15

Somewhere in the house, a grandfather clock chimed four, and Anastasia stirred, murmuring a protest at even that minimal an intrusion.

Interpreting her action as a sign of discomfort, Damen gathered his strength and rolled to one side, taking her with him. "I'm hurting you," he murmured.

She smiled, shaking her head against his chest. "You never hurt me. Not before. Not now." She stretched, then leaned back, gazed up at him. "I never imagined feelings like that were possible."

"Nor did I." His knuckles caressed her cheek. "Then again, I never imagined *you* were possible. Thank God I was wrong."

Tenderness softened Anastasia's eyes. "You're turning out to be quite the romantic, you know."

"I know." Regret slashed his handsome features. "And the romantic in me wishes I'd walked you down the aisle, made you my wife, and gave you the wedding night you deserve."

"You will." She lay her palm against his jaw. "Damen,

dashing off to Gretna Green is not my idea of a wedding. As for what just happened between us, how could anything have been more romantic, or more perfect?"

He turned his lips into her palm. "It couldn't. Nor could you." He bent down, kissed her tenderly. "At least I compelled you to get some sleep."

An impish grin. "If that's your technique, you're welcome to encourage me to sleep any time you want—now, and for the rest of our lives."

"I'll remember that, with pleasure." He tucked a strand of hair behind her ear, noting the reminiscent light that glimmered in her eyes. "What were you just thinking?"

"About something Breanna said earlier. She said Grandfather would be delighted that you and I found each other. And I agree. He would."

Damen reflected on his memories of the late viscount, then nodded slowly. "I think you're right. Your grandfather was an exceptional man—intelligent, shrewd, and compassionate. To find all those qualities in one person is a rarity, believe me." A corner of Damen's mouth lifted. "He must have adored you—your spirit, your fire. And that incredibly sharp mind that puts the rest of the world to shame."

Anastasia smiled at Damen's assessment. "I don't recall putting *you* to shame. Try though I will, I've yet to best you."

"Ah, but I fully expect you to keep on trying," Damen teased. "Think how exciting our marriage will be—in bed and out."

"True." Her smile softened. "As for Grandfather, he adored Breanna *and* me—each for different reasons. He was the only person, until you, who never confused us. I suppose he saw differences that escape most people."

"He also saw the equally important similarities. Your loyalty and love for each other, your determination to preserve the Colby family. That's why he entrusted you both with that huge inheritance."

"Yes, I know." Anastasia sighed. "I think about that money often, about what Breanna and I can do with it that would ensure Grandfather's wishes are carried out. I feel as if the answer is right here in our own backyard, only we have yet to see it. But whatever it is, it has to be something that would bind our family together, not only now but for generations—actually, forever, if I had my way."

"I notice you don't speak of investing the money."

Anastasia's chin shot up and she gave an adamant shake of her head. "No. That's not what Grandfather wanted. He didn't regard the inheritance as an impersonal avenue through which to increase our funds. He regarded it as a uniting force, a means to entwine Breanna's and my futures, and the futures of our children. Allocating it to a business venture, or worse, to several different business ventures, is out of the question. If we divide it, it loses its impact. And if we invest it, however wisely . . ."

". . . all you could reap is more money," Damen finished for her. "When what you're really determined to secure is something far more valuable." He kissed the pucker between her brows. "I think you've just begun to answer your own question. The rest will come with time. You and Breanna will see to it."

Absorbing Damen's words, Anastasia recognized not only the truth they held, but Damen's part in helping her arrive at that truth. Emotion formed a tight knot in her chest, emotion inspired by his innate understanding of her, heightened by their earlier intimacy. Fervently, she leaned up to kiss him. "I love you, Damen Lockewood. More than you could possibly know."

He rolled her to her back, his own expression mirroring the profound intensity of hers. "Show me."

The knock startled them both.

Anastasia jolted out of a light doze, automatically reaching for the bedcovers as Damen sat up, swung his legs over the side of the bed, a black scowl darkening his face.

"Who could it be?" Anastasia whispered.

"I don't know. But I intend to find out."

He yanked on his trousers, striding to the door and opening it just enough to address whoever was on the other side of the threshold.

"What is it, Proust? I thought I made it clear that I wasn't to be disturbed."

Proust. That was Damen's valet. Anastasia popped her head out from beneath the bedcovers, straining her ears to learn what the servant wanted.

"Forgive me, sir. I wouldn't have intruded, but you said to advise you the instant your response from the Paris office arrived. The courier just delivered it." He slipped a letter through the partially open doorway. "I took the liberty of bringing it up. I hope that was the right decision." A tactful silence.

Damen snatched the sealed correspondence, his entire demeanor having altered from infuriated to relieved. "It was absolutely the right decision. As usual, you know me well."

"I try, sir." Proust cleared his throat. "If that's all, I'll leave you to your privacy."

"Yes, that's all. I appreciate your diligence, Proust."

Anastasia heard the servant's footsteps fade away. Simultaneously, Damen shut and bolted the door, tearing open the envelope as he walked across the room.

"It's from Dornier," he informed her, perching on the edge of the bed and angling the correspondence toward the window to catch the late-afternoon sunlight. "He runs my Paris office."

By now, Anastasia had guessed that this letter concerned Damen's inquiries about Rouge, and she leaned forward eagerly, watching his face as he smoothed out the single sheet of paper. "What does it say?"

Damen scanned the letter, then reread it carefully, his brows knitting more severely with each passing word. "This makes no bloody sense," he muttered. "Dornier says he's totally baffled by my questions about Rouge and his background, given that I'm the one conducting extensive business with Rouge—business that's highly confidential in nature."

"What?" Anastasia sat bolt upright.

"According to Dornier . . . here, I'll read it to you: 'Some months ago,' Dornier writes, 'I received specific instructions from you advising that the Paris office would be receiving numerous sealed communications to one M. Rouge. Those confidential communications, you directed, were to be set aside and held while a note was immediately dispatched to a specific address . . .'"

Damen paused, reading the address aloud as if hoping that by doing so he would trigger some memory of its significance. "'4 Rue La Fayette.'" A blank shrug. "'In that note'—" He resumed reading Dornier's words. "—'I was to state that a message addressed to M. Rouge had arrived and was waiting at the bank's main office. Soon after that, I was to expect a courier to appear, presenting my note for identification purposes. At that time I was to give the courier Rouge's envelope, no questions asked.

"'Conversely, should a courier arrive at the Paris office bringing correspondence addressed to the House of Lockewood in London, with the designation, *To Lord Sheldrake, confidential—M. Rouge*, I was to dispatch that letter immediately, again no questions asked.'"

Damen looked up, an odd expression on his face. "Dornier closes by assuring me that he's followed my instructions to the letter, and asks whether my latest inquiry means I've decided to alter these arrangements. If so, I should advise him immediately. He's awaiting my reply. Dammit!" Bolting to his feet, Damen raked a hand through his hair and began pacing about the room. "Do you have any idea what this means?"

Anastasia's mind hadn't stopped racing since Damen had begun relaying the contents of the letter. Now, she nodded, feeling utterly sick—not only for the situation, but for Damen. "It means that someone is using the House of Lockewood as a conduit for sending information to and from Rouge." She pursed her lips. "Could it be my uncle?"

"No." Damen shook his head emphatically. "Although I'm sure whoever it is is working with your uncle. But there's no way George would have access to the bank's correspondence, most particularly to any letters addressed privately to me. Whoever sent Dornier those instructions has to work at the House of Lockewood." Damen stared at Anastasia, his expression pained. "Someone at my bank is using his position to undermine me and to help your uncle in his sick endeavors with

Rouge. Well, I intend to find out who that is. And when I do, I pity him."

He stalked over to the writing desk, yanking out a quill and paper.

"You're writing back to Dornier," Anastasia deduced.

"Indeed I am."

"What are you planning?"

"I'm planning to beat this M. Rouge at his own game."

Anastasia inclined her head, considered Damen's statement. "How? By having the French police storm 4 Rue La Fayette? I doubt Rouge lives there. My guess is that it's just a meeting place."

"I'm sure you're right." Damen dipped his quill and started writing.

"Then what are you advising Dornier to do—snatch the courier when he arrives at the bank? Damen, there's no guarantee the lad turns the letters directly over to Rouge. In fact, there's no guarantee he's even met Rouge. Nor, for that matter, is there reason to believe that Rouge sends the same messenger each time. Anyone who's clever enough to buy and sell women without getting caught is certainly clever enough to cover his tracks with the couriers he uses."

"Again, your logic is excellent. Grabbing the messenger would be futile." Damen paused, his features taut with concentration. "The only way to beat a man like Rouge is to catch him by surprise. I'm going to tell Dornier to continue business as usual. The next letter that arrives from *me* addressed to Rouge is to be handled precisely the way it's been handled up until now. With two exceptions . . ."

His jaw set. "One, that I'm to be notified immediately

of the letter's arrival by a courier waiting to leave for London at a moment's notice. And two, that a private investigator—one hired by Dornier the instant he receives this reply—is to follow Rouge's messenger from the bank to wherever he takes the correspondence I supposedly sent. Even if Rouge himself doesn't meet up with his messenger, another of his paid lowlifes will. I don't care if this investigator has to follow a chain of gutter rats through Paris and all the way up to Calais— which is where I'm sure the shipments of women first dock. He's going to unearth Rouge. And when he does, we'll grab him *and* implicate your uncle. Correction—*further* implicate your uncle. By then, I'll have had George arrested on charges of theft, kidnapping, and Lord knows what else. I'm just getting started."

Anastasia pursed her lips thoughtfully. "How are you going to manage that? With what proof? Never mind," she added quickly, supplying her own answer. "I can guess. You intend to find out who the traitor is at the House of Lockewood and link his activities to Uncle George. I should have known you'd never wait long enough for Rouge to be captured and supply you with his informant's name. You want him now."

"You're bloody right I do. I'm going to expose that bastard myself." Damen stared at the tip of his quill. "My father started the House of Lockewood, Stacie. He opened our very first bank. He also invested a good portion of his money and all his heart and energy into making us the thriving merchant bankers we are today."

A small smile touched Anastasia's lips. "I think you're being a bit modest. From what Papa told me, you're the family genius—the one who made the House of Lockewood the most influential merchant bankers in England, maybe even in the world. Your business acumen, your powerful connections—why, every European nation seeks your advice and counsel. You might not have opened the bank's first doors, but I'd say you had a hand in establishing the House of Lockewood's reputation."

Damen waved away the compliment. "My financial insights enhanced our bank's reputation. But they didn't establish it. What established it was what brought people in initially, what convinced them to entrust us with their money, their investments. And that something was integrity. My father's integrity. He fostered loyalty and trust in our clients, and he did it by being a fine, decent, and honorable man. Shrewd investing might have increased our number of clients, expanded our number of contacts, but it was the knowledge those clients and contacts had—the knowledge that they could count on us, count on our honesty and dedication—that built our reputation. Well, no one's going to take that reputation away, certainly not some miserable scoundrel who's using his position in my bank to achieve his own crooked ends."

Anastasia watched Damen's face as he spoke, seeing, feeling his fervor, and realizing for the first time just how it was he understood so much about family loyalty and commitment.

His allegiance to his family ran as deep as her own.

"You've never spoken of your father," she said softly. "Were you close?"

Damen gave a vague lift of his shoulders. "Not in the way you mean. Not like you and your parents. In all fairness, we didn't spend very much time together. I was away at school most of the time, and he was either building up the bank or traveling abroad with my mother. When she died, he threw himself into the House of Lockewood. When I came home on holiday, I worked alongside him. He wasn't a demonstrative man, nor was he given to conversation. But he was a good man, a decent man. So were we close? Not tangibly. But we shared the same principles, maybe even part of the same dream."

"Expanding your bank."

A nod. "The House of Lockewood was a symbol of who my father was, what he believed in. I shared that commitment. The difference is that my father was driven solely by his dedication and integrity. Whereas I . . ." Damen shrugged, considering how best to explain. "Dedication and integrity are at the core of every good man, every worthwhile endeavor. But they're not the only factors that drive me. I revel in what I do. Running the House of Lockewood is a perpetual challenge, one that stimulates my mind and fires my excitement. It's so bloody fascinating—taking a sum of money, analyzing the possibilities of where it can be invested, choosing the right place to invest it. Then, watching that investment as it increases and thrives. That's where my father and I were different. He savored the end result, because it benefited people. I savor that, too. But I also savor the process of getting there." Damen quirked a brow in Anastasia's direction. "Do I make any sense?"

"Oh, a great deal of sense." She grinned. "You're talking to the one woman in England who finds business, investments and earning profits riveting—even if that does get me labeled a bluestocking."

Damen's chuckle was husky. "A very beautiful, very passionate, very brilliant bluestocking." His smile faded, as his attention returned to the matter at hand. "In any case, perhaps now you can understand why I can't let that traitor at my bank go undetected—or worse, unpunished."

"I understand completely," Anastasia responded, pride welling up inside her. "You needn't explain. And, Damen, we'll figure out who that snake is. I promise you that. He and Uncle George will both be locked up at Newgate—soon."

For the tenth time, George reread the note Wells had given him earlier that day, muttering each word aloud as if to confirm it. Then, he crumpled the page and shoved it into his pocket, crossing the study to pour himself a much needed brandy.

Anastasia was gone. Anastasia had left England and gone home to America to supervise the opening of her new bank. And she'd gone at the request of Lord Sheldrake.

With a bitter oath, George tossed back the contents of his goblet and refilled it.

Who was the little bitch trying to fool?

She'd no more left England at Sheldrake's urging than he had. Damen Lockewood handled his own business matters; he didn't send a woman to manage them for him—even a woman as astute in business as Anastasia. No, if she'd left England, it was for another reason.

But what?

And given her sordid affair with Sheldrake, their supposed attachment for each other, why would she leave England at all?

On the other hand, why would she lie? Was she planning something, plotting something at his expense?

Another vicious oath escaped George's lips, and he dismissed his own stream of useless questions.

What the hell difference did it make *why* Anastasia had gone? The fact was, he had to get her back. *Now.* Because without her staged death, without her transport to Paris, there would be no payment from Rouge, no inheriting Henry's money, no Sheldrake as his son-in-law.

No future.

Dammit, he had to find her.

Furiously, George polished off his next brandy, then slammed down his empty goblet and abandoned it, for the time being.

There was only one place to turn to for answers. Because if anyone knew Anastasia's plans, her whereabouts, it was her loving cousin.

Fine. He'd get his information from Breanna.

He made his way down the hall and toward the stairway, pausing to grip the banister and right the dizziness in his head. He probably shouldn't have had that last brandy. He needed his wits about him so he'd recall every word Breanna said, as well as what she didn't say. And if she dared lie to him . . . His hand balled into a trembling fist. If she did, he'd thrash her.

"Can I help you with something, sir?" Wells approached the stairway, hands clasped behind his back.

"H-m-m?" George scowled at the butler. "Help me? No . . . yes. You can tell me where Breanna is."

Wells pursed his lips, his astute gaze flickering over his employer, taking in his besotted state, as well as the fact that he was angry. *Very* angry. "I believe Lady Breanna went upstairs to rest, my lord. She'd gone for an afternoon ride. And the sun is unusually strong today. She looked quite peaked when she returned. My guess is she's already asleep."

"Then I'll just have to awaken her." Ignoring Wells's protest, George climbed the stairs, rounded the second-floor landing, and marched down to Breanna's chambers.

He rapped purposefully at the door, simultaneously twisting the handle, only to find the door was bolted.

"Yes?" Breanna's voice was muffled, as if she had indeed been asleep.

"It's your father. Let me in at once."

Some muffled sounds, then footsteps as Breanna crossed the room. She turned the bolt and opened the door, peeking into the hall, her wrapper clutched tightly about her. "Can it wait, Father? I was resting."

"No. It can't." He shoved past her, striding into the room and veering about to face her. "I want to hear everything you know about Anastasia."

Breanna blinked, smoothing back her hair. "I don't understand what you mean. She explained everything in the note."

"Don't toy with me, daughter." George massaged his temples, feeling rage pound through his skull like gunfire. "I don't believe a word of that note. I want the truth. And I want it now."

With a wary expression, Breanna walked back toward her bed, doubtless considering her answer. She perched on a side chair, reaching for the cup of chocolate that was sitting atop her nightstand. "I don't know what truth you mean, Father. As I told you, Stacie didn't confide in me. She probably knew I'd try to talk her out of leaving—which I would have, given how long we've been apart. But you know how headstrong she is. She must have decided this was the best way to follow Lord Sheldrake's instructions without upsetting . . ."

"Sheldrake would *never* have sent her to oversee that bank," George bit out.

"He trusts Stacie," Breanna reasoned quietly. "She understands business better than most men do. And it is half her investment she's protecting."

"And what of the investment she's leaving behind?" he sneered. "Her *personal* financial adviser, the marquess. Her partner in business and in bed."

Breanna's eyes widened. "I don't know what you mean."

"Damn you, Breanna." George lunged forward, grabbing her shoulders and hauling her to her feet. He shook her—hard—sending her cup and saucer clattering to the floor. "I won't be lied to, do you understand? I want to know where Anastasia is. Did she really leave England? Where did she go—to the Continent? Is she doing something with that inheritance of hers?" His hand drew back, and he slapped Breanna across the face, not once but twice, sending her head jerking sideways from the impact. *"Where is she?"*

"You've had too much to drink, Father." Breanna twisted herself free, a defiant light flickering in her eyes as she rubbed her smarting cheeks. "I think we should discuss this later."

"We'll discuss this now." George reached into his pocket and flourished a strap. He gripped Breanna's arm, twisting her around so her back was to him. "I'll ask you again, where is Anastasia, and what were her real reasons for leaving?"

Breanna went rigid. "And I'll answer you again, I don't know anything more than you do."

The strap lashed out, striking Breanna's back and biting through the delicate material of her gown and wrapper, which did little to buffer the pain. She flinched, cried out.

"*Answer me!*" George bellowed.

It was as if something inside her snapped.

In one swift motion, Breanna wrenched herself away and yanked open the nightstand drawer. Whirling about, she faced her father, a pistol gripped tightly in her hands. "Don't strike me again," she commanded.

George's jaw dropped, and he stared at her, as taken aback by the vehemence of her tone as he was by the weapon in her hand.

"I mean it, Father. I won't be used as a whipping post."

"Why, you presumptuous little . . ." He took a step toward her, then hesitated as her fingers tightened, her jaw set in harsh, unyielding lines.

"Don't doubt that I'll use this," Breanna assured him. "I will—if I have to."

"You're not a killer, daughter." George's statement was absolute, but his voice held the tiniest shred of uncertainty. "You don't have it in you."

A shrug. "Perhaps not. At least not under these particular circumstances. Then again, I wouldn't have to kill you. I'd simply have to wound you. Just enough to incite an investigation—*and* the ensuing scandal that would occur. A daughter, so brutalized by her father that she'd be forced to shoot him to protect herself. That would do irrevocable damage to the reputation you're so eager to preserve. Or to restore."

Twin spots of red stained Breanna's cheeks as she watched the stunned amazement on her father's face. "I may be reserved, Father, but I'm not stupid. I've always understood your motivations. More often than not, I've bowed to them. But not this time. I won't be beaten to satisfy your belief that Stacie is anywhere except where she claims to be, or that I know more than I'm telling you. So it's up to you. Are you going to promise not to strike me again, or shall I shoot?"

Again, George hesitated. He massaged his temples, grappling with this insane twist of events, wondering if he was imagining this whole encounter, if it was really just some absurd nightmare—a product of his liquor-clouded mind.

He refocused, saw Breanna aiming the pistol at him, and realized this was no nightmare. It was real. Very real.

Disbelief surged to the forefront, penetrated his besotted state. "You'd threaten your own father?" he sputtered. "With bodily harm?"

"Only if *he* threatened *me* with the same. If you don't strike me again, you have nothing to fear—not a bullet or a scandal."

George dragged a shaky hand through his hair, wishing like hell he was sober. "I just want to know . . ."

"I have no information for you," Breanna interrupted. "Stacie's gone to Philadelphia. She'll be away several months." A tiny smile. "Perhaps she'll be back in time to help me celebrate my twenty-first birthday; it's less than four months away. And then Stacie and I will both be independent women."

Splotches of color suffused George's face as the reminder found its mark.

"What's more, I don't know why you're so upset about Stacie's leaving," Breanna added dryly. "We both know you're hardly fond of her."

Another swift glance at the pistol. "Regardless of my personal feelings, Anastasia is my responsibility."

"Not any longer, she's not. When she returns, she'll be of age. You'll no longer have to look out for her. Why, I should think you'd be celebrating."

George's jaw set, his gaze flickering to the nightstand as he considered his options, and how to effect them.

"You're right," Breanna acknowledged, reading his mind aloud. "I won't always have my pistol handy. But if you should try to strike me when I'm unarmed, I'll simply scream loud enough to alert the servants, then make it look as if you were beating me senseless. The staff is very fond of me, so they'll be more than willing to support my story. And if you're wondering how that could possibly harm your reputation, I'll explain. Hard as it is for you to believe, there are some noblemen out there—Lord Sheldrake, for one—who'd be appalled to learn how violent a man you are, how unduly cruel you and your strap are to me. Appalled enough to reconsider their alliances—both business and personal. Are you willing to take that risk, just to gain information I don't have?"

A choked sound of frustration and anger emerged from George's throat.

Simultaneously, a knock sounded on the bedchamber door. "Miss Breanna?" Wells's voice called out. "Are you all right? Are you hurt?"

Breanna inclined her head, staring down her father. "It's your choice," she prodded.

Drunk or not, George couldn't deny the truth of Breanna's logic. He'd obviously underestimated her; she'd anticipated his course of action, and developed tactics to combat it. And though he loathed her for putting him in this position, he was lucid enough to realize that to push her any further could yield disastrous results. It was also possible that Anastasia had acted without telling anyone her real plans, that Breanna was indeed speaking the truth, as far as she knew it.

And a scandal, at this particular time—he shuddered to think what damage that would do. No, livid or not, his best recourse was to back away, to let Breanna be. Then, he'd keep an eye on her, go through her mail each day to make sure she had no contact with Anastasia. And, in the meantime, he'd find that bitch himself.

"Miss Breanna?" Wells knocked louder. "Are you all right?"

"Answer him," George snapped.

"I'm not sure what to say," Breanna replied. "You tell me—am I all right?"

George shot her a dark look. "Physically, yes. But your behavior—I don't know what's happened to you. You're no longer my obedient, dutiful daughter." His eyes glittered with resentment. "But I do know who prompted the change: Anastasia."

"No, Father, Stacie didn't prompt my behavior. *You* did." Breanna never averted her gaze. "Just a minute, Wells," she called out. Another pointed look as she awaited her father's decision.

"Fine," George conceded, taking a symbolic step backward. "I'll do as you ask—even if it is my right as your father to discipline you as I see fit."

"Not any longer, it isn't," Breanna retorted. "I'm a grown woman, not a child. I've endured all the *discipline* I intend to from you."

He forced himself to nod.

Satisfied, Breanna lowered the pistol, pivoting about to replace it in her nightstand drawer. "Coming, Wells," she called. Walking boldly past her father, she crossed over and opened the door. "I'm fine, thank you," she assured the anxious butler. "Just clumsy. Father and I were chatting and I dropped my cup. I didn't mean to worry you." She made a wide sweep with her arm, throwing open the door so Wells could see everything—and every*one*—in the bedchamber.

Wells's gaze shifted from Breanna to George to the broken fragments of china on the floor, then returned to Breanna's face—and the clear imprint of her father's fingers on her cheeks. "As long as *you* aren't hurt. I'll summon a maid to clean up the mess."

"I'd appreciate that." Breanna smiled. "And then I'd like to resume my nap." She inclined her head quizzically in George's direction. "Unless, of course, there's something else you need to speak with me about, Father."

George cleared his throat. "No. As a matter of fact, I have some business to arrange." He left the room, pausing when he'd reached Wells's side. "I'll be gone a good portion of the day tomorrow," he said quietly, for the butler's ears alone. "Keep an eye out for the mail carriage. When it arrives, collect all correspondence, but distribute nothing. From this moment on, I want everything addressed to this manor to be held for my inspection. Is that clear?"

"Perfectly clear, my lord."

With a brooding glance at Breanna, George stalked off, his footsteps echoing down the hall.

Wells watched him go, then turned to meet Breanna's gaze.

A current of communication ran between them.

"I'll send up a pitcher of cold water and a cloth," the butler said in a tight voice. "It will take away the sting."

Breanna walked over, squeezed his arm. "Thank you. And don't look so worried. This won't happen again."

Over his spectacles, Wells's brows rose fractionally. "With all due respect, Miss Breanna, how do you know that?"

A twinkle. "Because I just threatened Father at gunpoint. I told him that if he ever struck me again, I'd shoot him and make sure it resulted in the scandal of the decade."

Wells started, studying Breanna as if to ensure she was telling the truth. At her emphatic nod, his lips began to twitch. "I'm sorry I missed it."

"So am I. It was a long time in coming." She leaned up, kissed the butler's weathered cheek. "I can't tell you how much I appreciate your rushing to my rescue."

"My pleasure." He cleared his throat, waited until his emotions were in check. "Now, if you'll excuse me, I'll arrange for the water and the clean-up. I'd do both myself, but I have a letter to dash off."

"A letter?"

"Indeed." The tiniest spark glinted in his eyes. "I want to advise Lord Sheldrake that tomorrow afternoon would be a splendid time for a visit—from him, and any other surprise guests he'd care to bring along."

16

Awakening in a man's arms was a novel experience.

But given those arms belonged to Damen—the experience was sheer heaven.

Anastasia smiled, snuggling farther beneath the bedcovers, reliving the exquisite hours that had flanked the arrival of that disturbing missive from Paris. First, there had been the dreamlike hour before Proust interrupted, the once-in-a-lifetime moment when Damen had made her his. And then, much later, after the return message to Dornier had been sent, after their immediate plans had been discussed and a late dinner consumed, they'd gone back to bed, spending hour after glorious hour discovering the magic their bodies made together.

Three A.M. had come and gone by the time they fell asleep, wrapped in each other's arms, their future a beckoning wonder they had only to reach.

After the obstacles blocking their way were eliminated.

That reality jogged Anastasia awake, and she shifted, wincing a bit in response. Her body ached in places she'd never known existed before last night, and it was strangely comforting to have those lingering twinges to remind her of the beauty she and Damen had shared, especially in light of the trying events that lay ahead.

Stretching, she opened her eyes, noting the weak sunlight that filtered through the windows. It couldn't be much past dawn, she mused in relief. And that suited her just fine. She and Damen had a lot to accomplish today which, much as she wished otherwise, meant they couldn't loll away the day in bed.

"Good morning." Damen's husky voice came from just above her ear, and she twisted around to see him propped on one elbow, gazing down at her. He looked uncharacteristically disheveled, his hair mussed, a shadow of a beard covering his face.

It was nice to know that the unrufflable Lord Sheldrake could sometimes be ruffled after all.

Nicer still to know it was only she who could manage that feat.

"Good morning," she replied with a radiant smile.

A corner of Damen's mouth lifted. "Don't we look self-satisfied this morning." He lowered his head, brushed her lips with his. "Any reason in particular?"

"M-m-m." Anastasia sighed, twined her arms around his neck. "Several. Most of which are self-explanatory." She caressed his hair-roughened jaw. "But at the moment I was thinking how smug it makes me feel to know that I, and I alone, can demolish the composure of the ever-commanding Damen Lockewood."

"Indeed you can." He rolled onto his back, pulled her over him, and dragged her mouth down to his. "Again and again, if I remember correctly," he breathed into her lips.

Anastasia shivered, giving in to the demands of her

watery muscles, which clamored to relax, melt into Damen's solid strength.

Damen made a husky sound of approval, tangling his hands in her hair and slanting her mouth to accept the full penetration of his.

Their tongues met, stroked, melded, and Anastasia's breath came faster as their kisses deepened, turned more urgent. Her nipples hardened against his chest, tingling as the hair-roughened surface rasped against them. Damen's thighs slid between hers, nudged hers wide apart, and she whimpered aloud as his rigid shaft probed the entrance to her body.

"Is it too soon?" he managed, his voice rough with passion. "Can you take me again?"

Anastasia tried to answer, but the words lodged in her throat. Instead, she let her body speak for her, her knees straddling his hips, her thighs lowering her slowly, maddeningly onto him. He glided into her, a rumbling groan vibrating in his chest, and his mouth devoured hers as he eased into her tight, clinging passage. She sank down farther, begging him wordlessly for more, and Damen's hands slid down her back to her bottom. He gripped her buttocks, hard, and pushed up and into her trembling wetness, burying himself to the hilt inside her.

Talons of pleasure shot through her, and Anastasia tore her mouth from Damen's, arching her back and taking him deeper still. She began the instinctive motion—up, down, up, down—the resulting sensations too acute to withstand. She felt wild, frantic, her entire body burning with a fever she'd only just discovered and couldn't imagine living without.

Clutching her waist, quickening the motion of his hips, Damen raised up, capturing her nipple between his lips.

He drew the entire peak into his mouth, lashing at it with his tongue until a harsh sob escaped Anastasia's lips. Still, he didn't relent, shifting to the other breast, lavishing that nipple with the same attention as the first.

"Damen." She cried out his name, so desperate for release that she hardly knew what she was saying. Her thighs gave out, the muscles too weak to keep setting the pace. She was close, so close, hovering right at the brink of where she needed to be, and yet unable to get there. Each tug of Damen's lips sent fire shooting from her breasts to her loins, each lunge of his hips brought her one degree closer to fulfillment. And yet . . . God, she couldn't reach it.

Her entire body tightened, reaching, shuddering with unappeased hunger. "Damen," she gasped again, his name an unspoken plea.

Damen understood it.

Abandoning her breasts, he dropped back down to the bed, his own body screaming its need for release. Staring into Anastasia's passion-flushed face, he raised his knees, pushed her backward until she was anchored by them. "Let me," he commanded. He grasped her waist with one hand, continuing the frenzied rise and fall of his hips as he thrust even higher, farther, into her, nudging the very mouth of her womb. "Stacie, look at me," he rasped. "I want to watch you. I want you to watch me."

She complied instantly, meeting his blazing silver gaze, his handsome features taut with unsated passion. Just seeing how close he was made her own need even sharper, and she whimpered again, quivering as she kept her eyes on his.

His other hand moved to the spot where they were

joined, his fingers unerringly parting her, finding the straining bud. His thumb caressed it, scraped over it, then circled it with erotic precision. Her insides clenched violently and, the instant he felt her response, Damen lunged upward, lifting her off the bed with his total possession, his fingers burning into her as he filled her, stretched her, penetrated her, beyond bearing.

Her climax slammed through her like cannon fire, and she screamed, grabbing Damen's shoulders and watching his face as his own release took over, stormed through him. He threw back his head, the tendons in his neck straining, and he shouted her name, thrusting into her once, twice, then holding her there as he pumped his hot seed into her, meeting each of her wrenching contractions with a scalding burst of heat. She watched him until the pleasure became too acute, until she had to arch, fling back her head, then toss it from side to side as the spasms intensified, clasped rhythmically around Damen's turgid length as he poured himself into her.

She fell forward, collapsed against the wall of his chest, felt it heaving with the exertion of their lovemaking. She was shaking uncontrollably, her heart racing, her emotions as raw as her body.

Damen's arms closed around her, enfolded her tightly against him, and he pressed his lips into her hair, willing his senses to right themselves. "God," he panted, barely able to speak. "My God."

Anastasia closed her eyes, lay her cheek against his hot skin. "I love you," she whispered. "More than I ever thought possible."

"And I love you; although those words—any words—seem inadequate after what we just shared."

A lingering shiver rippled through her, along with all the romantic yearnings of a woman in love. "I wish . . " Her voice trailed off.

Damen hooked a forefinger beneath her chin, angling it until her gaze met his. "So do I. And we will." He brushed damp strands of hair off her face. "We'll have it all, Stacie—a lifetime like this. Beginning with a church wedding, and all the guests you want to fill it. Once we've taken our vows and the entire world has witnessed you becoming my wife, we'll have a wedding breakfast fit for a king and his queen—most of which we'll miss because I'll be sneaking you off to a local inn, making love to you until you can't breathe and don't even want to. We'll leave for our wedding trip the next day, very little of which you'll remember because I'll be keeping you abed throughout it. And when we come home . . ." His fingertips caressed her lips. "When we come home, you'll be pregnant with my child, and I'll spend the next nine months doting on you and watching you grow more beautiful and radiant with each passing day. How does that sound so far?"

Tears glistened on Anastasia's lashes. "So far? Have you planned more than that?"

"Of course." A profound smile touched his lips. "I'd like four, maybe five, children."

"Five—is that all?" She smiled through her tears. "Girls? Or boys?"

"Both. The girls will look just like you; beautiful miniatures of their mother, with burnished hair that won't stay up and jade green eyes that flash when they're angry and glow when they've conjured up a brilliant idea."

Anastasia kissed his fingertips. "And the boys will be impossibly handsome and independent, and so astute in business that it will be obvious from the day they're born that they're destined to be brilliant." A peppery spark. "Then again, the brilliant part applies to the girls, too. After all, they'll be *our* children. Besides, we have more than enough companies for them to manage: the House of Lockewood, Fidelity Union and Trust—soon to be open and thriving—and, of course, Colby and Sons . . ." Anastasia halted, the very mention of her grandfather's company acting as a blatant reminder of the ugly dilemma they now faced.

She stared at Damen, apprehension eclipsing all traces of humor.

"We'll make things right, Stacie," he said softly. "I promised you that, and I meant it."

"We have to. Because none of the beautiful dreams you just described can happen until we put Uncle George and all his colleagues in prison." Fear knotted her gut. "By now, I'm sure he's interrogated Breanna to see if she knows anything more about my disappearance. I hope to God she's all right, that he didn't try to beat information out of her."

Damen gave an astute shake of his head. "Have faith in your cousin, sweetheart. I think she'll surprise you. She's stronger than you realize."

"I know." Despite the certainty of her words, Anastasia frowned, her brows knit in worry. "Breanna is very strong. But Uncle George is irrational. Lord knows how desperate he'll become when he discovers I'm gone, and to what lengths he'll go to find me."

Equally troubled as she by the prospects that conjured up, Damen rolled to one side, taking Anastasia with him. "Let's get our strategy under way. You'll feel better and, frankly, so will I." He kissed her ever so softly, held her for one more tantalizing minute before reluctantly withdrawing from her clinging warmth. "Remember where we left off," he murmured.

A watery smile. "Just try to make me forget."

He framed her face between his palms, brought her mouth back to his. "I'd rather make you remember. And I will, just as soon as we've destroyed your uncle and brought him and his crooked associates to justice."

It seemed days rather than hours before the grandfather clock in the hallway chimed twelve, heralding the noon hour and the time Damen had said he'd be returning to his Town house.

Anastasia spent the morning the only way her frayed nerves would allow her: she paced through every room in the house, covering both levels and never sitting down.

The servants were kind and understanding, offering her meals, tea, a library of books to read. But all she could think about was Damen and what he might be finding out at the bank. That, and Breanna, and whatever had taken place between her and her father yesterday.

Although she was significantly less worried about the latter since Wells's note had arrived this morning.

Actually, it had arrived last night, but Proust had waited until morning to present it to Damen, handing it to him the minute he and Anastasia strolled into the dining room. The two of them had read it together, and Anastasia had nearly wept with joy at how cheery the message sounded. According to Wells, he was writing at Miss Breanna's request. She was feeling lonely since her cousin's departure and would like some company. Therefore, she was cordially inviting Lord Sheldrake to either tea or a late lunch the following day.

Which meant today.

"That's Wells's way of assuring us Breanna is all right," Anastasia declared, rereading the message. "He's also suggesting that afternoon would be the best time for your visit. Uncle George probably has business away from Medford Manor." Anastasia sighed with relief. "I only wish Proust had delivered this note the instant it arrived. I would have slept much better."

Damen had cocked a brow, glancing about to make sure the dining room was deserted. "May I remind you that I practically accosted Proust the first time he interrupted us? I hardly think he'd choose to take me on again, especially when I hadn't mentioned expecting another piece of urgent correspondence last night." A provocative twinkle. "With regard to your sleeping better, that's a moot point since you didn't really sleep at all. I can attest to that fact."

Anastasia had been cheerfully unable to dispute that logic.

Right after breakfast, Damen had put their plan into motion. He'd gone to the bank as usual, ready to act as if nothing was amiss while keeping a keen eye on the mail, and on whoever touched it. Later in the morning, he intended to announce that he had an afternoon appointment, after which he'd ride out to Medford Manor.

Making an unscheduled stop at his Town house to pick up a passenger.

It was ten past twelve when Anastasia heard the key turn in the front door.

She flew to the entranceway, nearly knocking down Damen's butler in the process. "You're home," she gasped, seizing Damen's forearms and tugging him inside. "Tell me what happened."

He glanced back over his shoulder, then gestured for his butler to shut the door. "You're supposed to be staying out of sight," he reminded Anastasia with a dark scowl. "What if it hadn't been me at the door?"

She shot him a defiant look. "Just who else has a key to your home?"

He couldn't help but grin. "Good point. No one." He guided her into the sitting room, then drew her close, covering her mouth in a slow, lingering kiss. "Just so you know, that's how I'd like to be welcomed home each day."

"With pleasure, my lord." Anastasia leaned back in his arms, searched his face. She could see beyond the bantering, sense the strain beneath it. "You didn't figure out who he is."

Damen shook his head. "I know as little as I did yesterday. I saw the mail arrive. No one went near it during the quarter hour it sat up front. Then, Graff distributed it, leaving my personal letters on my desk. I glanced through my correspondence the moment he walked out. There was nothing from M. Rouge. I then intentionally left my door open and my room unattended to see if any of the bank officers went in, inspected my mail. They're the only people with access to that private section of the bank. Although it's hard for me to believe any of them could be guilty. They've been with me for years. Still, I can't be influenced by sentiment. I intend to catch this bastard, whoever he is. In any case, the point was a moot one."

"No one took the bait?"

"Not a soul so much as stepped into my office, much less examined my mail." Damen sighed, dragging a hand through his hair. "It was a wasted effort. In fact, the only productive thing I did all morning was to put on a convincing show. Anyone scrutinizing me would think it was a day like any other. That way, should my scrutinizer meet with your uncle, he can truthfully say I behaved in my typical fashion. George will have to conclude that your absence came as no unwelcome surprise to me, which would support your claim that it was I who advised you to go to Philadelphia."

"Or indicate that you haven't an inkling that I've gone at all," Anastasia pointed out. "Uncle George will probably try to find out, either directly or through his informant, which of the two it is. Not that it would alter his plans. Either way, I'm sure he'll be sending Meade after me." An ironic smile touched her lips. "But while it won't alter his plans, it will certainly improve his humor if he decides the latter is true. Just think, if I acted on my own, with no urging from you, Uncle George would have the pleasure of telling you what I'd done. You'd doubtless be furious at the recklessness of my actions, and more than ready to wash your hands of me."

"Turning my full attentions to Breanna."

"Exactly."

Damen sucked in his breath. "Every time I think about what that bastard has planned, what he means to do to you, I want to choke him with my bare hands."

"I know," Anastasia responded quietly. "But then you'd be the one in prison and I'd have to live without you. I don't intend to do that. Nor do I intend to let whoever's deceiving you continue on at the House of Lockewood, unknown and unpunished. The same applies to Bates, Lyman, Meade, and whoever else is involved in this."

"Like M. Rouge and his contemptible clients," Damen

muttered. He straightened, shot Anastasia a probing look. "Are you ready to go on our little jaunt?"

A terse nod. *"Very* ready."

Damen's closed carriage rounded the drive at Medford Manor, coming to a halt before the front steps.

"Don't forget," he cautioned under his breath. "Stay under that blanket. Don't move or poke that curious head of yours out to see what's going on. We don't know for sure that your uncle is away. Nor do we want any of the servants to see you. Remember: you're on a ship on your way to Philadelphia."

"And you're alone in a carriage having a conversation with a horse blanket," came the muffled retort from beneath the opposite seat.

Damen rolled his eyes, torn between amusement and worry. He knew Anastasia. And she wasn't going to stay still for long—especially after a lengthy, cramped carriage ride from London, during which she'd been allowed to emerge and stretch her legs only when the roads they'd been traveling were deserted enough to ensure she wasn't detected—and, even then, only after the carriage curtains had been tightly drawn.

Oh, Damen knew how much Anastasia loathed confinement of any kind. But he wasn't taking any chances with her safety.

"I'll linger inside only as long as I have to," he advised the horse blanket. He bent down, as if to retrieve his glove. "Promise me you'll stay put."

"Promise me you'll bring Breanna."

He grinned. "I promise."

"Then so do I."

"Good." Damen straightened just in time for his driver

to come around, open the door. "Wait here," he instructed the driver in a normal tone, as he alighted from the carriage. "I'll be out shortly. You'll be taking Lady Breanna and me for a ride in the country."

"Very good, my lord." The driver nodded, shutting the door and resuming his seat at the reins.

Damen climbed the steps and knocked.

Wells opened the door at once. "Ah, Lord Sheldrake," he greeted. "Lady Breanna will be delighted to see you."

"I'm looking forward to seeing her as well." Damen glanced down the hallway, trying to determine if George was at home.

"I hope you don't have pressing business to discuss with the viscount," Wells continued. "He had an appointment in Town and won't be back for several hours. He'll be sorry he missed you."

"Ah." Damen shot Wells a grateful look. "That's quite all right. My business with the viscount can wait. I really came to see Lady Breanna."

"Then I won't keep you waiting." Breanna reached the bottom of the staircase, smiling as she approached Damen. "I'm so glad you're here."

"As am I." Damen cleared his throat. "I realize you invited me for tea, but it's such a beautiful summer day that I thought perhaps you'd enjoy a ride in the country instead. Unless, of course, you haven't eaten."

"I've solved that problem," Wells interrupted. "Wait here." He hurried off, reappearing scant minutes later carrying a basket. "Mrs. Rhodes was kind enough to pack up these sandwiches. She'd prepared them for you to eat in the garden, but they'll taste just as good elsewhere. So long as you're enjoying the summer day, it doesn't matter where you are."

"Thank you, Wells." Breanna squeezed his arm.

"Go," he urged, gesturing toward the still-open door. "Have a good time." He leaned forward to hand Damen the basket, briefly whispering something to Breanna as he bent past her.

Her lips twitched, but she didn't reply.

Three minutes later, Breanna and Damen were both settled in the carriage, basket and all, and the driver was urging the horses around the bend.

"Not yet," Damen warned in a hard voice. "Don't move or speak. Not until we're beyond the gates and I've drawn the curtains."

Breanna blinked in surprise, thinking at first that Damen was addressing her. Then, she followed his line of vision and smiled as she spotted the lumpy blanket beneath her seat. "Why, Lord Sheldrake, is that for me—a token of your esteem, perhaps?"

"Don't sound so enthused," he retorted dryly. "You might return it once you see how much trouble it is."

A grunt of protest emerged from beneath the blanket.

Laughter bubbled up in Breanna's throat. "Does that mean *you* wish to return it?"

With a profound shake of his head, Damen leaned forward and stared at the blanket, all teasing having vanished. "No. You see, as fate would have it, this is one gift I can't seem to live without."

"Then, indeed, it should be yours." Visibly moved, Breanna followed Damen's gaze, her own filled with the joyful knowledge that Anastasia had found her future. "As you should be hers." She reached down, touched the blanket ever so lightly. "The gates are just ahead," she said soothingly. "We're almost there."

"Breanna, what did Wells say to you as we were leaving?" Damen asked curiously. "Or am I prying?"

"Not at all." Breanna's sparkle returned. "He said there's more than enough food in the basket to serve three."

Damen's lips curved. "So he *does* know."

"Wells knows everything." A smug lift of her chin. "Except when Stacie and I are switching places."

An impatient thump resounded from beneath the blanket.

"We're driving through the gates now," Damen answered. "I know you're eager. But I've got to make sure you're not seen. Concealing your presence by switching places with Breanna is one thing. But it would be a little hard to explain you away by claiming you're Breanna if you're both sitting beside me at the same time. Give me a minute or two to create the illusion that Breanna and I are seeking some privacy. Then you can come out."

The ensuing silence signified Anastasia's agreement.

They rounded the corner onto the road, and Damen rose out of his seat, jerked the curtains closed on both sets of windows. He squatted down and yanked the blanket off Anastasia's head. "You're free, little hellion." He offered her his hand. "Come on out."

Anastasia squirmed out of her hiding place, blowing strands of hair off her face. She accepted Damen's assistance, clutching his fingers and scrambling out and onto the seat beside Breanna.

The girls hugged, and Anastasia heaved an enormous sigh of relief. "Thank God you're all right."

"*I?* *You're* the one who dashed down to the London docks alone."

"I wasn't alone for long. Damen rode in and rescued me like a knight-in-shining-armor."

Her analogy made Breanna smile. "Still the same romantic Stacie. Clearly, you're none the worse for your adventure."

"And you?" Anastasia asked quietly. "Are you any the worse for yours?"

Breanna didn't pretend to misunderstand. "I'm fine. I thought you'd figure that out from Wells's note."

"I did." Anastasia drew back, gripped her cousin's hands. "But I needed to see for myself." She studied her cousin's face closely, seeing remnants of evidence that Damen had missed. "Uncle George hit you."

Breanna's shrug was nonchalant. "At first, along with a fair amount of shouting and threats. But that's over now."

"What do you mean?"

With more than a touch of pride, Breanna recounted her showdown with her father.

"You threatened to shoot him?" Damen repeated in amazement.

"I certainly did. Very convincingly, if I must say so myself. Believe me, Father won't touch me again. He's too terrified of a scandal, and of the possibility that he might lose you as an ally and future son-in-law."

"An ally," Damen muttered. "I'm hardly that."

"But Father doesn't know that, at least not yet."

"Where is Uncle George now?" Anastasia asked.

"With Mr. Lyman," Breanna supplied. "Wells said that's who Father dashed off a note to last night."

Anastasia and Damen exchanged glances.

"He's arranging for Meade to find me," Anastasia murmured, catching her lower lip between her teeth. "That doesn't give us much time. The ship I allegedly took is only one day ahead of him. And how many ships could have left for the States in that amount of time? Not many."

"You didn't necessarily have to have boarded a packet ship. You could just as easily have paid your way on a smaller craft," Damen pointed out. "Lyman will have to check every ship's manifest. He and Meade still have their work cut out for them."

"I'm not sure they'll be looking at all," Breanna inserted.

Anastasia's head whipped around. "What do you mean?"

Her cousin frowned, rubbing her gloved palms together. "Something Father said last night really puzzled me. I haven't been able to get it out of my mind."

"What did he say?"

"While he was accusing me of knowing your whereabouts, he demanded to know if you'd truly left England. He seemed to think you might not have. I tried to convince him that it was perfectly natural for you to be going to Philadelphia since it was half your investment you'd be protecting. He sneered at me and asked, 'What of the investment she's leaving behind? Her *personal* financial adviser, the marquess. Her partner in business and in bed.' I realize Father was drunk, but his words were quite lucid." Breanna gazed anxiously at her cousin. "He wasn't guessing, Stacie. It's as if he *knew* you and Damen are involved. But how could he?"

A ponderous silence, punctuated only by the *clack-clack* of the carriage wheels.

Abruptly, Damen muttered an oath, his fist striking his knee with furious awareness. "He *did* know about Stacie and me," he bit out. "How? From his informant."

"What informant?" Breanna demanded.

"The one in my bank."

Breanna sucked in her breath. "You'd better explain."

Tersely, Damen told her about the letter he'd received from his Paris office, and the information it conveyed, as well as what that information signified. He leaned forward, growing more definitive as he spoke. "Think about it. For the past few weeks, you and Anastasia have switched places every time I visited Medford Manor. Your father believed it was *you* I was courting, and he was thrilled with our presumably whirlwind courtship. If he'd realized the truth . . . well, suffice it to say, he would have made us aware of that realization. So, up to and including my latest visit, he had no idea it was really Stacie I was with. Right?"

"Right," Breanna concurred.

"Now let's get to Stacie and me. It was only during the last few days that we've let down our guard, spent any intimate time together. And where were we? At my bank, in my office." A muscle worked in Damen's jaw. "Which means that our secret is out. And that it was discovered at the House of Lockewood."

"Of course," Anastasia breathed, her eyes wide with realization. "That explains what pushed Uncle George over the edge. Not only was he worried about losing Papa's inheritance, he was now frantic about losing you, too. That's what he meant when he told Bates about his plan, and added the part about how he'd be getting the perfect son-in-law from this transaction. He must have just found out we'd been deceiving him."

"Yes. And he found out from one of my bank officers." Damen's voice was rough with anger and betrayal. "There's no other explanation, Stacie. No one but my officers have keys to that door marked 'Private.' Only they have access to my office area, which was the only place we talked and acted in any intimate manner. Whoever this son of a bitch is, he's someone I trust. He's also a duplicitous cad who's using my bank to communicate with Rouge and spy on me."

Anastasia inclined her head, her brows drawn in mystification. "There's a hole in that logic. If what you're saying is true, if this informant eavesdropped on our private conversations, then he'd certainly rush off and tell Uncle George everything he'd overheard, including our suspicions of my uncle's guilt. Well, if that's the case, why is Uncle George still counting on your welcoming him with open arms as your father-in-law? That makes no sense."

Damen stared broodingly at the carriage floor, analyzing Anastasia's well-taken point, and trying to remember the last few meetings the two of them had shared. "My office door was shut," he recalled aloud. "Maybe only snatches of what we said were audible. Or maybe George's snitch didn't wait around long for fear of getting caught. I don't know. But think about it. It wouldn't take more than thirty seconds of eavesdropping to figure out the way we feel about each other. That's the only explanation I can come up with. He knows some part of the truth, but not all of it." A scowl. "The question is, how much is some?"

Her mind darting from the issues to the suspects, Anastasia zeroed in on a possibility. "Damen, do you think it could be Booth? I've mentioned to you before how uneasy he makes me. He seems to hover around whenever you and I are together. On my last visit, he greeted me in the lobby and stayed right by my side, flattering my appearance, until you rescued me. A short while later, when Cunnings interrupted us to look for Mr. Crompton's portfolio, Booth magically appeared in your office doorway and flourished it. I told you—there's something about that man, the way he ogles me, rambles on and on about my beauty, and about Breanna's." Anastasia paused, chewed her lip. "Maybe he hasn't been ogling me at all. Maybe he's been spying for my uncle."

"Mr. Booth?" Breanna interrupted in surprise. "I never thought of him as anything but harmless. You're right about the flattery; he's been very solicitous of me on those few occasions when I visited the bank with Father. Still, a spy for Father? That's hard to imagine."

"I agree," Damen said. "And not out of a stubborn sense of loyalty, by the way. Hell, at this point, I don't know who to trust." He considered the notion, shaking his head ever so slightly. "Booth has a keen mind when it comes to managing money. But he's very awkward around people—*too* awkward, I think, to serve George's purpose." A slight shrug. "Then again, my instincts are apparently more flawed than I realized. Maybe Booth is guilty. Maybe he's a superb actor. I don't know."

"We'll figure it out." Gently, Anastasia wrapped her fingers around Damen's. "I'm sorry," she said softly. "I know how hard this is for you. But at least what Breanna's told us narrows down our search." She paused, watching his expression. "Damen, this doesn't demean your instincts. None of us is clearheaded when it comes to those we trust. And in your case, the handful of men who are now potential suspects have been valued colleagues— and friends—for years."

"You're right." Damen kissed her gloved fingertips, his

brooding supplanted by determination. "And not just about my instincts. About the fact that we've narrowed down the choices. There are only four men—five, if you count Graff—who have access to my office. I'll do thorough checks on all of them, find out if they've come into any recent funds from unknown sources, if they've been seen coming and going from their homes at unusual hours. By tomorrow, we'll have our informant."

"In the meantime, I'll keep my eye on Father," Breanna said thoughtfully. "Something you just said piqued my interest—the idea of comings and goings at unusual times. Now that I consider it, Father's been guilty of that, and more so recently. I never gave it much thought, until now."

"What unusual comings and goings?" Anastasia demanded, swooping down on her cousin's words. "Why didn't I notice?"

"Because you've only lived with us since July. You wouldn't know Father's habits as well as I do." Breanna fingered the folds of her gown as she reflected. "Over the past months, he's been making late-night jaunts, usually after drinking to excess. I assumed he was going out to clear his head. Now I wonder. Could he be meeting this informant of his?"

"How frequently does he do this, Breanna?" Damen asked. "How late at night? And how long is he gone?"

"It used to be about once a fortnight. Lately, it's been more like twice a week." She frowned. "I'm afraid I never paid much attention to the hour or to the amount of time he was gone. I was usually in bed, reading, when I'd hear him drive off. So it had to be after midnight. As to when he'd return . . ." A shrug. "I was asleep. Lord only knows how late it was." Breanna broke off, a triumphant smile curving her lips. "Let me rephrase that: the Lord isn't the only one who knows how late it was. Wells knows, too."

"Of course." Anastasia's eyes lit up. "Wells knows everything. He'll give you any details he can."

"I'm sure he will." Unconsciously, Breanna smoothed a wisp of hair into place. "I'll talk to Wells—right away, if I can. I'll also keep an eye on Father. Maybe I can figure out how much he knows, and how much of the truth Lyman and Meade have pieced together by now. Damen, you do your checking into the suspects at the bank. Schedule another visit to Medford Manor for the day after tomorrow. That will unnerve Father, since he's now aware of the fact that you're not calling on me, at least not in the romantic sense." A triumphant gleam lit her eyes. "That doesn't mean we don't have things to discuss—things like Stacie's whereabouts. Which I'm sure is what Father will assume we're discussing. The very notion will throw him into a tizzy. The more off-balance we render him, the better. Because with any luck, after we combine whatever information we've uncovered, we'll have enough proof to confront him. And, if he's drunk enough, intimidated enough, we might just get a confession. Which would be the perfect finishing touch to the evidence we've amassed—and the perfect end to this nightmare."

"An excellent plan." Damen looked sufficiently impressed. "You and Stacie are more alike than I realized."

"At times, yes." Breanna grinned. "Although you've rarely seen that side of me. I must admit I find it much easier to be myself around you now that I know you're to be my cousin and not my husband." She shot him an apologetic look. "At the risk of sounding too brazen—even more so than Stacie—you and I are terribly suited."

Laughter rumbled in Damen's chest. "True. But there's a lucky man out there somewhere who's going to feel very differently about the two of you. And once you meet him, you'll agree. Unfortunately, he'll have to win both Stacie's and my approval before he can win your hand. Ah, the poor fellow." Still chuckling, Damen leaned over the basket. "On that intriguing note, let's enjoy some of Mrs. Rhodes's delicious sandwiches."

"Wait." Anastasia held up her palm, halting Damen in the process of unpacking the basket.

"Why?" Damen's head came up, and he frowned as he saw the rankled expression on Anastasia's face, the indignant set of her jaw. "What's the matter?"

"I'm delighted that the two of you have successfully worked out your strategies for capturing Uncle George and his colleagues," she retorted, folding her arms across her chest. "Just how am *I* supposed to contribute to all this?"

The lighthearted banter of the past moments vanished in a heartbeat.

"You're supposed to remain in hiding, unseen and undetected by the men who are trying to find you—*and* sell you," Damen replied, his expression grim. "Or have you forgotten that unpleasant tidbit?" Warning glints flashed in his steel-gray eyes. "I'm not taunting you, Stacie. I'm dead serious. Your life is in danger. You're going to stay put until that's no longer the case. Is that clear?"

Silence.

"Anastasia . . ."

"It's clear," she replied, her gaze as direct as his. "For now."

17

"*T*hat's the last update, Medford. And still no luck."
Lyman slapped the scribbled note on his desk, dismissing
the lad who'd delivered it by tossing him a shilling, then
gesturing for him to go.

He waited until the office door had shut before turning
back to George, who was pacing furiously near the
windows overlooking the docks. "My contacts have been
at it all night, ever since I got your message. They've
checked every bloody manifest. The fact is, no Lady
Anastasia Colby booked passage to the States yesterday.
Not in London, anyway. I won't know about Liverpool for
a few days. But you and I both know how unlikely that is.
Your driver said he brought her to the London docks. I
doubt she found her way to Liverpool from there."

"I wouldn't put anything past Anastasia. Maybe she did
that just to steer me in the wrong direction. Or maybe she
boarded in London, but used another name." George
halted, slicing the air with his palm. "Damn that miserable chit! Where the hell is she?"

"I don't know." Lyman looked grim. "But I don't think

a false name is our answer. I had Meade and a few other men ask around at the docks. And no one matching Anastasia's description was seen boarding a ship, or even walking along the wharf or around the warehouses. So, unless she paid a coach to take her to Liverpool, my guess is your niece didn't leave England."

"Dammit. *Dammit!*" For the third time in the past hour, George crossed over to the sideboard and refilled his glass, taking two healthy gulps as he resumed pacing. "I've got to know for sure. There are so many ways she could have managed this—stowing away, disguising herself. You don't know Anastasia. She's the most resourceful female I've ever met."

Lyman drew a slow breath, then released it, crossing over to refill his own glass at the sideboard, then hurrying back to stand behind his desk. When Medford was in this kind of mood—drunk, irrational, angry—he was more comfortable putting some distance between them, even if it was only half a room and the comforting presence of his desk that separated them.

Because when Medford was like this, there was a dangerous quality about him, one Lyman wasn't interested in provoking.

"I don't doubt your niece's resourcefulness," he replied in what he hoped was a soothing tone. "I've seen her attempt to charm a roomful of men to finance that bank of hers. The question is, why would she go to so much trouble to keep you from finding her? She left you a note, told you where she was going and why. Why would she suddenly decide to become secretive?"

"Maybe because she knows something—something that could lead to something more, and then more, and then more . . . all of which could eventually spell my end." George gulped down the remainder of his drink, slammed the glass down on the window ledge. "Maybe that's why she's sailing off—to protect herself while she assembles the pieces she's uncovered. Or maybe that's why she's not leaving England at all—to assemble the pieces here and now."

The shipping owner had gone very still. "Knows something?" he asked carefully. "As in, about us? What we've been doing?"

George stared broodingly across the room at the pile of papers on Lyman's desk—all letters stating that Anastasia Colby's name had not been listed on any ship's manifest. "Yes, about us," he bit out. "And what we've been doing. At first, I thought she was running off to squander more of Henry's money before I could stop her. Then, I thought about it more carefully, in light of some information that's recently been brought to my attention."

"What kind of information?" Lyman asked in a shaky voice.

"I have reason to believe Anastasia suspects I'm involved in something criminal. How many of the details she's privy to, who else she's told . . . all that is pure speculation, as is whether or not it ties into her reasons for disappearing."

"Christ." Lyman had gone white. "You never mentioned any of this."

"I just told you, I only recently found out. It's one of the reasons I'm so eager to find her, and to get rid of her."

"Under those circumstances, you should be glad she's gone. Instead of brooding over where she's gone, be grateful it's not to the authorities. Instead, concentrate on figuring out who she might have shared her suspicions with. They could be far more dangerous to us than

Anastasia. She's your *niece*, for heaven's sake. Your brother's daughter. She might condemn you, but she'd never turn you in. Hasn't she proven that by running off? She wants no part of your illegal activities—or of you. Whereas someone else, someone outside your family, wouldn't hesitate to send you to the gallows." A cold shiver ran up Lyman's spine. "Getting rid of Anastasia should be secondary to . . ."

His mouth snapped shut as the meaning of George's words sank in, and he stared at him as if seeing a ghost. "By 'get rid of,' do you mean—kill her?"

An ugly laugh. "Yes and no. Figuratively, yes. Actually—well, actually, I mean for her to begin a brand-new life. Only *not* in America. And *not* at my expense. At my profit, as a matter of fact. My fifty-thousand-pound profit."

Realization struck, and Lyman sagged into his chair. "The ship . . . the falsified destination . . . the whole damned arrangement you're working on with Bates to supply Rouge with the girl he needs. My God, Medford, you're planning to send Anastasia?"

George shot him a disgusted look. "Stop looking so horrified. We've been sending women to Rouge for months."

"But your *niece* . . ."

". . . could be our downfall," George finished for him. He strode over to the desk, gripping the edge until his knuckles turned white. "Did you hear what I said?" he ground out, leaning forward to glare at Lyman. "She might know enough to send us both to prison. And you're a fool if you think she won't. My *niece* . . ." he spat, ". . . has no loyalty to me—hell, *Henry* had no loyalty to me. As for selling Anastasia to Rouge, stop sounding so bloody self-righteous. You've been more than content selling women all this time."

"But they're . . . she's . . ." Sweat was beading up on Lyman's forehead.

"Ah. In other words, it's acceptable to sell strangers, workhouse girls we don't know, but you're offended by my selling the one girl who could see us both in Newgate."

"Does she know what you intend . . ." An inadvertent shudder. ". . . what you intend to do to her?"

"No. That much, she's blissfully unaware of."

"Thank God for that."

"Stop thanking God. We've got to find the little bitch before she causes any more trouble."

"She could be anywhere," Lyman put in weakly.

"Not according to your sources." Rage against Anastasia was rebuilding inside George until he could taste it. "According to your sources, she's still right here in England." His eyes narrowed. "And if she is, I intend to find her."

"How?"

"To begin with, by keeping a close eye on my daughter—something my butler is taking care of in my absence. Breanna knows more than she's telling me. Although, in her case, she'd never be stupid enough to actually help Anastasia destroy me, not unless she was privy to my plans for her wretched cousin. In *that* instance, she would protect Anastasia with her life." George scowled, remembering the shocking confrontation he'd had with Breanna last night. Clearly, his daughter had more pluck than he'd given her credit for. "Fortunately, Breanna hasn't any idea what I intend for Henry's brat."

"And speaking of Anastasia," he continued, "assuming she's still in England, she doesn't have that many friends, certainly not friends who'd keep her from her legal guardian. I'll start with Fenshaw, see if he's heard from her. Then, I'll stop in at the House of Lockewood, find out what Sheldrake knows." He paused, rubbed his palm across his chin. "On second thought, that's too obvious. If Sheldrake knew anything about what we're doing, he'd have sent Bow Street over here to collect us by now. That's the only reason I'm sure Anastasia isn't with him. He's too damned ethical to ignore our crimes, even for a short while. No, she hasn't told him yet—either because she's only just figured it out or because, as I said, she's still missing pieces and dropped out of sight to do a little investigating on her own."

"Or maybe you're overreacting and she doesn't know a thing," Lyman burst out, his composure drawn taut to breaking.

"Then why did she run off?" George shot back.

"I don't know!" Lyman's control snapped. "To spend Henry's money! To see the world! Why does any young woman run off? Maybe she's with child!"

George recoiled as if he'd been struck. "With child?" Everything inside him went numb. "I never thought . . . but given their trysts . . . and if she is . . ." He could see it all dissipating before his very eyes—not just Rouge's payment now, but everything: Henry's inheritance, the balance of power from his own descendants to Henry's, not to mention Sheldrake . . .

Sheldrake.

White shock vibrated through George's being.

If Anastasia was pregnant, Sheldrake was the father.

"Dammit." His hands balled into fists, pounded the

desk with all the rage of a wounded animal. "It can't be. *It can't be!*"

Lyman backed away, breathing heavily. "Take it easy, Medford. I only meant . . ."

"Give me a quill." George's tone was lethal, a drowning man clawing his way to the surface. "I've got to get a letter off. *Now.*"

"Fine. Here. Whatever you say." Lyman shoved a quill and some paper across the desk. "Who are you writing to?" he ventured.

"To the one person who can tell me just how Sheldrake fits into all this. Because if Anastasia knows something, if she puts the rest of the pieces together, she'll run straight to him. And if she's with child . . ." A bitter laugh. "She'll definitely run straight to him. Either way, I've got to get to her first. Even if it means taking a chance and passing off some substitute to Rouge. My wretched niece has got to be stopped."

In Medford Manor's sitting room, Breanna moved the heavy drapes aside, peeked out the window, and watched Damen's carriage disappear around the drive. She felt a sense of emptiness, of loss, knowing Anastasia was in there, leaving her home yet again. It shouldn't be this way. Stacie belonged here. Not just here, but safe, happy.

Breanna drew herself up, her chin set in staunch determination. It was *her* father who was responsible for this nightmare. And it was up to *her* to stop him.

"Miss Breanna?" Wells addressed her from the sitting room doorway. "Lord Sheldrake has taken his leave. You wanted to see me?"

Slowly, Breanna turned and nodded. "Come in, Wells.

And please shut the door. I want this conversation to remain private."

The butler complied, looking not the least bit surprised at Breanna's request.

"I suspect you know what this is about," she began.

Wells's expression softened. "I suspect I do."

Breanna cast a nervous glance over her shoulder, scanning the deserted drive.

"We have another hour or so before your father returns," Wells supplied. "So you needn't worry."

"Good." Her mind at ease, Breanna turned her attention back to Wells, who was regarding her with an expectant look on his face. "I hate involving you in this," she said honestly, her brow furrowed. "But I'm afraid we no longer have a choice."

"I'm already involved, Miss Breanna." Wells adjusted his spectacles, then stood up straight, hands clasped firmly behind him, as if stating his position on the subject. "I've been involved since the day your grandfather died. I know what he wanted. And I mean to see that he gets it."

Tears glistened on Breanna's lashes. "Thank you," she managed. "From Stacie and me. And Grandfather, as well." She composed herself, clearing her throat to steady her voice. "I don't know how much you're aware of . . ."

"There's something *you're* not aware of," Wells interrupted. "Until your father returns from London—which, as I said, should be in another hour or so—I've been assigned to keep a close eye on you, to report back if you should meet with anyone unusual . . ."

Breanna gripped the back of the settee. "Anyone meaning Stacie."

"Or someone who knows her whereabouts."

Her eyes widened. "Does Father suspect Damen?"

"I don't know, Miss Breanna." The butler shrugged. "I'm sure it's occurred to him that Lord Sheldrake is somehow involved. From what I've gleaned from the viscount's mutterings, he realizes Miss Stacie and Lord Sheldrake are . . . close friends."

"Yes, he does." Breanna sighed, smoothing her palm over the settee's textured cloth and polished wood trim. "Wells, I want to use this time wisely, since Father will be home soon. I need to ask you some questions about his actions. Or, more specifically, his destinations—if you know them."

"I'll tell you anything I can. But *you* tell *me* one thing first: is she all right?"

A soft smile touched Breanna's lips. "She's fine. Eager to have this ordeal over with, but fine. And Wells—" For an instant, Breanna put the unpleasantness aside to tell their lifelong friend something she knew would delight him. "When all this is behind us, there's going to be a wedding. An incredibly joyful wedding."

Wells's smile was broad, but a fine mist veiled his eyes. "Our Miss Stacie—a bride. It's hard to imagine her as a wife—the little girl who climbed trees and spoke her mind no matter what the cost."

"She still speaks her mind, only now she speaks it to Damen." Breanna's eyes twinkled. "They're perfect for each other, Wells. Grandfather would be so happy."

"Indeed he would." Wells's gaze grew sober. "What questions can I answer to make this wedding happen more quickly, and more safely?"

"Father's late-night outings." With equal gravity, Breanna resumed their original subject. "The ones he's been taking more and more often these days. Do you have any idea where he goes? Who he meets?"

The butler pressed his lips together, contemplating his employer's activities. "I don't know the viscount's precise destination, nor the name of whomever he meets. What I can tell you is that he's only gone a few hours each time, which means he can't be going far. And, if I had to wager a guess, I'd say his meetings take place at a pub."

That brought Breanna up short. "A pub? Why would you think that?"

"Because whenever your father returns, he reeks of smoke, and there's a certain stench clinging to his clothing." A distasteful shudder. "The last time he got home, the smell of cheap ale was on his breath. It doesn't take a scholar to add up all those clues."

"That fits," Breanna murmured. "If Father were meeting a contact for some secret, unscrupulous purpose, he wouldn't want to be recognized. And what better place to remain anonymous than in a seedy pub filled with riffraff who don't know you and, quite frankly, don't care?"

Wells nodded. "There are only three or four such places I'm aware of within a half hour's carriage ride from Medford Manor. But then again, I'm not exactly an expert on taverns."

Breanna couldn't help but smile at Wells's offended tone. "Of course you're not." She reflected on what she'd just learned. So her father met his snitch at a pub. *Which* pub she'd have to determine later, perhaps by intercepting the next message between the two men.

And that led to her next question.

"How does my father make arrangements for these late-night excursions? I assume he communicates with his colleague by messenger."

"A courier brings the messages straight to Lord Medford."

"What about those messages initiated by Father, or his responses to those he receives?"

"One of our footmen delivers the viscount's correspondence directly to the courier's address. Where it goes from there, I have no idea."

"I see." Breanna's thoughts were racing. "They go to a great deal of trouble to keep the recipient's identity unknown." She pursed her lips. "This courier—I assume it's the same one each time?" She waited for Wells's nod. "Tell me, does he come here often?"

"Not too often. Other than to dispatch word on the late-night excursions we've just discussed, he generally comes only when the viscount receives business correspondence from the Continent." A frown, as Wells reconsidered his words. "Actually, that's not true. He handles only the viscount's most pressing business correspondence to and from the Continent."

Breanna jumped on that distinction. "How do you know the business involved is pressing?"

"Several reasons, the most obvious being that the letters are marked 'urgent.' Also, the viscount's instructions are that I bring these letters to him immediately, no matter what the hour or circumstances." Wells's frown deepened. "And they do arrive at the oddest hours. For instance, one such letter was delivered during Miss Stacie's coming-out party. Your father rushed off, closeted himself in his study, and read it. The next morning he arose at dawn, and dashed off an equally urgent reply."

"And this courier delivered it for him?"

"Again, our footman brought the letter to the courier's address. I assume from there it was dispatched to the Continent. I don't know who these messages are from or to, but they cause your father great agitation. Could that tie into anything you and Lord Sheldrake are considering?"

"Rouge," Breanna muttered. "That must be who Father is corresponding with. The courier you're describing is obviously hired by the informant at the House of Lockewood. It stands to reason he'd use the same person to handle everything else pertaining to these vile transactions." She met Wells's gaze. "I need that courier's address."

"Of course. It's number 17 Fleet Street." Wells's eyes narrowed a bit. "You're not thinking of doing something foolish, are you? Because confronting the courier . . ."

"No, no." Breanna waved away Wells's concern. "Confronting the courier would be stupid. He wouldn't tell me anything, since I don't pay his bills. And I'd only succeed in making him suspicious enough to go to Father. No, what I intend to do is give the address to Damen. I'm willing to bet that courier is someone who does frequent business with the House of Lockewood. That way, no one would notice a few extra charges on his bill—charges incurred by the snitch Father's working with. Damen can use the address as evidence when he confronts whoever that turns out to be."

"You've lost me, Miss Breanna."

"That's all right." Breanna released her grip on the settee, and began walking restlessly about the sitting room. "The sordid details can wait. Planning our tactics can't." She paused, pivoting slowly to face Wells. "My father's with Mr. Lyman. He's probably trying to locate Stacie, which we both know is not going to happen. So, Father's going to be unnerved. My guess is he'll want to find out exactly how much Damen knows, and how he factors into Stacie's plans. He won't ask Damen flat out;

that would be too risky. Instead, he'll probably get his informant to do a bit of spying. After which . . ."

". . . after which, the viscount will need to meet with this snitch of his, to get the information he's seeking," Wells finished for her.

"Exactly." Breanna pressed her palms together, tightly interlaced her fingers. "Wells, I need you to tell me the minute Father gives you a message to send off to that courier. I'm going to steam open the seal and read it."

"There won't be time. Your father expects those particular messages to be dispatched posthaste. He'd notice even the slightest delay."

"Fine. Then I'll read his informant's reply."

"He'll be waiting for it." Wells gave an emphatic shake of his head. "It's not only implausible that you could manage to intercept the note without being spied, it's hardly worth your effort to try. Think about it. The viscount and his snitch have been holding their late-night meetings for months now. My guess is that their meeting place has remained the same. Why, then, would they bother spelling out the address in a note? Their communications are probably cryptic—stating the time they should arrive and the urgency of the topic."

"You're right." Breanna gave an exasperated sigh. "But I've got to . . ." Abruptly, she broke off, her jade green eyes darkening with resolve. "Fine. I'll accomplish this in a bolder manner. The instant Father exchanges a message with this courier or informs you that he'll be going out late at night, tell me. I suspect we haven't long to wait until that happens. Things being as they are, I'm sure Father will want his answers right away, either tonight or tomorrow night."

"Why are you so eager to know when this meeting is going to take place?" Wells asked cautiously.

"Because whenever Father goes, I'm going, too."

Wells sucked in his breath. "You're going to follow the viscount to . . ."

"Yes. It's the only way I can learn who Father's meeting, how much he assumes we know, and what he's planning."

"Miss Breanna." Wells looked ill. "Do you understand how dangerous that is?"

"I understand it's the only way we're going to get the information we need quickly enough. Even if Damen figures out the name of my father's contact by tomorrow, all we'll have is an uncooperative snitch whose confession we can't count on. And even if his confession is genuine, there's no guarantee he can piece together the whole plot. Damen, Stacie, and I know aspects of my father's plan that this informant might not. I need to hear Father's conversation with him firsthand, hear what his instructions to him are. Then, I can combine what I learn with what I already know, and figure out the full scope of what Father's done—*and* what he plans to do next. Especially the latter, if we're going to ensure Stacie's safety and bring this nightmare to an end."

She hesitated, searching for the right words to explain to Wells how deeply, how personally, she felt about all this. "I'm his daughter, Wells," she said in a small, dignified tone. "It's up to me to stop him." Her chin set, and she met Wells's gaze with unyielding conviction. "Please don't try to deter me. It won't work. I can be as stubborn as Stacie when I want to be, if I believe what I'm defending is important enough. And this *is* important enough. It's more precious to me than anything else in my life. It's my family."

Wells cleared his throat, his lips pursed as he contemplated his reply. "I'll make sure the second phaeton is ready, both tonight and tomorrow night," he declared, the essence of efficiency. "We can follow behind, at a discreet distance, so we won't be spied."

"We?" Breanna's jaw dropped.

One of Wells's brows raised ever so slightly. "You didn't think I'd let you do this alone, did you? Now . . ." He continued as if that subject were closed. "Neither of us can go in our customary attire. Certainly not you, who'd be devoured by the pub's lowlifes, before your father could even recognize you to thrash you. And I . . ." He glanced down, scowling at his dignified uniform. ". . . I look far too stately to fit into the crowd we'll be mingling with, certainly if I hope to do so without being spotted by your father." A decisive sniff. "I'll borrow the necessary clothing, have it ready. We can leave at a moment's notice."

Emotion clogged Breanna's throat, made speaking difficult. "It's obvious that Grandfather realized something I've only just begun to comprehend," she managed. "Something that explains why Stacie and I are still blessed enough to have you looking out for us: that family isn't necessarily defined by ties of the blood. Family is defined by ties of the heart." She crossed over, abandoning protocol entirely to give Wells a huge hug. "Thank you, my dear friend. Thank you for being part of our family."

George stormed up the front steps of Medford Manor, pounding on the door with his fist.

Wells opened it, stepping aside to allow his employer to enter. "Good evening, sir. I didn't know you'd arrived."

"Obviously, I have." George marched inside, trying for the fifth time to smooth the wrinkles out of his coat. He hated wrinkles. They looked damned untidy, even if one had been drinking.

Besides, whatever liquor he'd consumed had long since worn off. As had its dulling effect.

"Is my daughter home?" George demanded, peering about as if expecting to see Breanna awaiting his return.

Wells stifled a cough. "She's in her room, sir."

"And the mail—did you put it aside for me?"

"Just as you asked, yes."

"Good. Were there any private messages delivered to Breanna?"

"No, my lord." This time, Wells relented, giving one or two raspy coughs. "But Miss Breanna did have a visitor."

George's head shot up. "Who?"

"Lord Sheldrake."

"Sheldrake." Suspicion and fear clouded George's eyes. "He came to see Breanna?"

"Actually, he was looking for you, as well. Something about business you two had to conduct. But I told him you'd be gone all day, so he said he'd return in a day or two to meet with you."

"That's all he said?"

"Sir?" Wells cleared his throat, looking puzzled.

"Did the marquess say anything else?" George snapped. "Was he in a good humor?"

"We exchanged pleasantries. And, yes, he seemed cheerful enough."

"I see." George digested that fact, although sweat still broke out on his forehead. Why the hell had Sheldrake come to Medford Manor—to get answers or to provide them? What had he and Breanna discussed?

Who, he could guess.

"You say Sheldrake visited with Breanna?"

"Indeed he did, sir. They took a picnic lunch and went off for a ride in the country. Lord Sheldrake thought Miss Breanna might need some cheering up, given that Miss Stacie had to leave so suddenly."

George's eyes narrowed into slits. "So Sheldrake knew Anastasia was gone?"

"Why, yes, sir." Wells plucked out a handkerchief, coughed discreetly into it. "As I understood it, she left at his suggestion. Nonetheless, it was clear he sympathized with Miss Breanna's loneliness. I'm sure he appreciated how much she missed her cousin—how much we all miss her. But then, I needn't explain that to you, my lord."

"No, you needn't," George muttered, wishing he had more concrete information, determined to get it. "I want to see my daughter," he barked.

Almost instantly, he realized his error, as he saw Wells start, tense ever so fractionally. *Dammit*, he berated himself. *I have to watch my tone.*

The very notion made him furious. *He* was the master of this household, the bloody head of the family. Why the hell shouldn't he rule it with an iron hand, or any other way he chose to? Worse, why should he allow his actions to be dictated by his acquiescent slip of a daughter?

Not so acquiescent, he reminded himself, recalling yesterday's incident, as well as the reproving look on Wells's face when he'd glanced into Breanna's bedchamber, assessed whether or not she'd been hurt—by her father.

Silently, George swore. The little chit was not only bolder than he'd realized, she was also smarter. Because she was right. He couldn't afford to alienate his servants, not given the precarious state of his life right now. The staff adored Breanna; they had since she was a child. If they believed he was physically harming her . . .

No. He couldn't risk the kind of scandal that would ensue. It could push things over the edge, eliminate any remaining chance he had with Sheldrake. There was no choice to be had. He must curb the severity with which he approached Breanna, lest she follow through with her threats. Besides, she wouldn't tell him a damned thing if he thrashed her. But if he was civil, perhaps that would yield different results.

So be it. However, when all this was over, when Anastasia had been found and his own world had been righted, then things would return to normal. Then, he'd once again be master of Medford Manor, and of his fate. And when he was—well, God help Breanna if she upset his plans for her future.

Inspired by that thought, George drew a slow breath, sought a more acceptable approach.

"Wells," he began, this time keeping his tone composed and even. "Give me a few minutes to peruse the mail. Then, ask Breanna to come to my study. I have a few questions I'd like to ask her."

He could actually see Wells's rigid stance relax a bit. "As you wish."

"Thank you. Oh, and once Breanna and I have finished talking, I'll take my dinner in my study. Alone. I'm not to be disturbed all evening. And Wells . . ." George leaned forward, lowered his voice to a secretive pitch. "I'm expecting the courier. When he arrives, bring his message to me at once. That also means I'll be going out tonight. At half after midnight. Have the phaeton ready."

"Of course, my lord." Wells winced a bit, his fingers shifting reflexively to his throat. "Pardon me, sir, but may I ask permission to retire early tonight? After I've taken care of your arrangements, that is. I'm feeling a bit under the weather. Of course, I'll direct one of the footmen to attend the entranceway door, if needed."

As grateful as George was that Wells's misgivings had been appeased, he wasn't interested in hearing about the butler's health. He had more important things on his mind. "H-m-m?" he asked, distracted by the reminder of all that had yet to be resolved. "Oh, that's fine. And don't bother with the footman. Other than my dinner, I won't be needing anything more tonight. Once the courier's gone and the phaeton's been readied, you can take the night off."

"Thank you, sir. I'll go see Mrs. Rhodes now, make sure she sends your dinner directly to your study. Then, I'll return to my post and await the courier."

Wells headed off to the kitchen, acutely aware of the viscount's footsteps as they moved down the hall in the direction of his study.

By the time the study door had clicked shut, and the bolt had been thrown, Wells had finished speaking with Mrs. Rhodes and was halfway to his own quarters.

Once there, he paused long enough to yank open his bureau drawer and scoop up the smaller of the two stable hands' outfits he'd found earlier in the laundry yard and had hidden in his room. He spread the clothes out on a serving tray, then draped a fine linen napkin over them, making the overall presentation look like an elegant dinner.

With a gleam of approval, he left his room, made his way calmly to the front hallway, then up the stairs. He rounded the second-floor landing, nodding his acknowledgment to the passing servants, who bowed respectfully and hurried on their way.

Without incident, Wells knocked on Breanna's door.

"Yes?"

"I have your refreshment, Miss Breanna."

A quick rustling sound, and Breanna tugged open the door. "Thank you, Wells," she said, her gaze searching his face. "Would you kindly put it on my nightstand?"

"Certainly." Wells walked over, placed the tray beside her bed. "I think you'll find everything to your liking," he assured her. He straightened, met her stare head-on. "Tonight. Half after midnight," he breathed, his voice nearly inaudible. "I'll bring the phaeton around and meet you on the east side of the drive, the side concealed by that awning of trees."

Slowly, she nodded, a glint of anticipation lighting her eyes. "I'll be there," she whispered. Then: "Thank you, Wells," she said in a more normal tone.

"My pleasure, Miss Breanna." The butler clasped his hands behind his back, a flicker of distaste crossing his face. "Your father wishes to speak with you. Please give him a quarter hour, then go to his study." A scratchy cough, followed by a meaningful look. "I'm feeling a bit under the weather, and the viscount has given me permission to retire early. But should you need anything, I'll be in my quarters."

"I appreciate that," Breanna replied, nodding her understanding. Wells had freed himself of having to man the entranceway door by claiming to be ill. But that didn't mean he wouldn't be available to her, if her father lost control. "I'll be fine," she said, giving his forearm a reassuring squeeze, then shooing him toward the door. "Go. Get some rest. That way, you'll be yourself again in no time."

Waiting only till Wells had gone, Breanna retreated into her chambers, tugging the napkin off the tray and nearly laughing aloud as she viewed her "refreshment." A shoddy pair of breeches, a threadbare shirt, some scuffed but serviceable boots and—ah, bless Wells's keen mind—a cap.

Breanna gathered up the clothes, tucked them away in her wardrobe. Then, with a thoughtful glance at her nightstand, she reminded herself of the one other article she'd need to bring with her.

Her pistol.

Given the risk involved in tonight's excursion, the full extent of which she didn't dare ponder, a little protection was in order. Because if her identity were discovered, she'd need that protection—not only from her father, whose wrath would be too fierce to imagine, but from his informant, with whom she was doubtless acquainted and could therefore identify, and from any riffraff who became unruly once they realized she was a woman.

In short, discovery was unthinkable. But, should it occur, the pistol was necessary.

As for now, her father had asked to see her. Well, that came as no great surprise. By now, Wells had doubtless told him that Damen had been at Medford Manor during his absence, which would make him frantic to find out what Damen knew of Stacie's whereabouts.

And what he knew of her father's guilt.

Bitterness surged through Breanna's veins. *Very well, Father. I'll come to your study. I'll play this cat and mouse game with you. But if you think you'll learn one wretched thing from me, you're wrong. Even I can't be browbeaten into helping you, not when it's lives you plan to sacrifice. Innocent lives—including Stacie's. No, not this time. This time you're going to get what you deserve.*

18

*G*eorge swore under his breath, examining each worthless letter that had been delivered today, then slapping them onto his desk. All trivial invitations and foolish announcements. Not one of them pertinent to the dilemma he now faced.

He *had* to find Anastasia.

Dragging a hand through his hair, he dropped into his chair, contemplating today's latest development.

Sheldrake had been here. He'd spent hours alone with Breanna. Why? Certainly not to woo her. That he knew, thanks to the information he'd received from his reliable contact. Then why? Did Sheldrake know where Anastasia was? Had he come to tell Breanna? Or was he corroborating Anastasia's story that it was he who'd sent her to America?

Tonight's meeting should yield some answers with regard to Sheldrake's involvement, not only in Anastasia's disappearance, but in whatever incriminating search she'd undertaken.

Perhaps, in the meantime, he could acquire a few of those answers from his daughter.

As if on cue, a knock sounded at the study door.

"Yes?" he responded impatiently.

"You wanted to see me, Father?" Breanna called back.

George rose, crossing over and unlocking the door. He gestured at his daughter, who was hovering on the threshold, eyeing him warily. "Come in." He stood aside, waiting for her to comply.

She took a few tentative steps into the room, then halted.

"Stop staring at me as if you expect me to whip you," George ordered.

"Do you?"

George drew a slow, calming breath. "No." He shut the door, but refrained from locking it. "There. This is a private conversation, or I'd leave the door ajar. But the bolt isn't thrown. You can escape any time you fear for your safety." He paused, giving her a pointed glare. "Or did you bring your pistol as protection?"

"My pistol is in my drawer." Breanna interlaced her fingers in front of her. "I told you, I don't intend to walk around the manor armed."

"Ah. You'll just shout for the servants if need be, accuse me of thrashing you within an inch of your life." George walked across the room, stood before his desk, and leaned back against it. "Well, don't worry. I want only to talk."

Breanna's delicate brows rose. "About what—Stacie?"

"No, about Lord Sheldrake. He did visit you today, didn't he?"

"You must know he did. Just as you must know we went for a carriage ride."

"Indeed I do." George folded his arms across his chest, watching Breanna's face. "And tell me, how is your courtship progressing? I did advise you to encourage the marquess as much as possible, if you remember."

"I remember." Breanna never averted her gaze. "But, as I tried to tell you last time, no one can force feelings. Lord Sheldrake isn't in love with me. Nor, to be honest, am I in love with him. He's a fine man. But he's not destined to become my husband." A small smile played about her lips. "However, I do suspect he'll be a member of our family, nonetheless."

George's brows shot up. He'd expected to catch Breanna in a lie. Dammit, was she actually going to tell him the truth? "What does that mean?" he asked carefully.

"It means that Lord Sheldrake and Stacie are in love. I expect they'll be getting married. Whenever Stacie gets home, that is."

"I see." George's fingers dug into his sleeves, anger surging through him in wide, hammering waves. What kind of game was Breanna playing, admitting something she knew would enrage him? Was she testing him to see if he'd strike her?

He wouldn't. Furious or not, he'd keep this to a battle of words.

"Your cousin and Sheldrake," he said icily. "Interesting. Tell me, when did they become so enamored with each other?"

"Over the course of their business meetings, I suppose. I really don't know the details. Stacie hadn't time to divulge them to me before she left."

"If she and Sheldrake are so smitten with each other, why did she leave him and make this trip to the States?"

Breanna sighed. "We already discussed this, Father. I told you: Lord Sheldrake felt Stacie would be the right one to protect their interests in that new banking venture. Frankly, I think Stacie agreed. She's as leery as the marquess is about trusting others with their investments."

George leaned forward, scowling at Breanna. "Why didn't Sheldrake go himself?"

"I couldn't say. Probably because he's a busy man. He has dozens of clients who count on him."

"Yet he found time to see you."

"He came to see you, Father. But you weren't home."

"So he took you on a lengthy carriage ride?"

A grateful nod. "He's a very compassionate man. He guessed how much I miss Stacie, and tried to take my mind off it. Now that I've stopped trying to win his affections, I feel far more relaxed around him."

Good, George thought silently. *Then you'll slip easily into the role of the Marchioness of Sheldrake once I've rid myself of your cousin.* Aloud, he asked, "What did you and Sheldrake discuss during your ride?"

Breanna shrugged offhandedly. "Nothing special: Stacie. You."

George's insides clenched. "Me? How did I factor into this conversation?"

The slightest hesitation. "To be frank, Lord Sheldrake is relieved that Stacie will be of age when she returns to England. He didn't want to offend you by whisking her off to Gretna Green, but he is determined to wed her. Now you'll have several months to accustom yourself to the idea of their marriage and, upon Stacie's return, it will no longer be an issue. She'll be twenty-one and she and

Lord Sheldrake can have the formal church wedding she wants so much, along with the presence and the blessings of those they love."

Over my dead body, George thought bitterly. *It's you who will be Sheldrake's bride. He'll get over Anastasia, learn to live with the closest substitute. Just as I did. And I'll get my respectability back, along with Henry's inheritance, and all the benefits of Sheldrake's wealth and acclaim.*

"Father?"

George blinked, refocused on Breanna. "What?"

"Was there anything else you wanted?"

Swiftly, he gathered his thoughts. "Sheldrake—did he say when Anastasia would be returning?" A pointed pause. "From the States, that is."

If Breanna felt flustered by the question, she didn't show it. "She'll leave the minute the bank is open and running smoothly. She'll be back before the holidays. After all, she won't want to be away for *too* many months. She has so many exciting announcements to make, so many life-altering events to look forward to—not only her wedding, but beyond."

A hard knot of dread gripped George's gut. "Beyond?" he echoed, unable to keep the strain out of his tone. "What kind of events are you referring to?"

Breanna met his gaze, her expression unreadable. "Fate is a miraculous thing, Father, whether or not you believe it. It takes a hand in putting the right people together, and seeing that the right people get what they deserve."

George could hear the thundering of his own heart. "What the hell does that mean?"

"Mean?" Breanna's brows drew together, but there was an odd glint in her eyes. "It was a philosophical statement. I don't think it requires further explanation."

The rage was beginning to take over. George could feel it. "I'll ask you again," he said, unconsciously pushing away from his desk, taking a step toward Breanna. "What life-altering events are you referring to? And who is it you expect to get what he deserves?"

Like prey being cornered by a hunter, Breanna tensed, swiftly assessing her father's approach, the controlled violence of his motions. She reacted instantly, reaching behind her to twist open the door handle. "I'm going to my room," she pronounced. "Before you do something you'll regret."

"Not before you answer my question." In three strides, George was beside her, slamming his palm against the door and holding it shut, his eyes blazing as he glared down at his daughter. "What events? And what *deserving* people?"

Although Breanna was clearly unnerved by the vehemence of his response, she didn't cower, nor did she evade the question. "Stacie's beginning a new life with a new husband here in England, the country she loves but spent ten years away from. If those aren't life-altering events, I don't know what is. I realize you don't feel about her as I do, but I happen to think Stacie is wonderful. She and Lord Sheldrake deserve a long and happy future together." Breanna drew a slow, shaky breath. "Now please take your arm away and let me pass. I'd like to go upstairs and rest."

"In a minute," George ground out from between clenched teeth. He grabbed her arm, his stare probing hers with seething intensity. "And don't bother shouting for the servants. I don't intend to thrash you—not this time. But I *do* intend to get an answer. You say you were referring to your cousin's future, her right to be happy.

Let's say I accept that. But I *don't* accept that ludicrous explanation about your comment regarding fate." His grip tightened. "What do you know that I don't?"

"Nothing." Breanna shook herself free, wearing that same determined look she'd worn when she aimed her pistol at him. "You know everything I do, and you have for far longer than I. But knowing and accepting are two different things."

"Knowing and accepting what?" George shouted, abandoning his last filaments of control.

"Just what I said." Breanna raised her chin, twin spots of color staining her cheeks. "That the right people belong together. Like Stacie and Lord Sheldrake." A pointed pause. "And Uncle Henry and Aunt Anne."

George went rigid, his air expelling in a hiss. Anne? What did his daughter know about Anne?

"I might have been a child, but even I could see how much in love she and Uncle Henry were," Breanna supplied. "Your bitterness was wasted. Aunt Anne cared only for her husband, just as Lord Sheldrake cares only for Stacie." An astute look. "Or is that repetition of history exactly what's bothering you so much?"

Fury exploded in George's skull.

"And *I'm* getting what I deserve?" he bellowed, grabbing Breanna's shoulders, shaking her violently, his fingers biting into her flesh until she whimpered. *"I'm getting what I deserve?"* He flung her away from him, knowing that in another minute, he'd beat her so viciously, he'd ensure his own undoing. "Get out of here!" he thundered, wrenching open the door and shoving Breanna halfway across the hall. "Get out of my sight!"

He slammed the door in her wake, his entire body shaking with the force of his rage. That little bitch

Anastasia had actually told the entire story to Breanna. It's the only way his daughter could have found out. Which meant that Anne, the faithless trollop, had confided the whole history of their lives to the child she should have had with him, but had given Henry instead.

Muttering an oath, George crossed over and sloshed a drink into his goblet. On the verge of tossing it down in a few hard gulps, he slammed it onto the sideboard and thrust it away. *No*, he ordered himself, eyeing his trembling hands. *I'm already out of control. I can't compound it by getting drunk.*

He gripped the edge of the sideboard, determined to stay, if not rational, then sober—sober enough to ponder all Breanna had just said.

And all she hadn't said.

Had she really told him all she knew? Or had that allusion to his getting what he deserved encompassed more than just her assessment of his bitterness, his solitary life? Had Anastasia confided in her cousin, told her she was close to exposing him as a culprit, a thief—or worse? Had she told her about Bates's visit to his office, wondered what urgent business a magistrate might have with Colby and Sons? Had she found something suspicious in his files—something she couldn't yet prove? Had she noticed anything out of the ordinary about his bills from Lyman and the few other shippers he had special financial arrangements with? Was it even worse than that? Had she actually managed to fit together enough pieces to deduce what was *really* being transported to the Continent?

And what the hell had Breanna meant about the life-altering events Anastasia had to look forward to after her wedding? Oh, she'd explained it away nicely with that drivel about her cousin becoming a bride, starting a whole new life. But George sensed there was more—a lot more.

Icy fear prickled up his spine.

Could Lyman be right? Could Anastasia be with child? Could *that* have been what Breanna was alluding to? Had Anastasia divulged that to her, then sworn her to secrecy? Was his wretched niece giving Sheldrake a child? Is that why she'd run off, yet remained in England?

No. Dammit, no. If she was pregnant, she'd have gone straight to Sheldrake.

Maybe she had.

Not according to Breanna.

But Breanna wouldn't admit such a truth—not if it meant betraying her cousin.

Still, Sheldrake was so bloody noble. If Anastasia had gone to him, told him she was carrying his child, it would have been Gretna Green he'd be driving to today, not Medford Manor.

So where did Damen Lockewood fit into all this? What did he know, about Anastasia, about the illegal activities going on at Colby and Sons? How involved in Anastasia's investigation was he? And what life-altering results might have resulted from this liaison of theirs?

All the unanswered questions led back to Sheldrake. As did George's future. Because the minute Anastasia showed up on the marquess's doorstep, either with the news that she was carrying his child or with proof of her uncle's guilt, George's hopes, and his life, would be over.

Which meant one thing: He had to get to Anastasia before she got to Sheldrake.

And when he did . . .

When he did—what?

A better question would be how, he berated himself. *How do I find her? How do I get rid of her when I do—especially if the time frame on Rouge's requirement has elapsed?*

George scowled at the sideboard, ran his forefinger around the rim of his goblet. He'd questioned dozens of people today: from Lyman, Bates, and Fenshaw, to a slew of innkeepers in both London and Kent, not a single one of whom had an Anastasia Colby—or any young woman matching her description—staying in their establishment. George had even gone into shops, into coffee houses, and made inquiries. Nothing. And, as of his last check with Lyman, made late in the day, not one of the shipping company owner's contacts had turned up anything, nor had Anastasia's name appeared on a single ship's manifest.

The bloody chit had vanished into thin air.

Unless she was with Sheldrake.

According to the marquess's conversation with Breanna, she wasn't. Unless, of course, Breanna was lying. But she wouldn't be that stupid. Not when she knew bloody well he'd confirm the story with Sheldrake the very next chance he got.

So, if Anastasia wasn't with Sheldrake, where was she? Where had she disappeared to? And who was equipped to find her?

That question incited a flash of recall, and George's mind darted to the conversation he'd had—the one about the professional assassin. Abruptly, he found himself considering the prospect.

A hired killer; one who'd hunt Anastasia down and end her miserable life.

It sounded more enticing by the minute—and more necessary.

Of course, it would mean forfeiting Rouge's money, but that was a moot point anyway, since if Anastasia didn't surface, there would be no fifty-thousand-pound compensation. Besides, perhaps a suitable substitute really could be found. He still had some time.

But not if Anastasia incriminated him.

Which she couldn't if she were dead.

With her demise, the threat to his freedom would be gone, Henry's inheritance would be his.

And hell, the bitch would be gone forever.

Wouldn't that be divine justice, Anne, George mused sardonically. *Destroying the one person you loved even more than you did Henry. Killing off Henry's legacy, his sole heir. Marrying Breanna off to Sheldrake, and having the Colby name to myself. Savoring the sheer joy of knowing I do.*

On that thought, George stalked over to his desk, dragging open the drawer and shoving everything aside until he found the miniature portrait. He glared down at Anne's likeness, loathing her with every fiber of his being, wishing he had her in front of him, alive and well, just so he could choke her to death with his bare hands.

Savagely, he flung the portrait across the room, watched it strike the wall and topple to the carpet, not giving a damn that its clutter upset the room's perfect sense of order. Fine. Anne was dead. Perhaps it was time he accepted it.

Perhaps it was also time for Anastasia to join her.

19

*I*t was ten minutes past midnight.

Breanna shoved in her last hairpin, then tugged on the cap Wells had given her, relieved to see it was deep enough to cover all her hair, its brim reaching halfway down her forehead.

Excellent. She pivoted in front of the looking glass, grinning at the image she made. If someone didn't plant himself directly before her, they'd think she was a scrawny but wholly realistic sailor or workman.

Mentally, she reviewed what was left to do.

Her bed.

She crossed over, rearranging the bedcovers and stuffing the pillows beneath it until it looked as if someone was not only there, but deeply asleep. That way, if her maid should check on her, all would seem normal.

With a satisfied nod, Breanna completed the final detail of her attire. She slid open the nightstand drawer and extracted the pistol, shoving it into the pocket of her coat. Now she was ready.

Twelve fifteen. Almost time.

She wandered about the room, running her fingertips over her porcelain figures and reflecting back over the cryptic war of words she'd had with her father—a war that had ended with him exploding in a manner so irrational that it made her wonder if he'd truly gone over the edge. The enmity in his eyes, the trembling fury in his voice, the frenzied way he'd thrown her out . . . Even now Breanna shuddered.

Maybe she'd pushed him too far. She'd sensed his surprise and his anger when she freely offered him information on Stacie and Damen's feelings for each other. Clearly, he'd expected her to lie. Which also meant he had no recollection of what he'd blurted out yesterday while in a drunken rage—the reference to Stacie as Damen's partner in bed. If he'd recalled saying it, he would have known why she'd called his bluff, given him the truth she already knew he possessed.

But the rest of what she'd said to him . . .

Breanna frowned, unconsciously picking up the figure of the two little girls, holding it tightly in her hands. She'd known she would provoke him with that reference to people getting what they deserve. But she hadn't been able to restrain herself. It had been a stupid thing to say—she was fully aware that she'd made him suspicious of how much she knew. Nevertheless, she couldn't regret it. She hated him for what he was doing, and in some small way, she needed him to know that.

However, his control had snapped when she mentioned fate putting the right people together. She hadn't planned on telling him she knew about Aunt Anne; that had just slipped out in the heat of anger. Still, even she had never anticipated the intensity of his rage.

Well, it was too late now for regrets. She couldn't retract her words even if she wanted to. Whatever her father believed, however furious he was, the damage was done, the die cast.

As for his reaction to her statement about life-altering events, obviously he was worried about how Stacie's future would affect his. She'd be marrying Damen, joining her life with his . . .

Having his children.

Breanna's head shot up, the realization accosting her. Of course. *That's* what her father's fears stemmed from. He knew Stacie and Damen were intimately involved. He was probably terrified that she was pregnant. In his mind, that would explain why she'd run off.

It would also explain his absolute determination to find her. To find her and rid himself of her—especially if she was also carrying a child he wanted gone, its conception undiscovered. She could almost imagine her father's thoughts: If he shipped Anastasia off to Rouge quickly enough, he could pass this child off on another man and no one would ever be the wiser. But if he waited too long . . .

A surge of fear shot through Breanna. Her father's panic was escalating. He stood to lose more and more with each passing day. Lord only knew what lengths he would go to to find Stacie and transport her to Rouge.

She had to stop him.

Biting her lip, Breanna replaced the porcelain figure on her bureau, pausing only long enough to caress the edge of the silver coin, which was gently nudged in its slot between the little girls and the flowers. "Help me, Grandfather," she whispered aloud. "Help me find the strength to do what I must. And please—help Stacie."

She turned away from her bureau, dashed away the moisture from her lashes.

Her glance fell on the clock.

Twelve twenty-five. Time to act.

Savoring the reassuring weight of the pistol in her coat and her grandfather's presence in her heart, Breanna went to the door, eased it open.

The hallway was deserted.

She made her way to the landing, hiding in the alcove and listening for noises below—noises that would indicate her father's departure.

Three minutes later, she heard them.

Quick, purposeful strides—her father's—walked the length of the front hall to the entranceway. The door opened, then shut, its firm click echoing through the empty hallway.

Breanna counted to ten. Then, she scooted down the staircase and darted in the opposite direction, down the corridor that led to the manor's side door, and the eastern portion of the drive.

She glanced into her father's study as she ran by, shivering as she remembered the rage on his face when he'd shoved her out.

A shiny object near the threshold caught her eye.

Without the slightest notion why, Breanna stopped long enough to bend down and pick up the object. It turned out to be a small, ornate picture frame, one that housed a tiny portrait. The portrait was of a woman, one with delicate features, fair skin, and a cloud of honey brown hair.

At first glance, she thought it was her mother.

Instinct made her look more closely, and she realized her mistake in a flash.

It wasn't her mother. It was Aunt Anne.

Trepidation gripped Breanna's gut.

Her father had kept Aunt Anne's portrait all these years. Clearly, he'd been consumed for decades by a woman he adamantly believed should have been his.

But what really frightened her was that he'd chosen tonight to destroy it, as if he'd finally banished Aunt Anne from his life.

Just as he intended to banish Stacie.

Time was running out.

Stuffing the miniature into her pocket, Breanna took off at a tear, bolting down the hall and bursting out the side door.

Wells and the phaeton were waiting. Panting, Breanna climbed into the passenger seat, adjusting her cap and peering around the drive.

Silently, Wells pointed, indicating that her father's carriage was nearing the gates.

Breanna nodded.

They waited only until George's phaeton had turned the corner, disappeared from view.

Then Wells slapped the reins.

Damen's contacts were as good as their word.

By one A.M., they'd compiled and delivered personal details on every one of the five men—his four bank officers and Graff—who had access to the private offices at the House of Lockewood.

Proust brought the final papers to the sitting room, where Damen and Anastasia were already poring over what they'd received.

"That's the last of what you requested, sir," Proust announced.

"Thank you, Proust." Damen glanced at the grandfather clock, which heralded the hour as ten past one. "Go to bed. Anastasia and I can manage from here."

"Very good, sir." The valet bowed and took his leave.

"I see absolutely nothing incriminating about Booth," Stacie murmured. She was curled up on the settee, papers strewn all around her, and she frowned as she read and reread the pages on Booth. "He lives a simple life, doesn't gamble or attend parties, and resides in a modest flat several blocks from the bank. Even his savings account is adequate but not huge, although I doubt this snake would be stupid enough to deposit his illegal earnings in your bank."

"Probably not." Damen crossed over, sank into the armchair beside Anastasia. "However, you'd be surprised how arrogant some people become when they feel they've outsmarted the world. They become lax, make careless mistakes. I see it every day in business." He peered over Stacie's shoulder. "In Booth's case, though, I think we're barking up the wrong tree. I've reviewed everything three times, and I see nothing to label him as anything but a quiet, honest man."

With a frustrated sigh, Anastasia tossed the pages aside. "We've also reviewed the pages on Valldale and Lockhorn. They, too, appear to be as innocent as babes. Which means that all we have left are Graff and Cunnings. Both of whom have been with you longer than any of the others. Both of whom have handled your confidential papers for nearly a decade."

"All the more reason we have to investigate them." A muscle worked in Damen's jaw as he tore the seal of the newly delivered envelope. "I can't let sentiment interfere with learning the truth."

"Damen, I can't imagine . . ." Stacie broke off, waving away his oncoming rebuttal. "I know. We have to be sure. Fine. Let's be sure. But I'm beginning to wonder if this is all a waste of time."

"Someone told George about us. Someone is corresponding with Rouge. If these papers don't tell us who that someone is, we'll find another way. But I want that son of a bitch stopped."

Anastasia heard the pain in his voice, and she put aside her doubts, aching for what this part of the investigation was doing to him. "I love you," she said quietly, reaching out to caress his forearm.

Damen looked up, the tension on his face softening, although the fiercely protective light in his eyes seemed to intensify rather than diminish. "And I love you. I don't think you realize how much." He caught her palm, brought it to his lips. "I want my ring on your finger," he said fervently. "I want to flourish you before the world as my wife. I want my child growing inside you. And I mean to make all those wants realities the minute you're safe and those bastards are in Newgate. I intend to move heaven and earth to see that that happens."

Anastasia's fingertips caressed his jaw. "I hope you realize something, Lord Sheldrake," she murmured in a watery tone. "Brilliant as you are, some things are not even in your control."

"Such as?"

"Such as the last want you described." Her misty gaze met his. "It's very possible our child will decide not to wait for your permission to go ahead and be conceived. Especially if he's half as impatient as his mother." Anastasia's voice quavered. "Or *her* mother, as the case may be."

Damen put the envelope aside long enough to pull Stacie off the settee and drag her onto his lap. "That thought . . . the very possibility of you carrying my child . . ." His eyes darkened to a smoky gray, his hand tightened around the nape of her neck as he lowered his mouth to hers. "God, you don't know what it does to me."

"I think I do." She twined her arms around his neck.

"I love you," he breathed, burying his lips in hers. "And if I had my way I'd forget these bloody papers and carry you off to bed, create our first child. Tonight. This minute." A shuddering sigh, as he brought himself under control. "But I won't. Because I intend to have *all* those 'wants,' Stacie, not just one. And there's only one way that can happen."

"I know." Anastasia kissed him tenderly. Then, she leaned over, scooped up the envelope, and extracted the remaining papers. "Let's find him."

The pub was a forty-minute drive from Medford Manor, tucked off a dilapidated road in a village near Canterbury.

"As I suspected," Wells muttered, pulling the phaeton into a nearby alley, nestling it in the shadows between a carpenter shop and a blacksmith shop. "A shabby alehouse; one that's close enough to get to, but far enough— and crude enough—not to be recognized in."

"I see your point." Breanna peered about, tried to see around the corner. "Is Father already inside?"

A terse nod. "His phaeton is on the far side of the pub. I saw him leave it there and make his way inside."

"Good. Then we can follow." She began to descend.

"Wait." Wells stayed her with his hand. "Give the viscount an extra minute or two to get settled. I realize you're anxious. But he's not going to elude us, not at this point. And we certainly don't want to come face to face with him."

"You're right." Breanna hovered at the edge of her seat, poised and ready.

"Miss Breanna, maybe you should stay here while I . . ."

"Wells, I'm going in there with you," Breanna interrupted. "I came to find out who my father is meeting and what they have planned. And I'm not leaving until I do." She leaped lightly from the phaeton. "We've given him enough time. Let's go."

Wells alit as quickly as his less youthful bones would allow. Then, he walked around the phaeton, studying Breanna intently and ensuring, for the tenth time, that her identity and her gender were totally concealed. "I'll do the talking," he instructed. "I have only to remember to speak in a less refined manner. Whereas you'd have to do that *and* lower your voice to a much deeper pitch."

"I can manage."

A troubled frown creased Wells's forehead. "Miss Breanna," he said unsteadily. "If anything should happen to you, your grandfather would never forgive me." A deep swallow. "I would never forgive myself."

"Nothing will happen to me, Wells." Breanna squeezed his arm. "I promise. As for Grandfather, he's with us. I can feel his presence. Besides," she added, trying to soothe Wells's misgivings. "We'll fit right in. We both look like common workingmen." She patted the worn sleeve of his coat. "And our shillings will qualify us as patrons."

Accepting, however uneasily, her unwavering decision, Wells nodded. Together, they strolled out of the alley and toward the pub.

"We've got to act natural, as if we're used to frequenting alehouses," Breanna instructed. "The less attention we draw to ourselves, the better. We'll find Father, sit as near to him and his colleague as we dare. And remember . . ." She tapped her pocket. "If necessary, I have my pistol."

The butler's lips thinned into a grim line. "I haven't forgotten. I only pray you won't have to use it."

The pub was smoky and dim, the latter of which Breanna was thankful for. She scanned the room, scrutinizing the darkest corners first—the tables where it made the most sense for anyone trying to avoid detection to sit.

Sure enough. There he was. He and another man, whose back was turned toward them.

Silently, Breanna nudged Wells, jerking her chin in that direction so he could follow her gaze.

Wells's eyes narrowed as he saw the viscount and his associate, and he pointed to a table just beside theirs— one that was equally concealed by darkness, but that was close enough to attempt eavesdropping.

Pausing only to order two ales—which they paid for at the counter to avoid any immediate interruptions—Wells and Breanna carried their tankards to the table, lowering themselves to the rickety stools.

"You're sure Sheldrake acted normal? He didn't slip off during the day or receive any suspicious missives?"

It was her father's voice, audible even over the thrum of voices, clanking of glasses, and occasional bursts of raucous laughter.

Breanna leaned closer, listening for the reply.

"Perfectly normal. And the only time he slipped off was to go to your house. I'm telling you, he thinks she's on her way to the States. Whatever your niece is doing, she's doing it alone. Or with your daughter."

Clenching her teeth, Breanna stifled the anger that rose inside her.

She knew that other voice. And so did Damen. He knew it well.

"Dammit."

Damen uttered the word in a hiss of disbelief, his finger tracing the number of purchases listed on the page he was reading: jewelry, clothing—all bought over the past several months. In addition, there was a large quantity of food purchased and people hired—extra footmen, a cook, maids, a trio of musicians—for an extravagant party that had been held a fortnight ago at a private house. The house, whose address Damen had never before seen or heard mention of, was the property of the same man who'd paid for the party, a fact that was verified by the attached documents.

In short, John Cunnings was spending more than ten times what he was earning.

He was also conducting extra business with one of the House of Lockewood's couriers—business the courier believed to be sanctioned by the bank but which, upon closer investigation by Damen's contacts, showed no bank authorization whatsoever. And that business involved the delivery of messages to and from Medford Manor.

"Oh, Damen." Anastasia lifted her head, her stunned eyes meeting Damen's. "I can't believe this."

"Cunnings." Damen dragged both hands through his hair. "Of all people." A bitter laugh. "My senior officer, the man in charge of all my overseas investments. He's been with the House of Lockewood since before my father died, and he was by my side from the day I took over. I considered him to be my right-hand man, my friend. Yet it appears I don't even know him."

Anastasia interlaced her fingers with Damen's. "To some people, money means more than anything, including friendship and integrity," she reminded him softly. "I know that's foreign to you, as it is to me. But just look at Uncle George. Look at the extremes he's willing to go to for wealth and position."

"Yes. George." Damen's jaw set. "I wonder how deeply involved Cunnings is in his sick scheme. Is he just George's spy, his connection to the fastest courier? Or is he fully aware of the cargo George deals with? Worse, is he getting paid to help find you, ship you off on the next vessel to Rouge?"

"I don't know. But we'll have to . . ." Anastasia broke off, an odd expression crossing her face.

"What is it?" Damen asked.

"I'm not sure." She pressed her lips together, shifting restlessly on Damen's lap. "But I have the strangest feeling something's happening. Something that involves Breanna."

"You think she's in danger?"

Contemplating that possibility, Anastasia frowned, slowly shook her head. "No. At least I don't think so. I don't feel panicked. I feel . . . fidgety." Her gaze met Damen's. "Whatever it is, it won't be long now. My instincts tell me that this whole nightmare is beginning to unravel."

In the alehouse, Cunnings straddled his stool, lighting a cheroot and eyeing George warily. "Medford, isn't it time you told me what's going on? I know you want Sheldrake to marry your daughter. You've been doing everything you can to keep him and your niece apart. Well, now she's gone. So why aren't you celebrating?"

"Because I don't think she's gone." George's laugh was bitter. "And because 'gone' is no longer good enough."

"You're talking about your brother's inheritance."

"I'm talking about all of it: the inheritance, the company, Sheldrake. Everything. But I can't get my hands on those things as long as Anastasia's missing."

Cunnings brought the cheroot to his lips, inhaled. "I thought you had a plan."

"I did."

"But you need your niece for that plan."

"Exactly."

Cunnings took a swallow of ale. "She'd have to be dead for you to get any of what you want—including Sheldrake, at this point. I told you, he's head over heels in love with her."

George stared at his clenched hands. "If my plan had worked, the world would have believed she was dead."

"Where *would* she have been?"

"On a ship. En route to the Continent."

One of Cunnings's brows rose. "To Rouge?"

"Yes."

A low whistle. "That sounds like a damned good plan. How much were you getting paid?"

"It doesn't matter." George shoved aside his untouched tankard of ale, glaring at Cunnings. "What matters is, Anastasia's gone. I *know* she's still in England—although where, I haven't an inkling."

"And if she reappears—without your being able to grab her before she gets to Sheldrake, ship her off to Rouge—then your plan is a thing of the past. As, given your current financial situation, are you." Cunnings inclined his head. "Have you considered sending a substitute? Or is Rouge demanding only Anastasia?"

"What Rouge is demanding is a well-bred young woman who's chaste, beautiful, and highborn. And I've got five days to deliver her."

"Really." Cunnings stabbed out his cheroot. "Let me look over the bank's client list. Maybe we'll get lucky and find a lady we can send in Anastasia's place—someone who fits Rouge's specifications, *and* who won't be missed. How would that be? Would it be worth ten percent of whatever Rouge is paying you?"

"Fine. Fine." Whereas yesterday George would have jumped at that opportunity, today he was more preoccupied with finding Anastasia and eliminating her—permanently. "But first we deal with the problem of Anastasia. Which brings me to the other business we have to discuss tonight." He gripped the edge of the table, leaning forward to regard Cunnings intently. "That associate of yours—the one you mentioned last time—how good is he at tracking people down?"

Cunnings raised his chin, met George's stare head-on. "There's no one better."

"So he'll find her."

"No matter where she's hiding, yes. He'll find her."

"And then?"

"He'll kill her."

At the next table, Breanna bit off a cry. She grabbed her tankard of ale and pressed it to her lips, taking an enormous gulp to quell her shock.

Kill her? He was going to kill Stacie?

The bitter taste of ale burned its way to her stomach, but she scarcely noticed it.

Her horrified stare met Wells's.

"I've known him for quite some time," Cunnings was continuing. "And I'm well aware of his accomplishments. He's an expert tracker and an even better shot." A meaningful pause. "He's also expensive. *Very* expensive."

George waved away the warning. "That doesn't concern me."

"It should. You owe me almost a thousand pounds, plus that ten percent if I find you another girl for Rouge. You owe a fortune to your colleagues and your creditors. How the hell are you going to pay the kind of professional we're discussing? His fees are a lot higher than mine."

"You forget about Henry's inheritance." Triumph curved George's lips. "You yourself told me Anastasia only invested twenty-five thousand pounds of that money. That leaves over one hundred seventy-five thousand pounds for me. I can pay you double what I owe you, and I can pay your friend. I'll be a rich man, Cunnings. I'll also be sole owner of Colby and Sons. In fact, handle both these assignments successfully—ending Anastasia's life and securing another candidate for Rouge—and I'll give you the notoriety you've always craved. No more second place. You'll have a seat on my Board of Directors. Why, you'll be right up there with Sheldrake."

Cunnings tossed off the rest of his ale with a flourish. "I've served like a faithful dog at my rich master's feet all these years. And what has it gotten me? Nothing but an occasional pat on the head. I deserve better. And I'm going to *get* better. You've got yourself a deal, Medford. Give me a day. I'll dig through the bank's files and contact my associate. Your niece is as good as dead."

George's eyes gleamed. "When can I meet this gifted assassin?"

"You can't. He never meets with anyone—other than

me." Cunnings shoved back his stool, aiming a pointed look at George. "Surely, given his line of work, you can understand his desire to stay anonymous."

"I suppose so." George nodded reluctantly. "How long will this take? It must happen quickly."

"If she's nearby, as you claim? A day. Two at the most. Relax. The next time you see Anastasia, it will be at her funeral."

Breanna's breath was coming in sharp rasps as she dashed down the alley and jumped into the phaeton.

She'd had to dig her nails into her thighs to keep from leaping up and lunging after Cunnings. But she had to stay level-headed—for Stacie's sake. So, she and Wells had nursed their drinks, lowering their heads as Cunnings walked past them and exited the alehouse. Not long after, her father had followed suit.

They'd given it another five minutes—enough time for George to reach his phaeton—before they acted.

Making their way outside, they'd peeked to the right, ensuring George was out of sight, before veering off to the left.

Wells hadn't come close to keeping up with her pace.

Breanna huddled in the phaeton, watching the elderly butler hurrying toward her, blood pounding in her veins. There was never a doubt what she had to do.

"Miss Breanna . . ." Wells hoisted himself into the phaeton. "Are you all right?"

The poor man was sheet-white, and Breanna lay her hand over his. "No," she replied honestly. "Are you?"

Mutely, he shook his head.

"Wells, listen to me. I've got to get to Stacie. I know

how exhausted you are, not to mention you're reeling with shock. I'd never ask this of you, but . . ."

Jaw set, Wells snatched up the reins. "I assume Miss Stacie is with Lord Sheldrake?"

"Yes."

"I recall the address. We're on our way."

It was still dark when the phaeton sped up to Damen's Town house.

Inside the sitting room, Stacie's head shot up, and she gently disengaged herself from Damen's arms, climbing off the chair and trying not to awaken him. He'd nodded off less than an hour ago and, after the emotional upheaval of the night, she was determined not to disturb him until it became absolutely necessary.

It was about to become necessary.

She'd expected something significant to occur ever since that feeling had come over her. She didn't know what, but the very knowledge had precluded her from relaxing into sleep.

Well, she was about to get her answer.

She peered out the window, tensing as she saw two shoddily dressed men climb out of a phaeton and dart up the Town house stairs.

Whatever she'd been expecting, it hadn't been this.

"Damen . . ."

He was awake and beside her before she'd finished uttering his name. His jaw clenched as he scrutinized their two surprise visitors. "Who the hell . . . ?"

"You don't know them, then?"

"No. I don't know who they are or what they want. But I'm sure as hell going to find out." He stalked over to the small corner desk, unlocked the top drawer, and extracted a pistol. Clutching the weapon in his hand, he headed off, pausing only to glare at Stacie. "Stay here—out of sight," he ordered. "These men might work for your uncle."

She opened her mouth to protest, then thought better of it. "All right. But be careful."

"I will."

Stacie listened as Damen strode down the hall and yanked open the front door. She couldn't keep herself from venturing as far as the sitting room threshold, peeking around the corner to watch.

"Who are you?" Damen was demanding. He flourished his pistol, blocking the doorway, and whoever was standing at it. "What are you doing here at this hour?"

"Damen." Breanna's voice was muffled but urgent. "It's us."

20

*S*tacie was across the threshold and down the hall in a heartbeat.

"Breanna!" She grabbed her cousin's arms, pulling her into the entranceway, and staring in amazement as she assessed Breanna's unexpected attire. Her gaze shifted to the tall, shabbily dressed man behind her, and her eyes widened. "Wells? Is that you?"

"Yes, Miss Stacie. Indeed it is."

"Why on earth are you dressed like that?"

It was Breanna who replied. "We followed Father to his meeting place. We saw and heard everything: who he met, what they talked about—oh, Stacie . . ." She stared at her hands, realized they were still shaking.

"You . . . what?" Anastasia gasped. "Are you all right?"

"Were you followed?" Damen interrupted to demand. "Is anyone after you?"

"No, we weren't followed and yes, we're fine." A pained pause. "Physically."

Damen leaned past them, peering suspiciously out into

the night and seeing nothing but a deserted street. "Let's not take any chances. Don't stay out in the open. Come in." He gestured for Wells to enter, shutting the door behind him, then leading the way to the sitting room. "I'll pour you each a drink. You look as if you've seen a ghost."

"More like a demon," Anastasia muttered. "A demon named Cunnings."

"You know?" Breanna's head jerked up as she sank into a chair.

Anastasia nodded, glancing over at Damen, who was pouring drinks at the sideboard.

"So, it really is Cunnings." He handed a glass of Madeira to Breanna, then one to Wells, a bitter scowl darkening his face. "Yes, we knew. My contacts uncovered some ugly facts about him. But I suppose I needed confirmation."

"You have it." Breanna tugged off her cap, her burnished tresses, for the first time, a bit disheveled. "He's my father's informant. That, and a great deal more."

Anastasia was too unsettled to sit still. She paced about the sitting room, looking from Breanna to Wells, a thousand questions crowding her mind, clamoring to be asked.

Her curiosity was diverted when she saw Wells lean his head wearily against the wall, looking so utterly depleted that it broke her heart.

"You're spent, my friend," she said softly, walking over and guiding him into a cushioned armchair. "You need rest."

"I'll get rest," he stated flatly, taking a healthy swallow of his drink. "*After* all this is resolved. Don't worry about me, Miss Stacie. I'm hardier than I look."

"Wells was heroic tonight," Breanna declared. "I don't know how I would have managed without him."

"Tell us what happened. How did you come to follow Uncle George? What did you overhear?" Stacie began blurting out her stream of questions.

Quickly, Breanna filled Stacie and Damen in on the talk she'd had with her father, on the plan she and Wells had conjured up, and on where it had taken them.

"So you actually saw Uncle George and Mr. Cunnings together?"

"Oh, we more than saw them," Breanna affirmed. "We sat at the table next to them. We eavesdropped on their entire conversation." She took an unsteady sip of Madeira, then lifted her chin, met Stacie's intent gaze. "Stacie, there's no easy way to tell you this. So, I'm not even going to try to soften the blow. Father's hiring an assassin. He means to have you killed."

A ponderous silence filled the room.

"Killed," Anastasia repeated woodenly—although her surprise was less acute than Breanna's. Any man who'd sell his niece—or any woman, for that matter—as a whore, was capable of anything. "What about Rouge? What happened to Uncle George's plan to export me?"

"Apparently, Father's fear that you're closing in on him, figuring out the full extent of his criminal activities, has overshadowed all else. He's convinced you're still in England. Probably to finish the investigation you began, and see him in prison. Either that, or . . ."

"Or?" Anastasia prompted.

"This is just a feeling on my part. But, judging from some of the things Father said to me, I suspect he's contemplating another reason you might have dropped out of sight—a reason that intimidates him almost as much as your plans to incriminate him."

"And what's that?"

"I think he's afraid you're with child—Damen's child. That would be almost as destructive to him as being found out. With the exception of prison, the rest of his sentence would be the same: he'd lose Uncle Henry's inheritance, control of Colby and Sons, and, of course, Damen. As for Rouge, Cunnings solved that problem for him."

"Cunnings did," Damen echoed, a vein throbbing at his forehead. "How?"

"By making some adjustments to my father's original plan. He offered to find Father a substitute for Rouge—one of the bank's female clients who, as he put it, won't be missed. That way, Father can collect his huge fee *and* get his hands on those things he'd need Stacie dead to acquire."

"I don't believe I'm hearing this."

Breanna nodded bleakly. "I don't believe I'm saying it."

Damen rubbed the back of his neck, trying to come to terms with everything he was learning. "You said George is hiring an assassin. How is he managing that?"

"He's not." There was genuine pain in Breanna's eyes, spawned by the realization that she was about to deliver a cruel blow. "Cunnings is."

Shock jolted through Damen's body, and he recoiled from its impact. *"Cunnings?"*

"Yes. I'm sorry, Damen. But Cunnings is the one with this particular contact. Father instructed him to make the arrangements."

"How the hell is an officer at my bank acquainted with a paid killer?"

Breanna spread her arms helplessly. "He didn't say. In fact, he was very secretive about the matter. When Father asked to meet with this man, Cunnings said no, that this assassin would do business only through him."

A muscle was working furiously in Damen's jaw. "What's Cunnings getting in exchange? A huge amount of money?"

"Several thousand pounds, plus ten percent of whatever Rouge pays Father. Oh, and one thing more." Breanna swallowed. "A seat on the Board of Directors at Colby and Sons."

"Which Uncle George will have sole ownership of, if I'm eliminated." Twin spots of red tinged Anastasia's cheeks. "That monster will then have just what he wants, what he's always wanted—to triumph over Papa, and to wrest away everything Grandfather held dear: his company, his name, and everything good our family represents."

"Not to mention acquiring Uncle Henry's inheritance," Breanna reminded her. "And Damen, who Father assumes will seek solace in my arms once you're gone." A bitter gleam flashed in her eyes. "Does that course of events sound familiar?"

"It's the path he took when he married your mother," Anastasia supplied, gripping the folds of her gown as if by doing so she could stem her rage. "He's decided Damen will do the same: love a woman he can't have, and marry her closest replica."

"Exactly. Father all but admitted that to me during our argument tonight. Which reminds me . . ." Breanna shoved her hand into her pocket, extracted the miniature portrait. Its frame was somewhat mangled, but the image inside remained clear as day. "I found this in Father's study after he left tonight. He'd obviously hurled it at the wall." She stretched out her arm, offered the portrait to Stacie. "I believe it's self-explanatory."

Stacie took it, her eyes widening as she recognized the likeness. "Mama," she murmured, angling the picture for inspection. "He's kept a portrait of her all these years?"

"And destroyed it the very day he decided to destroy you."

"I can't listen to this another minute." Damen strode over, refilled his drink. "Not without riding to Medford Manor and choking that son of a bitch with my bare hands." He sucked in his breath, then released it, fighting for the restraint necessary to resolve things. "However, we still have one problem—the same problem we've had since the onset. Proof. Or lack thereof. What concrete evidence, other than hearsay, do we really have against George?"

"I believe we can tie the viscount to Mr. Cunnings," Wells put in, his color somewhat restored from the Madeira. "I gave Miss Breanna the address of the courier who delivers messages between the two of them. Surely that will help."

"Thank you, Wells," Damen replied, staring broodingly into his goblet. "Unfortunately, it's not enough. Oh, I have more than enough proof that Cunnings is involved in personal business with George." He gestured toward the pile of papers on the end table. "My contacts supplied me with dates and times when that courier ran personal deliveries back and forth between Medford Manor and my bank—at Cunnings's authorization. And Cunnings has been living like a prince, buying property, jewelry for women, you name it."

Damen's hands balled into fists. "The problem is, we still haven't gotten hold of documents that directly incriminate George. Nor have we closed in on any of his colleagues to the point where we could squeeze a confession out of them, one that would implicate George, as well. If we went to Bow Street, had them seize George, he'd slip right through our fingers. They'd have only our testimony, and a few suspicious actions, to go on. Doubtless, George would have Bates exert some judicial influence—Bates, who's nearly as crooked as he is. After which, George would walk out a free man."

"What if we had a confession?" Anastasia interrupted. "A confession made directly to the authorities?"

Three pairs of eyes riveted to her.

"Stacie, have you lost your mind?" Breanna responded. "Father would never confess—not when he's sober and never to the authorities."

"He might. If he didn't know he was confessing."

"You've lost me." Breanna inclined her head quizzically in Damen's direction. "Do you know anything about this?"

A dark scowl. "Only that I'm not going to like it." He set down his drink, folded his arms across his chest, and leveled his stare at Anastasia. "Let's hear your plan. And Stacie—it had better not involve you."

Her chin jutted up. "I'm already at risk, Damen. As of tomorrow, a hired assassin will be out hunting me down. How long do you think I can hide in your Town house?" She rubbed her palms together, growing more determined the more she contemplated her plan. "Breanna, did Cunnings say anything to Uncle George implying Damen played a part in my disappearance?"

"Cunnings is convinced that Damen isn't involved. He's satisfied that Damen believes you're really on your way to the States."

"Excellent. I suspected as much, given Damen's acting performance today at the bank. So whether I dropped out of sight because I'm pregnant with Damen's child or because I'm close to exposing Uncle George as a criminal, he thinks I haven't yet gone to Damen with the news."

Still baffled, Breanna nodded.

"What if I found the evidence I was looking for? What if I got hold of exactly what it would take to throw Uncle George into prison?" A smile curved Anastasia's lips. "I'd share that proof with Damen immediately, wouldn't I?"

"But we don't have any proof."

"Your father doesn't know that."

Breanna's brows drew together. "Do you want me to plant a seed in Father's mind?"

"Absolutely not. He'd never believe you. Uncle George already knows your loyalty lies with me. No, we'll let Cunnings take care of that for us."

"How?"

"That's easy." Anastasia grinned. "Remember our pact. I'll go to the bank in the morning, pretending to be you. I'll insist on seeing Damen, alone, in his private office. Mr. Cunnings will be unbearably curious about the nature of my visit—pardon me, *Breanna's* visit. Damen and I will make sure he overhears every word of our private talk. I'll tell Damen that Anastasia contacted me, saying she found the evidence she was searching for, but that she was reluctant to deliver it to Bow Street without first getting my—Breanna's—permission. After all, turning over this evidence would mean sending Breanna's father to prison, and thereby tainting the Colby name, neither of which

Anastasia felt right doing without securing Breanna's consent first. Being the moral person Breanna is, she'll fully support Anastasia's decision once she sees the evidence."

Stacie turned to Damen. "Damen, you'll gallantly refuse to have Breanna meet Anastasia alone. You'll arrange to be there with her when she reads Stacie's evidence—which will be, say, at the docks, at ten o'clock that night. You'll tell Breanna that, once this damning proof is in your hands, *you'll* be the one to turn it over to the authorities, sparing both her and Anastasia any potential risk. Cunnings will hear this entire plan. He'll rush off to contact Uncle George, alerting him to the fact that he'd better intercept whatever evidence Anastasia has before she shares it with you and Breanna—and you present it to the authorities. Uncle George will panic. He'll arrive at the docks at nine-fifty P.M.—he's *always* prompt, and this time he'll want to be early so, hopefully, he can grab Anastasia, destroying her and her proof before you and Breanna even lay eyes on it. Sure enough, you both won't have arrived yet, giving Uncle George just the advantage he needs. When I show up, as myself, we'll have a little scene. I'll provoke him into admitting what he's done. It shouldn't be hard, given his high opinion of himself and the fact that he believes we're alone."

A triumphant smile lit Stacie's face. "What Uncle George won't know is that Bow Street has been alerted to the situation, and has men hiding behind the warehouses and listening to every word that's spoken. Once he's confessed, they can take him away. Now, are we all ready to enact my plan?"

"Absolutely not." Damen sliced the air with his palm. "Your plan neglects to take into account a few minor details. Such as, what if this assassin Cunnings hires is watching the bank when *Breanna* visits? What if he figures out it's you, not she, who's calling on me, and he decides to carry out his job then and there? He's a professional killer, Stacie; there's no guarantee you can fool him."

"We don't have to try." Breanna's eyes were glittering precisely like Anastasia's. "Stacie will stay here, in your home, safe. *I'll* come to the bank."

"And what will you tell your father?" Stacie demanded, hands on hips. "Before he thrashes you, that is?"

"I'll tell him nothing. I won't see him. I'll spend the remainder of the night right here. Then, I'll borrow one of your gowns, take our phaeton, and ride to the bank as soon as it opens."

Anastasia's jaw dropped. "And how will you explain your absence at Medford Manor?"

"I won't have to." Breanna's lips curved, and she explained to them how she'd stuffed her bed to make it look slept in. "My lady's maid will peek in, and think I'm still asleep. By the time she realizes her mistake, I'll have finished my business in London and be on my way home. Given the speed of your courier—Cunnings's courier— Father will have received his warning message before I return, so he'll already know where I've been. Beating me for it would be counterproductive: it would only alert me to the fact that he's aware of my plan, which would give me the opportunity to warn Stacie. So he'll save my whipping for *after* he deals with her." Breanna's smile widened. "But, as we all know, there won't be any 'after' for Father. He'll be en route to Newgate."

"And if he brings a weapon?" Damen demanded.

"Father's no marksman," Breanna assured him. "I'm a far more accurate shot than he is. He's also a coward.

That's why he's paying an assassin to do his dirty work, rather than taking care of things himself. When it comes to violence, Father uses his fists, not a pistol.''

"Which brings me back to the assassin." Damen's scowl deepened. "Obviously, Cunnings will alert him to our plan at the same time he alerts George. He'll respond by being right there at the docks waiting for Stacie to show up."

"I'm sure he will be," Anastasia concurred. "But Cunnings will also instruct him not to shoot me until Uncle George gets the written evidence he's there to collect. So I'll be safe until that happens. And once this assassin sees Bow Street swarming about, I doubt he'll rush forward, pistol aimed and ready."

"It's bloody risky," Damen said, with a hard shake of his head. "I don't like it."

"You'll be there to safeguard me," Anastasia reminded him. "Bring your own pistol, if it makes you feel better. Give me one, as well. But this is the only way we're going to catch Uncle George. Before he makes sure I'm . . ." She wet her lips, not eager to finish her own sentence.

"Dammit," Damen bit out, only too well aware of Stacie's implication, and the fact that she was right.

"What about Wells?" Anastasia suddenly realized aloud. "He's been at his post every morning for three decades. If he and Breanna stay here overnight, he'll be glaringly absent at dawn. That will make Uncle George suspicious."

"That's true." Damen rubbed his chin, considering the issue thoughtfully.

"I told the viscount I felt ill," Wells protested. "He won't be surprised if I'm not up and about at dawn."

"We can't take that chance," Damen replied, studying

the tired but determined butler. "Listen to me," he continued gently. "Don't be stubborn. You're exhausted. You need some rest. And Stacie's right—you'd better be at the entranceway door tomorrow morning. Even if George believes you're ill, you can't be sure he won't check on you. If he does, and finds you missing, he'll most certainly become suspicious, especially since he knows full well how deeply you care for Anastasia and Breanna. That's a risk we can't take."

Seeing the butler's oncoming protest, Damen held up his palm, warded it off. "If you want to help us, go home. I'll arrange for an appropriate change of clothes. Then my driver will take you to Medford Manor. He'll use the closed carriage, so you can get a few hours' sleep on the way. It will be later than usual when you reach your post—which is understandable, given how ill you felt the night before—but the important thing is that you'll be there. Everything must seem in place."

"That's perfect," Breanna agreed. "If Wells goes home, I won't have to face Father until ten o'clock tomorrow night. I'll stay here, drive the phaeton to the bank, then return here, spending the rest of the day with Stacie. I'll fill her in on what happens at the bank, keep her inside and out of view—" A pointed, no-nonsense look at Stacie. "—until it's time for us to leave for our rendezvous at the docks. In the meantime, Wells can tell Father I left Medford Manor right after breakfast, took the phaeton, but mentioned nothing about where I was going. Once Father receives Cunnings's message, he'll know my destination, and why I didn't disclose it to Wells."

She gazed pleadingly at the butler, appealing to him in a way she knew would ensure he went home, got the rest he so desperately needed. "Please, Wells. You'd be sparing me Lord knows how severe an argument and how painful a beating. Do it for me."

The butler's protective instincts won out, just as Breanna knew they would. "Very well, Miss Breanna. If it will shield you and help Miss Stacie, I'll do as Lord Sheldrake asks." He rose, looking tenderly from one girl to the other. "I'll do my part," he assured them, his voice quavering a bit. "And then . . . I'll pray."

As always, the House of Lockewood opened its doors at nine A.M.

And, as always, Cunnings was there at half after eight, doing his paperwork in preparation for the day.

His first client arrived promptly at nine.

A half hour later, their business together was completed.

Leaning back in his office chair, Cunnings nodded, satisfaction gleaming in his eyes. "Excellent. You'll take care of it, then."

A smug smile curved the lips of the man sitting on the opposite side of the desk. "For such an enormous sum and an even more enormous challenge? Of course."

"Good." Cunnings felt a surge of triumph, a premonition that, at long last, he was about to come into his own. "I've given you all the information I have. I realize it's not much, but . . ."

"It's all I need."

"I rather suspected as much." Cunnings rose, handing the man a sheet of paper. "By the way, here are the figures you requested. If you glance at them, you'll see . . ." His head snapped up as a din from the hallway accosted his ears.

"Please, Graff. Hurry. I left Medford Manor at the crack

of dawn in order to get here this early. I must see Lord Sheldrake now—no matter who he's meeting with. My business simply won't wait."

It was Breanna Colby's voice, Cunnings realized. Clearly, she was standing just outside his closed office door, or rather, rushing by it. She sounded breathless, and terribly distressed.

"I alerted Lord Sheldrake to the urgency of your visit, my lady," Graff was reassuring her. "He's agreed to see you at once. I assure you, I'm walking as quickly as I can."

"Good. And please see that we're not disturbed."

Her voice moved in the direction of Damen's office, and Cunnings took an inadvertent step toward the door, wondering what the hell this was all about.

"That's Breanna Colby, Anastasia's cousin," he muttered, half to himself, half to his visitor. "I'd better find out why she sounds so flustered. Maybe she's heard from her cousin. Will you excuse me?"

"By all means. I'll wait here, in case there are developments I should know about."

"Good idea." Cunnings scooped up some paperwork. Then, he crossed over, opened his door, and wandered casually into the hall.

Graff was on his return trip, shaking his head in puzzlement as he headed back to his post.

"What was that commotion?" Cunnings inquired.

"Lady Breanna," Graff supplied. "She has some critical business to discuss with Lord Sheldrake." An exasperated sigh. "Women can be so excitable at times." He shrugged, continuing on his way until he disappeared from view.

Cunnings moved down the hall, pausing a few feet from Damen's office. He leaned against the wall, scanning his papers as if he were actually reading them, in the event someone walked by or Sheldrake abruptly emerged.

The marquess's door was shut nearly all the way, a slim crack being the only open space.

It was enough—not for observing, but definitely for eavesdropping.

"She's *here*? In England?" Sheldrake was asking incredulously.

"Yes," Breanna replied. "Apparently, she'd uncovered information that implicates Father in some horrible crimes. But she had no proof. So she pretended to leave the country, only to stay right here and gather the evidence she needs to send him to Newgate."

"I don't believe this." Sheldrake sounded badly shaken. "Is she all right? Did you see her?"

"She's fine. And, no, I didn't see her. She sent a messenger to Medford Manor late last night, instructed him to throw pebbles at my window until he got my attention. I was lucky. Father had gone out after midnight and Wells was feeling ill and had retired early. I slipped downstairs and met the messenger at the door. He gave me Stacie's note. Then, I sent him on his way, quickly, before Father could return and ask questions. No one saw him but me."

"Did Anastasia's note tell you where she's staying?"

"Only that she's somewhere in London. Her note said that knowing her exact whereabouts might put me in danger."

"Did she tell you what proof she had?"

"Not specifically. Just that it would shock me and strip Father of everything—including his freedom. So it must be despicable. In any case, Stacie insisted that I see it with my own eyes and decide what I want her to do. She won't turn the evidence over to the authorities without my permission." Breanna drew a shaky breath. "It is, after all, my father she'd be relegating to Newgate. Not to mention the scandal this entire affair would cause our family."

"Lord," Sheldrake muttered. "Whatever George did, it must be contemptible. Otherwise, Anastasia would never ask you to betray your own father."

"Exactly."

"What do you intend to do—or need I ask?"

"I'm going to support Stacie's decision," Breanna responded instantly. "Our grandfather would want nothing less. If Father is guilty of some horrible crime, he should be punished. The Colby name will survive, and ultimately prevail." A troubled pause. "But Damen, to be honest with you, I'm terrified of what Father will do to me if he finds out I'm involved. Despite my false show of bravado—waving that pistol around as I did—I'm truly afraid of the man. I don't know why I ran to you, but the truth is, I had nowhere else to turn."

"You did the right thing." Sheldrake's voice was taut with strain. "I'll help you. Tell me when and where Anastasia expects you to meet her."

"Tonight. At the London docks—the deserted southwest section nearest the Tower. At ten o'clock."

"Fine. I'll go with you."

"What?" Now Breanna sounded panicked. "But, she's expecting only *me*. If she sees someone else, she might bolt."

"Not if that someone is me. I love her, Breanna. Anastasia knows she can trust me." Sheldrake paused, blowing out his breath slowly, thoughtfully. "On the other hand, you have a point. Between the night and the fog, she'll see the silhouette of a man and, unless I have time to call out and let her know it's me, she'll take off. The best thing would be if we both went. You can coax her out, and I'll be there to lend my support—to both of you."

"And what about the evidence?"

"I'll take it directly to Bow Street. You and Anastasia will wait for me in my carriage. We won't venture back to Medford Manor until the authorities have arrested your father."

"After which we'll all be safe." Breanna emitted a shaky sigh. "I don't know how to thank you."

"No thanks are necessary." A hesitant pause. "I suggest you spend the day in Town. Feel free to use my house as your own. Shop, call on friends, do whatever you most enjoy. But don't ride back to Kent. The last thing you need is a confrontation with your father. Answering his questions was bad enough when you knew nothing. Now that you've actually heard from Anastasia, I'm not sure you'd be able to successfully lie about it. And if George should suspect . . ."

"Say no more," Breanna interrupted, an audible tremor in her voice. "I can't face Father. Not now, knowing what I know, planning what I've planned. I'll do just what you suggested—stay in Town, then go to your house until tonight's meeting." A rustle of material, alerting Cunnings to the fact that Breanna had risen, was heading for the door.

He edged back toward his office, head cocked as he listened to Sheldrake and Breanna's parting words.

"I'll see you tonight," she murmured.

"I'll be home in plenty of time," Sheldrake vowed. "We'll be at the docks promptly at ten."

Breanna opened the door, stepped into the hallway.

The area was deserted.

"How did it go?" Stacie pounced on Breanna the instant she walked into the Town house.

Her cousin grinned, slipping off her gloves as she strolled toward the sitting room. "Like a perfectly acted play."

"Cunnings was there?"

"He arrived at half after eight, just as Damen said he would. By the time I dashed into the bank, he was ensconced in his office with a client."

"You're sure he heard you?"

"Oh, he heard every word," Breanna stated confidently. "I began my speech when I was right outside Cunnings's office—the third door to the right, just as Damen instructed me. Poor Graff," she added, laughing. "He's never seen me so overwrought. I think he was torn between consoling me and choking me to death."

Anastasia's eyes sparkled. "It sounds like you were very convincing."

"Oh, I was. But then, so was Damen. Once Graff delivered me to his office—after which he darted off like a prisoner who'd been granted his freedom—both Damen and I played our parts superbly. At first, we waited."

"Three minutes, as planned?"

Breanna's brows lifted. "It only took two. We shut the door all but a crack, positioned ourselves near enough to be heard, and watched the outside wall. Less than thirty seconds later, we saw Cunnings's shadow hovering on the wall not ten feet from Damen's office. That's when I launched into a recounting of my dilemma."

"And Cunnings didn't budge?" Anastasia prodded, circling Breanna like an anxious parent. "The entire time you and Damen talked, he stayed outside and listened?"

"Up to the very last word, yes. In fact, I actually spent an exaggerated moment shaking out my skirts to give him enough time to get back to his office. When I emerged, he was gone."

"Wonderful," Anastasia breathed. "Then, by now, the note is on its way to Uncle George, and Damen is on his way to Bow Street."

"Yes, and a paid assassin is out combing the streets of London looking for you," Breanna reminded her, all humor vanishing.

Rather than terror, Anastasia felt a surge of impending victory, a sense that the end was in sight. "Yes, but he won't find me. Not until we want him to." Her eyes glittered with anticipation. "At which time, Bow Street will grab him."

"And if he spies them first and escapes?"

A careless shrug. "Then, after tonight, it's *he* who will be the hunted. With Uncle George in prison and Cunnings a cornered rat—pressured into revealing the names of his contacts—this assassin is all but captured."

Breanna nodded, trying hard to share Anastasia's optimistic appraisal.

Still, she thought, an uneasy prickle crawling up her spine. Gut instinct warned her it wouldn't be that simple.

21

It was nine forty-five.

George steered his phaeton through the last of the rutted roads that led to the docks, gripping the reins more tightly as he neared the end of his journey. The fog was too thick to see clearly, but he could smell the Thames, hear the screech of gulls circling overhead. He was trembling, whether with apprehension or relief that this would finally be over, he wasn't sure.

Cunnings's message had been terse and to the point. Anastasia would be here tonight, carrying with her some unknown proof that was damning enough to send him to Newgate. Cunnings had alerted the assassin, who would be there to give her a proper farewell, *after* she'd relinquished the evidence to George.

How Cunnings had learned about Anastasia's impending appearance was the infuriating part.

Breanna.

George's insides clenched with rage every time he contemplated the fact that it was *his daughter* Anastasia was meeting with, *his daughter* to whom Anastasia was turning over this proof.

His obedient little Breanna meant to betray him.

She actually intended to turn him over to Bow Street, relegate him to prison—and at her precious cousin's bidding.

Well, he'd deal with Breanna and her lack of loyalty later, after the proof was in his hands and Anastasia ceased to be a problem.

Then there was Sheldrake.

The fact that he was joining Breanna here tonight was the main reason George had arrived so early. It was imperative that Anastasia's evidence be destroyed before Sheldrake could see it. That was the only prayer George had of seeing his plan through, regaining all that was his, and still acquiring Sheldrake as a son-in-law. Oh, the marquess would never really trust him again, of that he was certain. But Damen Lockewood was a pragmatic man. And without proof, he wouldn't do anything to ruin George, not given the strong history that existed between their families. Nor would he allow whatever indiscretions George might or might not have committed to cloud his opinion of Breanna. After all, even if her father wasn't all Sheldrake had hoped, that was in no way Breanna's doing. She was as honorable as the day was long. Sheldrake knew that firsthand. He might not love Breanna, but he most certainly liked her. Moreover, despite Anastasia's intrusive presence hovering between them, he and Breanna had grown much closer these past weeks.

And they'd grow closer still as a result of Anastasia's tragic death. Why, within a few short months, Breanna would probably become Mrs. Damen Lockewood.

The very notion eased George's rage.

But not his trepidation.

He had to carry tonight off perfectly. He'd get the proof from Anastasia, hold it high over his head so the assassin could see it, then watch Anastasia take her last breath.

With any luck, he'd be gone by the time Sheldrake and Breanna arrived. If so, the marquess would never know he'd been here, much less that he was involved in Anastasia's shooting. As her uncle, he could grieve beside Sheldrake at her funeral. After which, the marquess would need some time to mourn her death—a period of bereavement Breanna could help him through.

If things happened that way, then everything could turn out just as he'd planned.

But if not, if Breanna and Sheldrake burst into view before he had time to bolt, he'd play the scene of a lifetime. He'd rush over to Anastasia's lifeless body, lament her untimely passing, caused by a smuggler's stray bullet. Hell, he'd shed real tears if he had to. Between those tears, he'd explain how Anastasia had summoned him, expressed her regret over being too impulsive, believing him guilty of trying to wrest away her inheritance, only to find she'd been wrong. The proof she'd been so sure was incriminating had turned out to be false.

It had been her intention, he'd claim, to offer him a formal apology at tonight's meeting with Breanna—a meeting she'd scheduled before she realized her mistake.

But now she was gone . . . and it was too late . . .

George's lips thinned into a grim line. No matter what happened here tonight, he had to convince Sheldrake or, at the very least, give him pause, make him contemplate the possibility of George's innocence. He *had* to.

Reaching the end of the road, George pulled the phaeton over and left it behind a warehouse.

He'd go the rest of the way by foot.

Warily, he headed toward the Thames, trying to see through the fog and make out the shape of a woman moving along the docks.

All was still.

Pebbles crunched under his feet, and the smell of the river grew stronger, the silence thicker.

The Tower of London was just on the other side of this section of warehouses, he thought, veering to his right. She had to be hiding near here somewhere.

He peered around the corner of the first building he reached, eyeing the deserted area beyond, strewn with empty bottles and a few scurrying rats.

"Breanna?" a tentative voice called. "You're early."

A slender shadow eased out of the shadows about twenty feet away from where George stood. She took a step, then halted when she saw the larger frame of her arrival. "Damen?" she tried. "Is that you?"

"Yes," George hissed back, his whisper too fleeting to be differentiated as his and not Sheldrake's.

"Where's Breanna?" Anastasia took a few more cautious steps in his direction.

It was enough.

"With Sheldrake, I presume," George replied in his normal tone. He lunged forward, grabbed Anastasia's arm. "What's the matter?" he bit out, seeing the shock register on her face. "Aren't you pleased to see your uncle?"

"What are you doing here?" she managed, struggling to free herself.

"You know the answer to that. I'm here to collect what's mine."

"I don't know what you're talking about."

"Stop lying, Anastasia." He dragged her to him, his eyes blazing with rage. "And don't play games with me. Whatever proof you've found, I want it. I want it *now*."

"And then what?" Anastasia shot back, abandoning all pretense. "Will you throw me on the nearest ship to Calais, ship me off to Rouge?"

George started, but recovered himself quickly. "You are well-informed, aren't you?" He glared at her, loathing the rebellious glint in her eyes that refused to be extinguished, despite the fact that she was obviously afraid. "So bloody defiant. I pity the man Rouge would have sold you to."

"Would have?" Anastasia stopped struggling, went very still. "Does that mean you've reconsidered? That you're not going to sell me as a whore?"

A thoughtful pause. "Perhaps not. *If* you give me that proof you have." He glanced about, seeing no documents in her other hand. "Where is it?"

"You're frightened," Anastasia taunted softly. "I don't blame you. Selling women as chattel to warm the beds of strangers. Stealing from the company your father founded. Plotting to stage your niece's death so you could get her inheritance. I'd be frightened, too. Especially if that same niece had evidence of my crimes. Not to mention confessions by Lyman and Bates. Why, as we speak, both those men are signing statements incriminating you. Then again, what choice did they have? With proof that Lyman accepted illegal payments from you *and* that Bates supplied you with workhouse girls to export to the Continent as whores, your two colleagues were desperate to save their own skin. They happily turned you over to Bow Street in exchange for leniency."

"*Shut up!*" George shouted. His rage was spiraling out of control. He could feel it. "*Shut up and give me that proof!*"

"Why should I? I'm not stupid. Neither were Lyman and Bates. They realized that, as accomplices, their necks weren't pulled nearly as tight in the noose as yours is. You're the head of everything." Anastasia's smile was mocking. "As for their loyalty—it didn't extend as far as sacrificing their own freedom. Especially since their incentive to do so has worn a bit thin. Let me think—how long has it been since you paid them what they're owed?"

George drew back his arm, struck Anastasia across the face with such force that her head snapped back. "You lying bitch," he snarled. "Lyman and Bates would never confess. They're as involved with Rouge as I am."

"Not quite," Anastasia refuted, teeth clenched against the pain shooting through her cheek and down her neck. "Granted, Lyman supplies the ships, and Bates the women. But it's *you* Rouge communicates with; *you* who orchestrates all the exchanges. And it's *you* who reaps the largest profit. Also, neither Bates nor Lyman are stealing from their companies or attempting to steal from their dead brother."

"That money is mine!" George bellowed through the savage red haze coursing through him. "All of it. Henry's, the company's. I'm entitled to it. And I intend to have it—the minute I get you out of the way."

"Why are you entitled to it? As compensation—because Papa stole Mama? He didn't steal her, Uncle George. She loved him."

With a violent curse, George's free hand whipped out, wrapped around Anastasia's throat. "Your mother was a whore," he roared, his fingers biting into her tender skin. "*You're* a whore. Whatever Rouge had in store for you was too good. You should be thrashed until you bleed, taken until that brazen spark is snuffed out of your eyes, the life snuffed out of your body. And I intend to see that it is." He began walking, dragging her toward the warehouses with him. "Damn you, Anastasia—where is that proof? Do I have to choke you to death to get it?"

A silhouette lunged out of the shadows, and a fist shot out, slamming George in the jaw and sending him reeling. "Get your hands off her, Medford," Damen commanded, shoving Anastasia to safety and advancing toward a wild-eyed George.

"Sheldrake," he gasped.

Damen's fist shot out again, this time sending George toppling to the dirt. "You filthy bastard. I'd like to kill you here and now."

"Don't, Lord Sheldrake." A uniformed Bow Street runner strode out, gesturing for two of his colleagues to follow. "It's not worth dirtying your hands. We'll see that the viscount gets what he deserves. We have everything we need to do that."

The three officers stalked forward, yanking George to his feet, then grabbing his arms, jerking them behind his back.

"You arranged this?" George managed, looking bewilderedly from Anastasia to Damen. "Both of you?"

"*All* of us, Father." Breanna walked forward, coming to stand beside her cousin.

"*Breanna?*" George's eyes looked like they were going to bug out of his head. "*You?*"

Her nod was emphatic, bitter tears glistening on her lashes. "How else would Mr. Cunnings have known where and when to direct you?"

George swallowed convulsively—once, twice. "You're saying . . . this morning . . . your visit to Sheldrake . . . your conversation . . ." His eyes widened in sudden realization. "The evidence Anastasia has . . ."

"All fabricated," Breanna supplied. "At least until we get into your private files to confirm it. We simply set the trap. You walked into it." She signaled to the Bow Street men to take him away. "Maybe now Grandfather can rest in peace."

She turned her back to him, his furious verbal assault falling on deaf ears, growing more indistinct as Bow Street dragged him off.

Her head held high, Breanna turned her attention to Stacie, who was standing in the circle of Damen's arms.

"Are you all right, sweetheart?" he was asking, tracing the red marks on her cheek with gentle fingers.

"I'm fine," she assured him, kissing his palm. "I'm more than fine. I'm thankful and I'm relieved."

"You were incredibly brave," Breanna declared.

Anastasia gazed proudly at her cousin. "So were you. My ordeal lasted only a few minutes. Yours lasted a lifetime. Your inner strength never ceases to amaze me. Right down to the way you just faced your father, told him the part you played in his capture, when you could so easily have stayed in the shadows, spared yourself the ugliness of his reaction. And why? Because it was important to you that he knew of your commitment, not only to doing what was lawful and right, but to our family and to Grandfather." A glowing smile. "You're the most courageous woman I know."

"*One* of them," Damen corrected her. "I'm holding the other." Anger slashed his handsome features. "I almost charged out and beat George senseless when he hit you. But I promised Bow Street I wouldn't interfere until they signaled to me that they'd gotten enough of a confession to do what they had to." His voice grew husky. "I'm sorry he hurt you."

"It was worth it," Anastasia replied fervently. "Because now he'll never hurt anyone again. Also, as Breanna just said, Grandfather can finally rest in peace. As can Mama and Papa." She reached up and kissed Damen, then turned to hug Breanna fiercely. "Let's go home."

She took a few steps, Breanna and Damen following suit.

Breanna had no idea what made her glance back. All she knew was that that eerie sensation she'd experienced earlier returned, crawling up her spine like some odious insect, propelling her to act.

She could feel a pair of eyes boring through her.

She pivoted. Her fingers slipped reflexively into her pocket, as her gaze swept the docks beyond the warehouses.

A silhouette emerged from the fog. A glint of metal flashed in the night.

It was a pistol.

Breanna never hesitated.

In one smooth motion, she whipped out her own pistol, aimed, and fired.

A scream of pain split the darkness. The dark figure

grabbed his hand, his gun thudding softly as it struck the ground.

He bent, recovering his weapon just as Damen whirled around, pulling out his own pistol.

Damen never had the chance to shoot.

The silhouette melted into the night.

"My God," Anastasia breathed, shock reverberating through her. "The assassin. But I don't understand—why would he go ahead and kill me when he obviously wasn't going to get paid?"

"He must not have seen Bow Street," Breanna murmured, still staring at the spot where the armed killer had stood. "The fog is thick. He must have heard Father's voice, then saw the three of us standing alone. I guess he assumed the proof had been confiscated and the deal was still on."

"He'll find out the truth soon enough," Damen muttered, equally shaken. "If he survives that wound you just inflicted. Judging from his scream, it was pretty bad."

"Bad, but not fatal," Breanna corrected. "The bullet struck his hand. I saw him grab for it. The important thing is that I stopped him from doing what he came here to do. When he finds out Father's been arrested, he'll seek an assignment elsewhere."

"Oh, Breanna." Anastasia went to her cousin, grasped her arms. "Do you realize you just saved my life?"

Still trembling, Breanna smiled, although a fine mist veiled her eyes. "Consider it repayment, then. For all the times you saved mine. Beginning with that night we made our pact."

Cunnings was working later than usual.

It was half after ten, and he was still at the bank,

perusing the files to select just the right woman to send Rouge.

Once he found her, he'd haul her onto that ship himself, arrange for her immediate passage to Rouge. That would certainly earn him extra points with Medford. Why, the viscount would be eternally grateful for his assistance. After all, as of tonight, Medford would be mourning the death of his precious niece. He couldn't very well conduct business. Cunnings, on the other hand, could. So he'd visit Medford Manor, pay his respects, and offer to take care of the whole process. Rouge would get his shipment, Medford would get his son-in-law . . .

. . . and he would get his spot on the Board of Directors.

Leaning over his desk, Cunnings doubled his efforts, smiling as he imagined Sheldrake's expression when he learned they were going to share equal roles at Colby and Sons.

Finally. He'd have all the wealth, influence, and position he deserved.

Cunnings's thoughts were interrupted by the telltale click of his office door—a click that told him he was no longer alone.

His head shot up, and he started as he saw who his visitor was.

"What are you doing . . . Dear Lord!" he exclaimed, jumping to his feet as he saw the stream of blood flowing from the man's hand, seeping through the torn forefinger of his glove and trickling down his wrist, saturating his coat sleeve. "What the hell happened?"

"Breanna Colby happened," the man snapped, sweat

pouring from his face as the pain of his wound lanced through him. "The little bitch shot me."

"She shot . . ." Cunnings wet his lips with the tip of his tongue, his mind racing. "Before or after you killed Anastasia?"

"I didn't kill Anastasia, you stupid fool. It was a trap. Bow Street was there. Anastasia goaded Medford into confessing everything aloud. They took him away."

The color drained from Cunnings's face. "Medford arrested? Then why did you . . . ?"

"I never fail, Cunnings. Money or not. I waited for the perfect moment. Then I acted." Fury darkened his sweat-drenched face. "I didn't make a sound. I don't know how the bitch knew I was there. But she did. I would have killed them both—one bullet per cousin—if Sheldrake hadn't gotten in the way."

"Sheldrake saw all this?" Cunnings asked with a sick sense of dread. "He heard Medford's confession?"

"Every word." A determined glint flashed through his physical agony. "Including the part about you."

"Christ." Cunnings sank into his seat, burying his head in his hands. "How the hell will I . . . ?"

The click of a trigger. "You won't."

Again, Cunnings's head snapped up. This time, his eyes widened with terror as he saw the pistol aimed at him, the assassin's blood trickling from his mutilated forefinger, which hung limply beside the gun's barrel, his middle finger against the trigger.

"You're the only one who can identify me," came the icy assessment. "You'd give them my name in a heart-beat."

"No," Cunnings whispered. "I wouldn't."

"You would." A wince, and the man swallowed, fighting to combat the excruciating pain. "Besides, I've never failed before. Until now. And you're responsible."

"Please . . ."

A bitter smile curved the man's lips. "Don't worry. My failure is only a temporary setback. I'll finish it. At the same time that I torture and kill the bitch who did this to me." A mock salute with his good hand. "Good-bye, Cunnings."

The shot echoed through the walls of the bank.

The assassin slipped into the street, ducking into an alley and doubling over with pain.

Cunnings was taken care of. In addition, the intriguing set of notes on his desk had been confiscated, to be put to use at a later time.

Now he had to get this wound fixed. Not in England. Somewhere else. Somewhere where they didn't know him. He stared at his saturated glove. The wound was bad. His entire forefinger had been severed. He'd had to shoot Cunnings with his middle finger. It was awkward. He'd need his weapon modified. Fine. He'd take care of that, too—*and* master the new weapon. There were no other options. His craft, his incomparable skill, would overcome this setback. He was a genius. And no amateur chit was going to take that away from him.

He'd do what he had to.

After which, his first order of business would be to come back and even the score, take care of that bitch. She'd die slowly, with the maximum degree of anguish.

Completing tonight's unfinished business would be part of that anguish—relatively easy to accomplish. Those two damnable cousins were rarely apart.

Another agonizing pain shot through him, and he emitted a muffled groan. He groped in his pocket, pulled out a handkerchief, then gritted his teeth as he tied a ruthlessly binding tourniquet around the wound. There. That would have to do, at least until he could get himself to a doctor.

He needed passage on the next ship leaving for the Continent. He had no time to waste.

But he'd be back. Lady Breanna Colby could count on it.

Another gathering pain shot through Sara, and she emitted a stifled groan. He groped in his pocket, pulled out a tumbler-like... hand puller, the brushes, he ran a culinary... surface to the next... amount of wound. Then... could turn to an orderly and decant all... to a doctor...

I'll recited to urge on the work... time through... to the Colonel. He had do... to water.

But he d... in 1942. I say license doing... and sniffing at it...

Epilogue

The south gardens at Medford Manor had never looked more exquisite. Despite the fact that summer was at an end and the cooler days of September had arrived, the blossoms had never been brighter, the oaks' branches never more green.

Or perhaps it only seemed that way to Anastasia.

"My, you're looking euphoric," Breanna teased, as they strolled toward their favorite oak. "That wouldn't be because next week at this time you'll be the Marchioness of Sheldrake, now would it?"

With a glowing smile, Anastasia gazed about the gardens. "It just might. Actually, I pinch myself each morning to make sure I'm not dreaming. For weeks I wondered if the time would ever come when we all could put our fears behind us, when the nightmare we've been living would stop haunting us, and we could bid the past goodbye. I guess I'm only now starting to believe it's possible."

"Oh, it's possible, all right," Breanna assured her. "And no one deserves the resulting happiness more than you and Damen." A twinkle. "What's more, I think your betrothed agrees. In fact, judging by the way he stares at you when he thinks no one is watching, I suspect he might just drag you down that aisle to become his wife."

"He won't have to. If Wells doesn't restrain me with a firm grip, I'll probably run to the altar at breakneck speed."

Laughter bubbled up in Breanna's throat. "That might be one shock too many for our guests. Most of them still haven't recovered from your unorthodox business proposals at your coming-out ball. And now—a streak of silver and white, rushing down the aisle to accost her bridegroom—I don't think they're quite ready for that. Why, dozens of swooning guests would litter the aisle, blocking your return path."

Anastasia grinned. "Shocking the *ton* yet again. It sounds appealing. But for Wells's sake, I'll control myself. He's nervous enough about giving me away. But I can't think of anyone Grandfather would rather have represent him or Papa at my side."

"Nor can I. Wells is the perfect choice." Breanna glanced about them, savoring the beauty of the garden. "And this is the perfect spot for your wedding breakfast. There are so many happy memories here. It's fitting that we add one more—one extraordinarily important one."

"I agree." Anastasia reached the oak, traced its bark lovingly as she gazed up at the canopy of leaves. "Not to mention that if the guests become too tiresome, I can always scoot up here and try again to touch the sky."

A reminiscent smile touched Breanna's lips. "Don't stretch too high. You'll fall and reopen that scar of yours. And I have no intention of tending my cousin's injuries on her wedding day." Tenderness softened her features.

"Besides, I think your climb will be unnecessary. The way you and Damen feel about each other, you're closer to heaven than any oak could take you."

Anastasia nodded, twisting a tumbled strand of hair about her finger, a look of wonder in her eyes. "I always knew love would be wonderful. But I never imagined *how* wonderful—not until Damen." Concern darted across her face, and she regarded her cousin with probing intensity. "Breanna, I want the same for you. I want you to find someone who loves you every bit as much as you deserve. I want your heart to skip a beat every time he walks into the room, and to pound furiously every time he takes you in his arms."

Breanna gave a tolerant shake of her head. "Stacie, I know what a romantic you are. And I love you for it, and for wanting me to be happy. But please try to understand. I *am* happy. Oh, I want all those things you just described—someday. For now, though, I'm so thrilled to be free. Free from Father's cruelty, free from the isolation he imposed on me. For the first time, I can do things like meet new people, visit their homes. I can invite other young women to tea. Why, Lady Margaret Warner and her friends aren't nearly as snobbish as I thought. These diversions may seem frivolous to you, but that's because you've been able to do them all your life. I haven't. So, I don't mind waiting a little longer to meet the man of my dreams."

A grudging sniff. "Damen said you needed time to come into your own. He likened you to a butterfly emerging from its cocoon." Anastasia rolled her eyes, folded her arms across her breasts. "The insufferable man is right again."

Breanna's eyes sparkled. "This marriage is going to be a lifetime of fireworks. Neither you nor Damen will ever be bored. Nor will I, just watching you." She gathered up her skirts and lowered herself to the grass, relishing the fact that grass stains were no longer a horrifying prospect, but a welcome result of a brush with nature. "I, in the meantime, will have the chance to flap my gossamer wings. You have no idea how excited I am."

"I think I'm beginning to." Anastasia dropped unceremoniously to the grass beside her. "Will you be all right while Damen and I are away? Three months is a long time for us to leave you alone."

"Alone?" One of Breanna's brows shot up in amusement. "I have a houseful of servants who are as elated about being released from bondage as I am. And I have Wells looking out for me—Wells, who's more of a father to me than my own ever was. I'm fine, Stacie. I promise you. There are no lingering scars from Father's actions. He and his colleagues are locked up. Cunnings is dead, and his paid assassin gone. Rouge has pulled up stakes and vanished. The ordeal is over. I want you and Damen to leave on your wedding trip as planned. Open that wonderful new bank of yours. Take long moonlight walks in Philadelphia. And try not to start another revolution—that is, during those scant hours when you're not abed." She blushed at her own comment, blurted out before she could censor it.

Anastasia dissolved into laughter. "The butterfly is already out of its cocoon," she observed. "By the time Damen and I return, you'll be soaring the skies like an eagle." She took Breanna's hand in hers. "We'll be back before Christmas. Then, as soon as we return, we'll hold a huge party at Medford Manor—to celebrate the holidays and both of our twenty-first birthdays. By that time we'll both be of age."

"Yes we will." Breanna plucked a blade of grass, an air of gravity settling over her. "I'll miss you, Stacie," she said softly. "Not so much on your wedding trip, but after. We're finally reunited after ten long years. Selfishly, I suppose I'm not ready to say good-bye. Even if you're only off to London, where you and Damen will be living. It's still not the same as having you here."

Anastasia swallowed deeply, her grip on Breanna's hand tightening. "I'll miss you, too. Terribly. And I'll miss Medford Manor." Tears blurred her eyes as she gazed, once again, across the acres and acres of beloved grounds. "Part of my heart will always be here. Because you, Wells, Mrs. Rhodes—and everyone from Mrs. Charles to Lizzy—are my family. And family is the most precious gift life has to offer. No matter where I go, Medford Manor will always be home . . ." She broke off, a certain conversation she and Damen had shared on a moonlit balcony resurging like the tide.

Is it possible to miss home even when you're right there in it?

Yes. When that home is no longer the same as the one you remember. And the one you remember is the one you miss.

And then the second conversation, the one they'd had in bed, after their long hours of lovemaking.

I think about that money often, about what Breanna and I can do with it that would ensure Grandfather's wishes are carried out. I feel as if the answer is right here in our own backyard, only we have yet to see it. But whatever it is, it has to be something that would bind our family together, not only now but for generations—actually, forever, if I had my way . . . a uniting force, a means to entwine Breanna's and my futures, and the futures of our children.

I think you've just begun to answer your own question. The rest will come with time. You and Breanna will see to it.

Once again, the brilliant Marquess of Sheldrake was right.

Anastasia jerked upright so abruptly that Breanna started. "That's it!" she exclaimed, jumping to her feet, shading her eyes as she peered across the manicured grounds. "That's absolutely it!"

"What's it?" Breanna demanded, rising as well.

"Grandfather's money. *That's* what we'll do with it." Anastasia turned, gripped both Breanna's hands in hers. "Damen said the answer would come with time, and it has. Breanna, let's build another manor, several more manors, right here on these grounds. There are hundreds and hundreds of acres here, more than enough to accommodate a half-dozen houses. The first will be for Damen and me—our new home. Oh, I know his Town house is right near the bank, but this is one inconvenience I know he won't mind suffering. Besides . . ." Her grin was impish. ". . . I have a feeling my soon-to-be husband will be spending a lot less time at his desk and a lot more time working at home. Building a home in Kent will ensure that."

She paused, only to suck in her breath. "Anyway, after our new manor is complete, we can wait awhile, then begin construction of the others—the ones for our children and their families. Each manor will have plenty of privacy, yet be part of the growing Colby circle. What do you think?"

Breanna's mouth finally snapped shut, and joy exploded across her face. "I think you're more brilliant than Damen, after all." She whirled about, surveying the grounds, then turned and hugged Anastasia fiercely. "Choose the spot for your manor," she urged, drawing back to regard Stacie with spiraling exhilaration. "Now. Immediately. If we hire an architect right away, he can begin while you and Damen are on your wedding trip. You'll be able to move in that much sooner."

An emphatic nod. "Damen will be here in an hour. I'll talk to him the minute he arrives."

Anastasia fell silent, feeling a sense of rightness so profound it made her ache. Slowly, she raised her eyes to the heavens, sharing the feeling with the man who'd inspired it.

"He knows, Stacie," Breanna whispered, following her cousin's gaze. "Grandfather already knows. He's sharing our joy, just as he always will."

Breanna's words sang inside Anastasia's heart a week later when, on the arm of a proud, beaming Wells, she walked down the aisle and joined with the man she loved.

The chapel was filled, the approving murmurs and stares all directed at her as, clad in a shimmering gown of silver and white, Anastasia took Damen's hand, declared her vows to him, and he to her.

The wedding breakfast, held in the very spot where Stacie and Breanna once climbed, and where they'd made their all-important decision last week, was a veritable paradise of flowers, an endless stretch of manicured greenery.

One that was theirs forever, Anastasia reflected joyously, separating herself from the throng of guests long enough to gaze across the grounds, to savor the fact that her future with Damen lay right here.

"Admiring the site of our new home?" Damen asked huskily, coming up behind his bride and wrapping his arms about her waist.

"Treasuring it," Anastasia amended, leaning back against her new husband's solid strength.

"I love you, Lady Sheldrake," Damen murmured solemnly, burying his lips in her hair. "More than you'll ever know."

Anastasia turned, gazed up at him, all the love in the world shining in her eyes. "And I love you. More than I ever dreamed possible."

A wicked gleam. "Enough to slip away from your own celebration?"

An impish grin. "Definitely enough." She traced his lapel with her fingertip. "See? If our new manor were already completed, we wouldn't even have to waste time riding to London."

"If our manor was already completed, I would have whisked you into it an hour ago."

Anastasia searched Damen's face, a trace of anxiety clouding her own. "You really are pleased about the way Breanna and I are spending Grandfather's inheritance, aren't you?"

A look of fierce pride darkened Damen's gaze. "I'm more than pleased. I'm so bloody proud of you I could burst. You picked the most fitting tribute, the most rewarding investment in yours and Breanna's future that your grandfather could ever wish for. He was blessed to have you. And now, so am I."

Tears dampened Anastasia's lashes. "Damen . . ."

"Come, my beautiful bride," he breathed, brushing her lips in a soft, poignant caress. "It's time to seal our vows in the most magnificent way possible." He glanced beyond her, at the very spot where their manor would soon stand. "Those workmen had best toil round the clock," he muttered. "Because by the time we return from our wedding trip . . ." An insightful spark flickered in his eyes, and he drew Anastasia to him, his hands settling on her waist, his thumbs skimming the layers of her wedding gown that covered her now flat abdomen. "Let's just say that my Town house is far too cramped for what I have in mind."

A watery smile. "And what is that, my lord? A dividend from our joint venture?"

"Oh, more than one, Mrs. Lockewood," Damen assured her. "This ultimate partnership we just committed ourselves to is going to reap more rewards than you can begin to imagine." He held her stare, his expression profound, utterly certain. "In fact, my instincts tell me that we're going to give your grandfather every bit of the extensive, loving family he prayed for."

Author's Note

I'm going to be very tight-lipped, so I don't give away a single clue about Breanna's story, *The Silver Coin*, which Pocket Books is releasing next month, right on the heels of *The Gold Coin*.

All I'll say is this: the few insidious, lingering embers of the crimes committed in *The Gold Coin* will re-ignite, blazing forth to threaten Breanna in the most terrifying way possible.

It seems there's just one man who can save her . . .

Enjoy the preview Pocket Books has provided of *The Silver Coin*. I hope Breanna and Royce keep you at the edge of your seat.

Happy reading!

Andrea Kane

P.S. If you'd like a copy of my most recent newsletter (keeping you up-to-date on all my titles—past, present, and immediate future), just send a legal-sized stamped, self-addressed envelope to:

P.O. Box 5104
Parsippany, NJ 07054–6104

Or visit my exciting web site and read the newsletter electronically at:

http://www.andreakane.com

My e-mail address is:

WriteToMe@andreakane.com

SONNET BOOKS
PROUDLY PRESENTS

The Silver Coin
Andrea Kane

**Coming next month from
Sonnet Books**

The following is a preview of
The Silver Coin. . . .

London, England
December 1817

She was going to die.

It was only a question of when.

He sat calmly at a corner table of the London coffee-house, sipping his tea and gazing out the window as he contemplated the busy cobblestone streets. London looked the same as always. It was chillier than when he'd left, with winter closing in. The fog had transformed from a clammy blanket to a raw mist—a mist that thickened as it mingled with the puffs of cold air emerging from the mouths of scurrying patrons and plodding horses. Everyone seemed in a hurry, including the shopkeepers who stepped outside in rapid succession, glancing about for any last-minute customers, then locking up for the day. One by one, they turned up their collars and hurried home to their waiting families.

How touching.

How convenient.

The throngs of people, while providing an interesting scene for an early evening diversion, made it easy to remain unnoticed. He'd intentionally picked this coffee-house, one whose customers were primarily artists and authors, none of whom would have the slightest idea who he was. So he remained, a solitary gentleman enjoying his solitary late-day tea.

And if, by chance, one of his colleagues happened to wander in, spot him at his corner table, that colleague would doubtless offer his greetings, inquire where his lordship had been, and learn about his prolonged business trip abroad.

Given his status and position, his explanation would be accepted without question or doubt.

Ah, anonymity. It came in many forms, each one of them satisfying indeed.

He set down his cup, tugging his gloves more snugly into place and studying his cloaked hands—his right one, in particular. The German physician had been remarkably skilled, he mused, turning his palms up, then back down again. Same size. Same shape. Right down to the tapered fingers. With his gloves in place, it was impossible to tell that his right forefinger was a mere replica of what it had been. Oh, it couldn't bend at the knuckle, of course—wood never did—but he had no cause to bend that forefinger anyway. Not anymore. Now he had a substitute: his second finger—a trigger finger impeccably trained, ready to perform on command. He also had a new weapon, one fashioned especially for him, made by the same craftsman who'd designed and constructed the original. Both weapons were unique. But this new version was a stunning, one-of-a-kind achievement. Mastering it had taken every ounce of his skill and concentration, given his physical impediment. But master it he had—as brilliantly as he'd mastered its predecessor—and almost as quickly.

Yes, the weapon, and the proficiency to use it, had been acquired within a month of leaving England. But conquering the pain—*that* had taken every day of the three long months he'd been away.

Still, it would surge to life, sometimes so acutely he nearly screamed aloud. It would never truly leave him. That he knew. Not even for a day.

But it also wouldn't stop him.

Nothing would.

As if to taunt him, the front door of the coffeehouse opened, admitting a cold blast of December air. He winced as the chilling wind shot through the room, found him in his corner, and set off the throbbing in his hand. Gritting his teeth, he waited for the worst of the pain to subside, bitterly acknowledging that the winter months were going to be excruciating. Cold intensified the dull ache that gnawed relentlessly at him, sharpening his agony with a piercing stab.

He had no choice but to endure it.

Damn the winter.

Damn the pain.

And damn Breanna Colby.

He finished his tea, cursing silently as the hot beverage did nothing to warm away his agony. A drink. That's what he needed. A good, stiff drink to dull the throb.

Tossing some coins onto the table, he left the establishment, shoving his hands into his pockets as he made his way through the tangle of people to the nearest tavern.

Inside, it was dark and smoky, but he paid little

attention to his surroundings as he ordered a brandy. He tossed it down in three gulps.

The liquor worked wonders, burning through his system and making its way to the raw nerve endings at his knuckle.

When all this was over, he vowed, he'd spend winters somewhere warm, where the pain was bearable. There he could live in solitude. There he could savor his victories.

Especially the one hovering just ahead—his ultimate triumph and long-awaited revenge. Doing away with that miserable bitch who'd done this to him, condemned him to three months of agony and a lifetime of physical torment.

She'd pay for each and every day he suffered, each and every night he'd awakened, drenched in sweat, pain spearing through his hand, shooting up his arm. Oh, yes, she'd pay. First, by watching her precious cousin die at her feet, then by waiting, wondering when the bullet meant for her would find its mark.

It wouldn't be immediate. Oh, no, it would be eventual. Torturing her had to be savored. He had to terrorize her to the point where she'd be crazed with fear.

Until she realized, with a final surge of panic, that she couldn't escape him.

Until she understood he never failed, never missed his mark.

Until she knew it would take one bullet, and one bullet alone, because he never needed a second.

And until she knew that he was watching her, toying with her, deciding when and where to end her wretched life.

Oh, Lady Breanna Colby, by the time I kill you, you'll beg to die.

And die you will.

Look for
The Silver Coin
Wherever Books
Are Sold
Coming Next Month
in Paperback from
Sonnet Books